The Search For Intelligent Life on Earth

A STORY OF LOVE

Gerry Pirani

This is a work of fiction. The characters, names, organizations, dialogues and incidents in this book are the product of the author's imagination and entirely fictitious; places that are real are used fictitiously. Any similarity to real or actual events, establishments, or persons, living or dead, is entirely coincidental and not intended by the author.

ISBN-13: 978-1497417748
ISBN-10: 1497417740
Library of Congress Control Number: 2014905727
CreateSpace Independent Publishing Platform
North Charleston, South Carolina

For C, whom I've missed for so long already.

ONE

Kenya, April 1982

Mark forged ahead, wiping dirt-laden sweat from his brow with his soiled hand. He focused on the remaining coffee shrubs, saw them at once brown and dry, and became conscious of the fallacy inherent in the name "evergreen." Mark liked to think he embraced the Buddhist concept of impermanence, but he wished it would leave his actual life well enough alone. Instead, everything was about to change. He took a deep breath and willed the rain to come.

About to move along, he saw a small beetle turned upside down trying to right itself. It was just an insect, but Mark couldn't help but take a moment to flip it over. As he did so, his thoughts flashed back to boys in grade school who tore the wings off of insects for amusement. He felt revolted, assuming any act of brutality toward life would naturally translate into bigger and more malicious acts, as if the condoning of cruelty even toward the smallest of things would somehow, insidiously, seep its way into the very essence of one's self. He was glad to have finished high school and to be rid of these same classmates. But, when his mind drifted in that direction, a chill electrified his spine as the realization hit anew that Kyle was leaving.

Annoyed by the constant strands of his jet-black hair, he stopped to tighten the small rubber band that held them at the back of his head. In honor of Sioux tradition, he had stopped cutting it—though he knew little about his mother's people. He wouldn't bother about his heritage at all if it weren't for Papap, his African stepfather, who impressed upon him the weight of tribe when he spoke of his own.

"Mark!" his stepfather called out from the house just beyond the field. The Kikuyu man was as great as a tree, but he no longer towered over Mark like he once did.

"Take a break," Papap said. He didn't seem as worried about the crop as Mark felt. In a sense, Papap never seemed as disturbed about anything—as if he had struck a deal with the universe and trusted in its reliability.

His stepfather came closer now and assessed him. "You never know when to quit. Even as a child, you were stubborn and had to do everything in your own way. See, in this manner, you remind me of your mother. Look at you. You're a mess." Papap shook his head and clucked his tongue. "Go rest now."

Mark's hand slipped to his bare chest, made darker by the equatorial sun. In his twelve years in Kenya, he had never felt Africa so parched. It left him feeling thirsty and overexposed. Still, he wasn't ready to face the evening. "No, thanks," he said.

"I wasn't aware that I was asking a question," Papap said, already heading back to the house. The absolute tone of the directive was clear, and Mark wouldn't have argued. He had too much respect for Papap to challenge him, but it didn't matter now because Kyle was pulling up in his jalopy.

The car made choking noises as it maneuvered its way to the house. When Kyle stepped out, Mark's stomach churned, taken by the slender build, the bronzed skin, and the revelation of neck under his short locks. His arousal was muted today by a resonant sadness.

"Can you stay the whole night?" Mark asked when they caught up. The sun had started to descend and allowed for an array of spectacular color on the horizon. The silhouette of Mount Suswa presented a foreboding darkness in the otherwise perfect blend of crimson and violet. Mark again felt for moisture in the air but found only the buzzing of gnats. The dry earth met him hard against his tired feet.

"Of course," Kyle answered as his eyes roamed over Mark's worn body. "What are you doing to yourself?"

"Working." Mark wiped his hands of commingled dirt and blood from scrapes, cuts, and broken blisters. "I guess I was grateful for the distraction," he said, shrugging at the confession. He felt a spasm in his back, but the knots in his muscles just seemed to mock the one in his heart.

"When is everyone arriving? Maybe you should shower or something," Kyle said. He laughed, but there was a nervous ripple to it.

"Might make for a more memorable evening if I don't." Mark winked, though playfulness never quite suited him. He started toward the house, and Kyle followed.

Mark's mother, Humming, was at the kitchen counter preparing a few snacks. "Thank you for having this bon voyage party for me," Kyle said. He leaned over and kissed Humming on her cheek. "It's nice of you to go through this trouble."

"It's no trouble at all. You're part of the family." She looked sad. "I wish it could be more of a dinner, but there were just too many mouths to feed." Humming turned toward Mark's half-sister and said, "Bella's received an award today at school. Tell your brother and Kyle about it."

Bella gave Mark a wide grin. "I'll get it and show them." She ran to and from her room and held up her award for best student in her class, not letting him take it in his dirty grasp.

"Well done," Mark said. Bella's high cheekbones and almost straight, black hair were made all the more stunning against the coffee color of her skin. She was a perfect fusion of Mark's mother and his stepfather. She looked at him with idolatrous admiration, and Mark felt a pang of guilt that he seldom had patience with her eight-year-old antics.

Kyle grinned at him. "She'll be smarter than you at this rate."

"I hope so," Mark said, and Bella appeared pleased enough to return to her play.

The slight breeze moved the fresh scent of jasmine as they walked along one of their favorite trails. Mark breathed in the fragrance, wishing his irritation gone. He resented the party for lasting so long because, as usual, he wanted Kyle all to himself. But, it was more than that. There was a persistent anger that any of this was happening in the first place.

"I don't know what to say," Mark said. In the past, the silence was a soothing partner in the African night, but now it just seemed to form a gap between them.

"I know. I feel it, too. It's my fault," Kyle said. "I'm trying not to cry. I know how you are about that."

Mark wrapped his hand around Kyle's neck and drew him close in a half-embrace. He wanted to say he didn't blame Kyle for leaving, but he choked on the words even as he tried. He pulled Kyle to a more secluded area in the bush, so they could sit and talk—and kiss—without anyone descrying.

"Everyone's so excited to get out of here," Kyle said. "My father's contacted some distant relative of ours in Kyoto and has been acting like he's suddenly more than one-eighth Japanese. I'd do anything to stay behind."

Mark felt Kyle's individual fingers grasping his back, seeming to fight for a hold. Then Kyle kissed him, and Mark's throat started to close up. He was sure this type of love, the kind that held no bitterness or turgid expectations, came around once in a lifetime and, then, only if one were lucky.

"I asked if I could stay," Kyle's voice was low and hesitant, as if he weren't sure he should divulge the rest.

Mark's heartbeat sped in response. He felt so disappointed in Kyle for not being more willful the past few months. When Kyle's father had been re-stationed to Tokyo, Mark knew it came as a relief to Kyle's family. They'd complained enough of the heat, the bugs, and the natives. For Mark, however, it was like facing a death sentence, and he repeatedly shook his head in disgust at his own sense of helplessness. He would have fought harder against his own family, a million times so. "You did? And?" he asked.

"What do you think? Maybe if they thought more highly of the American school here, I'd be able to convince them to let me finish in Kenya. Anyway, I guess it wouldn't matter because he knows and would never let me stay here with you." He shrugged. "I don't care what he thinks. Let him call me a fag. It's worth it. You're worth it."

Mark's head dropped. Kyle sniffled and then grinned. "He didn't actually use that word."

They were quiet again. What word *had* Kyle's father used? The man must blame Mark for corrupting his son, although in actuality, it had been Kyle who made the first move. He chuckled. "Remember when you grabbed me in the restroom at the library? The first time we kissed? You said, 'I realize I could get my ass kicked, but I have to take the chance.' I couldn't believe it." He looked over at Kyle now, awed because he had been too cautious to do it himself.

Kyle appeared to be absorbing the land with his eyes when he finally spoke again. "Will you remember me?" he asked.

"Of course," Mark said, trying again not to fear the looming, gaping cavity his friend's absence would create in his life.

"No, really? Will you remember me when you gaze at the stars at night? Or when you're walking out here? Or, eating with your folks? Or, just reading? I want you to actively remember me. Will you?"

Mark pulled him closer, almost protectively. "I can't imagine not."

The house was bathed in quietude when they returned. Mark's bedroom was created from an alcove off the main hallway. A mattress rested on the floor with books and articles strewn about it. The creaky floorboards and the hanging beads—a makeshift sort of door—made deliberate movement necessary. Snores reached them from down the short foyer. Mark didn't resent the circumstances because they had shaped their lovemaking into something hushed and almost sacred in his mind.

Tonight, of all nights, there was no intention to sleep. Mark moved to the window in the small living room, waiting for Kyle to finish in the bathroom. He became lost again in the thoughts that existed to camouflage his apprehension of daylight, thoughts of the drought, of the crop drying up, and then of imminent sex.

Kyle tiptoed to reach him and now embraced him from behind, wrapping one arm around his waist and the other around his neck, so as to hold his hands over Mark's heart. "You okay?"

"Yeah, sure." Mark laughed a little, low, and then closed his eyes. "I'll miss you more than I can explain."

"Me, too," Kyle said.

He turned around and kissed Kyle with forcefulness before letting up and gently pushing him through the beads and onto the mattress. His objective was to pleasure his friend as many times as possible because that's what he would miss the most. Kyle came too quickly once Mark started on him.

"Sorry, I've been thinking about you all day," Kyle said, a sheepish grin spread over his face.

Mark smiled but didn't respond. They still had the rest of the night. He stopped Kyle from grabbing him, wanting to prolong his anticipation.

Kyle took tobacco from his trousers and rolled a cigarette. "Smoke?"

"No. You know that." Mark chuckled.

"I'll light up outside." They pulled their pants on and stepped out the front door into the expanse of stars.

"It won't be like this, you know," Mark said, eyes skyward.

"What?"

"The night sky in Tokyo. There's too much light pollution to see the stars like this. You better enjoy it while you can."

"Oh, I'm enjoying it while I can, all right." They both laughed at his attitude, but Kyle abruptly stopped. "I'm so sorry about messing up our plans…No," he said when Mark was about to interrupt him. "I mean it. You could have started at university this coming year. Why didn't we think to have you apply just in case my father got transferred again? I should've known better. I've been dealing with this shit my whole life."

"I have plenty to do here. Besides, I don't know yet if I want to go to university," said Mark, his mind wandering to two step-cousins who had matriculated in Nairobi the year before. They concentrated more on recent communist activism than their schoolwork, and they'd been leaning on Mark for support the past few weeks. He felt guilty for thinking only of Kyle and his personal loss.

"Christ, don't be ridiculous, Mark. You have to go. It would be a waste of a brilliant mind."

Mark just laughed at that.

"What the hell else will you do?" Kyle extinguished his cigarette on the concrete slab that made up the front patio and glared at him. "Farm for a living?"

"Maybe," Mark answered. He wasn't sure where the resistance against school came from—probably his desire not to buy into Western principles and priorities. He told himself he disliked living by someone else's standards and that he would set his own, but he also feared losing the solace of home.

"The only reason why your parents saved this place was because Papap had the retirement pension. Once they're gone, you'll starve to death, even in the odd years you have a good coffee harvest. Shit," Kyle said with vehemence. "Promise me you'll be careful," Kyle added, slipping his arms around Mark's waist.

"What are you talking about?"

"The East African Communists League, as if you didn't know," Kyle said. "That recruitment meeting the other day was cryptic. I'm afraid for you."

"Cryptic?" Mark found it suitable to laugh again.

"You may not believe they're capable of murder, but my father is convinced the League isn't just an innocent political party," Kyle said.

"Your father works for the American embassy. Of course he'd forbid you to get involved with anything communistic."

"My point is precisely that he's a diplomat. Maybe he's privy to information he can't share. He really seemed upset when he warned me."

Mark looked down, allowed for the possibility, and rejected getting engrossed in such a debate on their last night together.

"If you stay here, you may get more involved than you plan to," Kyle said.

Mark pulled away enough to face him. "What am I going to do, become an explosives expert?"

The reference of the sarcasm was not lost on his friend, who gave him a serious and pleading look. They had wondered a few weeks ago if the League were responsible for an unexpected explosion in Nairobi. "Are you going to be careful or not?"

"Yes, I'm going to be very careful." Mark smiled, but both knew he meant what he said, and he always kept his promises.

"Are you going to join?" Kyle asked him.

"I don't know. How much longer do we have talk about this?"

"Do you really think you're a communist?"

"Yes. I do. Well, if there's a difference between the spirit of Marxism and the practice in Eastern Europe or China, I'd say so." He spoke sarcastically but changed his tone now. "I don't think it's right that dogs in America are getting fat, and people here are starving to death, and have no medical care."

"Jesus Christ, are you referring to that American article on canine obesity they handed out at the meeting? You can't believe that propaganda. It was taken out of context and had more to do with the effects of neutering and spaying."

"That's not the point," Mark said, wound up now.

"Yes, it is the point. And the League isn't about to change the States, you know, and you live in Kenya. Thanks to the Brits, as my Dad would say, there's still plenty of opportunity here," said Kyle.

"And a very large discrepancy in classes here, as well. It's not right. I don't know when I feel sicker: when I see the poverty, or when I see the club folk." Mark's voice crept louder as he referred to the British Kenyans and their oasis of privilege. He lowered it in response to the tentative look in Kyle's eyes. "We should at least try to do something. Why should some live with so much more than they need, and others with so little?"

"Some? Like we diplomatic families?"

"I never thought of you like that." He looked at Kyle, refusing to allow anything to come between them now. He sighed when his friend's response showed no signs of melting. "What do you want me to do?"

"I want you to resist joining the League, at least till you research what's going on with them, and at least a year," Kyle said, and Mark realized Kyle still had plans to persuade him to leave Kenya by then to attend college in the US together.

"A year?" Mark smirked again. Kyle rarely made any unreasonable demands. They had so seldom even disagreed. "How come you didn't say anything about this before now?"

"I did."

"No, you didn't. Not like this. Why are you so worried all of a sudden?"

"I guess because I won't be here to help you keep your perspective," Kyle said.

"You mean *your* perspective."

Kyle shrugged but showed no hint of relenting.

"All right," Mark made the requested promise, just like that, surprising both of them a little. He didn't voice the relief he felt that the decision would be out of his hands for now. Instead, he kissed his smug friend on the cheek and then lightly on the lips.

"I'll come back for you," Kyle said into his ear.

"Don't say things you can't guarantee, Kyle." Mark shook his head and swallowed hard. He refused to weep.

TWO

Jacques sat alone at his dressing table and began the ritual he'd practiced every evening for the last three years. He brushed his long blond hair until it hurt his scalp. Still wearing his silk, cream-colored robe, he opened the door a smidge, a message that he was ready to be prepped and groomed, made up and dressed. Then he returned to his cushioned, floral, and somewhat stately chair, unlike the fold-up ones the other performers had. Being the boss' son had certain advantages.

The stagehand Aimee stuck her head in the door and waved. She'd been told not to bother him when he was getting ready for work, but sometimes she seemed unable to stop herself. He smiled ruefully and returned his eyes to his own visage in the mirror. Where were they? There was usually no time for contemplation once the door was ajar, and too much reflection could be a bad omen. Jacques didn't have a whole lot to celebrate in his life, and his mind could too easily become wrapped in self-woe. He took a deep breath and started counting in his head as a distraction. Maybe he should have asked Aimee to keep him company.

Finally, a tall, gaunt man with little hair entered. He was one of the fill ins. "Bon soir," he said with a perfunctory smile. He apologized for keeping the star waiting. Jacques said it was nothing because he preferred not to appear ruffled in front of the help, both here and at home. What was his name? Not the usual makeup artist, not very friendly. There was always a cold edge to this man. He started to rub cream into Jacques' arms and hands, then his face.

"Did you see the costume for tonight?" the man asked.

"No, not really." Jacques wasn't in the mood for small talk. He wanted to crawl into a ball and play dead.

"Feeling blue?" the man asked as he slapped foundation on.

"Where is everyone?"

"Everyone who?"

Jacques sighed out of frustration. "Westhoff, Yves, my hairstylist, my assistant, the people who are usually running in and out of my room with last minute problems."

The man shrugged as if he didn't care. "The choreographer is prepping the dancers because one was injured. He has to rework the routines. Yves is sick. The stagehands are…sit still, look what's happened now." He huffed as he took a cloth and rubbed at Jacques' face.

Jacques grimaced and pulled away. "You'll make my face red. Where is my father?"

"He is not coming this evening. You don't know?"

Jacques felt too humiliated to answer, but it explained why the staff was running late. For a second, he deluded himself about walking out. What was it that American tourist said to him last week? *If you are not happy, just do something else.* Just do something else! Americans! They are so naïve. He didn't know anything else and was still underage. His father had too much pull in this part of France. What would he do for money? Work in a boutique and live in a flat in the dangerous outskirts of town?

He glared at his reflection again. Maybe he could sell his hair and make a getaway with the profits. Though, maybe it would only afford him a croissant and a coffee. He had no idea. As he was considering his escape strategy, the inept theater manager arrived.

"Come on, come on! You are on soon, and you are still not dressed."

"You are the one who was late, Westhoff," Jacques said with a bitter note.

"Not in the best mood, Jacqui?"

"Not in any mood. I'm just not the one who was late."

"Well, I was arranging a seat for your father's guest. He seemed very nice, by the way."

Jacques' stomach fell when he caught the makeup artist exchange a glance with the manager. How much did they know?

"Do you want something?" Westhoff revealed a small envelope from his breast pocket holding a few tablets.

"No, it's not necessary," said Jacques, although with less resolve than usual.

Westhoff slipped the gown over Jacques' head and then scrambled for the rest of the team. He clapped and whistled in the hallway to call attention to the dire need of a hairstylist in Jacques' dressing room. Jacques laughed for the first time that night as the makeup artist zipped him up. What a scene, what a lunatic bunch of people.

He really needed a new life. Recently his mind alighted on faith. He told himself to believe that there would be a sign. Something, or someone, would come into his life, and he would have a means to break out. Making appeals to St Jude, the patron saint of hopeless causes, had become another daily ritual.

The hairstylist ran in with curlers and products in tow. "You know what would be easier?" he asked no one in particular as he dropped the whole lot on the dressing table. "A style you can just live in. Not so much hassle every night. You see what I mean?"

Jacques had no idea what he meant and didn't bother to respond. If it was such a hassle to do his hair, why not leave it straight down his back the way it was? It might even look more authentic that way—but, then, that was the predicament, wasn't it? Authenticity was not what most people were after in life.

THREE

So many days went unnoticed after Kyle left that time could have accused Mark of being the most inattentive of lovers. He could see no beauty. He snapped at people one day for doing exactly what he had requested of them the day before, as if he were capricious. He'd always considered himself anything but. He had to accept that he would never find a friend like Kyle again. He didn't know any homosexual men, nor could he imagine seeking them out—even if it were safe to do so in the political landscape of his country. He began to hide behind angry and solemn moods. As a result, his few friends avoided contact to spare themselves his sardonic tirades, which were scathing enough to blister their idea of a good time even if not directed at them.

His friends' abandonment suited him just fine, especially because he promised to eschew involvement with the League. Instead of wasting time socializing, he read. He toiled. He studied. Books became his missing companion: books about history, especially where the African and the European versions clashed, books about ornithology and botany, books about physics and philosophy. He made lists of well-known authors and read literature: English, existential, Japanese, and modern Kenyan. He crossed subjects and titles off one by one compulsively, but the more he read, the longer the list became. In his mind whirled ideas of intricate design and pattern, but he rarely verbalized any of them, even when his family tried to lure him into conversation. He felt a glimpse of something akin to happiness only when he would see a connection among seemingly disparate subjects. At such moments, he would sense meaning in an otherwise chaotic existence.

This sense of interrelatedness extended to his personal fate. For instance, was it entirely random that his natural father decided to invite him to Germany several months after Kyle left? Was it a coincidence that he would have discarded the invitation had it arrived before, but that he now considered it despite his misgivings?

"What is it?" his mother asked as she joined him on the couch.

"Take a look for yourself." He handed her the white sheet of stationery. He'd wanted to tell her anyway but was too aware of the resentment she'd been harboring since she left Europe.

She was quiet for a while, as he thought she would be.

"Well, that's unexpected, isn't it?" she finally said.

"Yeah, I wasn't sure if I should say anything."

"No, no. I'm glad you did. It's not the worst idea to explore a little." When Mark rolled his eyes, she added, "Really, Mark. I think it would benefit you to go. You need to get away from here for a time. I'm worried about you ever since…you know. You need to make new friends and have some fun."

He felt pained by the encouraging front she put on. Still, it was time he acknowledged that his life had completely stalled. In the beginning, he convinced himself that indiscriminate reading was a valid way to go, but now he saw she had a point. In fact, his mother had commented on a few occasions that she could not keep track of his course of pursuit. When he was forced to travel to Nairobi to obtain rare texts, she expressed chagrin when he reported no serendipitous adventure. Why would he? But it didn't help that on top of his burdensome loneliness, he was disappointing her. When she threw another college application on his pile of unopened ones, she would sigh. He was reluctant to tell her that Kyle was the one who requested them.

"Well?" she'd asked last week, standing at his door-beads, not bothering to move them.

"Well, what?"

"What did you decide to do?"

"About what?"

"About college. About anything."

"I haven't decided."

"I don't see how all these books are helping you figure it out," she said accusingly. And so the conversations went.

This might be just the opportunity he needed, she told him now. "Go! What's here to hold you back?" she added, patting his knee.

"Thanks for reminding me." He stood to walk out, done with the conversation, angry again and wanting to break something. If only he were invited to Tokyo instead.

———

"Mark," Humming called after him, but he parted the beads to his room like a storm and didn't respond. She picked up the few accumulated newspapers on the coffee table and wondered how to proceed. Even after all these years, she could still conjure the frightened look on his face after she had a brutal fight with Andreas, the fear in his eyes that convinced her to leave her ex-husband for good.

She should probably go to Mark presently and make him talk about his feelings. But, her husband was the one who was good with that sort of thing. It was Kisau whose resolute devotion to them had renewed her faith in herself and her passion for life. And now, however improbable, it was Kisau again who carried her through her doubts and fears about her son's sexuality. If she pushed Mark to go to Europe, and then Andreas found out about him, it might make things worse. But Mark's penchant for other boys wasn't obvious, and it still might pass. If it didn't, she hoped he would at least find love.

Love was not what she had with Andreas, who had been an officer in the West German Army when they met. His commanding quality had been mistaken for confidence and strength instead of a need to control. It hadn't helped that she'd been so alone in Europe, or that she'd had no tribe in which to burrow and find, if not affection, at least cover. But, after her entire youth was spent struggling against their "way," as it had been called, she could not return to the reservation defeated. If only she'd considered how lonely she might be when she embraced the white man's idea of rugged individualism. She hurt thinking her son was feeling that kind of loneliness now. She hesitated outside his bedroom and sighed.

"What, Mom?"

There was a disheartened sound to his voice that made her want to cry. "You know, Mark, when I was young, I didn't want to identify with my people or see things from my mother's perspective," she started to explain to him, but she wasn't ready to consider aloud that she may have been foolhardy and ungrateful when growing up on the reservation, when she wanted to dismiss everything that smelled of Indian.

Instead, she skipped to the end of her thought. "Andreas is a part of you. Germany is a part of you. I think you should go. Sometimes you can't wait for the rest of your life to come to you. You have to go to it. Or at least meet it half way."

When he didn't respond, she retreated to her bedroom, hoping his silence meant he was more undecided than he'd let on.

FOUR

Mark agonized over how to greet Andreas after so long without contact. He hardly slept during the flight, and the one time he did, he woke startled at the idea of being so close to his natural father but still feeling so apart from him. For one thing, Mark worried they wouldn't recognize one other. Of course, he was the single individual on the flight who remotely looked American Indian, especially now that his hair was growing out. That should give it away.

Then he was distracted by customs for a short time, though carrying a German passport made that bit simpler. He didn't want to seem too eager to scan the faces when he entered the greeting area. He saw a variety of family members embracing before he eyed a lone man: tall, fit, with some gray blending into the chestnut brown hair. For a moment, Mark considered pretending to be someone else, but he refused to act like a coward. The man's lips formed a small, tight smile, and he walked over.

"I take it your trip was good." Andreas shook his hand, as if he were a business associate.

"Not bad," Mark said, noticing he reached his father's height.

"Baggage is this way." Andreas started toward baggage claim. "How is your German? Do you remember how to talk?"

"A little."

"Well, you were quite young when you left."

So, we left? Funny, I thought you left us. He could tell Andreas that he practiced his German at home, but he already felt like denying his father any satisfaction.

"How many bags?"

16

"Just one, there it is," Mark answered as he walked to the fair-sized, battered brown piece and pulled it from the belt.

"Good, that was fast. Tanja, my wife, has probably made us some breakfast." For a moment Andreas' eyes met Mark's, and Mark could swear he saw repulsion in them. Was it because he looked more like his mother than he did him? Did his father regret the invitation already? They were both quiet as they walked out to the car, which was a standard grey sedan, and as soon as they were in the car, his father turned the radio on. Mark could make out very little of the German reporting, but occasionally his father would grumble in response to the commentator. Mark remembered now how circumspect he had been around his father when he was five years old because they so often missed each other's meanings. Nothing had changed. Why had Andreas bothered to reach out at all?

They pulled up to an A-frame home, beds of flowers decorating the front yard. Mark was struck by the uniqueness of it for the area, as every other house in view was boxy with a squared-in front yard. Perhaps his father wasn't as conventional as he thought. After initial introductions of his new wife and two children, Andreas seemed preoccupied with the newspaper. Tanja, however, beamed at Mark incessantly and showed him around. She explained that the children were shy at first but soon would be unrelenting in their attentions.

Tanja poured Mark a tisane of peppermint and served bread with cold cut meats and cheeses on individual cutting boards. He could tell she was trying and was convinced it was she, in her youthful optimism, who initiated this invitation to Europe. He couldn't guess at her age but figured she was still under thirty. Her blond hair was shoulder length with soft curls. Their first breakfast together was spent mostly in silence, as her English seemed to degrade with time; perhaps she had practiced her first few questions and was now too challenged by the language barrier.

"Will you go to university soon?" she asked as an afterthought. His father looked up for a fleeting moment at this, which Mark caught from the corner of his eye.

He cleared his throat. "I'm not sure about school, but eventually I suspect I will."

His half-sister, Sabine, asked in German if she could be excused. She was born around the same year as Bella. Andreas exchanged words with his daughter. Although they didn't seem to be argumentative, the sound was still pretty harsh. He wondered if the character of a language developed over time to match the personality of the

17

people who spoke it, or if a culture arose in response to the tongue of its people. He felt differently when he spoke English than when he spoke Swahili. He was jolted back to the table by Tanja's English now.

"Well, you have time, ja? Here in Deutschland, your father complains about the age of the students living off his taxes." She tittered. "Will you study in Europe or in Africa?"

"Probably in the US."

"Oh, but it's so expensive there!" Tanja's eyes seemed to open wider. "I heard this, right?" She looked at her husband for confirmation, but Andreas seemed unwilling to engage.

"Well, I would probably get scholarships." And then seeing her confusion, Mark said, "The universities there have funding for students who need it, so long as your academic record is successful. And, anyway, as Sioux, or half-Sioux, I would also qualify as a minority student."

"It sounds like you did your research about this," his father finally commented. "What would stop you?"

"Several things. I'd miss my family, for one. Something you—" He stopped himself, hearing contempt pour into his voice and cleared his throat. "You wouldn't understand," he said, his abdominal area tight under his shirt.

"Ja, well," Tanja said quickly in German and with obvious experience in diverting confrontations. "I have maps and city plans for you, if you like, in your room. It's not difficult to get to the Bahnhof, and the Kinder and I can go with you when you like."

His toddler half-brother, Peter, smiled, dimples and blond hair making him a picture Mark thought even Hitler might have approved. These children at least had a chance at gaining their father's approval, but he chose not to resent them for it. It was obvious that Andreas found the adoring, submissive woman he craved. Mark's mother would never have fit that bill. What an odd pairing his parents must have made. He promised himself he would never make the same mistake.

To survive the summer in Andreas' house, Mark planned to isolate and read. A week went by like this, and Tanja started to encourage him more vocally to go out and see the sights. Andreas, on the other hand, treated him with growing aloofness at best. A second week passed, and Tanja insisted that Mark go someplace, so he started taking walks. He walked around the suburb, through several farms and open spaces, enduring the stink of manure at times in exchange for the seclusion these strolls provided him. Never before had Mark felt like anything but a white man, Mzungu.

18

Of course, nightlife was mostly an unknown entity to him, so the scene was very foreign, and he found himself both fascinated and dismayed by the skinheads and other characters. Sexuality seemed an open and immodest pursuit. Bars seemed to harbor heterosexuals and homosexuals alike, and at one club, Mark spent about fifteen minutes watching two men kiss before they noticed and waved him over. He walked away instead. If a passing hand touched him, or if someone winked, he seldom reacted with anything but analytic detachment.

Tonight, Mark sat and observed with his usual curiosity, except that he was in a pub in a seedy part of Hamburg because he was tired of the loud music and frenzied activity of the more popular clubs. A group of English-sounding fellows who'd entered a few minutes before were loud and obnoxious. They looked like punks, some of them with Mohawks and lots of piercings. They seemed to be dealing in drugs.

Presently, one of the finer looking of the group walked toward Mark and sat beside him uninvited. "Hello, mate," he said looking sideways at Mark. The young man's asymmetrical haircut appeared to cut off the vision of his right eye. Still peeping from under his blond bangs, he added, "You speak English?"

Mark looked away and ignored the question. The young man blurted out in sloppy German, "Ik heishe John," pointing to himself and laughing. Mark could smell alcohol from the young man's breath. "Unt du?"

"What do you want?" Mark asked as if swatting a mosquito with his words.

"Cheers, you speak English. I don't want anythin', mate. The question is, what do you want?"

"I want you to leave me alone," Mark said. He didn't want to buy any drugs, nor did he wish to continue speaking to a drunken Englishman. If the guy had any sense at all, he would realize these facts and move along.

"You speak like an odd chap. Where're you from, then?" John continued, apparently senseless.

"Africa," Mark stood up, picked up his beer, and began to leave when John grabbed his arm.

"Please don't go. What have I done to offend you?" His English was suddenly nasally snobbish. His eyes, or one visible eye, implored Mark.

Mark sat down with some trepidation and was quiet. He didn't want any trouble.

"I'm just lonely is all," said John. "I..."

"Are you on something?" Mark interrupted.

"Probably."

"You don't know?" They shared a smirk. "I'm Mark." He didn't think the Englishman was dangerous, but since he was accompanied by what looked like a group of thugs, he felt wary about how to proceed.

"Pleased to make your acquaintance, Mark," John lifted his glass in a toast and finished the remaining alcohol. Mark asked John what he was doing in Germany to which the young man replied, "Escaping that bloody country of mine. Also, the Beatles got a good start here."

"Oh, you're a musician," Mark said, thinking it might explain some of the eccentricity.

"Musician?" John asked with a raised eyebrow, "Not at all." The stranger offered no explanation, and Mark sought no clarification. He watched John rub his nose and sniffle and suspected cocaine use. John turned back to him and asked, "So, you don't like the English, I take it?"

"Not particularly, I suppose. Why do you ask?" Mark watched the gang at the bar harass other customers in turn.

"Dunno. Just seemed the type."

"Oh, yeah, what type is that?" Mark asked him.

"Suffice it to say, I wasn't wrong. So, why not? What about us gets under your skin?"

Mark disliked the British for their imperialism, their smugness, and for the manners they used to disguise their barbarianism. Compared to other imperialists, though, they were all right. "The usual," he decided to say.

"Ah, I see. You envy our charm and good looks, of course."

Mark laughed at the straightforward delivery of this line, and John looked at him in return. He was disarmingly handsome when you could see his face.

"Why are *you* here?" the Englishman asked now in a confrontational but flirtatious way. He leaned toward Mark until the two were face-to-face and added, "And what can I do to make your stay more pleasurable?" He sounded both sultry and cynical in a confusing way. Mark wondered how old he was and if he were a prostitute. He sensed his own attraction, but was simultaneously repulsed by the young man's behavior.

"How old are you?"

"What? Why do you ask?" John asked, turning away from him.

"What are you selling exactly?"

SEVEN

"Moechten Sie etwas zu trinken?" asked the bus boy on the train. Mark had had no trouble finding John that morning at the *Bahnhof*. After explaining the situation to Tanja, allaying her concerns about the condition of his right fist, and preparing his backpack, he left for town and the main station. There was only one first class car, and he had correctly deduced that his companion would be in it. Mark asked the bus boy for some mineral water and was grateful Tanja had insisted on giving him some cash.

John was asleep with his head looking uncomfortably pressed against the window, his mouth slightly ajar, and his body limp. His face was mostly covered by his hair, but Mark noticed the whiskers on his outer cheeks, the folds of his ear lobes, decorated with an assortment of crosses and chains, and the curve of his neckline. He became aroused against his will, not really over John, but over the memories of touching Kyle, and kissing him in similar places. He then immediately became sad. The letters arrived less often and with less affection and passion. They had not seen each other or talked in months. Mark wondered now what Kyle was doing, if he desired someone else, if he looked longingly at virtual strangers to ease the pain of loss and solitude. He reached into his pocket for the letter that awaited him on the kitchen table earlier that morning; it arrived yesterday.

Mark was not prone to reading these letters right away any more. He dreaded what they might say. He scrutinized the envelope for details and hints of what was written within. He saw only the crooked handwriting of his friend, the Japanese postage. This was new stationery–the wafer thin writing paper sold by Japanese merchants. He remembered the jokes he shared with Kyle over the small and neatly decorated "little things" of the Japanese culture: its reputation for the fine point pens, the dainty keepsake and novelty boxes, and the sheer stationery. Kyle had obviously grown acclimated to his surroundings. He opened the envelope.

Dear Mark,

For days now I've been waiting for a letter from you. When I last wrote, I mentioned how I was in a dreary state. My confusion over this decision to leave Japan and go to an American university (perhaps on my own?) has been weighing on my mind, and yet I hear nothing from you. Are you mad that I haven't planned to attend college in Nairobi? I thought we had already discussed the probability of going to the States. Please respond. I remain,

Yours truly

Mark folded the letter and replaced it in the fine envelope, feeling guilty. He wondered how the last letter Kyle wrote might have been lost. He still had no reasonable explanation for why he let those university applications go unopened. Peering out the window now as the train arrived in Brussels, its screeching halt awakening his traveling companion, he felt disoriented. It was announced, in French, that they had indeed arrived.

"Do we need to change here?" Mark asked in haste.

John grunted a negative and proceeded to ruffle his own hair, maybe in an attempt to make it appear fresh. Mark tried to appear pensive and distant in an effort to keep conversation to a minimum. As soon as John closed his eyes again, though, Mark's fixed on him. John had a fine, delicate look to his facial structure, so different from the broader, more chiseled features he had himself inherited. He tried to glean from John's face what ailed him but gave up after a time.

It left Mark to his own fantasies again. He recalled how when he had first met Kyle, his heart and groin seemed to smart at the same time. After they started to spend time together, Mark often stared at Kyle. He knew his feelings to be mutual because Kyle caught him several times and simply smiled with a longing Mark recognized. He allowed that same feeling of desire to rise up in him now, allowed himself to taste it fully despite the sorrow that often followed. In Kenya, he had wanted to be left alone, to feel how lonely he believed he'd be the rest of his life, so that he could get used to it—just as he was trying to adjust to the sense of pining that would be his from now on, too, unless…no…there could be nothing real with John. Finally, he let his eyes close.

The Englishman was staring at him when he woke up. Mark shifted in his chair and blocked his face.

"Sleep well?" John asked him.

"I don't know. I was dreaming." Mark looked out the window to disengage from discussion.

"It's almost like not having you here at all."

"Excuse me?"

"It's just that you're a bit of a bore as a travel companion."

"Am I?" Mark asked with an edge.

They glared at each other for a moment, but then John turned away, as Mark knew he would. But he hadn't meant for him to look as glum as he did suddenly. "What would make me more interesting?"

John shrugged. "We could talk."

"About what?"

"Tell me about your family."

Mark exhaled. He didn't like talking about himself, especially to near-strangers. "Well, my mother is Sioux, a tribal people from North America. My father, well, her husband, I should say, but I think of him as my father, is Kikuyu, a tribal people of East Africa. As you already know, my natural father is German. You've been to his house." He looked to John for recognition because he had no idea what John remembered, how stoned he'd been, or what was going on in his mind. John didn't respond but appeared very attentive. "Anyway, my stepfather helped raise me since I was six, after my mother and I left Germany..." he trailed off. The marriage between his European father and Sioux mother ended in a sour divorce and a conspicuous lack of custody dispute, but John didn't need to know that much detail.

"Afterward, in a bold move, my mother decided we would relocate to Africa." Mark saw their lives as a testament of Providence because they arrived far across the globe into the arms of their destiny, in the form of Kisau Gituma. Buried memories surfaced on the private movie screen of his mind. Memories of standing near his mother's side as they disembarked in Nairobi from the Alexandria train, of wanting to feel strong and protective of her, of a giant, almost tar-skinned man, heavy with the scent of unfamiliar spices and foreign ideas.

Mark had nearly forgotten that John was waiting for him to continue. "That's it, basically," he said. "I have two half siblings in Germany and one in Kenya. All younger."

John shook his head as if he understood. "I don't get on with my father, either. Nor my mother, really. I have one sister, perhaps I've mentioned."

"And you're wealthy." Mark's eyes swept the first class car.

"Yes, well, not I. My parents keep threatening to cut me off but haven't so far."

John remained quiet for a while after the brief exchange, and Mark was glad to look out the window again, alone with his thoughts. He missed Africa—not just his family, but the mood of the continent itself. There was something so alive about being there that even the new experience of traveling in Europe didn't compare. He'd heard white settlers complain about having to leave, 'having to leave' being a euphemism for not-being-able-to-stand-native-African-rule, and then lament the loss of something they too couldn't quite name. How could he leave it to go to university in the United States? Everyone knew Americans were ignorant about people from other lands—and addicted to television.

Once they arrived, John insisted on going the rest of the way by taxi. Mark was still pensive and rather tired, so he acquiesced. On either side they caught glimpses of historically notorious locations, buildings and monuments, but Mark glowered despite the beautiful impact this city usually had on visitors.

"What are you thinking about, mate?" John asked as he rummaged through his bag in obvious search of something.

"Did I mention I didn't think I'd like this city before we left?"

"Ah, here it is. What?" John pulled a long mitt over his right arm, ostensibly to cover the bandages. Mark eyed him with suspicion and then rolled down the window. "Good idea, some fresh air," John chortled. "And, yes, you did intimate something about disliking the French, not just for their imperialistic conquests, but for their unique intellectual snobbery, much like the British in arrogance but historically lacking in the psychological inhibition which keeps us pitiable in your estimation. Do I have it right?" John cocked his head.

Mark glared at him but not without the slightest turn of his mouth, as if he would smile if he were just a little more generous.

Presently, they drove by a group of young people congregated by the Arc de Triomphe. Mark turned back to John. "Do you ever wonder if people spend their entire lives focused on insatiable grasping?"

John let out a startling guffaw. "I wouldn't dare judge, mate."

"Where are we going, anyway?"

John showed him a flyer advertising a famous Parisian theater known for cabaret.

"Why?" Mark asked, his voice cracking a bit.

"Don't get to panicking now," John teased.

"I'm not, I don't," Mark said. He questioned his decision to accompany John on this escapade, distraction or not. "I thought we were visiting a friend of yours here."

"We most certainly are."

"At a theater?"

"Yes. Drag show tonight. Big scene." He looked at Mark directly and asked, "Don't feel threatened by female impersonators, do you?"

"Maybe you should have asked me that before you lured me here."

"Is that what I did?" John looked away. "You're hurtful."

"And you're deceitful."

John took his sunglasses out of his breast pocket and placed them on. "All right, then, enough name calling for today. My friend, my sister's friend, really, is an *entertainer*," he stressed the last word affectedly.

"An entertainer?"

"Yes, he's 'Jacqui,' the well-known transvestite, or whatever you call it. Gay, I think, in case you're interested."

"I won't be."

"You're sure, then? Have you seen any of the posters on the billboards?"

Mark believed he actually had seen an advertisement in the train station of a blond-haired, green-eyed beauty, who, he presumed, was female. He glared at the Englishman again, "You failed to mention this."

"Do you speak French?"

"What?" Mark asked, distracted momentarily by the bright lights and the crowd outside the show house.

"French?" John repeated, as he grabbed his baggage. Mark followed his companion's lead and reached for his backpack. He offered half the fare, but John ignored him and stepped out of the cab first, shouting for Mark to follow. They reached the ticket collector, and John spoke in near-fluent French. Mark heard something about being personal guests of "Jacqui." They were accompanied swiftly backstage and directed to the star's dressing room.

"Speak in French. He'd like that."

"I will not," Mark said defiantly. "I mean, I just don't care for the language." He wasn't sure how else to explain how uncomfortable it was for him to speak in French, how sensually unlike himself it felt.

The door to Jacqui's dressing room was swung open as soon as John knocked. John and Mark both stared at the creature before their eyes: the slim, decidedly feminine figure outlined in a draped gown. The flat chest gave Jacqui the appearance of a French fashion model rather than a drag queen. The long blond hair was braided in cornrows, a style that had become popular in the West in recent years. Was it possible that this guy could be so beautiful? Mark had been called laconic at times, but he was rarely at a loss for words. He was relieved when suddenly the rapid French of the entertainer interrupted the silence. The voice was soft, delicate, enticing, welcoming them, kissing John on both cheeks with penciled perfect lips, smiling at Mark and evidently accustomed to the astonishment of men.

Mark heard, as if in a vacuum, John's apology for his companion's inadequate French. His palms were sweating, and he recognized the damn adrenaline flow again.

"You don't speak French?" Jacqui eyed him flirtatiously. "You will excuse my English terrible, n'est-ce pas?" And with his sexy lack of orthoepy, he turned away from Mark and concentrated on petting John and soliciting compliments.

"You look frightfully lovely," John said, among others.

"Have you not seen me dressed like this?"

"No, not in person. I definitely would have remembered."

Mark's heart continued to race. He wanted to lash out at both his travel companion and the anomalous beauty. He moved as far away from them as he could and tried not to look awkward despite his flip-flopping emotions. He was opposed to everything they stood for and was trying to cover up his initial infatuation with every possible excuse and denial. It had just been too long since he was with Kyle; he was lonely; the situation was unusual.

John and Jacqui were engaged in dialogue in French now about John's sister Lily, who was reportedly concerned about John. Jacqui urged John to call her and to take any medication that had been prescribed. John reassured the entertainer he'd had no "episodes" and was fine. He would call Lily, if Jacqui insisted.

Just then, a man was standing in the doorway pointing to his watch and staring at them.

"Ah, you will see the show?" Jacqui looked at Mark who was fixated on the Frenchman's pronunciation of the English sound "th."

contact. Then he remembered he had dreamt of the Frenchman, after the limo had driven John and him to a Parisian hotel the night before. He could feel himself blush.

"American Indian," he answered as he followed Jacques around the corner. There was music, drumming, on the other side.

"These two men are Cherokee street performers. I love their dance," Jacques said.

John reached them and started laughing. "I doubt Mark will share your appreciation for their art. He probably finds it degrading."

"You don't like dance?" Jacques' face dropped.

"Yeah, traditional dance I like. In Africa," Mark started but stopped at once, not wanting to speak of anything personal, like when Papap took him to see folk dance in Kenya. He shook his head to imply *never mind* and asked if Jacques had met the Cherokees. The headdresses were large and impressive, and the beat of the drum and the chant-like singing were intoxicating.

"Only once, I introduced myself. We talked for a little while about their home. They lived in…an area only for Indians, I forget the word, in, and now I do not remember the state," he sighed, seemingly disappointed in himself. "They were very," and he went into French with John asking how to translate something.

"Gracious," John smiled. "So, what do you think?"

"You're right, I find it degrading," Mark said, but there was also shame behind his words. He had no idea where a Cherokee reservation might be and wanted to steer clear of revealing his ignorance. He only knew that his mother had grown up in Pine Ridge and that his Unchee or maternal grandmother moved out of the reservation about ten years ago. He was pretty sure she resided in Montana, not too far from Yellowstone, but he hadn't paid enough attention to return addresses over the years.

"Ah, but a creative way to travel through Europe on a budget," said John.

"I am glad, too, because I am able to see it and learn about it. I probably do not otherwise," Jacques added, surprising Mark.

Had he not been so biased against him, Mark might have liked Jacques, but he did not allow himself the freedom. He separated from the two the next day, instead, and explored Parisian museums on his own. Jacques had predictably recommended the Louvre and the Musée d'Orsay, the former first because it housed one of the grandest collections of art in the world, the latter second because it was worth seeing the architectural design even if he were too tired by then to go inside.

Mark expressed no desire to see another of Jacques' performances and indicated that he would have to return to Hamburg soon in order to catch his flight to Kenya. He wasn't lying. He decided that he would return to Africa a few weeks earlier than planned because he couldn't bear to sightsee any more and because he couldn't tolerate feeling so unwelcome by his father. Maybe a part of him was running away from his new friends, too, but he didn't care. His experiences in Europe mobilized him, clarified imprecise desires, and geared him up to get on with his life, with or without Kyle.

NINE

"I'm Joshua." The about-twenty-five year old African stuck his hand out and shook Mark's with consideration.

"Hello. That's an unusual name for these parts."

"I'm from Ethiopia," the skinny, new acquaintance said as if it explained everything about him including his name. "I'm in charge of this area. I was told you're interested in joining our cause." He looked Mark over and then signaled someone to come with a jerk of his head. "This is Pierre." Pierre had been standing a distance away and had acted unrelated.

Mark recognized the older man's French accent, ascertained he was from the Ivory Coast. The three spoke about travel in Africa, the difficulties obtaining visas and the unreliable transportation. Overhearing them, one would think them tourists or travel agents. The streets in this part of Nairobi were packed with people, buses and cars, all competing for the same space.

Pierre leaned in and whispered, "There's something you can do for us. Can you make yourself available?"

"Sure, I'd like to help, but I just want to make it clear that I don't want any involvement with illegal activity." The two strangers exchanged a glance. "Are you able to assure me of that? If I join the League? My father has a government pension, and I can't risk anything happening to it, or them." Mark felt a jolt from behind him as a local tradesman ran into him with his produce cart and then proceeded to yell at the three of them. They were in the way and rather than argue back in their limited Swahili, they moved further in toward a storefront.

"We need committed activists for the sake of global change. We can't always be so careful about the means to reach our end. The capitalists have no scruples." Joshua lifted one foot behind him and rested it on the wall of the building. He reached into his shirt pocket, grabbed a hand rolled cigarette and lit it. He offered it to Pierre who took a drag and then stuck it out toward Mark.

"No, thanks."

"You're Robert's cousin, by marriage, right?" Joshua readdressed him.

"Yes."

"He's a good man. Cares about the cause, is willing to make sacrifices. Perhaps you need to consider your priorities. Do you have any children?"

"Chi—no." Mark had never been asked the question before.

"So, you don't worry yet what's become of our world, our continent."

"Well, I wouldn't say that."

"So, what is the hesitation?" Pierre asked.

"I just prefer—" Mark stopped, waited for car horns to cease. "I prefer passive forms of resistance," he said in a low voice.

"You strike me as a man of action; perhaps I'm wrong." The words arrived in puffs of smoke.

"What do you want me to do?"

"There's no point in talking about it. Nothing illegal, though. We have a lot of pressing matters to attend to. If you're not willing and able, we can't waste our time."

Mark shifted his weight from one foot to the other, suspecting an attempt to manipulate him but also painfully aware that he continued to have doubts about everything. Now almost four months back in Africa, he still tried to forget about the two unusual Europeans, but it wasn't easy for him. He was glad that the Englishman had called only once and then apparently forgotten him. John was likely mentally ill, and that's why Jacques had persuaded him to take his medication. Mark didn't wish to pry at the time, or risk further entanglement by questioning them about it. He forgave his own callousness now by choosing to believe that mental illness was a luxury afforded by the wealthy. Some statistical data supported the notion, although he was well aware of how numbers could be made to lie. Still, it served him to hold this conviction because it supported his hatred of capitalistic trends.

It didn't help that Jacques called him several times. He couldn't figure it out. What was it that the Frenchman wanted? He had everything and certainly didn't need Mark's interest. Embarrassed by the show of solicitude, he berated Jacques for wasting the money to call him. Inwardly, though, he enjoyed the sound of his refined voice, and this only fueled his confusion and anger. When Humming asked about the curious French accent on the phone, Mark ensured she received evasive responses. If she were to have eavesdropped, she would have heard nothing but "Hmm." Once he ordered the Frenchman distinctly not to call, and he hadn't since. Mark almost regretted it now. But, what did Jacques–or John–know about suffering and things that mattered? That's why Mark was meeting with the communists–to relieve his sense of complicity. He felt wrong that a year hadn't gone by yet, but the inner pressure to act was growing stronger.

"You're right," Mark conceded finally, realizing he could put off the decision by a couple of months by keeping his word to Kyle. "I need to be sure I'm committed." The other two exchanged another glance. Mark had been quiet for so long, they'd probably miscalculated his intentions.

The fan-swept air felt dry and cool on Mark's face as he sat down to eat dinner that evening. His father was reading the newspaper from Nairobi as his mother dished out homemade dhal. The phone rang, and Mark quickly rose to answer it.

"Go ahead," Mark answered.

"Mark, is it you? C'est moi, Jacques."

Mark faced the other direction. "Yes."

"Something bad has happened. I think you should know."

"What is it?" he asked. Papap wanted to know who was on the phone. Mark said it was someone from Europe and his father went back to the paper. His mother slammed the lid on the pot she was holding. Then she let the pot down on the stove with a bang, forcing Mark to ask Jacques to repeat himself. He wasn't sure what his mother's anger was about, maybe the German connection reminded her of Andreas, maybe it was too ostentatious for the European to call whenever he wanted. Did his mother think he was being disloyal to Kyle? He didn't mean to give her that impression but had always refused to explain himself to anyone and wouldn't start now.

"John tried to kill himself," Jacques said louder. "Mark, did you hear me?"

"Yes, I heard. Why?"

"Why?" Jacques sounded incredulous. "I don't know. He is sick…you must know it."

"Hmm."

"Will you come to Europe? I fly to London tomorrow. Please come."

"That's not possible."

"I will pay for you," Jacques said.

"No."

Silence. Humming asked what was wrong, although the conversation must have sounded eerily similar to every other one he'd had with the French voice. Mark told her nothing was wrong.

"I have to go now."

"But he needs to see you."

"Why me? I don't even really know him."

"He doesn't have anyone else. His sister asked that we come because he mentions us to his family. He thinks you are his friend."

Silence.

"Please come. I will pay for you."

"That's not possible."

"Yes, of course, I can."

"That's not what I meant."

"Oh, alors…" Silence ensued except for the sound of Jacques' sigh. Mark wanted to say more but was trapped in the house with his parents' ears not five feet away. Now his father asked what was happening, what was wrong, and his little sister was staring at him from the table.

"I'm sorry, I have to go."

"I will call you back. I will buy the ticket and tell you the information later when I call."

"I can't."

"Please don't make me go alone," Jacques said. Neither said anything for a few seconds. Then Jacques said again, "I will call again later with the information."

Mark wanted to tell him to stop insisting. He hung up the phone without saying good-bye.

"Who was that?" asked his father. His mother was eating her dinner with her eyes downcast.

"Jacques."

"The French boy? What does he want?"

"That I go to see someone with him." Mark chose his words with caution.

"A friend?" Papap seemed merely concerned and not judgmental about it like his mother.

"Yes, well, I guess."

"He's in trouble?"

"Yeah, I guess."

"How?"

"He's in hospital."

"Why is he in hospital?" his little sister asked, her eyes wide. "Is he going to die?"

"Bella!" his mother admonished.

"I don't know." Mark avoided his father's eyes.

"We can't afford it. Unless your—unless Andreas pays for the ticket again," his mother added.

"Andreas doesn't know him. I met him in Germany, but he's…"

"He's what?" Papap asked.

"English." He thought to add that John was also crazy, but his mother might not want to explain to Bella what that meant. Besides, what *did* it mean?

"Maybe we could afford to send you," his stepfather said as his mother looked up sharply.

"There's no need. If I want to go, the French boy, as you call him, is apparently willing and able to pay my way."

"How come you don't want to go? It's not like you to disregard your friends."

"It's complicated, Papap."

"They aren't his friends. He just said he hardly knows them, and he doesn't want to go. Besides, we need him to work."

"We don't need him that badly." Papap and Humming stared at one another while both Mark and Bella stirred in their seats. "He's a grown man, my dear wife. He has to make his own decisions."

"We've been over this, Kisau. Leave it alone. He's nineteen, he's not a 'grown man,' for God's sake."

"Jesus, Mom, that's probably not the best direction to go with this argument." He looked at Papap and wondered what it meant they'd "been over this."

Papap was smiling suddenly and then laughing. "When are you leaving?"

"He'll let me know when he calls back." Mark couldn't help but join Papap when he broke out into a full laugh. He saw how his mother was trying to appear angry, but she couldn't resist Papap's charm any more than the rest of them.

TEN

Not only was Mark taking a trip with a rich Frenchman to see a British aristocrat who suffered ennui to the point of suicide, he was doing it first class. He was on his way to London via Paris. It meant that he'd been forced to decline helping the League. He wasn't sure exactly what they needed, since he didn't get to meet with them a second time, but it had been important, "pressing." He was too angry to sleep, and the self-inflicted castigations multiplied. How had he let himself be manipulated into running to the rescue of someone he hardly knew and didn't particularly like? His thoughts fell through trap doors and down circular staircases of his own concoction until he reached a barely tempered rage.

He boarded his next flight in Paris after a two-hour wait. It was four o'clock in the morning French time, and still he had not slept. He finally arrived in London, just as its citizens were preparing for a workday. The cold air blasted through his thin jacket as he made his way to the hotel.

The room was elegantly Victorian but nothing luxurious. There was only one bed. He figured he'd have his own room like he did in Paris. Why would Jacques have gotten only one room now, with one bed no less, unless he was making unsubstantiated assumptions?

Mark looked at the amount of luggage Jacques brought with him and wondered what the hell he planned to do with all of it. The idea of sharing a room with someone so dissimilar to himself was a little nauseating. Or, did his stomach feel sick because he was exhausted? Either way, he wasn't feeling well and wished he hadn't come. He decided to lie down for a while before he went to see John and hoped the trip would go by quickly.

Mark did not understand and said so.

"This will daze you," Jacques said, maybe sarcastic, "but there are many men who don't despise me, who want me, even married men, respected men. For their pleasure."

Mark leaned back in his chair again. He looked at the food on the table and then at the others sitting near them. Can they hear this? He leaned forward again and asked, "He prostitutes you?" The gnawing pain in his gut made his words bite.

Meanwhile, Jacques looked like he was trying to swallow a stabbing knot in his throat. He did not answer.

"That's appalling," Mark said, indignant.

"Please," Jacques grabbed Mark's forearm, his eyes alight, as if he had just become aware of what he had revealed, "Do not tell anyone this."

But, Mark was too fraught with his own reaction to heed the request. "Christ, it's inconceivable. Have you reported him?"

"My father?" Jacques looked shocked.

"Yes! He doesn't deserve your protection."

"I am afraid of him." Jacques began to cry again. "Please, just forget it. My father does not know, probably. I do not know why I told you this." His accent was thickening and sounded vulnerable to Mark. "I was upset because of John."

"You have more than that to be upset about," Mark said.

"Please do not pity me. I would rather you hate me."

Mark shook his head. "That's fucking horrible," he said, oblivious to Jacques' request. Maybe that was why the Frenchman kept in touch. He needed help. "And what do you mean he doesn't know? How could he not?"

"Like everyone else. People do not know not the things they do not *want* to know," Jacques said, as he wiped his eyes dry.

They returned to the hotel without exchanging words. Mark contrived vengeful plots against Jacques' father but attempted to brush aside his own level of involvement.

———

When later that evening Mark climbed onto the bed and stretched out in his briefs, Jacques felt less enthusiastic than he imagined he would. He hadn't been able to get Mark off his mind for the majority of the last couple of months. It was so rare for him to feel attracted to anyone, and even more extraordinary for him to know desire that he interpreted it as falling in love. He'd not seen the coldness with which Mark addressed him with clarity. He'd blamed his own flaws and had felt unworthy of someone like Mark, someone who seemed so free, wild, and not without passion. Perhaps he'd wanted Mark's strength to rescue him. Jacques had convinced himself that he needed the African there because he'd never traveled alone, never been without the servants, drivers, and assistants employed by his father, but the grander truth was that he wanted Mark to be his boyfriend, the lover he'd never been afforded. After today, he had doubts for the first time but still dropped to his knees by the side of the bed.

"What are you doing?" Mark grabbed Jacques' hand just as it started to tug on his briefs.

Jacques' breath was caught, and he could feel his face red-hot.

"Shit, I'm sorry, Jacques," Mark said. "Really. But, this isn't going to work for me. I didn't mean to mislead you or anything. I plan to sleep on the floor."

Was he serious? Now Jacques knew he'd never met anyone like this white African, and that's when it hit him. Mark represented the notion of *far away*. Mark could be the sign he was waiting for, the very thing that would lead him from his unwanted life into something new. The sense of anticipatory liberation kept him awake for hours.

TWELVE

Jacques had his dressing gown wrapped with a loose bow around his waist when he walked out of the hotel bathroom. He wasn't used to taking care of his own hygiene; his valet would run his bath water and lay out meticulously selected clothing. A personal care assistant would dry and style his hair. Left on his own, he was less particular. After his father's initial outburst at Jacques' intended "vacation," he agreed to pay for either one to join Jacques on his trip. By then, however, Jacques had made other plans and did not want the intrusion. Presently, he was busy repacking his bag after having spent an hour stretching.

Maintaining his dancing skill took many hours every week, something foreign to his new companion. Mark seemed to be curious about every stretch, what its intended purpose was, how often Jacques practiced it, what it meant he'd be able to accomplish. Jacques had appreciated the attention, even if it seemed only educational.

"You want to have supper here tonight? At the restaurant, or perhaps room service? I have almost finished with my luggage," Jacques asked as he turned toward Mark. The African was already undressed for bed and wearing only briefs. There was an open box of biscuits on the small hotel table, an apparent dinner for one. Although it was a little disappointing, Jacques was used to skipping meals. As he got closer, Mark seemed to startle and hurriedly placed his thrown jeans in front of his crotch in an attempt to conceal his hard on. Jacques tried not to appear gratified. He backed off a bit because Mark had the look of a trapped raccoon. Then he wrestled with his choices and settled on offering Mark relief.

"Why not let me do something?"

Mark sighed. "It's not right. I can't get involved with you," he mumbled.

"I understand," he said, although he didn't, and it hurt that Mark stated it so emphatically. "What if I just use my mouth, to help you, so you will sleep better?"

Mark shook his head no but his eyes were less resolute.

"No obligation to get involved with me. It's just sex," Jacques said. He had his own fears to quell. Ever since John had brought this young man to him, he had hardly been able to think of anything else. The faceless men had been superimposed by Mark's image, and, in turn, Jacques had enjoyed his sexuality for brief moments, crediting the strange African instead of his own imagination. He kept his romance with Mark to himself for the duration.

He could now see the head of Mark's penis pressing for freedom under his cotton briefs, and he wondered how he could be so otherwise offensive that Mark would refuse the offer in spite of such supplication. He smiled when he saw Mark finally reach to remove the barricade and lowered himself to the floor next to him. Adept at fellatio for reasons he did not like to contemplate, Jacques devoured him for the short time Mark could contain himself. When he came, Mark released an emancipated roar, the likes of which Jacques had never heard before.

Wiping his lips with the back of his hand, Jacques asked, "That is better, n'est-ce pas?"

Mark had a satisfied grin and look of amazement. "Thank you," he said. He then stood and pulled Jacques up as well, leading him over to the bed. They lay down, foreheads touching. "I just want to stay like this for a little while, if that's okay."

Jacques felt happy and sad at the same time. He wanted something more than Mark appeared willing or able to give him. He debated with himself whether or not to reveal his feelings. He decided he had nothing to lose and said, "It was about you, some of it."

"What?"

"The letter John wrote before he hurt himself. It shows how crazy he was, but also it speaks a little about you." Seeing Mark's confused expression, he added, "Because I had mentioned you to him when I wrote."

"Oh. What about? I mean, you don't have to say. I'm sorry, I didn't realize before that you meant it was personal on your end."

"I told him I had dreamt of lying here like this with you, and his response was… well, the whole letter was truly…" Jacques sought an appropriate word.

"Nuts?" Mark asked.

"Oui." Jacques wondered if Mark would have the courage to acknowledge what he had really just told him, so he waited. Finally, he looked away. "Will you stay with me in Paris for a time on your way back to Africa?"

"I don't know if I should…because there's work to be done at home."

"Yes, I understand," Jacques said.

"But, maybe I could stay for a short time," Mark said.

Jacques suppressed a grin, not wanting to seem overeager. He longed to kiss the African but was too afraid of rejection, and of pushing his luck. Besides, Mark seemed to like to be in command of things. He should wait for him to lead.

THIRTEEN

"Are you going to keep fussing the whole flight?" Mark asked Jacques after they were seated in the first class cabin. He only pretended to be vexed. What he really felt was something more like agitated desire. He was discovering a side of himself engaged in watching Jacques. After a final visit with John, as hopeless as the others, they took a cab to Heathrow and boarded a jet to Paris. Mark had been a little rough in his rebuke about not being in economy class, and here he was expressing judgment again. He reminded himself that he was starting to like this unusual guy.

"Sorry," Jacques said, but then a warm smile lit his face when Mark grinned at him. "I cannot find my book."

"If you had fewer bags…"

Jacques stood up and opened the overhead storage bin. The flight attendant walked over with an air of urgency asking if she could be of help. Jacques declined but asked for a diet soft drink. "You want one?"

"No, thanks. I didn't think you'd drink cola."

"Only when I travel," Jacques said, and Mark nodded, pretending it made sense. "Ah, voila." Jacques held up the paperback in a superfluous gesture.

Somehow he made the Frenchman nervous, which was hard to believe when he thought of Jacques' life and experience. He turned his head away and retreated inward, considering the futility of their plan to spend more time together. What was the point? Their lifestyles were incompatible. They lived on different continents. He'd have a problematic time integrating Jacques into his world even if the Frenchman lived in Nairobi. And, what of Kyle? Was there no chance they would reunite?

The plane started to taxi from the gate and later took to the air effortlessly. Mark thought it was convenient, to do just what you were meant to do. He wished he had a clue about his own purpose in life.

When permitted, Jacques extended his seat and stretched, book in hand. He accepted the blanket offered by the flight attendant and spread it over his body.

"What are you reading?" Mark asked him.

"*Les Miserables* by Victor Hugo. You know it?"

"Do I know it? Yes," Mark said, taken aback. "Why are you reading it?"

Jacques just shrugged and looked back at the page.

"You don't know why you're reading it?"

It took a bit more prompting on Mark's part before Jacques finally said, "My valet gave it to me. He selects books for me."

"What's a valet?"

"Ah, oui. He is one of our staff at home. He is like my personal butler I think in English. I'm not sure if there is a more specific word for him."

"What does he do exactly?" Mark asked. The conversation so far seemed to solidify his belief in his own stupidity. He shouldn't be going to France with Jacques, and he felt his blood vacating his upper extremities. What on Earth would an eighteen-year-old need with a butler?

"Many things."

"Like?"

"He helps me with my clothing and personal care, and he is my friend. But, that part is not customary. He also recommends books to balance what my tutors teach me, like this one. Anyway, it's a classic, n'est-ce pas?"

"So it is." Mark smirked, but with no real disdain. He was curious about this relationship with Jacques' valet. Maybe it was like having a nanny, who just stayed on after Jacques grew up.

The Frenchman extended the blanket over Mark's arm then, and before Mark could complain or throw it off, Jacques slipped his hand into Mark's. His first thought was to pull away, but he was glued by the magnetism between them. Not since Kyle had he felt this kind of energy. He squeezed Jacques' hand but looked away.

"Why can't we just go through the front entrance?" Mark asked. They were standing in the dark on the impeccable grounds of Jacques' family estate. He was holding Jacques' bags and luggage and felt like a coat rack. There were smaller bags shoved into intimate crevices of his arms and a strap around his throat leading to Jacques' garment bag.

Jacques offered him a nervous shrug and knocked lightly on his valet's window. A light appeared, and Mark saw the older man donning a robe and waving them around to another entrance, apparently the servants' entrance.

His valet gave Jacques a warmer hug than Mark expected, and both turned to look at him.

"Mon Dieu!" the man exclaimed, seeing Mark weighed down as he was. Mark chuckled in response, and Jacques gave him the most beautiful smile. He introduced Louis, who quickly helped remove some of the bags. They shook hands.

The two Frenchmen spoke rapidly, almost conspicuously so, as if plotting in secret. Louis led them to the guest wing.

A little while later Mark leaned in the doorframe of a kitchenette, his head resting on the wall, his arms crossed, his right hand on his chin Rodin-like. He watched Jacques. The Frenchman stood as a sentinel by the stove and seemed concentrated on the teapot. Mark wondered what he was thinking. Jacques became more enigmatic by the minute. He wasn't sure why they were in guest quarters and didn't want to be nosy by asking. After helping them settle in, Louis bade them good night, and Jacques went to the small kitchen to prepare a snack. He said he didn't want to disrupt his valet any more than they had already, and Mark was glad for it.

Jacques' hair was down and gathered over his right shoulder. Mark felt so aroused, he had to fight the impulse to touch, or even grab, what was right there for the grabbing.

"Shall I serve you something to eat, too?" Jacques looked over his shoulder as he spoke, and the "th" in the word *something* bounced like a soft and jubilant z sound.

Mark was riveted to the lips that made that sound. There were so many implied complications he couldn't recount right now. His eyes moved up Jacques' face while his emotions reeled for a long moment before settling on pure want. His reason all but deserted him.

The whistling kettle interrupted, and Jacques turned away to quiet it with dispatch. Mark moved in and touched, softly at first, a hand on the waist, met by a welcoming, almost imperceptible, turn of the torso. Jacques trembled, and Mark thought of sex, actual sex, as in fucking. He dropped his hand to the Frenchman's ass and squeezed it hard while his heart pounded against his ribs. His mouth found the bared neck, and groped, while his free arm wrapped itself around the Frenchman's chest, pulling him in until Jacques gasped.

Mark swirled him around then, and Jacques inflamed him by meeting his eyes provocatively. Finally, he pressed his mouth to Jacques' lips, their eyes still locked. Jacques' scent was sweet, like rose water, and Mark didn't move. He just kept breathing this magnificence in, their lips open, but barely. Jacques started beckoning him further, letting the tip of his tongue entice him, so he grabbed the nape of Jacques' neck and forced his tongue into him, sucking with passion, biting his lips. Was it blood he tasted suddenly? Damn, he'd bitten too hard and cut the soft skin of the bottom lip. "Sorry," he whispered.

"I don't care," Jacques said, kissing Mark harder and holding him around the waist.

"I want you," Mark said as an involuntary confession. But then in a flash, he sensed the Frenchman tense up. He used his thumb to caress Jacques' moist lips before asking him what was wrong.

"I don't know how you want me to act," Jacques' voice was so low that Mark had to work at discerning the words.

"I don't get it," Mark said, struggling against feeling annoyed. He had been led to believe that this was what the Frenchman wanted all along. Jacques held his grasp on Mark, which softened Mark's irritation but didn't mitigate his confusion in the least.

"Did I do something wrong?" he asked. Jacques held his face down, so Mark pulled away slightly, lifted Jacques' chin and kissed him on the cheek. It was a gentle act that came naturally to him. "I don't know why you're upset, but you better tell me before I start believing you don't like this."

Jacques laughed through his watery eyes. "I am stupid. *Idiot*," he said in French.

"Why?"

"I don't know. It's hard to explain. With other men, I sense—"

"No...I don't want to hear about that. Not ever." He shook his head vigorously to emphasize his words. "Please don't ever mention it."

Jacques looked down again, and Mark was sorry for what he said. "This is different for me. I am nervous should I not satisfy you."

Mark considered how that could be possible when Jacques seemed so good at what he did. He struggled to find a way to console him without sounding trite. "I'm not worried," he said. Then he lifted Jacques off his feet and carried him to the bed.

"You are very strong," said Jacques.

"And you thought you wouldn't know how to please me," he said, chuckling. He laid Jacques on his back and stretched his own body on top of him, kissing him again, his hardness shoving against his companion's counterpart.

Once in bed, the Frenchman's inhibitions seemed to dissipate. He told Mark that he had never made love to anyone in his own home, which pleased Mark more than he would have guessed.

Mark believed in the intensity of homosexual love, of the mirror image of self. He had never been with a girl; in fact he had never been with anyone but Kyle. He feared he may seem inexperienced, but he didn't doubt that Jacques had surrendered to him. Everything about this guy turned him on, and he hoped he would last longer than he had at the hotel in London.

Mark laced their hands over Jacques' head and kissed him everywhere he could reach. He told him to strip, and the Frenchman stood up and complied.

Jacques was thinly muscular; his belly button was hollow. Mark took it all in, taking his time. He lowered himself to Jacques' pelvis with overwhelming desire to consume him. Before the Frenchman could come, though, he pulled him back to bed and on top. He enjoyed the pressure Jacques' body exerted on his, and he vocalized something guttural, feeling both more fully present and more out of his body than ever before.

When Jacques swept him into an almost frenzied yearning with his very competent mouth, he looked at Mark triumphantly and then positioned himself to be entered from behind.

Mark did enter, with caution, unsure if he was hurting the Frenchman by pushing into him. He hesitated to let his full size take hold.

"Wait," Jacques said as he leaned to the side and handed him a lubricant that had slid out of one of his bags. Jacques kissed him, lingering at his lips, and told him he did not have to be so gentle.

Mark blushed and hoped the dim lighting hid his embarrassment. He squirted gel onto his hand and stroked himself. Then he placed an extra dollop on Jacques, gingerly sticking a finger in, then two, testing what he had to work with, actively suppressing stray thoughts of distaste for such an act by losing himself in his desire once again. Next time he grabbed Jacques' waist, he thrust more thoroughly and with a little more abandon, astonished at the new sensations it stirred. He leaned over Jacques' back and ran his tongue along his spine.

"I wish we could face each other, so I could kiss you."

"We can," Jacques said, sounding happy to accommodate his every wish.

Mark pulled out and waited with fascinated interest as Jacques rolled onto his back and lifted his bent legs toward his chest. Re-entering the Frenchman this way brought shudders. The snug, yet welcoming, grip of Jacques' depths accentuated the delight in viewing him so openly spread out before him. When he came, the sound started in his abdomen and crawled through him till it escaped from his raspy throat between spasms of breath.

The Frenchman came without further stimulation, appearing to mirror Mark's pleasure. Emotionally, he didn't feel finished with him at all, but his body was exhausted, and he succumbed to lying quietly, cradling Jacques.

He tried to sleep. He let the fact that he and Kyle never had intercourse slip from his consciousness earlier but now felt twinges of guilt. They had considered it once or twice, but neither of them liked the prospect of being the recipient. He hadn't known it would feel that great. Kyle had asked him to remember him.

"I wish we could stay like this forever," Jacques whispered, bringing Mark back to the present.

"I'm afraid you're just smitten."

"I cannot deny it. I do not know that word."

Mark laughed heartily, a little smitten himself and not wanting to define it. He could feel his mouth dry and his loins dehydrated, but he refused to leave the bed for water.

"It means, I think you are like a dream?"

"Sort of, yes. But I'm far from perfect, you should be warned," Mark said.

The remainder of that night, Mark dreamt of Kyle. Not erotic dreams, but rather long, intricate, and haunting ones. It was as if Kyle were everywhere. He was the produce salesman at a market in Nairobi, the librarian who refused him a book at school, and a cab driver in Paris. Mark came to a couple of times around dawn with a foreboding that he could not escape his past any more than the Frenchman could.

FOURTEEN

Mark woke with a start a few hours soon after when an obnoxious banging on the door resulted in Jacques leaping from bed. The Frenchman was at the bedroom door before Mark had time to roll over and face it. He could only see Jacques standing there with his head peeking out. Just then, a man's voice yelled at Jacques for his impudence, but Mark had not heard the preceding conversation and was having difficulty translating the rapid French. It seemed as though Jacques were being reprimanded for being late. He was apologetic. He sounded intimidated. He offered the excuse that he had not been feeling well the night before.

The other man asked if Jacques were hiding something or someone in the room, heard the man demand Jacques' reason for being there at all. He was curious about that himself and started to feel like a stowaway. The older man threw the door open and gasped at the sight of Mark, who would appear somewhat wild in the bed with his lengthy, uncombed hair and a bit of dark stubble. Mark rose from the bed and was glad he was wearing briefs. He had no idea what to do in this unusual circumstance. His instinct was to come to Jacques' aid, so he walked over to him ready to fight if needed.

"Papa—" Jacques started.

"What? This is your father?" Mark was stunned. The man was shorter than he'd assumed, nowhere near Jacques' height, but bulkier, like a boxer. He wore a blazer with a paisley scarf, and had a beefy mustache. There was no family resemblance whatsoever.

Just then the older man slapped Jacques' face hard, throwing him upon the door. Mark helped Jacques to full standing and asked him if he was okay.

"How dare you, you..." Jacques' father apparently searched for the proper English pejorative.

Mark suppressed his desire to grab the man by the throat. He settled for glaring at him.

"Get ze hell out of my house and do not return," the man commanded.

"Please go, Mark. Please. It's fine," Jacques said.

"Really? Are you sure?" Mark asked him. He was having a tough time thinking with all the adrenaline now coursing through his system.

"Yes. I'll be fine."

Mark thought Jacques' eyes said otherwise, but he couldn't be certain. "I'll go only to make less trouble for you." He held Jacques' face tenderly and meant to kiss him, but Jacques pulled away from him. His father grunted and threatened to kill Mark, but this threat barely registered next to Jacques' unexpected retreat. Mark threw his jeans on and made sure he had his wallet and bag. But, he almost left without his shirt, so beside himself he was. Jacques grabbed it and handed it to him on his way out.

As Mark walked from the gates that surrounded the chateau, he remembered that he had no place to go. His plane ticket was not valid for a few days and he was not sure he could get on an earlier flight. Nor did he have a map. Nor did he want to get on an earlier flight. If he had to, he could take a train to Hamburg to see Tanja and his little sister and brother. There could be worse things, he mused. But, then, why did he feel like crying?

"Monsieur!" he heard presently and turned to see Louis huffing his way to Mark's side. He clenched a note written by Jacques in his gnarled hand and put a finger to his lips as if to bid Mark never to reveal his participation. He ran quickly back through the gate. The note read, *Mark, please go to Hotel Les Trois. I will call ahead of you and tell them to hold a room. I will pay the fee. I am very sorry. Please go to the hotel, and I will meet you there tonight. Jacques.*

FIFTEEN

Mark bit his lower lip and felt a tidal wave of anger rise and then fall within him. He had slept most of the day. He had just showered and was donning his jeans when he noticed how unbearably laden with gratuitous amenities the Hotel Les Trois was. Couldn't Jacques have chosen something more modest for him? How was he going to reconcile his value system with his new friend's life? On top of his personal dilemma, he could hardly stop replaying the scene at Jacques' home. He wanted revenge on the man who would prostitute his son and then beat him for loving someone. He finished dressing and was glad to catch some French news before there was a knock on the door.

Jacques was exquisite. He wore his costume from work at the club: a light blue sequined gown with a low backline. His face was smooth, blushed, and colored, but not overdone. Mark had no reason to believe that Jacques was actually transsexual, which was a relief. Still, he seemed so at ease in the garb that Mark now questioned it.

"May I enter?" Jacques asked when Mark just stood in awe at the doorway.

"Yes, of course. I guess I expected you would have changed before coming." He considered asking about the show but was too uninterested.

"Oui, perhaps I should have, but," Jacques looked down, "I can't stay the whole night with you." He walked toward the bed and sat on the edge.

"Oh," Mark said with an effort to seem unbothered. "That's fine," he said but felt immediately remorseful. The lie revealed his disappointment the way an exaggeration always betrayed the truth.

"I wish I could stay."

"I understand," Mark said. He leaned against the armoire, avoiding Jacques' eyes.

"I am sorry about this morning. My father is very stubborn and—"

"It's not your fault."

"Are you angry?" Jacques asked him.

"Not at you," he said. He felt angry with himself and wasn't sure what was happening. "Are you okay? Your father hit you pretty hard."

"Yes, I'm fine. There is a little mark but the make-up covers it."

He joined Jacques on the bed, felt his heart begin to pound and wondered why this anomaly of a Frenchman dressed as a woman was having this effect on him. He also felt a bit impish since he had masturbated in the shower earlier, fantasizing about making love as they had the night before. He was self-conscious in placing his arm around Jacques' waist and brought the Frenchman to laughter.

"What's so funny?" Mark asked, almost scared at how fragile and feminine Jacques looked.

"You want I should take the dress off, so you are more *confortable?*" The last word was pronounced in his native tongue. At that, Mark pressed his lips against Jacques' with a pressure he didn't intend. He pulled down on the shoulder of the gown and tore it slightly.

"Oh, non!" Jacques jumped up to inspect the damage.

"I'm sorry, I didn't mean to. I guess I don't know how to get this off you," Mark picked at the sequins and apologized again.

"It's not bad, do you think?" Jacques ran his finger along the small tear. "Not remarkable?"

"Noticeable," Mark corrected.

"Excuse me?"

"The word is noticeable, and it isn't very."

"Is not?"

"Noticeable." Mark turned away. He could see Jacques blush slightly, and he hadn't really meant to be so pedantic or hostile. "Where do you have to go tonight?"

"Back to work."

"At the club?" Mark was seated on the bed still and tapped a hand on the spread to invite Jacques to join him again. Instead, Jacques excused himself and went to the bathroom. He returned with a hotel robe wrapped around him, tied at the waist.

"This is better, n'est-ce pas?"

"Sure," Mark said. "I really am sorry about tearing your dress." He meant it, surprising himself again at the mere reference of the attire.

Jacques sat next to him and kissed him on the neck while pulling his T-shirt up over his head. They leaned back into a soulful kiss.

"I missed you today," Jacques said as he searched Mark's eyes.

"Can't you stay with me? Can't you get someone to fill in for you?"

Jacques averted his eyes to the side, as if somehow fascinated by the bedspread embroidery. "I can't stay," he said simply.

"You're not going to the club, are you?" Mark asked. A wave of heat walloped through his core when it hit him. How stupid of him to think things would have changed just because of their newfound romance. He pushed Jacques away and stood by the window, hoping the slight draft would cool him off. On the streets he saw French and tourists alike as they went about their evening. They all, no doubt, had their own stories, pain, and dreams, but Mark saw only automatons through his hateful glare.

"Please don't be angry," Jacques said, walking over to him. "I don't want to fight."

"Last night was just another trick, *Jacqui?*"

"Of course not."

"Why would you do this? Why would you leave me to…" Mark stared at him, unable to complete the thought aloud. Jacques stood motionless, as a deer caught in headlights, but the French beauty was nothing hackneyed despite his sexual history. It caught Mark off guard, which angered him further. "Why?" Mark yelled this time, quite literally throwing Jacques back a few inches with his energy.

"I don't have the choice."

"You always have a choice," Mark choked a little on the last word and turned away.

"Please…" Jacques muttered, but Mark did not look back. For the first time in his life, he felt mean and strange to himself. A lone tear rolled down his cheek by how he had betrayed Kyle. Did he really think he could remodel the life of this lost soul standing behind him, waiting to be told what to do, how to act, which to be?

Finally he said, "Just leave, Jacques. This would never have worked out. Your life disgusts me, and mine would never have been extravagant enough for you."

"Please believe me, I don't want this," Jacques mumbled, but he started toward the marbled floor of the bathroom to change, just as he was told to do.

The thought occurred to Mark then that he could have sex with Jacques first. He didn't want to have the thought, but there it was. He wondered if he could debase himself enough to yield to the inexplicable, compelling desire to fuck him as he had the night before, and the heat of the image burned his groin and flushed his face.

"Wait," he said as he turned to look at Jacques. "I want you so much, I can't think clearly. You decide."

"Prends moi," Jacques removed the robe and stood naked. "I am yours."

Mark walked over to him, remote from his usual sense of self, and too forcefully pushed Jacques face down over the ornate desk. He pulled his jeans down, separated the Frenchman's firm cheeks, and then rammed himself inside, feeling dry friction at first, then using his spit to ease it somewhat. Jacques gripped the corners of the desk. Mark thrust hard and angrily, unwilling to restrain how deep, while Jacques' position left his scarcely distended penis to whack against the desk drawer in rhythm. Mark didn't bother to stop or to move them. After he came, he left himself deeply encased for as long as he could, panting, biting Jacques' back less gently than he would have consciously chosen to do.

Then, as if waking from a trance, he took a step back and noticed Jacques' clinging form, his legs shaking. Mark's hands cupped his eyes, then covered his whole face, as the shame of his actions hit him. He didn't know what to do. He turned away from the Frenchman and did not look back. He was afraid of himself.

After Jacques got dressed, it looked like he might say something, but he must have changed his mind. Jacques must hate him now, after the way he acted, and his confusion was so thick that he really couldn't tell if he was glad or if he was devastated.

———

Jacques departed the Hotel Les Trois missing a critical component of self. The doorman made sycophantic remarks that went unanswered because the grief he felt took up all the space in his throat. Someone helped him into the limousine which would take him to the four star hotel not far from the Eiffel Tower.

Usually he dissociated whenever he was to rendezvous with someone his father scheduled. He was officially to perform, maintain the illusion of being the beautiful, young woman he appeared to be. He was never sure if his father knew that most of the men expected some kind of sexual activity. After it happened the first time, after a business associate of his father raped Jacques and then signed a lucrative contract the next day making his father the most pleased Jacques had ever seen him, Jacques couldn't tell him what had happened. He couldn't get past the shame to tell anyone. It had burrowed itself into his heart and made a home there.

To a more intuitive ear, Jacques had intimated plenty to his father. For instance, he was never feeling well whenever his father announced he had booked a "private show." Over the last year, Jacques believed it was an inner strength that allowed him to remove himself from the events as they occurred. Tonight, however, a detachment overtook him in a deeper way. Mark would probably never speak to him again because he didn't have the nerve to stand up to his father. If he weren't afraid of going to the real Hell, he would consider killing himself to escape the one in which he was living.

"Well, don't just stand there. Come in," the half-dressed businessman said. He was no more than forty-five but already had a flabby gut. He sounded mean. He'd been drinking. Jacques had walked to room 223 noticing almost nothing, but his senses were awakened now by fear. He felt it like acid along the length of his spine and into his already strained throat, multiplied when he saw two other inebriated men at the table. The door shut behind him. He knew he was in danger and that it was too late to do anything about it now.

SIXTEEN

The psychiatrist held a clipboard closely to his hip and walked into John's room with an air of authority. Nurse Mildred followed behind him in her usual attentiveness. John had been transferred almost two weeks ago to St. Katherine's Hospital for the Mentally Ill in Dover. When he'd arrived, his newly assigned doctor, Cornelius Comer, had declared him over-medicated and titrated him off the antipsychotic drug. Some of the unresponsiveness could have been iatrogenic—a result of the medication used to treat the young man, especially because he was on such a high dose in London. After reviewing his history—his whole history—he diagnosed John with psychotic manic-depression, labeled his last physician a complete incompetent, and hoped to prove John was not schizophrenic. He prayed he was right, as Dr. Comer, to the mortification of most of his colleagues, was a spiritual man and frequently prayed for the well-being of his patients.

The confident doctor had seen lithium carbonate work magic in patients with severe manic-depression, so he prescribed it as soon as he could. For the first time since he started treating the young man, the handsome, thirty-seven year old psychiatrist began to worry he'd been wrong. If so, the prognosis was much worse. He'd added a benzodiazepine just yesterday, which, although counterintuitive, would relieve some of the potential anxiety responsible for John's catatonia, pseudo-catatonia, or whatever this was.

"Good, then, how's John today?" he asked the nurse as if they hadn't just met to discuss the lack of progress in the corridor. "Any movement?"

"No, Doctor, he continues in the same state, I'm afraid."

"All right, then, let's do the, um, beanthacin hydrochloride," Comer said, wishing he hadn't forgotten to come up with the name of some powerful pharmaceutical.

"All right, then. Should that be the injection or the IV?" she asked with extemporaneous creativity.

The psychiatrist turned to view the older lady with a new respect and enjoyed the relationship they'd developed over the last year. "Let's go with the injection. We don't need him hyperactive, just active. Of course, if this medication doesn't work," his voice trailed off to captivate the right dramatic pause.

"What are you getting at?" Nurse Mildred asked with a suspicious tone.

"We'll have to go with ice water therapy if this doesn't work."

"Ice water therapy! Oh, no, I'm sure he's a nice young man…"

"It's not a punishment, Nurse, it's a treatment, and the only one we have left." He wondered if it was unethical of them to manipulate a patient back to health. He questioned for a moment how much his own ego rested in the outcome. He didn't want John catatonic and enjoyed thinking of himself as unique in his field.

"Yes, Doctor, I understand, but I have no doubt that he'll be better tomorrow, so I'm not going to fret over it much."

The doctor made a few notations on his clipboard and walked out without ceremony. The nurse, however, lagged behind to adjust John's bed and sheets. "Don't worry, the injection will work," she said as she stroked his hair back. "You'll be almost good as new in the morning."

She joined Comer at the nurse's station. "Let's hope this works." The nurse winked at the psychiatrist as she filled the syringe with a placebo. "I hate to hear what the board would say if we asked to use the old tub."

Dr. Comer laughed but not freely. He was appalled that it wasn't too long ago that a patient could be placed into shock by lowering his body temperature in such a way. Even the electroconvulsive therapy of today was sometimes more than he could stand. Still, he might have to consider repeating shock treatments if John didn't respond to the placebo. Without the heavy medications complicating matters, they might help.

"Dr. Comer," Sam, the night orderly, approached in his usual affable manner. "How are you? Hey, did you hear about the bloke who was told his wife had a severe case of OCD?"

"No, I'm afraid I haven't heard that one," he responded with an air of patronization.

"Yeah, all upset, he was. First thing he asked was if it's contagious," Sam roared almost before getting the last word out, and Dr. Comer laughed in spite of the silliness of the joke. Nevertheless, it brought to mind the affliction of his young patient, his compulsive cutting and burning. He wondered what was behind that violent need to relieve tension.

Mildred rolled her eyes as she walked toward John's room. Dr. Comer watched through the doorway as the nurse swabbed John's right deltoid with alcohol and inserted the needle. "Remember, first thing you do when you wake up is move your fingers and toes, then lift your hands and arms as high as you can. Don't think about it. Just do it." She paused for a moment and added, "Even if you wake in the middle of the night."

———

John watched her peripherally as she walked out and closed the door, wondering what 'ice therapy' was. He wanted to move, and remembered that at first his frozen state had been voluntary, a defense against his situation, maybe a little defiant, and certainly influenced by the heavy medication doses, but now it was as if an inertia locked him into immobility. Even when the physical therapists came to his side and exercised him against atrophy, he felt as if he were disconnected from his own nervous system. As if there were no signals. He fell asleep begging a God he didn't know to make this medicine bring him back to life.

The following morning woke John by broadcasting sunlight into his room and onto his bed, as if Mildred had specifically left the blinds open in hope that John would move his head by instinct to shield his eyes. He didn't, but he did immediately recall what his instructions were and that he might be "iced" if the medication didn't work. He took a deeper than usual inhalation and moved his right fingers, slightly, and then his left. He smiled inside. Then he moved his toes, although not as well. He lifted his right forearm off the bed sheet, marveling at the sensation it sent through his entire body and that it had worked.

Then he lifted his other arm bringing a gasp to his throat as both hands stood before him. He wasn't quite sure he was ready to share his voice, but a gasp in the privacy of his room was all right. Tears threatened to fall from his eyes as he rocked his left foot back and forth, slowly at first and then with more determination. It's not so hard. I can move if I want. Just then he thought to check out the time, but he'd have to turn his head almost ninety degrees to see it. Again, he started slow, like an icicle melting at the first upward rise in temperature, amazed at how exploratory the feeling of movement now seemed, and how miraculous. He made it half way before Nurse Mildred popped her head in on her regular patient rounds.

"Mr. Chatfield," she said, appearing somewhat surprised despite her declaration of faith in the injection. "Well done!" she exclaimed. "I'm glad you woke before my shift ended. I'll go ask the doctor for his instructions." She scooted out. John wondered what it must feel like to be that normal.

She returned with two syringes, announcing she was giving him more of the medication from the night before plus something to keep him relaxed. John questioned why he would need help relaxing but was still unable to bring himself to speak.

The next few days were spent in preparation for John to transfer to the more psychotherapeutic part of the hospital. Most of the staff seemed taken by him, almost all by his smile once it returned. His first words, uttered to Nurse Mildred the following evening, were "Thank you." John was a very well mannered young man, when he wanted to be. And he desperately wanted to be, if for no other reason than to be found dischargeable.

He hoped that once he started moving, he'd be able to leave, but his speech was still so limited, and his psyche so raw, that Dr. Comer had no quick plan to release him. Rather, it had been decided by the staff that he would be immersed in group therapy and individual work even before he was walking on his own. First he was transferred to another ward. Nurse Mildred wheeled him over herself. She handed the transfer paperwork to John's new nurse, and bade him farewell. John's eyes followed her as she walked straight away, not turning around again to look at him, and he wondered if she'd really cared about him or if she was just doing her job.

Nurse Maggie smiled warmly at him. "We've heard a lot about you." Then as if remembering to address all new patients as if they were paranoid, added, "All good things, of course."

John looked down, forlorn all of a sudden at losing the only stability he'd known for what seemed like years.

"Here's your daily schedule," Maggie said as she handed him a bright blue sheet of paper. John glanced at it:

8:00 Hygiene
8:30 Breakfast / Outdoors time
10:00 Group Therapy, atrium

11:00 break
11:30 Physiotherapy
Noon Lunch / Outdoors time
2:00pm Recreational Group, craft room
3:00pm break (individual appointments)
4:00pm Alcohol and Drug-Free Support Group, meeting room B
5:00pm Supper / Outdoors time
7:00pm Group Therapy, atrium
8:30pm Hygiene
9:30pm Lights out

"You'll see your regular doctor in the morning. This afternoon, though, you have a physical exam to check your progress." She pointed to the private appointments time on his calendar as she wheeled him to his room. "You're expected to arrive on time for groups. Please smoke only in designated areas. If you need help, press the call button," she said as she walked out of his room.

John sat where she left him for the next forty-five minutes, watching the clock and waiting for group time. He was scared, almost deathly afraid; the temptation to slip into his cocoon of silence and immobility enticed him. How would he get to group, no less on time?

He looked around the barren room. There was no television or any color. Everything was either white, or looked like it had once been white and had faded into nothing. There were unnecessary bars outside the windowpanes, reminding him of his involuntary status lest he forget. He was on the first floor overlooking a concrete courtyard, so there was no danger of his jumping to death even if he got any skinnier.

He thought of Lilith and if she would come visit him now that he was among the living again. He felt like crying out of shame and frustration for everything he had failed at and for being mental.

An orderly walked in looking for someone named Sam and announced to John that he was "the wrong patient" before walking back out.

"Oh, excuse me?" John called after him, but he mustn't have heard or bothered.

"All right, then," it was Nurse Maggie at the door another ten minutes or so later. "Let's get you there on time."

John sighed with relief. She wheeled him into the atrium, which was a large room with sky lights overhead to draw in as much light as possible in a country often cloudy. There were plants in one area by a pleasantly large, albeit barred, window, and a piano in one corner. About fifteen chairs were placed in a circle, some occupied by patients. John looked at them inconspicuously, fearing the start of group.

Just then the therapist entered the room carrying a clipboard with several papers flapping by the brisk pace she led. "Good, can we get started? Maggie, who's missing?"

"Looks like a few. I'll tell an orderly to round them up."

"Good day, everyone." She glanced at the paper in her hand and smiled. A few people responded by saying hello, most did not. She quickly counted heads and then took attendance. A very large woman walked in and sat outside the circle by the piano. She was wearing a loosely fitted housedress. Then an orderly, a young and muscular black man named Chip, accompanied an elderly gentleman in and helped him sit down. Chip had keys on a necklace around his neck, the type of chain that would break off if grabbed in a chokehold, the only type permitted in the asylum. He announced that no one else would be attending group that day, to which the therapist nodded.

"For those of you I haven't yet had the pleasure of meeting, my name is Teri and I'm one of the therapists on this unit. Let's go around the room and introduce ourselves, giving one thing we're grateful for today."

"You didn't say what you're grateful for," an impoverished looking man to her right commented.

"Okay, Ralph. I'm grateful for a visit from my sister last evening. She was here from London, and we enjoyed a lovely dinner together. Now, you want to go next?"

"Sure," he slurred. "Well, I'm Ralph, obviously... umm...should I say why I'm here?" He rubbed the whiskers on his face and looked at Teri sideways.

"Oh, yes, let's do that, shall we?" She looked around the room.

"Okay, I'm here for depression. To treat my depression," he corrected himself. "And, to stop drinking, and I'm grateful that I haven't had a drink in a couple of weeks. Since I've been here, obviously." He smirked, making it hard to read if he were in fact grateful for his abstinence, or resentful of it.

"Good, next."

"I'm Pat." The woman's right hand shook noticeably as she spoke, and she had odd, jerky mannerisms about her, with a fat, flattened face, and stringy, unkempt hair.

"I'm here for schizophrenia, and for being real anxious." She stopped and looked to the next person with eagerness.

"And what are you grateful for today, Pat?"

"Not really anything," she responded with timidity, still looking at the next person and shrugging.

"Can you think of something? Can anyone help?"

The large woman by the piano started singing. She was tugging at her unruly afro-like hair.

"Okay, Maria, you need to listen to your peers now."

"She should be grateful that God loves her and she's still alive. Come to me, baby, I'm the Lady of Guadalupe," Maria had a heavy Spanish accent. She started to quote the Bible.

"Can you make her shut up?" a young man asked. He was dressed in something like pajamas and looked agitated.

"Maria, would you do that after? It's time for group."

"The psychologists of the world are working for Satan! Come to me before it's too late!" Maria wailed at her peers, but it was the eerie singing when it began that stirred John to goose bumps.

"Chip! Chip, can you remove Maria from group? She's being disruptive."

"Come on, Maria," Chip said in an even voice to her screams. He attempted to lift her by the arm, but she was a large woman, and he was obviously afraid of agitating her further. Another orderly walked in, and the two tried together to coax her out of the room.

Finally, they gave up when she promised she'd be quiet. "I'll let the devil finish his work!" she added, looking at the therapist with accusation.

John recoiled into himself throughout the scene, afraid of what were now his "peers."

"Sure, they let her get away with anything. Last night, the beasts had me face down on the floor, just because I refused to take my medicine. I'm going to file a complaint."

"Now, Roberta, we can talk about that after group," the therapist addressed the young, black woman, whose hair was cut in a crew. "Let's move on. Will, do you want to go next, please?" She asked a middle aged, well-groomed-for-this-crowd, male patient.

"Sure," he smirked. "I'm Will, I have manic-depression, and I'm glad I'll be going home soon," he laughed. "They don't call it a mad house for nothing."

Maria shot him a look of pain and waved the sign of the cross in his direction.

"I'm Roberta. I'm a drug addict, or so I've been warned. And I've got some other problems, whatever. I'm not grateful today," she stated. "I'm angry, and I'm filing a complaint."

"Okay, next." Teri shook her head at John with encouragement.

He sat still.

"Are you John?" she asked.

"Yes." He looked around nervously. "I'm not sure what's wrong with me."

"Can you name something you're grateful for?"

He shrugged.

"You have lovely hair," Pat noted. "I wish I had your hair."

John wasn't sure how to respond to that. He was grateful when Teri went on to the next person, obviously giving him a break on his first day.

"Yeah, what do you want?" The elderly man wrapped a blanket around himself more tightly. "I'm Pete, I'm depressed, I have nothing to be grateful for."

"I heard that your daughter came to visit yesterday," Teri offered.

"Yeah, she wants me to get better. They all want me to feel better. Don't they know it's an imposition? I just want to wallow. It's too late for me... it's too late." His eyes fell to the floor in a despondency that matched his words. John looked to the therapist to see what she would do.

"You feel it's too late for you, and it's a nuisance that anyone is trying to help you," she said.

The old man shook his head slightly without raising his eyes.

"You bring up an interesting point, Pete," the therapist addressed the group. Pete's eyes lifted suddenly as she continued. "We're all products of the thoughts we conceive. When I have a thought over and over again, it solidifies in reality. Some people believe it's through biochemistry... or belief, but either way, it becomes real. For Pete, it's that he's never going to get better, and this has become real."

"What if he wants to change it?" asked Roberta.

"He needs to have another thought, and then he needs to have it often enough that it creates a wider road for his feelings to travel than the one he's already built. But, Pete has decided he doesn't want to change it, and we must respect that."

SEVENTEEN

John had a lot of questions following group but not so much time to think about them. During the only period of unsaturated time, Will accosted him to fill him in "on how things go around here." The man gave him warnings about some of the "less gentle" staff and told him whom to ask for favors. He also told him he could procure almost anything for him—for a price, of course. "Of course," John repeated. Will swept his right hand through his salt and pepper, closely cropped hair every four or five words. He explained the alliances on the unit and quickly added his "rules for release." John would have liked to go over these in more detail, but Will's train of thought was swift and too crisp for interruptions.

"It's like this," he moved on to why hallucinogenic drugs were important, indeed how they offered salvation, when Roberta came a little too close. "What I tell you? Stay away from me, if you know what's good for you. Go on, sod off!" He hissed at her like an animal. Roberta gave him the finger, ejaculated a "Stuff it!" and moved on.

"Right, so it's like this—oh, and stay away from her, she's trouble, real trouble—anyway, where was I? Oh, yeah, drugs. Like, in the 1960's you know, here and in America, all those kids doing drugs, it served a purpose."

John's brow arched slightly at the news.

"Think about it, mate. It's like everyone's living in an old house, right, and there are no windows anywhere. And, then someone comes by and makes a hole in the wall, calls it a window, right? Well, there's a lot of bother after that, right? A lot of fear, worry about all sorts of hazards, some may be real, right? But, then, it's like the whole, bloody consciousness of the household starts to lift, yeah? See what I'm gettin' at? Before you know it, there are babies being born *outside* the house, like, not just lookin' out the window, right? These newborns are outside the structure itself, see?" He grinned with self-satisfaction and lit a cigarette. "Now, it's harder to confound the whole populace when you got people living outside the four walls, right?" He looked at John for an answer.

John nodded.

Later on, after he'd been prodded and poked, stuck with needles for blood draws, and weighed, John was expected to attend the drug and alcohol group. He ascertained from the crowd that not all patients were "invited" to this group; those without a history of excessive drinking or illicit drug use attended another group. He also quickly learned that the substance abuse group was partly educational, with information on the medical detriments of cocaine and other chemicals. John and another new patient were advised that the group discussed a different drug every day, and that the patients themselves were expected to research and present material. They then talked about their own difficulties with abstaining from the substances they used, and ostensibly provided support to one another on their recoveries. Will caught John's eye and winked.

As it was his first day on the subacute unit, John was permitted to dine alone in his room, although it was clarified that he'd be expected to eat with his peers thereafter. The solitude and quiet were like water to a parched tongue. He still required a little encouragement to eat, but he was, after all, handling the utensils himself, a feat, by the way, he was told was no less than miraculous progress. Also, he moved to soft, but solid, food today, another small miracle. He felt grateful for several things by time he was ready for bed. Maggie was still there, and she helped him get dressed and into bed. He wondered how long her shifts were, if she had family, and what her private life was like, but he lacked the energy and initiative to ask. She reminded him that he would have more physiotherapy starting tomorrow and should be strong as new before long. He smiled at her compassion, feeling at once like a little boy and a slightly aroused man. She nearly tucked him in with her enthusiasm.

The following day in group, another therapist, Mary, facilitated. She seemed a bit high strung to John, and loud, as if she assumed that the mentally ill were also seriously hard of hearing.

"Are we ready for the hope scale?" she shouted. "Will, will you begin, and explain to the others please?!"

"Yeah, right. On a scale from one to ten, how do I rate my ever-abiding hope?"

"No commentaries, Will, please!" She was short and plump, with big cheeks and a hooked nose. Her dark hair was curly and seemed unsettled on her head. She had the appearance of utter exasperation, and John almost began to laugh for the first time in months, but he restrained himself.

"Right, no commentaries. What's the point of holding a group discussion, one might ask."

"Please!" she yelled, and again John restrained himself.

"About four, then, how's that? I feel a four today, Miss Mary, Quite Contrary." Several others did laugh at that.

"Next!"

Pat was twisting her hair and staring into space. "Three." The group laughed with no explanation.

"Pete? No laughing at each other, please!" Mary quieted them.

"Barely a one." Again, a chuckle. John noticed it was always Will, Roberta, and a couple of others he hadn't met who appeared to be enjoying themselves at the others' expense.

The question went around the room, and suddenly all eyes alighted on him. He had no idea how much hope he felt this particular day, or any day. Still, he had left the acute unit. He also noticed that higher numbers did not elicit jeers. "Six."

"Next!"

The young woman beside John shuffled her feet a bit and studied the floor. "I suppose a six is as good as any." Her voice was soft and sad, and John could not bring himself to immediately dislike her as he thought he would. She had long, very thin and fragile looking hair and was lovely, in an ailing sense.

It wasn't easy to address her after group, but John mustered the gumption to wheel over to her when she was alone on the couch by the piano. The others had mostly drifted to their rooms, or scattered about waiting for an outdoor break. Two of the patients were within earshot, negotiating with an aide for extra cigarettes.

"I'm John."

The young woman jumped.

"Oh, sorry," John whispered. "So sorry, I didn't mean to frighten you."

"It's all right, I'm just jumpy is all." She stood and looked down at him.

"I'm John."

"Yes, you said."

"Right." The fingers of his left hand combed through his hair.

"What do you want?"

"Nothing. I don't want…Jesus. Never mind." He started to turn away.

"I'm Robin."

He turned back. "Robin? That's pretty."

"Thanks much. I… I didn't mean to be rude. Just trying not to befriend anyone in the nut house." She gave a nervous chuckle. In the background, the sad horn of a train crossing caught their attention.

"Why are you here?" John asked.

"Well I should probably sit for that." She slid back down like a ballerina might. "I guess you weren't in the group the other night." John shook his head without verbal response. "My parents had me committed. They told the staff I was irredeemably depressed and in need of fixing when all I really wanted…" She looked down, melancholic, as he remembered her looking when he first laid eyes on her.

"What?"

"Oh, it's so bloody stupid. I just wanted them to listen to me, to care what I feel about things, to see how crazy the world is. It's a burden seeing the world for what it is, isn't it?" She hadn't looked up yet, and John would've taken the question rhetorically if she didn't now look straight at him.

"Yes, I suppose," he said, although he wasn't certain he understood.

"Now I feel like I never want to speak to them again." She folded her arms about her and pulled her legs up.

"Well, then we have something in common. I'm not fond of my parents, either."

"They said you were one of the crazy ones," Robin said.

"What? They who?"

"I don't know. The patient rumor mill, you know. They said you don't speak."

"I speak. Matter of fact, I can't bloody shut up sometimes," he mumbled. He looked away from her glare and scratched his left leg, consciously trying once again not to appear pathetic. The last thing he was ready to accept was that he was "one of the crazy ones" in a place like this.

"You seem all right to me. I have to go, though. It's my phone time, and I want to call a friend of mine, if she's on the approved list yet."

"Oh," he responded. Robin was gone in a flash. No matter, he was due for his own appointment.

He met with Dr. Comer in his private office. It was an institutional room made to look a little homier with a standing lamp, a few professional-looking photographs of dogs, and a painting of the sea. Scattered among the metal bookshelves were piles of paperwork and books.

"How do you like the new ward, John?" Dr. Comer asked, amicably enough.

John considered refusing to speak, but he didn't have the energy for such opposition. "It's all right, I suppose." He didn't want to rush into asking when he could go home.

"Are you having any hallucinations? Hearing voices no on else seems to hear?"

John appreciated the straightforward approach. He was tired of being spoken to as if he were an idiot. "No." He recalled how bad it had gotten before he ended up in hospital, how all he could think about was death and a release from the incessant suffering, and how the voice in his head had become so real, so outside of himself.

"Do you still feel that you want to die?"

"No, I don't." He knew better than to admit that, but the truth was that death was far from his mind these days.

"Are you having any dangerous thoughts or ideas of self-harm?"

"No, not any more." Dr. Comer kept looking at him, as if compelling him to continue, and he decided to do so once again to demonstrate his cooperative nature. "I remember that all I could think about before was how desperately I needed to end my life. I couldn't stop the thoughts from repeating over and over."

"It sounds almost hypnotic."

"Yes, in a way it was."

"How do you find the groups? Are you availing yourself of this type of therapy by really opening up?"

"They're different. Funny, really."

"Funny, how so?" Dr. Comer asked him.

"Everyone seems to fit in here somehow, as strange as we all are. But, also, there's a lot of derision."

"Does that bother you?"

"Which part?" John's guard returned.

"Either part."

"I don't know. It's all right."

"Does derision bother you?"

John was silent after that. In fact, for days afterward he kept quiet most of the time. Most of what he thought to say seemed absurd, especially when he was with Robin. Music was actually the language he most understood. When he tried to explain this "musical thinking," to her, he became tongue-tied, so mostly he listened to her fluent expressions instead. Having any kind of tender feeling toward a young woman was so inexplicably anxiety-producing for him that he would revert to his illness as a defense when it became too much for him, would ask Maggie or another nurse to tell Robin that he was too tired or "not mentally right enough" to leave his room. The nursing staff believed these excuses.

After a comparatively brief stay, Robin left, as she hadn't really convinced anyone but her parents of her insanity. She wrote him, though, long letters about her misery and, surprisingly, her dreams. John responded with notes interspersed with music he'd write in her honor and memory. Sometimes the lyrics were the only literary messages available, but they were honest and revealing without plumbing: just as his sessions were, to the disappointment of his doctor, who had openly expressed so wanting to give John a profound opportunity to move beyond his sorrow and self-contempt.

Day after day, John grew stronger and more restless. His physical condition progressed quickly, as expected, and he was up and about. Lilith visited him once, bringing books and other personal items. She seemed reluctant to engage in any real discourse and stuck to giving him news of family, friends, and the world.

Toward the end of his stay, he was allowed to take walks on the grounds, during which time he stayed mostly within his own mind—that is to say, he rejoined the human species and its baffling lack of true presence. He accepted this conformity as par for the course of recovery. Dr. Comer asked him about the seeming friendship he developed with Robin, if there were any romantic interest, but as a result, John only grew more uncommunicative around him. He couldn't explain his opposition to exploring the subject, but he could most definitely swear to the peril in it.

EIGHTEEN

Mark did not contact Jacques since his return to Kenya, but he thought of him almost every day. He felt disappointed when solicitations from France failed to arrive by phone or post. Presently, he lay in bed, unable to sleep, having difficulty resisting fantasies of the Frenchman. He worried about Jacques when he allowed himself to see past his loathing. Their irreconcilable differences filled him with so much anxiety that he almost pledged allegiance to the East African Communists League the week before.

His mind returned to the covert meeting he attended under the guise of an ornithology club. The British educated Ethiopian who was visiting Nairobi decreed, "We will not let the capitalist greed of Western men thwart our efforts to create an equitable society here in Kenya." His speech was met with enthusiastic applause. The room was muggy, a basement classroom at the college in Nairobi. Most of the participants were young students there.

After the talk, Mark walked around looking for his cousin. He saw Robert near a water fountain outside the classroom talking to a white man.

"Hey," he said, squeezing through the crowd.

"Hey, Mark. Good to see you," Robert said, shaking Mark's hand. "This is Gael. He is working on a PhD in political science, in Europe."

Mark shook his hand. "What brings you to Kenya?"

"My father is a Belgian diplomat here," Gael said. "I'm visiting my parents."

Mark thought of Kyle. He wondered if Kyle would have come tonight, or if he would have convinced Mark to stay at home. He had finally written him back and told him he'd apply to Kyle's school of choice, but for the following year. That meant he would be two years behind his age group.

"Where do you study?" he asked the Belgian.

"At the Sorbonne, in Paris."

Mark inhaled sharply and swallowed the sadness that enclosed him at the sound of the French city. He blinked.

"I'm almost done, just working on my dissertation on economic politics," the Belgian continued.

"What about?" Mark asked. What was Jacques up to these days? Why hadn't he called yet?

"The future implosion of capitalism. It explores in historical context how profit takes precedence over everything including human decency and rights. Eventually, the corruption and exploitation will spread until the society crumbles. I'm debating whether or not to present it as a mental illness."

"Like the economically insane?" Robert asked with a smile, and Gael nodded.

Mark nodded back, but his mind was preoccupied with Jacques again, especially at the Belgian's mention of exploitation. How could he have just left Jacques in Paris to fend for himself?

Mark accepted an assignment that evening, a test of his commitment to the cause. It seemed an innocuous, almost banal, one at that: to deliver a package to the South African Embassy after hours on the eve of the twelfth, the most difficult piece of the job being to avoid state police on the streets of Nairobi with no more than a forged slip of a document explaining who he was, an alias, and why he was out so late in that area of town.

That night, Mark had met briefly with a white fellow outside the side gate of the embassy, recognized by the description he'd been given. He showed the slip of paper, which must have meant something to the man, and gave the package as directed. Mark was dismissed, but then his heart quickened when a severe looking officer looked at him with mistrust just half a block away. He asked in English for Mark's ID and grinned at the forgery.

"I should be on my way," Mark said to him.

The man stared at him in response and looked about ready to haul him to the nearest station when a car pulled up and pressed the officer urgently in. He took the paper from Mark, leaving him without any identification to make his way back, not a small challenge and one he managed only by staying overnight at a school friend's home in town.

The phone rang, and Mark jumped out of bed quickly. He hadn't expected to hear back from Kyle this soon.

"Go ahead," he answered hopefully.

"Mark?"

"Jacques?"

"Oui, c'est moi." Jacques' voice shook, although maybe it was the connection.

"It's two o'clock in the morning here."

"I'm sorry."

Mark kept silent. He didn't want to sound cold and knew he would if he spoke.

"How are you?" the Frenchman asked.

"Almost three months older."

"You are upset with me still?"

"Still?"

"Oui, you were angry with me when you left Paris. Anyway, you were right, I should not gone that night."

"Have gone," Mark said.

"Excuse me?"

"Just correcting your English."

"Oh." A sigh.

Mark was unaccustomed to being speechless, as he was with many things regarding Jacques. When had this thing with the Frenchman begun to mean so much? He started to ask how Jacques was but changed his mind.

"Oui? You want to say something?" The "th" sounding pretty, Mark again simultaneously annoyed and aroused.

"Yeah, I'm sorry for what happened that night. I'm sorry for how things turned out."

"Moi, aussi. Me, too."

"Is that why you haven't called? Because of how I acted?" Mark asked, fully aware that he would have beaten the crap out of someone for acting how he did, maybe worse. He had the feeling Jacques was more forgiving, though.

"Maybe a little. I am not been well."

"What's the matter? Are you crying?"

"It is long, and, how do you say, involved?"

"Complicated?"

"Oui."

"I was just disappointed you didn't call."

"You told me not to. Anyway, I want to…" Jacques trailed off.

"What? You want to what?" Mark's heart was actually racing. "You're still there?"

"Yes," Jacques sniffled. "I want to come to Africa, to you."

"Oh. Christ, I don't think that's a good idea," he said, barely breathing. "This isn't a good time, and really the accommodations are not what you're used to."

"Please, Mark."

"It's extremely hot and rainy. I have to work. Please don't be upset."

"The rain season passes soon, I read. Please, Mark. I have no place to go." Jacques started to cry more audibly.

"What's going on? Are you okay? Did someone hurt you?" Mark asked, trying to remain calm. The thumping in his chest reverberated in his ears.

"Yes, that night. There were a few men, and they did vicious things to me. I was not back at the club yet, but now my father wants me to work again," he said between tears. "I am desperate. Please. I don't know what else to do."

Mark had listened with no comment. The phrase, "they did vicious things to me," repeated in his head. What about staying with Lilith, he was going to ask. But then he realized just in time that he wanted the Frenchman more than anything. "Okay, fine. Call me when you have the flight information, and I'll come get you in Nairobi."

———

When he hung up the phone, Jacques felt elated but nervous. He hadn't thought the conversation would go that smoothly. For the last several weeks, nothing else was that easy, not recovering his sense of self and not the healing of his flesh. He had endured not only the assault, but also humiliating procedures, trying to avoid the eyes of the medical personnel, trying not to hear the scorn in their comments. And then there was the emptiness of his father's consolation. How could the bastard have hardly said a word to him about the attack? And how could Jacques forget how cruelly his mother ignored him, his mother, who had been on holiday in the Riviera for the better part of the last year, even when he was in hospital? Louis was his only contact, the only person in his daily life who cared for him. Running away was the sole manner in which he could, possibly, punish his parents for their neglect. Maybe they'd feel sorry once he was gone, but the dread in his heart told him that they wouldn't really bother to care.

He picked up for the thousandth time the tourist book on Kenya that Louis had secretly purchased for him the week before. He turned again to the pages on potential complications all tourists should know. *Cholera is caused by bacteria and is transmittable person to person or through ingesting something contaminated*, it read. *It is a self-limiting illness, and, if the individual does not allow himself to dehydrate, almost never fatal. The diarrhea is often spotted with white mucus.* His stomach turned as it often did at this passage. Would Mark know how to keep him safe?

The fact that you can never really control the whim and instinct of a mosquito was another overwhelming consideration; he just prayed that the prophylactic pills he'd obtain from the doctor would protect him from malaria, along with the light colored slacks and long-sleeve shirts he was supposed to bring. He read on, again, about typhoid, hepatitis, and other pathogenic topics until he almost retched. He could be making a huge mistake leaving France, but it would be his to make, and he sensed that now was the time to act. A door opened, especially when Mark agreed to the visit. If he failed to take advantage of it, he may be stuck in this life forever, probably addicted to drugs just to get through the day. Such a fate was far worse than a lousy virus or bacteria, he convinced himself. Besides, Kenya wouldn't be such a popular tourist destination if it were really so dangerous.

He wished to but couldn't sleep, too worried that somehow Mark would change his mind and forbid him to go. He moved slowly into stretches and breath work, trying to regain the composure he used to feel on stage. Louis would offer to help him make the arrangements tomorrow, he was sure, even though it would threaten his own livelihood if he were ever found out. He feared for his valet, so he strategized how to leave Louis out of the plans as much as possible. He would simply ask him for instructions, whom he should call to purchase a plane ticket and the like. People did these things for themselves all the time; it would be easy. He would pay a fortune if he had to, if it meant getting away sooner rather than later, anything to avoid another fatherly-arranged disaster, and a potential rejection from Mark. He had caught Mark in the middle of the night, probably woke him up. What if he realized in the morning he didn't want him there, and changed his mind? He returned to bed realizing he was having the same thoughts over and over again. He could feel the bursts of adrenaline like little packets of raw fear detonating at intervals as he waited for the sun to rise.

NINETEEN

Mark stood outside international arrivals awaiting the passengers of flight 2260 from Paris. Jacques should have been one of the first people to disembark because he probably flew first class, but he hadn't come through yet. Mark started to worry that the Frenchman's strange beauty might have attracted too much attention in customs. Over the past few days, Mark had prepared himself the only way he knew how. He made a few plans but mostly worked till he was too exhausted to think about it. He managed to avoid questions about the nature of his relationship with Jacques, but then Papap asked him directly on their way to the Jomo Kenyatta International Airport. Mark said, "He's very rich and a little odd," sidestepping the matter altogether. He reproached himself now. His father had just been trying to help him feel less agitated.

His spine stiffened as he watched Jacques advance through the barrier. The Frenchman looked pale; he wore khaki colored slacks and a long-sleeved white pullover, neatly tucked in. His trousers were belted. His long hair was tied in a ponytail at the base of his head, and his features could easily have been feminine. Mark's heart raced, betraying his adopted façade of indifference.

They were both tentative in their approach, first Jacques moving forward to kiss Mark on the cheek and Mark jerking back, then Mark wanting to embrace as Jacques held out his hand for a shake. Homosexuality was taboo here. Although Papap was tolerant, Mark kept the subject safeguarded for his own protection and probably overcompensated at times. He assumed Jacques would understand the restrictions.

"This is my father," Mark said and explained that almost everyone called his father Papap.

"Hello, young Frenchman," Papap said with a broad smile and warm countenance.

"Hello," said Jacques. Mark noticed Jacques already seemed more at ease now that he'd met Papap. His father really had a gift with people.

"Only three bags? I notice the French like to pack when they travel," Papap said.

Jacques looked offended until Papap smiled and patted him on the back.

"I left in a hurry," Jacques said, deadpan, and both Mark and his father laughed.

"I'll take this," Papap offered, pointing to one of the black leather bags strapped around Jacques' shoulder.

"He can carry it himself," Mark said as he started toward the door.

Papap motioned for Jacques to hand him the bag, anyway. "You look delicate. Do you eat?"

"Yes, sometimes." Jacques smiled as he took in his surroundings. From the inside of the modern airport, you wouldn't know you'd left Europe. He worried somewhat that Mark was already irritated with him, but his body relaxed in Papap's presence. It had been a long time since he could say that.

Outside was terribly hot, and the truck ride was bumpy. Papap had insisted he would drive and that Jacques would sit next to him up front. Then he smiled at Jacques whenever Jacques started to feel nervous or self-conscious, as if Papap had access to his psyche. He wanted to turn around and look at Mark but thought better of it. Mark seemed put out by his arrival.

It was easy to note the British influence in the city, even in the attire of its dwellers. Jacques had expected to see barefoot women wrapped in minimum cloth and sharp street vendors pushing their carts of trinkets at white tourists. Only once did his nose pick up the uncertain stench of urban living. The colors, sounds, and scents all seemed to work in harmony. His eyes took in scenery that was at once startling and new, and Papap pointed out the jacarandas, euphorbia, and baobabs.

"What do you think?" Papap asked with a smile.

"It's quite lovely here."

"Beautiful, yes?" Papap looked proud and Jacques again felt better.

After leaving the city limits, the noise dwindled, and the redolence of frangipani and jasmine overtook Jacques' senses. They moved into an affluent suburb where guards stood at most entrances. Before he could ask anything about the area, they entered a postcard of African landscape. Jacques wondered if Mark was watching him from behind. Was there such a thing as mental telepathy? Was Mark thinking Jacques was scared to leave the wealthy neighborhood behind? If so, was he right?

Jacques shook his head to rid himself of his anxiety and tried to enjoy the miles of African plain stretched out before him. After they'd been on the road for about forty-five minutes, they stopped in front of a two-story building advertising a Gasthaus and restaurant at its entrance.

"We reserved a room for you here," Mark said, like an afterthought. Jacques was surprised but easily feigned graciousness. Mark hadn't said a thing the whole trip, so Jacques still had no idea where he stood with him. "It's the only hotel near where we live."

Jacques stepped down from the truck as Papap was already exchanging laughs with a white man and woman on the property. "How far do you live from here?" he asked.

"About forty kilometers or a twenty minute car ride," Mark said. "You'll have your own bathroom and some air-conditioning, please turn it off when you leave, and they have clean, filtered water, of course."

"Thank you for thinking of my comfort," Jacques managed to say, feeling his palms begin to sweat.

"And Europeans operate this, so you should feel more at home."

"When will I see you?" Jacques asked just as Papap was within earshot.

"How about you take some time to rest, and we pick you up in a few hours for supper?" Papap suggested.

"Supper at our house?" Mark asked Papap like he was unaware.

"Yes, of course."

"Why don't you stay with me?" Jacques requested of Mark and then turned to the man Mark didn't seem to repudiate and asked, "Is it okay?"

"A very sound idea. You two must need to get reacquainted," Papap said. Jacques studied Mark for signs of disapproval and noted none.

Mark introduced him to the German owners, Herr and Frau Gruener. They made small talk and he learned that the Germans had moved to Kenya four years ago after vacationing there several times. The couple gave them a tour of the grounds and then walked them through the restaurant to get to the check-in desk. Mark had generously prepaid two nights. Herr Gruener gave him his key and the rundown on breakfast.

Afterward, Mark hauled the luggage up the stairs for him to the second floor. The room was bland: white sheets with no spread on the metal frame bed, an old wooden dresser against the wall, a vinyl lounge chair in need of refurbishment. It resembled his image of an orphanage, which seemed apropos. He started to unpack quietly, relieved there was at least a tightly secured mosquito net over the bed. He wondered if he and Mark would have to start all over again.

"It's a little cooler in here than outside," Mark said, almost to himself, as he sat down.

"I am sure this will be fine."

"What's wrong?" Mark asked him.

"I thought...never mind."

"My house would be uncomfortable. My mattress is on the floor. Really, I thought you would be better off here."

"Yes, I understand," Jacques said.

"We don't have guest quarters, for God's sake," Mark snapped at him.

"Of course not," Jacques answered. He looked at Mark and wondered why the African seemed so irate with him again. "Anyway, I thought it was different with us. The last time, je veux dire." Jacques' English always became more tentative when he was nervous and presently his hands trembled slightly, but he continued. "I know you were not happy with me when you left, but—"

"I wasn't happy with me, either, Jacques. Don't you get that?" Mark cut him off aggressively and then leaned back in the chair, his right arm sheltering his brow from further scrutiny.

"I see," Jacques said, suspecting that he was expected to pay for Mark's actions as well as his own. Otherwise, wouldn't Mark be apologetic instead of angry? He sat on the bed and waited for a sign that things would improve.

———

Mark blew out hard, clasping his hands now between his knees. He felt remorseful at his ability to hurt someone and yet out of control of his moods. Furthermore, he'd been watching Jacques with lascivious glances as the Frenchman unpacked. He was more ashamed of himself than he was of Jacques, but he had to admit trepidation over the reaction he might get for having Jacques as a friend: a rich, French entertainer. He kept repeating this description in his head to justify his lack of compassion. He looked out the window. "Listen, let's just make the best of this trip, okay?"

"That is it? That is your response?"

"Sorry it doesn't meet your standards, Jacques, but I'm busy worrying about other things, too."

"Like how to fix everything that is wrong with the world?" Jacques asked, maybe sarcastically. With his accent and second-language handicap, it was hard to tell, but Mark heard recriminations in that question he couldn't sort out at the moment. He pushed his desire to hold Jacques to the dark edges of his mind. Maybe the Frenchman just brought out the worst in him. Or maybe Mark was just like Andreas, after all, and that made him feel queasy.

"Alors, you did not miss me at all?" Jacques asked both innocently and provocatively. Mark wondered how the two could coexist like that. He refused to answer; in fact, he was a little afraid to. Jacques lay down and seemed to fall asleep.

Despite his concerns about the invitation to his parents' home, Mark was grateful when Papap pulled up. He needed the distraction and was sure Jacques felt the same.

"All settled in, I hope," Papap said in his thickly accented English to a quiet audience. He reminded Mark of the large fan they had at home, which he proceeded to pull out of the back seat.

"Let me run this upstairs for you. It should help some more," Mark offered Jacques in a conciliatory way. He grabbed it from his father and ran back up to the room. Physical activity always helped soothe him when he was stressed, and he was glad to do it. Although the past hour had been strained beyond his expectation, he was aware that he didn't actually regret Jacques' presence.

TWENTY

They drove west into the dazzling sunset that made the African plain appear even more beautiful. Mt. Kenya wasn't far away. Jacques had never been outside of Europe, and he allowed himself a moment to enjoy being a tourist. Papap pointed out a few things worthy of note over the din of the truck.

Mark's mood must have lightened by the beauty of the landscape because he joined his father in giving suggestions for tours. He even reached from behind and briefly touched Jacques' shoulder to point to landmarks. Jacques smiled, delighted more by the simple gesture than by the sights.

They stopped in front of a modest single family home. In a cloud of dust kicked up by the tires, his fears began to dissipate. Inside, the houselights were all lit, as if the home were a veritable beacon.

"Mom, this is Jacques."

"Hello. I assume your English is pretty good," Humming said, but she didn't look up at him, so he couldn't offer his hand to shake.

"Yes, it is."

Humming continued to busy herself with the many pots on the stove. Mark looked as affronted as Jacques felt, and he caught Jacques' eye for a moment before shrugging and introducing his little sister.

Bella started pulling Jacques toward the small kitchen table, agog with questions. Jacques had never shared a family dinner, and he hoped Mark's family would not pick up on that fact. Mark grabbed his sister playfully as if not to be left out.

"Would you speak some French? Do you like Africa? How did you meet my brother?" Bella continued to rattle off despite Mark's teasing interference.

"Enough, Bella," said Humming. Jacques couldn't help notice how stunning Mark's mother was. Although she had some gray adulterating the straight, black strands of her hair, she couldn't be older than forty. He watched her peripherally and more obviously observed Mark for clues on how to proceed. Following leads was one thing he did very well.

Papap started to fix Jacques' plate once they were seated and explained that he and Humming made "local fare, for a new experience," for Jacques as he piled small heaps of spiced vegetables on their best flatware.

Jacques was about to protest that it was too much when Humming handed him a dish of barbecued goat and ugaly, a boiled cornmeal that supposedly tasted better than it sounded. He took a little and passed it to Papap. Despite her cold reception of Jacques, Mark's mother had prepared a small feast.

"How long do you plan to stay?" she asked him. The simple question brought silence to the otherwise clamor of utensils.

Mark cleared his throat while Jacques attempted to swallow half-chewed food. "I'm not sure we've figured that out yet, Mom."

She gazed at the both of them.

Bella, who had a multitude of suggestions for Jacques' to-do list, picked up the conversation. "Will you go to Victoria Nyanza? And to the Highlands?" And before he could answer, she said, "I went on a field trip to Ngong Hills last year. You can go! That's easy enough, right, Papap?"

"That's right, Bella. There are so many beautiful things about our country." He smiled brilliantly at Jacques. "Few other countries on Earth can boast the ecological variety and natural history of Kenya."

Mark explained that animal species were disappearing at alarming rates as a result of human overpopulation, subsequent habitat encroachment and illegal poaching, but that Kenya and its neighbor, Tanzania, still had a wealth of wildlife and fascinating natural mysteries that were irresistible.

"In fact," Papap explained to their guest, "even scientists arrive in droves, from animal behaviorists to archaeologists." He explained how a European entomologist accidentally and quite literally fell into the site now known as Olduvai Gorge located in Tanzania, and how the bones found there revealed a previously uncharted course of human evolution. "If you're interested, there is an extensive museum of natural history in Nairobi to visit."

All eyes were on Jacques, whose head was swimming in information. He turned to Mark for refuge, beckoning him to respond on his behalf. "Everything sounds so fascinating," Jacques said when Mark failed to meet his appeal.

"Well, you did come all this way. You shouldn't just hang around here, I guess. There are plenty of safari tours for Westerners. You could go to Serengeti and to see Kilimanjaro," said Mark. "We could get you a visa for Tanzania, if you don't already have it."

"Why not take him to Ambesoli and to Masai Mara? You don't have to leave the country to see the best safari," Papap said to Mark.

Jacques nodded, sensing he'd make a friend if he agreed. Besides, he preferred to stay by Mark's side as long as he could.

"I suppose you should go to the Lodge at Mt Kenya, too," Humming chimed in.

"Oh, yes, that's most charming and very historical. You would enjoy it," Papap said.

"Have you ever seen a herd of elephants?" Bella beamed. "It's spectacular."

"I would like that," Jacques responded as the rest of the family chuckled at the girl's enthusiasm and her new vocabulary word.

"You have a lovely family," said Jacques as Mark was showing him around their land.

"My father seems to like you."

"Yes, why?" Jacques was also curious why Humming apparently did not but was too polite to ask.

"I don't know. He has his own ways," Mark answered with uncommon respect in his voice.

"I like him, too," Jacques said, and Mark smiled. He suddenly pulled Jacques off the path by his waist and led him into the bush.

"I want to show you something. Look up there." He pointed above the horizon to what appeared to be a hole in the side of a hill, although Jacques strained to see it in the waning light. "It's a cave with a hidden pool I discovered a while back. Not many people know of it. Kyle and I used to go up there."

"Kyle?"

Mark looked away for a moment. "Yeah, a friend. He's in Japan now, but I still go to the cave alone sometimes."

"Maybe you can take me?" Jacques said, at first remorseful and then surprised when Mark smiled and responded he'd intended to.

"I like when you're like this."

"Like how?" Mark asked.

"Kind."

Mark lowered his eyes and turned away, and Jacques wasn't sure if he'd offended the African again. But then Mark turned back, placed his hands around Jacques' waist and lifted him off the ground slightly before holding him close. Without heels, he was about four centimeters shorter than Mark, who now kissed him tenderly on the mouth, then again with more determination. Jacques melted into Mark's grip. He desperately wanted to feel safe with someone. Their faces parted enough for Jacques to stroke Mark's lips with his fingertips and brush his mouth along Mark's lower jaw and neckline.

"You feel so good," Mark said. "Why does it have to be you?"

"Why am I so unacceptable?" Jacques pressed his face against Mark's neck, but Mark lifted his chin and kissed him on the bridge of his nose.

"If we're going to be together, we need to define it."

"How?"

"I just mean," Mark paused, "If you're mine, you're only mine. You can't be with other people."

Jacques agreed readily. That's what he wanted. That's why he left everything he ever knew behind.

"No, this is serious, Jacques. I can't deal with that, your lifestyle. And you'll have to be willing to do with less extravagance."

"I am here, n'est-ce pas?"

"Yes, you're here." Mark kissed him again, a flurry of pecks ending in a passionate, almost jaw-aching merger. Then he grabbed Jacques' neck with his left hand and pulled it back, revealing Jacques' Adam's apple. Mark's right middle finger toyed with the gold chain around Jacques' neck, and Jacques squirmed a little thinking Mark might get rough. "Do you promise?" Mark asked him instead.

Jacques smiled, relieved, and reassured Mark, who briefly seemed young and naive to the Frenchman. "I hope you believe I really had enough of it. The men and *my lifestyle*, as you call it."

"All men?"

Jacques laughed. "Alors, there's one perhaps…" He kissed Mark, pleased by his scent and how he tasted.

"I'll take you back to the hotel."

"And stay?"

"And stay."

The door slams behind him; loud noises seem intrusive. Like an echo, he hears, Don't just stand there! Other yelling ensues. Somehow the scene is recognizable; a hand grasps his waist. Bottles of liquor are strewn about. Suddenly movements become larger than life: tornado-like motion of a dress. Sounds of ripping, laughing, and crashing.

Pain, in the holographic context of his dream, overwhelmingly real.

———

"Jacques!" Mark called, shaking Jacques in his sleep. "You're dreaming. It's okay."

Jacques sat straight up in bed and wiped sweat from his brow, shaking and breathing heavily. Mark put his arm around him.

"It was a nightmare. It's over," Mark said, trying to sound confident. He wiped tears from Jacques' eyes before Jacques excused himself to use the bathroom.

"Are you okay?" Mark asked, knowing he should have asked Jacques earlier. When they arrived at the Gasthaus, Jacques' lovemaking was almost timid, not at all like he had been in France. On second thought, he seemed more insecure in general. "Tell me what's going on."

"I don't want to. I told you, I was attacked the last night you were in Paris."

"Yeah…by whom?"

"It doesn't matter who they were," he said, starting to cry. "They beat me…they beat me from the inside out. That's the best I can explain it." Mark leaned over and wiped his lover's nose with his own previously discarded t-shirt.

He found the compassion to reign in the onslaught of questions, which arose from a sense of morbid interest. He adjusted Jacques to a horizontal position and held him close. The notion that anyone he cared about could be raped was intolerable. Churning inside were homicidal thoughts toward Jacques' violators, and he was furious with himself for not having been there to protect him. When he calmed down, he said, "Jacques?"

"Oui?"

"I'm sorry."

"Pourquoi?"

"I don't know. For what I did that night, and for not taking you away with me."

Jacques kissed him on his cheek. "I would not have gone. It's not your fault."

But, Mark did feel responsible. What he had done to contribute to Jacques' trauma that night most certainly was his fault. Had he handled his jealousy better, maybe things would have ended another way.

TWENTY-ONE

Days passed with the drifting sands in Africa. Now a couple of weeks later, Jacques was accustomed to the routine. He rose early every morning and watched Mark get dressed to work at the farm, which he was managing for the summer. Then he would share coffee and some breakfast with other guests, usually Europeans, and sit in the common room to read or watch the news. Mark returned by late afternoon usually with a plan to visit somewhere magnificent or just new, and they would retire together when it grew dark. Yesterday, Mark mentioned overnight trips to Mombasa and Lake Victoria. Jacques acted the role of tourist because it seemed to bring pleasure to Mark to share his country, but he was glad just to be with him.

Presently, he was lying in a hammock in a t-shirt and jean shorts in a place between sleep and wakefulness. He smiled when he felt Mark slip onto the hammock and stroke his face.

"Whoa—" Mark exclaimed, as they toppled off, both laughing now. "That was some wake-up call. Sorry," Mark said, smiling, both of them on the ground. They kissed sheepishly, looking around them with caution.

"Ready to go to the cave?"

"Yes! Shall I change first?"

"We'll skinny dip, anyway, but, yes, you should put on long pants."

"Whatever you say," Jacques said, straightening up, his feet firmly on the ground. He slipped his sandals on.

"Oh, you should change your shoes, too. We'll be doing a little hiking to get there."

"Okay, I'll run up."

"I'll follow," Mark said with a mischievous glint in his eyes. Once in the room, Mark grabbed him and kissed him fully.

"You are very loving today," Jacques told him.

"You like?"

"Mais, oui."

"Good, but plenty of time for making out when we get to the cave."

———

They drove northwest, mostly to higher ground where the roads were primitive. Mark held Jacques' hand when he didn't need to have both hands on the wheel. Jacques looked very happy and kept watching Mark more than the view.

"What are you looking at?" Mark asked him.

"You."

Mark chuckled smugly. He kept wondering how long all of this could last. Loving Jacques brought him to both sexual and emotional heights. He wanted to tell him how much he felt for him but also enjoyed the leverage he maintained by not revealing too much of his heart. "What about me?"

"You are different. What you want is different."

"What does that mean?" Mark asked, a bit nervous. Did he mean he was some kind of pervert? His face must have revealed his uneasiness because Jacques laughed.

"Nothing bad," Jacques said after too long a delay. "Just that who you are is unique, what drives you. You are different from most men."

Mark bristled a bit at that, as he always did when Jacques said anything that reminded him of his past. He hated to think of his lover with anyone else.

Securing the truck well off the road, they walked the rest of the way through the bush. Mark recalled a time when he and Kyle would dare each other into acts of spelunking and again felt a pang of betrayal. Betrayal against his first love, his youth, his view of the world. He wasn't sure which of them. Gingerly he led the way to a well-hidden cavity, small and dark, as Jacques held onto his waist.

"It seemed much larger from below."

"That's because we're on the other side; there's no way to get to that larger entrance," Mark explained as they made their way into the narrow, dark space.

Jacques jumped when there was a squeal close to their heads.

"Bats," Mark said.

"Bats!" Jacques' voice echoed.

"Don't worry, they're harmless."

"I'm not sure," Jacques said. They reached another cavity. Mark flashed the light to all four sides of the opening to help orient Jacques.

"How did you find this place the first time?"

"From the vantage point on the farm, you know, where I showed you."

"Yes, but how did you have the courage to walk through this path without a guide?"

Mark laughed and started to remove his clothes. The flashlight, and the ingeniousness of the human eye, helped them adjust to their surroundings.

"Where's the water?" Jacques asked.

"Right here," Mark picked up the light and brought it down not two feet to their right. "It's hard to see maybe, but it's large. It extends all the way to the wall there," and he shone the light at another path. "That leads to the opening you can see from our land. What do you think?"

"It's like a pool." Jacques knelt down and stuck his hand in.

"Yeah, it's healing, must be mineral-rich."

"How do you know it's clean?"

Jacques seemed tentative as Mark removed his remaining clothing. Mark knew Jacques was worried about not being clean. He remembered Jacques telling him that he developed early on an almost obsessive cleanliness, sometimes showering or bathing as much as three times in one day. The idea of wading into a natural pool, with all that natural implies, brought a wave of uneasy disgust to Jacques' countenance that made Mark laugh again. He couldn't help but drag it out a bit.

"There are various clues that it's a fresh spring."

Jacques gave him a look of incredulity.

He laughed again, "Okay, and I had the water tested at a lab in Nairobi, at the university. Satisfied?"

"Why not just tell me that first?"

"Because I like to play with you." He helped Jacques undress. "Know what I mean?"

They kissed, Jacques with his hands on Mark's neck, and then jumped in together.

Finding buoyancy, Jacques hoisted himself up, and wrapped his legs around Mark's waist. "May I tell you that I love you?"

After Mark jerked back and then regained his composure, they both giggled.

"I didn't mean to shock you," the Frenchman said, holding a quality of both innocence and sarcasm.

"No, you didn't," Mark lowered his voice and drifted his gaze toward Jacques' lips and chin before returning to the Frenchman's impressive eyes.

"You don't love me too?" Jacques asked.

"It's just that everyone means something…individual…when they say those words. And it's trite, don't you think?" Mark tried to rationalize his response. He had seen some American television at Kyle's: married couples imparting *I-love-you*'s at every turn, made not the least bit impertinent by the lifelong vows they had ostensibly taken.

Jacques challenged him to describe what he did feel for him, in his own words, adding that he was not entirely a stranger to the reasoning with which Mark had just tried to dismiss the statement.

Mark blew out slowly, weighing his words. "I feel drawn to you and really good when I'm near you. I want you. I miss you when we're not together." He shrugged, embarrassed a little. "But, I still feel confused about us. That's as honest as I can be."

Jacques seemed satisfied by Mark's words. He smiled. "Tell me how to say 'I love you' in Swahili, or in your father's language."

"Why?"

"I am curious."

"It doesn't matter," Mark smiled as he pulled Jacques under, teasingly, to lighten the mood.

They made love as soon as they reached the Gasthaus, clinging to one another, sweating like crazy in the barely air conditioned space, and not caring in the least. When they were both spent, Mark went downstairs to request some iced tea and rolls because they were complimentary with the room. He was afraid everyone there would know his heart just by looking at him. He was afraid to know his heart himself, now starting to fear what a loss it would be if the Frenchman grew bored with Kenya and his little trip away from his life.

"Sir," the African girl knocked on the table to rouse him.

"Oh, thanks." He blushed, not having realized she had returned with the tray.

"Just leave the tray in the room. We'll pick it up tomorrow." She smiled broadly, nothing to conceal.

He greeted a German couple he'd met the day before. They were on their honeymoon and preparing for safari at Ambesoli National Park in the next couple of days. They exchanged a few words, but Mark rushed to get back to the room.

Jacques had fallen asleep…perhaps he was oversexed. Mark was concerned especially about the intercourse, wondered if Jacques were sore, and if it interfered with other bodily functions. He also feared that Jacques wouldn't be honest with him if it hurt. He never asked him to reciprocate, and Mark never offered. He felt afraid when it occurred to him again that he could lose Jacques as he had Kyle.

He slipped into bed with caution, not wanting to wake Jacques exactly, but not wanting him to be gone for the whole night, either. They hadn't had a proper dinner, and he was starting to feel too hungry to eat only bread. He placed his hand lightly on Jacques' arm and kissed his back. Jacques stirred, sighed, and Mark took the opportunity to move closer, spooning him. He could feel the Frenchman's slow heartbeat. He moved Jacques' hair over his head and blew on his neck to cool him. He drank from his glass and wet the Frenchman's lips with his fingertips. They'd been dry. He nudged him with his hips, wanting to wake him now, and then wanting to thrust into him again. Jacques' breath seemed to get caught in his throat.

Mark kissed Jacques' earlobe and let his exhalation whisk into the canal. Jacques responded as he'd hoped, his hips moving toward Mark, who then entered him lying side by side for the first time. He wished he had a mirror in front of them, so he could see the Frenchman from both angles as they rocked each other.

After he came, he remembered that he'd wanted to ward off dehydration in his lover before he was distracted by desire. Tourists seldom drank enough because they weren't used to the climate. He sipped some of the water, and then drained it again and again from his own mouth into his lover's until the glass was empty.

TWENTY-TWO

Jacques was a little startled when he was invited to Mark's house for another family dinner since he'd not been there since his first evening in Kenya. He had more insight this time, had been privy to more details of the African's young life, his stories. He could observe Mark's family with this new information. And, although Humming still seemed distant and aloof, he understood what she had left behind to start a new life, and how she must be upset that her son would soon leave her in the same way.

He idolized Mark. Try as he may, he couldn't picture his lover as a young boy, afraid, doing what his Papap told him to, being so alone and small in such a foreign place, not fitting in anywhere, least of all in his own imagination. At least that was his take on Mark's story, and it explained why he was so guarded, even with Jacques, who adored him more than anything.

With dinner over, they sat together on Mark's mattress listening to music on local radio. Mark did not own a phonograph, so he searched the radio for the station he liked. He suggested they borrow his cousin's record player next time.

"This show's usually good, alternative stuff, they're calling it in America."

Jacques cared little about such entertainment but was pleased that Mark was trying to be a good host. While browsing through Mark's books, journals, and newsletters, he wondered when Mark had time to read so much. There were pages earmarked, bookmarks everywhere, highlighted articles, and comments written in margins. He picked up a copy of a communist newsletter.

"Where did you get this?" Jacques asked with contempt.

"I'm a member," Mark said.

"You're joking, n'est-ce pas?"

Mark's eyes flashed angrily at him now, and Jacques became nervous. He wished he'd kept his mouth shut.

"No, I'm not joking. Wow, I forgot who you were the past couple of weeks."

"What do you mean?"

"Capitalist. Royal blood, right?" Mark stood up and started to pace.

"No! I mean, yes, but…I thought you were sensitive to the poor, but I…"

"The poor? Do you hear yourself?"

Jacques felt thrown while he tried to integrate this information. He wanted to see it as insignificant, certainly not worth arguing with someone he loved this much.

"You sound like…" Mark breathed out heavily and stopped talking. He looked horrified, his eyes aflame, like he was battling within himself or about to strike out. But, no, it couldn't be that serious, could it? He stood up and tried to get close to Mark, to smooth things out. He muttered how sorry he was and raised his arms to embrace Mark around the neck, but Mark pushed him away roughly, knocking him to the floor. Jacques winced, afraid suddenly not about the fate of the relationship but about his own safety. Mark grabbed him and pulled him up, but the gesture was not meant to comfort.

"Mark, what was that?" Humming was at the beads, and Mark let Jacques' feet drop to the floor below him. Jacques stifled his breath because he knew it would sound labored.

"Nothing. Jacques fell, tripped over all this crap," he said as he kicked several books across the room.

She parted the beads, "Are you all right? That was quite a bump we heard." Her voice sounded unsure.

"Yes, thank you," Jacques said, but he didn't look up, couldn't let her see what was in his eyes.

"He's fine. I'm taking him back to the Gasthaus," Mark told the wall opposite his mother. She hesitated but then slowly backed out.

"Get your stuff," Mark told him.

Jacques shrugged. "I don't have anything."

Jacques didn't hear from Mark the next day, and there was no answer at the house. He started to feel fraught with the same fear that had driven his young life for as long as he could remember. The ride home last night was spent in silence, and he was unable to break through the barrier that had gone up between them. Mark hadn't stayed the night, didn't even say good-bye when Jacques got out of the truck.

When he walked out of the house yesterday and waited for Mark by the car, he'd seen Papap sitting by himself on a bench looking out at the stars. He had approached quietly and then was afraid he'd startle the older man, so he pushed some stones and dirt with his shoe.

"I know you're there, French boy," Papap had said without turning around.

"Oui."

"Come," he waved. "Sit with me."

Jacques sat and looked where Papap's gaze pointed, not sure what he was seeing but feeling more at peace amidst the vastness of the cosmos.

"Beautiful?"

"Yes."

Papap breathed out meditatively and leaned toward Jacques on the bench. "You want me to drive you home?"

"Non, merci. Mark will be out in a minute."

Papap nodded. "If you're sure."

Jacques felt a couple of tears roll down his cheek. Mark's parents apparently knew that their son had a temper. "I said something stupid."

"Oh, I doubt it."

"I'm afraid..." Jacques did not complete his sentence for fear of losing control of himself emotionally.

"We'll all afraid sometimes."

"But, I'm afraid a lot of the times."

"Hmm."

"Now I am afraid I ruined everything."

"You can't always please everyone, French boy." A deep furrow crept into Papap's forehead. "Of course, there are those who would use that argument as an excuse to behave without scruples. But, you strike me as someone with a whole lot of principle." Then he smiled in that openhanded way Jacques loved.

Mark cleared his throat from somewhere behind them, so Jacques stood to take his leave and then spent the ride home in silence.

Presently, he was walking to the lounge phone to give it another try, Papap's words repeating in his mind. Was he really principled? Mark didn't seem to think so. His heart was replete with pleas and anxieties, and he could hardly breathe while the phone rang and rang. When Mark finally answered, Jacques felt unprepared.

"Jacques, is that you?"

"Yes," he answered, and then nothing else came out.

It was Mark who broke the silence. "I'm sorry. Could I come over?"

"Of course. I'm sorry, too."

———

When Mark arrived at the Gasthaus, having sped the whole way, he ran all the way up to Jacques' room. He knocked with more conviction than he would have owned and grabbed the Frenchman as soon as he opened the door. Jacques' breath seemed to catch in response, but he didn't say anything. Mark held his face and kissed him tenderly on the lips.

"Let's not talk about it," he said, as if in agreement. He had missed Jacques and regretted his behavior more than he wanted to admit aloud. "I have something I do have to tell you, though," he said between kisses.

"Oui?"

"You're not going to like it."

Jacques pushed back a little from Mark. "What is it?"

"Kyle's coming, in a couple of days. On his way to the States. He didn't know about you," he said as explanation.

"When did you find out?"

"This morning. He called and spoke with my mother. Apparently, another one of his letters was lost in the mail." Mark rubbed Jacques' lower lip with the soft side of his thumb in near reverie.

Jacques nodded in understanding, but he seemed to hold onto Mark more tightly than usual. Mark was dealing with his own demons that night, feeling external pressures exacerbating the tension already growing inside him. His delight in their love making, both sexual and otherwise, grew in ever-widening circles, equal in frightening proportion to the circumference of his anger. He hadn't wanted to talk about the argument because he knew he couldn't put right what was different between them, and it scared him almost senseless.

TWENTY-THREE

John walked out of the hospital, accompanied by his parents. Numerous times in therapy and later as preparation for suitable discharge, Dr. Comer asked him if he remembered his parents being abusive while he was growing up. "I don't remember them being much of anything," he'd answered.

Presently, he rolled his shirtsleeves down to cover the self-inflicted scars. He felt most embarrassed by the thickest one, the one that reminded him of his failure to end his life, and his failure to live it. His parents discussed his future as if he were still a child, unable to contribute to the plans intelligibly.

"You can't very well stay with us the rest of your life. You're nineteen years old now."

"I know how old I am," John said.

"Well, then, we considered renting you an apartment in London, but with your propensity toward illicit drugs," his mother continued, "well, dear, we thought it best to bring you to the country."

To bring me? Yes, I deserve to be spoken to like that.

"Surrey is, as you are well aware, too close to London and the vagaries in which you partake as soon as you're out of arm's reach. You'll love living at the cottage, darling. Wouldn't you agree?" his mother asked, looking over her shoulder to the back seat of their brand new luxury sedan.

"I don't remember," John answered.

"Excuse me? Surely you remember the cottage."

"The future is what I don't recall, mother," John responded to her, using obfuscation as a means of revolt.

He had spent eight weeks in hospital, the first two on the acute psychiatric ward of the London Public Hospital, where Jacques and Mark had supposedly visited, the next two or three on the acute adult psychiatric ward at the private facility, and then the remainder of the time on the therapeutic unit there, "subacute," the nurses had called it. He could remember the last five weeks. Prior to that, a combination of medication and electroconvulsive therapy robbed him of his experiences. He remembered virtually everything from the private facility in great detail, including a protracted journey back to himself, and the struggle to come out the other side feeling sane again, "back to baseline," written on his chart with a smile from the attending doctor.

The strongest feeling he harbored now was the pervading sense of dread he held toward his parents, and yet he was faced with depending on them once again for his arrangements. Beneath the contempt was his fear that they would ultimately grow impatient with their obligation toward him, and that he would be left alone, devoid of devices in which to save himself, and vulnerable. Empty, like a hand without a palm.

The world was too much for him, and yet, it was not enough. *My life will again be filled with the usual mishaps and eccentricities which define it, and I'll manage*, he assured himself, crossing his hands in his lap. He faced his sentence with equanimity, feeling he had nothing left for which to fight. He was wary of half possibilities and parallel worlds, and he would try to remain present instead. He tried not to invest much interest in whether Robin wrote him again, although she was the only person with whom he now felt anything but that peculiar sense of wariness.

Reaching home always brought on a deluge of emotion for him, not so much because of the last few rebellious years (during which he had displaced his anger toward the money and privilege itself) but because of phantoms he could never perceive long enough to decipher. His parents disengaged with dispatch: his father carried John's bag of personal belongings (a literal, plastic bag a nurse had obtained for him to gather his things once the discharge orders were in place), and his mother spoke to the housekeeper, something about John's temporary stay until they could relocate him to the cottage. John stood outside the imposing estate's entrance hall, gripped with sudden regret. Why shouldn't they have taken him straight away? The phantoms returned, but he was ready to shut them out. He had been taught to clamp down on the scary thoughts, replacing them with song lyrics or practiced poems, repeated by rote to ward off the evil spirits of his mind.

He walked in and onward to his room, wondering how his parents had managed to cover up his recent misadventure. Carpet removed, replaced with hard tile: he sneered in response. They've not been the type of parents to buttress a fall. If he attempted to kill himself again, perhaps he'd accidentally succeed as his skull hit the hard surface. Imagining all manner of revenge, he had momentary comic relief before thinking himself morbid. Then he dumped the contents of his bag on the chaise lounge.

At least they hadn't taken his posters down, rearranged the furniture and censored his literature, as they had done when he was sent to a drug rehab center in Scarborough. Far enough away to avoid imposing stigma on the family. The rehab center was where John learned of his association of sex with illegal drug use, notably that he never felt comfortable having sex without being high. He studied a photograph now that he had purchased at an art fair in London the year before, a few leaves, autumnal leaves, against the gray concrete of a sidewalk. John always liked the respite of that season. While everyone else mourned the passing of summer, he sighed contentedly at the elegance of a falling leaf. Nothing relieved his despondency quite the same as a just end.

His eye next landed on his music pad: pages and pages of notes and melodies that may never be played anywhere but in his head. He had forgotten he'd written a requiem, a bit melodramatic to him now. Studying the sheets of music before him, he saw that he'd left it unfinished. *This isn't done. It must be done, and soon. It shouldn't be left incomplete. God, what was I thinking? God? Did I just pray?* "How bloody ridiculous," he mumbled out loud.

The pages impressed him now. Could one write music more profound than oneself? He doubted that the compositions emanated from his own brain. Much more likely was that he managed to touch some kind of transcendent force deep within. The spate was just too powerful when it broke out, as it so often did over the past few years. It reminded him of a conversation he'd had with Robin. She was writing a story and had asked him if her characters could be more emotionally mature than she was. She had wanted to use their existence as a permanent marker of her insurgence against the norm, something to flaunt at the face of the world, when it would but thrust her into an institution for the mentally weak or beat her into submission. "Robin," he said, tasting her name aloud. She would be his secret. He jumped at the sound of the knock.

"John?" his sister was smiling, outlined by the frame of his door like a portrait. "Hey, Baby brother, are you talking to yourself already? That can't be a good sign." She smiled.

Twit. John turned his back to her and replaced the music pad on the end table.

"Do you need any help with your stuff? Mother said you'll be living in the cottage."

"No, thank you, and kindly refrain from entering my room."

"Sure," she looked down and then shuffled away, obviously hurt. He wasn't sure why he felt the need to be short with her. What would he do without her, after all?

On an excursion to London the next day, John decided to pick up some books and cassettes before leaving Surrey. In the underground he ran into a dealer he knew, a cockeyed, hair-spiking, ten-earring-wearing nut known as Freaky Pete.

"Haven't seen you about," the tattoo on Freaky Pete's face seemed to grimace at every word he spoke.

John eyed him with suspicion.

"What substance for your pleasure, mate?" the dealer asked him.

"The world has no substance but that which you impart upon it."

Freaky Pete forced a laugh, probably assuming his customer already high. But, staying clean was the meaning with which John now imbibed the scene. He saw his mental illness as a matter of moral impairment. His diagnosis had changed over the years, but with shame he regarded the roots: he knew his mind concocted paranoid fantasies to mask his own murderous rage. He knew he used drugs to hide from the phantoms. Now he also realized that the addiction had become its own crucifix. He managed to walk away.

TWENTY-FOUR

Jacques looked at himself in the mirror. He was dressed in conservative, black slacks. His long-sleeved dress shirt was rolled up to the elbows and unbuttoned enough to reveal his ribbed cotton undershirt. He held his hand on his stomach to quiet it and wished he could settle himself. Mark would soon arrive to bring him to dinner at his house, bring him to meet Kyle, who was staying there this week. He had tried for the last forty-eight hours to ignore this gnawing detail. He wondered how these seven days would impact his future, if he had a future. Where would it be? In Kenya? That was hardly conceivable. He missed Paris, the luxury of his home, but that was the extent of it. He couldn't return to his father's even if he wanted, as he'd been forbidden to leave in the first place. His father had cut him off financially, and his own funds wouldn't last much longer. He wished he'd been thriftier with his earnings from the theater, or rather the percentage he was given as an allowance. The rest of it should still be his, but he had no idea how to access it. What had he expected of Mark and this voyage to Africa? That Mark would really save him from his life?

He heard a car pull up, rushed to the window as Papap was stepping out of the truck. Mark was not with him.

"Ready to eat, French boy?" Papap was smiling as Jacques reached the Gasthaus entrance. He must have sensed Jacques' nerves because he placed his formidable hands on Jacques' shoulders. "What will be, will be," he said with equability Jacques wished were contagious. "Okay?"

He shrugged. He never liked the expression because it signified an inability to manipulate circumstances to his liking.

As they pulled up to the house, Papap spoke for the first time the entire ride. "Is there anything you need to know?"

The question came so unexpectedly that Jacques couldn't think of a thing to ask. Days later, of course, he thought of a multitude of queries which would have been useful had he only thought of them at the time.

They walked past a couple of unfamiliar vehicles and entered the kitchen. Bella, all aglow with enthusiasm and good will, introduced Jacques to her aunt and uncle. They were talking to Humming as she prepared the meal.

Jacques heard Mark's voice from the living room, where he was talking with his step-cousin, Robert. He'd only met Robert once—despite how close Mark said they were. They were presumably speaking with Kyle, who must have been sitting on the floor across from them. Jacques walked into the room unaccompanied and introduced himself to Kyle, humiliated that Mark ignored his arrival. He held his hand out to Kyle, a gesture Kyle completely disregarded. Instead, Mark's ex-boyfriend steadied his incredulous eyes on Mark's countenance.

Robert stood up and shook Jacques' hand because it had lingered afloat in the middle of the room. "Hello," he said.

Humming walked in with a glass of lemonade for Jacques, distracting them for a moment. Jacques noticed a small and whiny window air conditioner had been turned on. He walked toward Mark and sat beside him on the couch, squeezing in. Kyle glared at him, which he refused to acknowledge.

"Hi," Mark said to Jacques, and then he picked up the conversation where they must have left off, the two cousins asking Kyle about Japan, his family's well-being, and his plans. Jacques ascertained from the conversation that Kyle would have to leave Kenya in a week, whether he wanted to or not, to arrive on campus on time. He was too self-conscious to contribute anything to the discussion. Besides, he couldn't relate to it. He had nothing in common with Kyle, or with Mark's past, in general. He was even bored with it, truth be told, and found Kyle physically unattractive.

But, he couldn't help but scrutinize the glances, shared jokes, and nuances between Mark and his former boyfriend. During dinner, they flowed in a way that still eluded Jacques, sometimes due perhaps to the slight but ever-present language barrier. Jacques found further cause to fret when Mark asked his relatives to drop Jacques off at the Gasthaus for him when dinner was over. Mark then evaded Jacques' eyes as he bade him goodnight.

———

"Let's take a walk," Kyle suggested, putting his palm to Mark's mid-back. In unison, they walked toward their usual path. "I'm so glad to be back."

"You are?"

"Yeah. I've missed you more than I let on in recent letters. I was lonely in Tokyo. You wouldn't think that with the throngs of people, but…"

"You didn't say," Mark kept his gaze forward, feeling more confused and burdened than ever.

"There was a time I wouldn't have had to say."

"I'm sorry." Mark stopped and looked at him, his head tilted.

"No, I don't mean to make you sorry."

"I know you don't understand this thing I have with Jacques."

"You don't have to explain," Kyle said. Then he added, "Okay, yeah, let's talk about it. He doesn't seem your type, and I guess I can't believe you'd be serious about him."

Mark turned away.

"I know it's not my business."

"I guess it is, right? I never told you about him. I never technically broke things off with you. I didn't want to admit any of this was happening, in retrospect." They walked past a spot they'd often been intimate. Kyle dawdled behind him, and Mark knew it meant he wanted to stop and sit for a while. He'd always known what Kyle wanted.

"Want to sit?" Kyle asked superfluously, and Mark hesitated only briefly before going to his side. He was feeling torn in two directions so completely in opposition to one another. "So, what are you saying?"

"I don't know," Mark admitted. Kyle smiled as he touched Mark's face.

"I missed this the most, us being close." He kissed Mark on his cheek and kept his face close enough for Mark to feel his breath. "You didn't?"

"Of course I did," Mark said. He moved in and kissed Kyle fully but with remorse. He bent his head so that their foreheads connected, his hand held onto Kyle's neck. "I can't do this, I'm sorry."

"So you *are* serious about him," Kyle blurted as he jerked back a little.

"I don't know how I feel about him. Sometimes I don't even recognize myself when I'm with him."

"Doesn't that tell you something?"

"What? That I should end it? I ask myself that regularly."

Kyle let out a sigh and seemed to search for magical words. "Then do it. I came here to propose in person that you come with me to the States even if you're not enrolled yet."

"I never heard back from you, but I did get out a couple of applications," Mark said, feeling a little defensive because he didn't want to be perceived as the one who dropped the ball, as the one who let things end, if that was indeed what had happened.

"I know, but it was so difficult to coordinate without talking, and my father wouldn't let us call overseas much," Kyle said. "But, it can still happen. We can go, just like we planned. Think about it while we have fun this week. You don't need to decide right now."

"Deal. But," Mark hesitated again, "we do have to include Jacques when we go out, at least sometimes."

Kyle looked peeved but said, "Sure."

"And, maybe you can actually talk with him once in awhile," Mark said.

"I'll give it a try...for you."

"Thanks, Kyle." He was having trouble maintaining eye contact.

Mark undressed quickly while Kyle used the bathroom. He questioned his reasoning for staying at home with his guest, his ex-boyfriend, instead of at the Gasthaus with his current boyfriend.

Kyle rolled into Mark's bed-on-the floor the way a frankfurter fits into a bun, comfortable though tight, and commented, "Just like old times."

"Not just," Mark corrected.

"Well, right..." Kyle sounded disgruntled, and Mark realized he didn't need to remind Kyle that he preferred a shallow, pretty face to his.

Painfully aware of his error in judgment, Mark listened now for the rhythm of breath that would signal Kyle was sleep. His mind repeatedly wandered to Jacques as he fell into a restive sleep, and he berated himself for having fallen in love with someone so wrong for him. He dreamt he was a lion tamer in a traveling circus, all the time questioning why he would have chosen such a career, why he was trying to tame something so wild and beautiful. He woke with an erection and knew he was awake for the night. Even lying next to Kyle, he couldn't get his mind off of Jacques, so he went into the living room to read, hoping he hadn't disturbed his friend too much.

Mark went into town the next day with Kyle to shop for items Kyle's family wanted him to send back to Japan, trinkets and bric-a-brac they suddenly found themselves unable to live without. They ran into an old friend from school, joked with one another, ate lunch, and talked. Kyle had plenty to fill Mark in about, including his anticipated studies at university in Washington, D.C., and the details of his life in Japan. He spoke of his impression of Japanese boys their age and the cultural view on homosexuality. The conversation was refreshing but dreadfully one-sided, as Mark was unwilling to speak of his own new experiences. He shared nothing of his relationship with John, spoke naught of his impression of Paris or London, or his disappointment with his natural father. He kept his comments brief, feeling compelled to hide especially the intimate details of his liaison with Jacques. He dodged a suggestion that they pay a visit to their "private cave."

As Kyle spoke, animated, Mark found himself in agonizing critique of what he himself had become, of time wasted. He was older than Kyle and nowhere near as focused or ambitious. Kyle was eager to study political science. Mark found his own involvement with the communist movement superficial at best. He had been consumed by his work on the farm and by his infatuation with the Frenchman presently waiting for him at the Gasthaus. He would have to come up with an excuse to stop by there on the drive home.

But, Kyle made him promise to make one more stop first. Mark could read from his actions that his old friend didn't want their day together to end. They walked through Uhuru Park, reminiscing of times they'd shared.

"Anyway, I kept thinking I'd hear from you more often. Why didn't you write me more often, especially in the beginning?" asked Kyle with frankness Mark found disarming.

"I don't know," Mark tried to remember. "I rarely got any news from you, so I stopped."

"What are you talking about? I wrote a few times a week."

"You did not."

"I did, too." They both laughed at the exchange and slipped into more comfortable space.

"Maybe more were lost than I thought," Kyle said. "I didn't think the post was that bad here. I even sent most of them through the embassy, just to be sure on my end, although there's no problem with the Japanese postal service that I know of. I know the office is reliable. My Dad took my mail in for me," Kyle said.

They both stopped short and looked at each other.

"Oh, fuck, you don't think he would've..." Kyle swallowed and looked away.

"It would sure explain why there were so many gaps in the letters I did get. I kept wondering what you were talking about when I'd get your letters. And he may have kept letters of mine from you since I mailed all of them to his office. I know I wrote weekly at first. Did you get them?" Mark asked.

"No." Kyle seemed to be remembering something. "As a matter of fact, the only time I did seem to get a letter from you was when my Mom went to the embassy to bring my Dad lunch or something. Then I would curse the African mail system because it would be obvious a previous letter had gone missing."

"Wow." Mark stated emphatically. He proceeded to say "Wow" several more times as his mind raced from account to account of times he'd been confused by missing links in Kyle's notes, or hurt by lack of word from him.

They walked in silence for a while.

"What's done is done," stated Mark, although he was, of course, wondering what might have been. Interspersed with angry thoughts were feelings of deep sorrow that Kyle's father would have watched his son suffer with no qualms. What a torrent of grievances he could file if only there were some overseeing body that gave a damn.

"I need to pick up a book I lent him," Mark explained as he turned off the road and toward the Gasthaus. Kyle didn't respond. The truck pulled up jerkily in imitation of Mark's approach toward Jacques over the past year. He couldn't seem to help it.

"Coming in?"

"Sure," Kyle replied without hesitation. Mark hoped not to show his vexation at not having a few minutes alone with Jacques.

But, Jacques wasn't anywhere on the grounds and didn't answer his door. "I wonder where he is," Mark thought aloud, forgetting to mask his concern.

Kyle shrugged. "Probably went out with other tourists. You can ask the owners to let you in for your book."

"Right," Mark said before remembering there was no book. "Um, actually, I'll come back later on. I'm sure they wouldn't just let someone in to snoop around." He acknowledged peripherally that he was almost furious and most likely over-reacting.

On the way out the lobby door, he stopped short. "Hey, I'll meet you outside," and, in a manner preempting discussion, turned away and walked toward the small desk. Another native African girl was working there, younger than the one he'd met, probably hired during summer break from school. She said she hadn't seen Jacques but explained she'd been "out back serving tea" to other guests earlier. Mark understood she'd skipped out for a while.

He hurried home to see if Jacques had called, not caring now if Kyle sensed his agitation, or if his friend extrapolated from his behavior that his plans for them were truly jeopardized.

The truck screeched to a halt at the house. Mark tried to walk with an air of nonchalance to the door, but did not recover so well when he saw Jacques at the kitchen table with Papap and his friends. They were playing cards and laughing a lot. Jacques appeared to be enjoying himself.

"Hey, I was looking for you."

"I've been here." Jacques smiled at Mark warmly. "Did you two have fun today?"

"Yes," Kyle responded for Mark, who was too flummoxed to do so himself.

"How did you get here?" Mark asked.

"How'd he get here?" Papap laughed. "I picked him up with Matindo, of course."

"I hope it's okay." Jacques must have noticed his disquiet because his expression changed. Mark couldn't help but wonder what was causing the hostility he felt.

"Of course. Can I talk to you?" Mark pointed to the bedroom to imply alone.

TWENTY-FIVE

Now that Mark had him alone he wasn't sure what he wanted to say or do. Jacques smiled meekly at him. "What's the matter?" The Frenchman tried to maneuver closer to him, to kiss him.

"What's the matter with you?" Mark demanded in as soft a voice as he could muster.

"What do you mean?"

"Listen, I'm not sure this is working out."

"Why do you say this?" Jacques stepped back. Mark noticed how attractive the Frenchman looked in his casual clothes. His arms were toned and now tanned, almost hairless.

"I don't know what's wrong. You can't just come here, intrude on my life like this."

"Why are you so angry? Your father invited me."

"Because." Mark gripped his head and brushed against Jacques to look out the small window by the bookshelf.

"You don't want me to spend time with your father?" Jacques asked him.

"It's not that, no." Mark let out stale air. "I don't know if I can do this any more."

"Oh," Jacques seemed to buckle over in slow motion.

"Please don't make a scene. Can't we have a fucking conversation without you crying?"

"I'm sorry. I didn't know that you wanted to have a conversation." Jacques wiped tears from his face in a hurry. "Maybe after you're with him this week, you will want me again," he said in a pleading tone.

"What's that supposed to mean?"

"I didn't want to say anything about you staying with him last night. I thought maybe we will go back to how it was when he leaves."

"I'm not having sex with him, for Christ's sake." Jacques looked baffled, and Mark suspected he didn't believe him. "You know how strongly I feel about monogamy."

"About what? Oh, yes, I know. I just thought…" He leaned on the desk, the only other furniture in the room. "So, you are leaving me…so then you can have sex with him?"

Mark smirked and let out a grunt. "I hate when you do that."

"Do what?" Jacques sounded desperate to stop annoying him.

"Simplify something so childishly." *Tear through the chaff so easily*, his heart corrected.

"Is it not right?" Jacques asked.

"No!"

"What then? Why are you doing this?"

Mark was going to respond with the speech he had silently rehearsed several times. He thought it through now, *I'm breaking up with you because the very foundation of our relationship is wrong and shallow, because our worlds are 180 degrees apart from one another, because I can't ever love you the way everyone deserves to be loved,* or he could simply say *I can't be with a capitalist, we don't fit,* or if that's too impersonal, *you can never satisfy me.* But, all he saw were the brilliant gem-like eyes brimming in tears, the slightly quivering lips, and, most inviolate, the open heart before him.

"Forget it. I'm not doing anything. I, we, just need to get through the next few days," he said in a softer voice.

Jacques embraced him, Mark yielding to the pull of the Frenchman's energy, the two fitting suddenly very well into one another. "I can be more like what you want. Teach me," Jacques said.

Mark hushed him, and in a moment of slippery clarity, said, "Jacques, if I can't love you, it's my weakness, not yours."

"But it will be my loss. I want you to look at me the way you look at him."

"No, you don't," Mark said. "I look at him like I'm sorry it's over, that's all."

"But, sometimes you look at me like you're sorry it's not over."

Mark shoved Jacques' hips back from his slightly. "Don't say that. I can't guarantee this is for the long run, but I don't want to lose you, either. I just get so confused about us."

"I know. Je sais." Jacques nodded in a way that implied he'd heard *confused* several times before.

Mark took Jacques' ring finger into his mouth and sucked on it seductively, wanting to fix what he had done. "Maybe tonight we can make love."

"I hope so," Jacques said, a little less ardent than Mark expected.

He didn't know what else to do just now to assuage his lover's nerves, but he felt desire pouring into him again like a funnel. "Stick your tongue out."

Jacques complied, and Mark sucked on it with a force that brought a shrill noise to Jacques' throat. Mark released him. "Sorry."

Jacques cleared his throat and then said, "Me, too. I don't want us to fight."

"Come on," Mark took Jacques by the hand and led him to the others.

He saw that Kyle had joined the men at the table and had played Jacques' hand.

"Are you ready to go?" Kyle asked Mark. Kyle had arranged for them to meet some friends at a local pub, and Mark had forgotten. His palms started sweating, once again feeling pulled apart.

"I forgot. Are you tired? I can drop you off," he said to Jacques.

"No, I feel okay, if you don't mind."

"Oh," Mark said, looking at Kyle, who made no attempt to hide his disdain.

"It's not really your scene," Kyle said, out of line. All three fell quiet, and Mark encouraged them to move outside, as he was painfully aware of his father's frown even though he was turned away from him.

He saw Jacques kick some dirt under his feet on the way to the truck. Mark knew that his lover had failed to catch the jealousy behind Kyle's rude gestures because he was too engrossed in his own insecurities. He wasn't sure how to right any of this and wasn't used to being the center of conflict.

"How about I drop you off at the Gasthaus, go for a little while, and then come over?" he said to Jacques.

Kyle turned to face him abruptly, "You're not going to stay? It won't be much of a reunion without you." Kyle got to the truck first and pulled the front seat forward for Jacques to climb in back. The two exchanged a momentary but fixed stare.

"I guess," Mark agreed. "What do you want me to do?" he asked almost rhetorically to neither one in particular.

"Jacques, you don't mind, do you? I'll only be here a few more days, and then you'll have him all to yourself," said Kyle.

Mark now missed the time when Kyle wasn't addressing Jacques at all. Every word out of his ex seemed to alter his relationship with the Frenchman, tearing at it from the sides and corners of their already tenuous connection. He wished he were more in command of the situation.

"Do what you want," Jacques answered, looking at Mark through the rearview mirror.

At the pub, Mark joined his somewhat estranged friends in a toast, welcoming Kyle home and celebrating camaraderie. No one mentioned Jacques: his absence, well-being, or existence.

Mark's step-cousin, Robert, was deep in debate with a university pal Mark had not yet met. Mark and Kyle were discussing plans for tomorrow when Robert caught his attention.

"The only way to fight fanaticism is to surpass its fervor with your own. Make sure the blokes holding you hostage know you'd rather die for your principles than fear them." They were discussing the hostage situation in another country. "As a communist, I support the anti-establishment sentiment, of course, but I am ever so mistrustful of any movement with religious undercurrent."

"Yes, well Americans aren't going to demonstrate principles, are they?" The young, unfamiliar African laughed. "We're all anarchists as far as they're concerned." He dropped his eyes rather obviously when they lighted on Kyle and Mark, both American citizens, if not residents.

"I met a Belgian who referred to Americans as economic sociopaths," Mark added. "But, still, wouldn't you call bombing someone's embassy an act of terrorism?" he asked. The table was suddenly very quiet and Mark thought he'd opened Pandora's Box.

"What does this word mean, terrorism? I am not sure I know what it actually refers to," Robert, ever the semantic, posed to the group.

"It is any kind of counterstrike, obviously. We have to make them hear us! The big powers of the world are the terrorists. They are the ones who have colonized us and stripped us bare. We mustn't slip into that world of fuzzy gray that comprises most of the world's constitution. We must continue to fight for ourselves—fight for freedom from this injustice."

Of course Mark was acquainted with this argument, but he questioned the legitimacy of violent retaliation. He worried that his affiliation with the League would eventually implicate him. He used every excuse possible to put them off the past month or so.

"Nevertheless, I'd be terrorized if my embassy blew up," Mark said, disregarding the possibility of alienating himself or sounding like a white man. These points could raise contention even among the closest of friends. Still, wouldn't most men argue that there were substantial differences between terrorists and freedom fighters? Mark found himself at the core of those distinctions.

"Don't be so naive, Mark. You think revolutionaries would get far without a little violence? It's inevitable," his friend Wayne said as he finished his drink.

Mark looked over and caught Kyle rolling his eyes. Kyle was the most pro-West of the group, had in private argued that the so-called advancements since independence were debatable in his opinion. Mark raised his glass Kyle's way and flashed him a smirk. "Where do you draw the lines then?" he asked the group.

"How do you fight the juggernaut of the West on its own terms when you're small and politically insignificant?" Robert's acquaintance responded. "I admire the men of peace, men larger than life, men such as Mahatma Gandhi, as much as you do, but I question their potential in a world already so violent."

"Everyone seemed to question it then, too, didn't they?" Mark replied. His friends already knew he felt deeply about the power of civil disobedience and non-violent measures. They had, over the years, discussed nearly everything. It was what they did best. There were times when the more conservative and the more liberal in his country came to the same conclusions, despite that they came at those conclusions from very disparate angles. Mark wondered when the reactionary became the radical, and vice-versa, and when and why the words were more important than the people. He didn't like labels because he feared he would find himself on the uncomfortable side of them if not careful.

They all laughed at another clever remark, but Mark was only aware that the stakes had risen, had become both more intricate and more intimate. Nothing appeared quite so black-or-white to him as they once had.

TWENTY-SIX

In his bedroom that night, Mark felt Kyle approach from behind. He remembered a time he did not feel so separate from Kyle and leaned back, head on his friend's shoulder, wanting to move backward in time with the same effortlessness.

"I missed you so much," Kyle said, pulling Mark down to the mattress.

Mark had dreamt of this closeness often since they'd parted. On top of Kyle now, he enjoyed himself without being so defended, so in control, as he seemed to struggle to be with Jacques. As soon as his mind went to Jacques, he pulled away.

"Don't stop." Kyle encouraged him by rubbing his hand along the length of Mark's erection.

Mark held himself above Kyle, moving farther away from him.

"You can't do it?" Kyle asked with an edgy tone.

Mark shook his head no. He rolled over, so they lay next to each other.

"But, it's us. It's like nothing's changed."

"That's just it, Kyle, everything's changed."

"What hold does he have on you?" Kyle lay on his side, so that their faces would mirror.

Mark agreed to meet his eyes, but stayed on his back, shrugged and threw his hands up a bit. He couldn't begin to explain it.

"Is it the sex? Is it that good?"

Mark glared at him, "Yes, it's *that good*, but it's not why I'm with him. I thought you held me in higher esteem than that."

"You're only human, Mark. I'd be willing…"

Mark looked away, not wishing his friend to humiliate himself. There was actually nothing Kyle could agree to right now that would change his mind. "Don't..."

"It's just that I don't blame you for wanting to fuck his brains out, but you can't, absolutely cannot, be serious about him."

"Shut up, Kyle. Don't say another word about him."

Kyle pressed his head in his hands and huffed. "So, can we just be clear about this, think it through together?"

Mark did not overtly object because he wanted to get this over with, now that the truth was out.

"Let me preface this by saying that it's about you, not him. If it's not just that you fuck him, and I'm assuming you do," he paused. "Okay, so you're gonna be discreet," Kyle said with a sardonic air. "If it isn't just the sex, what is it?"

"I don't owe you an explanation."

"You don't have one."

"What's that supposed to mean?" Mark sat up, bent his head into his hands.

"You have no idea why you're with him. I bet you couldn't even tell me what you like about him," Kyle was whisper-shouting, obviously wanting to win this argument.

"It doesn't matter. It's late."

"No way are you going to pull that shit with me. I can't believe you'd throw away what we have for, for him."

"What we *had*. What we had," Mark stressed.

"So, we're not good together any more? I think we've done pretty damn well the past couple of days, especially considering how long it's been. We understand each other. We had plans."

"Kyle," Mark turned to him, "It's been great to see you, to be with you. And, you're right, I have no logical explanation for any of this, but I do know it's not just a physical thing with him, it's more."

"Can you honestly say you belong with him?"

"I haven't been honest with myself for so long," he said, the hour and the fatigue getting to him, empowering him to speak from his heart. "I don't know. It's been so weird for me. I was lonely when you left Kenya. All I did was try to engross myself in books. The visit with my so-called father in Germany was a bust, there's nothing there. He doesn't care about me and never will," Mark verbalized for the first time. He sat cross-legged on the edge of the mattress. "Stuff happened that led to my meeting Jacques, and I didn't like him at first, but," he stopped midsentence not out of a sense of suspense but out of ignorance. He wasn't sure what had happened. Kyle kept quiet while Mark processed what he could. "I did feel attracted to him, I guess," Mark said finally.

"He's quite effeminate. I didn't think you liked that," Kyle said.

"No, you're wrong. He's more feminine than we are, maybe, but he's definitely not effeminate. I do hate that," Mark said. "But, there's a difference. And, no, usually when I check guys out, they're regular guys, I guess.

"The whole thing is a mystery to me. What makes people fall in love, in lust? I don't know. There must be whole books written about it. I never thought much of it, seemed kind of silly and useless to think about things like that."

"Love does?" Kyle had apparently heard his use of the word. Mark himself had cringed when it slipped out.

He fought hard now to stay in his head, where he had more control, and he knew Kyle was doing the same. "Well, no, not conceptually, but romance does. It was yet another intrusion of Western culture, and I never bothered with it. And now I find myself in a minor, personal crisis because of it," he feigned the voice of a horror film narrator and tickled Kyle with affection.

"Stop!" Kyle laughed. They began to wrestle, playfully at first, but then Kyle slammed Mark abruptly against the floor, his elbow on Mark's sternum.

"Christ!" Mark said, losing the whispering in his shock. He gave Kyle the opportunity to release him, but when he didn't, Mark forced him off and into the wall, slamming him pretty hard and then throwing him face down while pinning his legs beneath him. Kyle didn't say anything, so Mark shoved his ex's face into the floor until Kyle finally submitted with a weak, "Uncle, God-damn-it, Mark, Uncle."

Mark smirked a little at the use of the give word. They were both breathing audibly, shaken up by the physicality of the argument. "We probably woke my folks," he said as he climbed off Kyle, then asked, "Can we sleep yet?"

"So to wrap up, if you don't mind my doing so, you don't believe in following your heart because romantic love is insignificant, yet for some reason," Kyle pointed out, "rather ironically, you're with someone your head would never have chosen or approved of. Is that right?" He was still breathing heavier than usual.

"Oh, for fuck's sake, Kyle. Can't you understand where I am with all this?"

"I have no desire to be in that world of, what was it? Fuzzy gray. I'm shocked it's..." Kyle shook his head. "Can you tell me what you plan to do?"

Mark stared at his ex in disbelief.

"I think I deserve to know."

Mark was quiet and lost in his own thoughts for a while. "He strikes me in places, in ways, I never knew before."

"Is that enough, though?"

"Yeah, it's more than enough." Mark realized the undercurrent of his life; his desire had repeatedly been definitive. "I want him. I don't want to hurt you," he looked at his friend with as much tenderness and respect as he could muster, "but I have to stop denying how much I want to be with him."

"Fine." Kyle stood and walked toward the partition.

"Where are you going?"

"Don't expect me to go through another night like last night," Kyle's words spat at him. "I'll sleep on the couch."

———

It was two o'clock the following afternoon when Jacques sat down to write John. He couldn't concentrate; when Mark failed to arrive last night, he tried to stay hopeful. *We just have to get through the next few days,* Mark had said. Jacques repeated it over and again in his head like a mantra. He was in the lounge area, *International Herald Tribune* spread out around him. He had considered calling a taxi and confronting Mark at his house. He had thought of calling the airline to ascertain if he could leave today. As if he had someplace to go.

"Jacques," Mark stood in front of him like a mirage. "Sorry about last night."

He didn't know what to say, so he kept quiet. He hoped his face did not look red or swollen from crying.

"Want to go up?" Mark tilted his head to the stairs.

Jacques shook his head in assent, pulled his newspaper, John's last letter, writing paper, and sandals together: the sole remains of his life. Mark moved aside to let him lead the way. He could feel his whole body tremble and hoped Mark couldn't see his hand shaking as he unlocked his room. But then Mark grabbed his hand, raised it to his lips for a kiss and shut the door with his foot behind them.

Jacques pulled his hand away as he backed into the small area of his room.

"I said I was sorry, Jacques." Mark sounded barely tolerant. "Anyway, Kyle's leaving tomorrow. I thought..."

"Tomorrow?"

"Yeah, he's leaving sooner than planned. He wanted me to go with him, but I'm not."

"I see." Jacques couldn't help but glower at him.

"This has been rough for me, too," Mark said in response.

"Yes? If my ex-boyfriend came to me, wanted me back, it would be rough for me, n'est-ce pas?" He didn't have an ex-boyfriend, but why mention incidentals?

"Come on," Mark sighed. "Give me a break."

"So, what do you want? Why are you here now?"

"Nothing, no reason. Just thought we could have some private time," Mark said as he tried to snuggle up to Jacques.

"Oh, I understand," he said as he pulled away again. "Let me, how do you say it in English, bend over for you, and then I'll see you, when? Day after tomorrow? Sooner, if you are in the mood?" Mark looked shocked when Jacques started removing his shirt.

Mark grabbed his hands. "Stop this!"

"Why? Why should you be any different?" he said the last under his breath but then looked at Mark directly, "Is it not why you are here?"

"No…I don't know," Mark enjoined.

"So, go on. The faster we're done, the sooner you can return to your real friends," he resumed undressing, knowing he sounded adolescent but unable to stop himself.

"I said to stop!" Mark shouted, then he looked at the door as if he were afraid people could hear them.

Jacques felt an unusual sensation just then, like heat and power combined. He was tired of being a source of embarrassment to Mark. "Pourquoi? You don't want me? Which position should I take?" Before finishing, he felt the back of Mark's hand crash against the soft flesh of his cheek. He instantly flashed back to the assault.

"Shit! I'm sorry," Mark reached out to him as he cowered. "I'm so sorry. I didn't mean to hit you." Mark held him firmly as if to pass on healing by osmosis while Jacques' face smarted in an exaggerated way.

"That's the last fucking thing I meant to do. Please believe me." Mark held his face, gently stroking his cheek. "I'll run and get some ice, okay?"

Jacques shook his head affirmatively and held back tears. He wished not to cry just now. He heard Mark running down the stairs and then back up after a bit.

"Here, hold this to your face."

Jacques was sitting on the chair and did as he was told. He was trying to take inventory of his situation. He wasn't sure what to make of Mark's eruptions.

Mark was kneeling by his side and spoke quietly. "I told Kyle last night that I wanted to be with you, not him, and it was late; he didn't take it well. I was sleeping this morning. That's why I just got here. The truth is, I missed you. I wanted to see you. Is that wrong?"

"No, of course not. I'm sorry I upset you," Jacques said.

"I'm sorry I hit you, truly sorry."

Jacques shrugged, feeling stupid and a little nervous still.

"I haven't really been myself for a while now. I get so angry, and I take it out on you. I don't know what to do with my life." Mark sat back on his heels. "I have to go to college, I guess, probably in the States. I'm not sure where you fit in." He didn't seem to be posing any kind of question, so Jacques remained silent.

Mark took a deep breath. "Are you mad?"

"Non. Just listening."

"Why are you so good to me?"

Jacques figured it was a rhetorical question and didn't know how to answer if it weren't, so he just looked down.

"Anyway, would you want that?"

"What?" He had lost Mark's train of thought.

"To go to America with me, to study. We could live together. Share expenses."

Jacques wanted to jump at the suggestion, but he still felt pain from the blow to his face.

"Well?" Mark's voice cracked a little.

"Is that what you want?" Jacques asked. "For me to move with you?" He eyed Mark with suspicion. "Because I want to be in your life. I would do anything, except make you unhappy."

"I won't be, I'm not. I want you with me. If I didn't, I wouldn't have suggested it." He moved to get up, expressed discomfort in his knees, and sat on the bed. "We're having a gathering at the house this evening, to wish Kyle well. You're welcome to join us. Okay?"

"Yes, sure. Does my face look hurt?"

"You look great," Mark smiled at him. "Was that a letter from John I saw before?"

"Yes. You can read it while I dress, I don't think he minds." He reached over and grabbed the envelope, stood up and handed it to Mark, who kissed his hand again and pulled him to his lap.

"You mean a lot to me, no matter how I act sometimes. You believe me?" Mark asked him.

"Yes, I think so," Jacques kissed Mark's cheek but stood again to dress, not wanting to stay on the bed presently.

———

Mark slid the letter from its envelope, grateful for the distraction, and embarrassed he'd lost control earlier. He told himself everything was going to be all right now that they had settled matters, that things would calm down and fall into place. The resolution about moving to the States and going to school would help him feel purposeful, and they could start a fresh life together with neither one being plagued by their past. He studied the odd script of their mutual acquaintance and began to read:

Dearest Jacques,

Notwithstanding the length of time I let lapse since you last heard from me, do know that I think of you often and wish you well. I'm quite grateful for the numerous letters you've sent, and I'm glad to hear of your recent happiness with my friend Mark. As for me, I continue to be in search for the real—haunted by my past and my unfortunate illness. Lilith, in her most frustrating optimism, believes I can lead "a normal life" if I stick to the regimen set forth by my doctor. I haven't the heart to tell her misguided soul that I'd sooner be dead than lead "a normal life." Alas, I remain tormented, knowing that in an attempt to preserve consistency, genius is killed, and that ultimately, if I am to survive, I would be utterly mad. I also remain almost entirely unsure about everything, the only unequivocal statement I could make. So, I will continue along, waiting for the elusive moment to hold me in place and wondering still whatever I've done to keep peace at such arm's length.

It was signed, "In admiration, John." Mark went through the letter a second time, perplexed somewhat about the strange young man, the same one who had referred to him as his friend. Was he being sarcastic?

Jacques was watching him. "Oh, you're ready. Trying to figure out if he's crazy or brilliant." Mark shook his head.

"Both, I think," Jacques said.

TWENTY-SEVEN

Later that evening, after weathering Kyle's open displeasure at his entrance, Jacques willed himself invisible. It didn't come natural for him, but confrontation was worse. The young men were sitting around the living room floor and furniture, having the house to themselves for a while. Jacques was seated next to Robert on the couch, with Mark on the floor between their feet. Kyle was also on the floor but across the room facing them. Jacques wished it were not so, but it was too late to get up and move. He could see a couple of goats in the twilight outside through the window and decided to watch them to help the time pass. He willed his grumbling stomach to quiet. He hadn't eaten even the little he normally did during the past week.

When he looked back, Kyle was staring at the gold cross around his neck. He pretended not to notice. He always wore it and didn't think it ostentatious. It was, in fact, a simple cross.

"Are you Christian?" Kyle asked from across the room, interrupting the conversation the others were having about curricula at the University of Nairobi.

Jacques was alerted, but still unsure where this was headed. "Yes." His hand went instinctively to the cross where Kyle's eyes were glued. "Catholic."

"Catholic?" Kyle almost coughed the word.

"Yes," Jacques said, looking at Mark for a quick assessment, but Mark was turned away from him.

"Is that a religion or a political party?" A young Kenyan, Njoroge, asked; he was a friend of Mark's from school. Kyle shared a look with him and laughed. Jacques opted not to respond.

"You do know that the Catholic Church doesn't allow for homosexual relation-ships?" Kyle asked.

"Yes, I know." Jacques was glad he sounded calm despite Kyle's instigation.

"But, you're Catholic, anyway." Kyle looked around the room like an attorney might look at a jury, and finally to Mark. "Maybe you two make a better couple than I realized."

Mark was looking down.

"Ah, yes, but the good news is that all people are sinners according to the Catholic Church, right?" Robert said, the apparent diplomat in the group. Jacques liked him.

"How is that good news?" Joseph, a new pal from college was perhaps trying to help him out since the tension in the space was rising. Jacques remained quiet to let them manage it.

"Because you can be homosexual or basically do anything you want and you're not any worse off than the rest of the Catholics." Almost everyone laughed, lightening the mood a little. Mark still kept his eyes downcast and Jacques squirmed. He knew about these things, he had thought about them, just as the rest of them had. Why shouldn't he argue?

"I pray you are making a joke, but... Perhaps the church, its politics, and the faith, are different, you know," Jacques' said, his English increasingly tentative in response to his nerves, and he searched for the word, "distinct? Maybe the church doesn't always represent the people, and if more homosexual, and, how do you say, tolerant people, were practicing Catholics, the church would change."

"That's rubbish," Kyle stated.

"I think he's qualifying the theology as distinct from the church's politics *du jour*," James explained, although Jacques was pretty sure he had just said that. Mark had told Jacques that James was the son of a national hero during the struggle for inde-pendence, that he'd completed a degree in theological studies before he switched to economics. Jacques breathed out with reprieve because James had at least understood his point. For a moment, he thought it meant that Kyle would back off.

"It's sophistic logic," Kyle said instead. "If you were Jewish in Nazi Germany, I hardly think joining the party would have helped re-establish the party line." Some laughed at this analogy, a ludicrous one, but Jacques doubted the others saw it that way. He hoped Mark would throw him a rope but was handed a line instead.

"Don't take anything personally, Jacques. We're prone to banter in this crowd," Mark said, then he very obviously tried to change the subject by talking about news he'd heard earlier in the day.

But Kyle did not drop the offense. He seemed to feed off a charge from his former lover that Jacques could feel in his gut. "Mark, you wouldn't be trying to change the subject? I mean, don't you think it's interesting that your boyfriend's a Catholic?"

"Not really. Lots of people are," Mark quipped.

"Yeah, but they're not people you tend to associate with," Kyle said.

There was coughing and a lot of nervous movement. Although the more-than-platonic relationship between Mark and Kyle was never ignored, Jacques knew it was never formally discussed, either. Would Mark blame him if his entire social network decided to ostracize him after this encounter? Kyle, uniquely, had nothing left to lose. The other young men sitting around that evening seemed much more comfortable sticking to intellectual exchange, so despite the hammering beat of his heart, Jacques searched for a glib response to throw Kyle off his scent. It wasn't the first time he felt like human prey. He handled men much more powerful than Kyle would ever be, but it was really Mark's potential reaction that unnerved him.

Robert cleared his throat to speak while Mark and Kyle stared each other down. "I've always found it difficult to resolve my political view with any religion. Faith tends to subjugate people. Yet isn't it the right of those very same people to believe whatever they choose?"

Again, Robert's college mate chimed in, "Yes, and if you think they cannot decide for themselves, you're, by definition, guilty of elitism, maybe of meritocratic sentiment."

"Of course, one could ask what's wrong with meritocracy? Why should the world be subject to the whims of the undereducated masses?"

Did they always talk like this? Was Jacques now considered a drooling undereducated? He wanted to know if any of them believed in God but was too timid to ask. He didn't even know if Mark did. Of course, atheism was inherent to communist philosophy, but surely that was just in theory.

"If there were such a thing as the devil, what greater ally would he have than the world's religions?" Robert asked.

"Religions can be dangerous, I agree," Jacques said, "but only when they become fanatical." All eyes were on him now, most of them incredulous. "Perhaps a little like political ideologies." His heart raced again, and he was horrified that someone might actually engage his statement in debate. He could feel the blood run to his face, and his throat close up. He was shocked at his own insistence and could see Mark had finally turned to look at him with a confounded expression.

"And what ideology do you champion?" Kyle asked, riveted like a vulture.

Jacques had no idea how to respond. He had little political opinion, and besides, his desire to flee was now overtaking his capacity to think. Once, when he was thirteen, his father imposed upon him by whisking him to the stage in drag without much warning or any rehearsal. They had needed someone to fill in for an ill performer. Brunelle, the former hair stylist, make-up artist, and fascist scheduler all in one, had fit him into a gown of black taffeta that had a sweetheart collar. He'd wrapped Jacques in padding to make him look like a young woman and was coaching him at the same time.

"You've been here every day this week, watching Madame Juliette rehearse. I know you know the score, and with your voice, you'll really excite everyone. Besides, you're so pretty, everyone will be too busy trying to figure out what sex you are to catch if you miss the lyrics. Just relax and breathe," he kept reassuring Jacques. A few minutes afterward, on stage and in the spotlight, the panic seized him and he fainted. The longtime theater crew still chided him about the auspicious beginning to his career. His mind recalled the debacle now, wondering if he was about to pass out again.

"Hey, boys!" Papap and Humming returned; Papap clapped his hands in celebration. "Let's eat like kings! We picked up a banquet of dishes in town for all to share."

Mark and several others jumped at the idea, relieved to end this conversation. Robert practically dragged Kyle off the floor and into the kitchen.

Soon Jacques was the only one left in the room, almost sulking, until Bella ran in and jumped on the couch. "Hello, Jacques," she accentuated the French in his name. "Aren't you hungry?"

Later that night as Mark was driving him back to the Gasthaus, Jacques decided to broach the topic once more but had difficulty getting started and rambled somewhat.

"What are you talking about?" Mark asked, yawning.

"Does it bother you that I'm Catholic?" he finally managed to ask.

"Oh, that. Well," Mark shrugged. "I need a mental break, Jacques, if that's okay."

"Please tell me. It's important to me."

Mark sighed. "Of course it bothers me. I don't believe in God, as you know. I guess if there is a God, he must be, or she or it or whatever, must be the most impotent one around. I mean, look at the world, Jacques. It's a great mess with a lot of suffering. Don't you think?"

"Yes, but..."

"And then the church tells people to keep reproducing. It's crazy. I don't know how you can subscribe to it."

Jacques was pensive for a while, the darkness encompassing them on the way back. Finally, he spoke again as they pulled in. "I guess the difference is that I don't blame God for what men do, and I was born Catholic, so I stay that way. What's important to me is that there is something more to this existence. Do you understand?"

"I understand exactly. It's the fear of alienation that causes the human mind to conjure a God in the first place. Just leave me out of it, okay?" Mark said as he pulled his overnight bag out of the car. Jacques was relieved to see it again.

———

The next day Jacques accompanied Mark and Kyle to the Nairobi airport despite Kyle's objections. The ride over was spent mostly in silence, but Jacques was seated in front with Mark this time. He didn't press it by holding Mark's hand or showing any affection, though he wished Mark would initiate it.

At the airport, Kyle delayed leaving, staying close to Mark after he checked his luggage, looking like he wanted to say something, but Jacques didn't budge. An announcement overhead obscured Kyle's request.

"What?" Mark asked, shaking his head and cupping his ear with his hand.

"Could we have a minute alone?" Kyle asked, edgy.

"Oh, sure," Jacques answered for Mark and walked a few feet away now. He couldn't hear them, but he did watch as they simultaneously opened up and into a hug.

After they parted, Jacques sped up to reach Kyle before he boarded. Surprising himself by his own strength, he grabbed Kyle and turned him around.

"What do you want?" Kyle asked.

"I did not have the chance to answer your question last night."

Kyle looked confused.

"My political ideology..." Jacques reminded him. "I'm a monarchist."

Kyle gave him a quizzical look.

"That's right. I am a descendant of the French crown. I was just surprised last night that Mark hadn't told you," he lied. Kyle's face lit up with bewilderment, questions, and hostility all at once. Jacques waved his competition good-bye as Kyle allowed fellow travelers to sweep him along.

"What was that about?" Mark had reached Jacques and looked curious.

"I wanted to tell him, how do you say, no hard feelings," he said, feeling scandalously satisfied for the first time in months.

TWENTY-EIGHT

Jacques watched as Mark's decision to attend college in the United States manifested into explicit opportunity. Details clicked into place with the precision of a finely tuned watch. Mark employed a sense of urgency to their plans because of the growing age gap between him and most freshmen. By extension, Jacques was expected to keep up. Mark accepted a full scholarship at Tufts University, and the administration decided to matriculate him with full benefits in the spring. On the other hand, Jacques still had to be accepted as a full-time student and had to prepare for all manner of exams, a daunting task for someone who had never stepped foot in an actual classroom or taken a standardized test. Mark was patient with him, helping him with his applications and exam preparations. For once, Jacques celebrated the rigorous standards of his tutors because Mark seemed so impressed.

It was the middle of November by time they arrived in the Boston area, and they spent most of their time working and saving for Jacques' tuition. Although Jacques declared independence from his family, funds for foreign students were not readily forthcoming from most schools. His financial resources were depleted. When he tried to convince Mark to let him audition for the Boston Stage, Mark was intransigent in his refusal. His stoicism excluded such options, but he treated Jacques' expenses as if they were his own, even if it meant keeping very long hours. Jacques was willing to yield to Mark's formidable will to avoid what would otherwise become chronic conflict. They were a bona fide couple. Being a couple had greater payoffs than inconveniences. As a result, though, he sometimes felt like an appendage of Mark's.

He was doing well enough so far that spring semester to presume acceptance in the fall as a full time student. He was sure Mark was pleased with his performance.

There were moments, rare but powerful, when he would catch Mark looking at him, and in his eyes would be the acceptance Jacques so badly wanted. He even felt happy at times. Once he grew accustomed to the waning *joie de vivre* of everyday life, the fact that he had found a home with someone became enough. In any event, it wasn't the first time he had inured himself to survive. With classes wrapping up, he anticipated a lighter summer schedule and perhaps more fun.

Presently, Jacques returned from a meeting with his English professor. He was working on his final term paper but was looking forward to a change in routine. Hearing the shower running, he began to undress. Their studio apartment consisted of a room, twelve by fourteen square feet, and two separate alcoves, one that contained a couch and desk, and the other a kitchen counter, stove, and miniature refrigerator. The center of everything was the full-sized bed. There was a small black and white television on the kitchen counter, and the windows were trimmed with yellowing blinds.

Jacques threw his clothes on the once again unmade bed. Before he left France, and his parents' estate, he never thought of such things as bed making. There was always someone there to take care of chores like that. But now the space looked cluttered and messy whenever the bed was undone, and it was certainly out of the ordinary when this was not the case.

He walked into the bathroom to join Mark in the shower stall, excited to make love for the first time in a few days. He felt closer to Mark when they had sex because he usually had his full attention then.

"Hey." Mark smiled, but then said, "I'm kind of in a hurry," jerking away slightly from Jacques' embrace.

"Where are you going?"

"To the lab. I have to finish setting some slides." Mark finished rinsing his now shoulder-length hair.

Jacques questioned why the molecular biology lab took precedence over him, again, but only in his mind.

"I'll be back early tonight." Mark stepped out of the shower and dried himself.

"It won't matter. I'll be at the restaurant. Remember?" Jacques had switched shifts with another waiter. He now let the water run down his face, then turned the faucet off before bothering to wash.

Mark threw him a towel, looked at him. "Oh, shit. I forgot about our afternoon together, didn't I?"

Jacques avoided eye contact and wrapped the towel around his waist.

"I'll make it up to you, okay?" Mark said as he walked out of the bathroom, not bothering to wait for an answer.

Jacques knew better than to make an issue out of Mark's thoughtlessness. What peeved him more than usual was that it had been Mark's proposal to spend the afternoon together after Jacques had boldly remarked on how little "quality time" they'd been sharing recently. He'd heard the buzz term on a television talk show.

He belabored the fiction that he could have made alternate plans, but in reality, Jacques had few social contacts. Most of the time, Mark so disapproved of his choice in friends that Jacques had acquiesced months ago and stayed to himself. He thought momentarily of Tony, a fun and flamboyantly gay Boston University graduate student he'd befriended when he and Mark first got to town. Tony had helped him get the job at a popular sports bar after they'd met at a club downtown. It had been one of only two times Mark had permitted such an outing.

At first, Tony used to call Mark "Jacques' hottie he-man," and embarrass Mark. He'd frequently taunt Mark with quips like, "Do tell us what it's like to be a real man," with exaggerated inflection whenever he thought Jacques was being bullied. After a while, Tony explained that Mark's desire to live in a social vacuum was typical in relationships of lopsided power, and the sting of Tony's words often enraged Mark. As a result, he had struck Jacques a few times afterward. When Tony noticed a bruised cheekbone after a particularly severe blow to Jacques' face, he called Mark abusive and started to pressure Jacques to end the relationship. Jacques had no taste for such 'American concepts' and was convinced he'd tacitly, if not outright, agreed to a life defined by Mark's rules from the start. It was too late now. He had no one else to lean on. The arrangement was somewhat familiar, and Jacques had all but abandoned the fantasy that he could chisel through the ice around Mark's heart if only he were patient enough. As for Tony, however, the strain pulled them apart. Jacques convinced himself it was a small price to pay to keep the peace.

The phone rang as Mark was walking out. He called out, "I'm not here," and closed the door behind him.

"Hello?"

It was Jacques' father. He had only spoken to his parents once since he'd left France, a conversation that didn't resolve any of the hurt feelings he'd been carrying. He'd refused to return to Paris. His father reminded him he'd be cut off from his inheritance. Jacques had asked for the money that was due him, but his father hung up the phone angrily, and Jacques never saw any of it.

His father sounded softer this time, more pliable, asked how he was.

"Fine," Jacques said. His curtness was not from feeling abandoned the last year but for the previous years of neglect and exploitation, the latter being Mark's description.

His father got to the point. A business colleague of his was visiting Boston, had been a big fan of Jacqui's, enamored even. Couldn't Jacques have dinner with him tomorrow evening? No performing, just dinner.

"I don't dress in drag any more," he said in French. He thought about the ease with which he could speak his native tongue; he missed it.

"Just this once," his father said. In exchange, he'd set up a bank account for Jacques in Boston. He could probably use some cash, a lot of cash. Just one dinner out, he promised.

Jacques quickly analyzed the request. His father probably found it untenable that his son was living as a poor man, or was he still giving him too much credit? Jacques also recognized the need for a separate bank account and resources of his own, although the reason he might need these things was held in a sequestered part of his mind. His palms began to sweat when he agreed to meet the man. He knew he could never mention this to Mark, nor use the money, but it provided a new security, one that he hadn't realized until this moment he wanted so badly.

His father gave him the name of the gentleman colleague and the broker who'd set up a financial portfolio for him.

Jacques had the presence of mind to ask for reassurance that he'd never be asked to comply with any other request in order to keep the funds.

"The money will be only under your name. But, a visit home sometime would be more than welcome," his father said.

Jacques hung up feeling proud for managing to alter the dynamic between him and his father. It was the first time he had ever negotiated any terms on his own behalf. But, he was afraid of Mark and the potential outcome of his choice. He buried this apprehension under the pressure to be ready for tomorrow evening; he would deal with other consequences as they arose. For now, he needed to obtain a costume, make-up, get his hair done (he wouldn't require a wig, as Mark had never made him cut his hair), and a facial. He kept thinking of all of the things he needed to do just to keep the gnawing fear at bay.

He went first to see the broker who had everything ready for Jacques to sign for the moneys to be transferred from an account in France. The accountant-broker, Harold Makin, was about 5'3" and almost entirely bald, dressed in a brown tweed suit. He seemed idiosyncratic but competent. Jacques felt giddy when Makin recommended putting half the funds, a mind-boggling sum, in a Swiss account and in foreign investments. There were enormous taxes to avoid. Jacques agreed to whatever Mr. Makin suggested, making a mental note to ask Mark if he could study economics in the fall. Any correspondence regarding his accounts would go to Makin's office, where Jacques would pick it up. Jacques was timid in explaining why the information could not arrive at his place of residence but was taking every precaution.

He couldn't resist feeling a little excited and reminiscent as he went shopping. He had more cash on him than they had had in their savings the past few months. He found a black, long-sleeved, almost satiny-smooth gown that fit him beautifully. He had to cover unshaven body parts because American women were obsessed with hair removal. The facial was a necessity, as he had neglected his skin over the last year and wouldn't have make-up artists and others fussing over him. Plus, his facial hair had become coarser as he'd matured. He'd have to shave as late as possible tomorrow afternoon.

The following day, Jacques skipped classes to have his hair and nails done, the latter shaped, cleaned up, but with no glossiness or anything obvious. His hair was blown dry; it looked full and straight. The color was touched up, made even lighter than his natural blond. He didn't really need to go to such lengths, but it had been so long since he had had the financial wherewithal to do so that he enjoyed it.

He had everything impeccably planned. Mark would be home between 3 and 5 PM and then would leave again. By the time Mark would return, Jacques would normally have left for work. He'd frantically pleaded with someone to switch shifts with him again and was due to pull a double twice in the remainder of the week, which meant he would need to skip more classes. Mark would be asleep as usual when he returned home. Jacques timed it all as precisely as possible. To be sure, he'd change in the cab or outside the apartment door before coming in. He needed an inconspicuous bag that looked dressy enough with a gown. He ran out to purchase one and made it back five minutes before Mark.

"Hi," Jacques felt nervous and exhilarated at once.

"Hey." Mark eyed him.

"What's that?" Jacques asked, pointing to a tote bag Mark had around his shoulder. He wanted the attention off himself but was not used to deceiving Mark.

"A bag." Mark smirked, putting it on the floor. "You look different."

"My hair. I needed a cut."

"Oh...did you go someplace expensive?"

"No." He knew Mark's question masked a compliment, in a way, and he felt wrong for lying.

"So, what are you doing the next couple of hours? I feel bad about yesterday, thought we could go out to eat, or something."

Mark put his arms around Jacques' waist, but Jacques tightened, worried they would get off schedule. Then again, Mark never went off schedule, not for him, anyway. Mark was wearing a black t-shirt, fitted so that it showed off his enlarged biceps, the result of spending a lot of time at the campus gym. He started kissing Jacques' neck.

"Are you hungry enough to eat now?" Mark asked, "Or, you want to fool around?" He lifted Jacques off the floor and laid him on the bed, more or less deciding for him.

"Let's stay here," Jacques said anyway. He wanted to be agreeable, and he wanted to watch the time.

Mark lay on top of him, kissed him with more passion than he had in a while, but Jacques was too lost in thought to enjoy it.

"Oh," Jacques stirred.

"What?" Mark lifted himself away from him. "Did I hurt you?"

"No, non. Nothing, just I forgot to take care of something, at school. It's okay," he said, pulling Mark back on top of him. Stockings. He'd forgotten to pick them up and needed them dark in color, to cover his legs and to slip into the shoes. He started strategizing while Mark stood to remove his clothes.

"Jacques?"

"Yes?"

"Wanna join me?" Mark laughed. "What are you thinking about so intensely?" He lay next to him.

"I'm sorry, it's nothing." He unbuttoned his own shirt and pulled Mark on top of him again, kissing him. He made his way to Mark's lower body, and, taking him into his mouth, blew him expertly to orgasm.

It was 3:55pm.

Mark seized him, pulling him up toward the headboard and started unzipping Jacques' pants when Jacques summarily grabbed his hand.

"No, I'm content, I mean, I'm satisfied," he almost stuttered as Mark gave him a quizzical look.

"What's the matter with you?"

"Nothing," Jacques said, trying to avoid direct eye contact. The sinuous sound of his "th" survived the fluency of his English.

"So, what if I'm not satisfied?" Mark asked him.

Jacques felt himself blush. "Oh. It's just that I think I better run back to school. I promised to return a book to a classmate today, and I forgot." Mark kept his eyes on him. "She'll be upset."

"Is there an exam tomorrow?"

"No, but she likes to be ahead of the class." He could see the disbelief in Mark's eyes.

"I thought you wanted 'quality time' together?"

"I did. I do!" he corrected, getting out of bed. "It's just—"

"You have to return a book," Mark interrupted him.

It was a ridiculous cover. If only he were more used to lying. He thought of asking Mark if he wanted to come along because he was almost sure he'd decline. Almost. He repeated how sorry he was and rushed out, barely remembering to grab a book.

TWENTY-NINE

Mark lay in bed where Jacques had just left him. He was having a hard time believing what had just happened and felt a twinge of anxiety. What if Jacques were having an affair? He had himself fantasized a few times over a young, Indian student who worked at the lab. Sanjay had beautiful, golden brown skin and delicate hands and often wore white shirts with his sleeves rolled up, the top button undone just enough to reveal a streamlined, hairless chest and a beautiful collarbone. They had spoken a number of times, always about politics or philosophy or molecular biology, never of anything personal. Mark thought for a moment there was a flirtation in his smile today when he caught Sanjay's eyes, but he wouldn't act on it. He was, above all ambivalence, devoted to Jacques, and even if he had a predilection toward infidelity in the past, it would've been curtailed by the AIDS epidemic by now. He just hoped that they hadn't already been exposed to whatever bug was causing the disease and that it wasn't dormant inside them.

But, perhaps Jacques was more reckless, or perhaps his feelings for Mark had changed. Mark leaned his head back and bumped it on the headboard. He hadn't been violent with Jacques, had not hit, pushed, or hurt him in any way for nearly two months. Although it had never been too much of a stretch for him to fault Jacques whenever he lost control, he still regretted the behavior. Recently, he couldn't bring himself to apologize following a transgression because saying he was sorry had grown too ephemeral, and he was ashamed of himself. He would never hit his partner if he were heterosexual. He wasn't sure what the difference was.

As soon as they had arrived in the States, he had determined never to be "gay" instead of homosexual. He recalled the club scene with dismay, and for a moment wondered if Jacques were frequenting such places without him. He always reeked of cigarette smoke after work, and maybe he was really going to bars with friends Mark wouldn't tolerate. When he considered it truly, he doubted it. After the last and final time they went together, Jacques had seemed almost pleased that Mark had forbidden them to return. Not having fully recovered from the assault in Paris, Jacques appeared overly frightened after he was accosted in the men's room of a club downtown. When Mark walked in to see why he was taking so long, he'd seen that two men had Jacques cornered and wouldn't let him pass. How aggressive they would have been in a public restroom was questionable (they had been insisting Jacques speak to them in French), but Jacques' eyes revealed almost wild fear when they lighted on Mark. He was oddly overjoyed to come to Jacques' rescue that night.

Mark felt comfortable in this city. His intellectual strength was anonymous here. *He* was anonymous here. But, he'd come to associate being "gay" with being promiscuous, materialistic, and perhaps even vapid. He wanted nothing to do with it, which mattered little since he was accustomed to having no familiarity of sexual culture around him. His intimate life existed in an enclosed bubble. It was separate from his academic pursuits and his goals. It was such an integral part of him that he didn't feel the need to be supported by others of similar preference. Intimacy was private, a world of its own with whomever one shared it. He didn't desire nor need to parade it. He didn't need acceptance by others. But, he did need Jacques. This had become increasingly apparent over the course of their relationship. He needed Jacques' loyalty, his love, even his adoration to some degree. And this bothered him.

Mark got out of bed now and dressed. Where had Jacques really gone? Could the absurd story be true? He still thought of his French lover as a bit of an enigma. Although he had no respect for Jacques' past or his upbringing, he believed him to be open and faithful, dumbfounded really at the level of steadfastness he'd shown Mark ever since they met. He convinced himself the story must be true, however incredible. The only viable alternative was that he was sulking about yesterday, but he'd never known Jacques to be vindictive. Finally, he settled on laughing at himself, at the uncustomary insecurity he felt. Jacques had never before chosen anything or anyone over Mark, and his ego had just been bruised. The day had simply flowed against the usual tide, nothing more.

THIRTY

Jacques waited outside the apartment building until he saw Mark leave. He was grateful and relieved he would never do this again; he could hardly brook deceiving Mark.
He watched his boyfriend disappear down the block and speedily ran upstairs to get
dressed. It had been so long since he was Jacqui that it felt foreign to play the role
now. He'd purchased two pairs of stockings in case he ripped one off the bat. He got
as close a shave as possible without nicking himself, applied the new make-up flaw-
lessly, and considered curling his hair. He decided to keep it straight since it had come
out so well at the shop. Jacques never thought of himself as transsexual even when
he was a locally famous Parisian drag queen. But, looking at himself in the mirror
now, after so much time had passed since it was Jacqui whose reflection looked back,
he was delighted–and beautiful. His chest was flat perhaps, but then that had always
added to the mystery. The other entertainers wore body suits and padding that made
them caricature-like.

The shoes were tricky at first because he was out of practice, but he adjusted
quickly. He called a cab, checked that he'd left nothing out for Mark to find, and left.
It was a little after six o'clock.

When he walked into the restaurant at 7:15, fifteen minutes late due to traffic,
he sensed the slight commotion he stirred. Men at the bar turned in unison at the tall,
thin, blond beauty. The dress created the illusion of a female figure. He let himself
enjoy the attention, realizing how long it had been since he had really felt seen.

"Jacqui!" A tall, graying man walked up. "What a pleasure." He kissed Jacqui's
extended hand, and hooked his arm under his own suited one. He was Canadian
French.

"Monsieur Claremont."

"I've been a fan of yours ever since I saw your show in Paris. You look just as lovely as I remembered. I was so disappointed when I'd heard you left France." Jacques noticed small sweat beads on the man's brow. "Would you like a drink before we dine?"

Jacques ordered a martini and took in the environment of the fine restaurant. He hadn't been in such a setting since he left Paris for Africa nearly a year ago. He was over the moon to be waited on, fawned over again. The lighting was dim, the tables clothed, and the china expensive.

Claremont was an 'enjoyable.' Jacques had kept categories for the men with whom his father did business. They ranged from 'most terrible' to 'enjoyable,' although he had almost forgotten about the latter category due to its lack of use.

Claremont spoke of his business mostly, his work-related travel. Whenever he asked Jacqui a question about himself, Jacques paused and fabricated an answer. After all, Jacqui hadn't existed in the last year, so he couldn't answer how she'd been doing or what she was up to, and he refused to confuse the role with his true life. His true life of drudgery. At one point, he actually wondered if Monsieur Claremont knew he wasn't really a woman, and he remembered how deeply people deluded themselves.

He watched the time during dinner. Since he'd usually return from work by 11pm, he'd have to be in the cab by 10:15pm. His heart accelerated when he thought of having to pull the rest of the evening off seamlessly. Monsieur Claremont would have loved for him to stay longer and asked if he could have the pleasure of Jacqui's company again, indicated he was in Boston fairly regularly on business. Jacques said, and meant, that he had thoroughly enjoyed himself but was unable to accept because of his involvement with someone. His dinner companion was a gentleman to the end, kissing Jacqui on the cheek as she stepped into the cab, and paying the driver a sizable amount for the fare despite Jacques' protest.

He had the cab drop him off on the corner instead of in front of the apartment building. He couldn't imagine what the driver must have thought of him as he pulled the stockings off and crammed his jeans and t-shirt on in the back seat. He must have believed Jacques female since he kept trying to catch a glimpse. As he walked closer, he saw the light was off in their studio and assumed Mark was sleeping as usual. He stopped in the corridor to remove his shoes. He made sure everything was neatly shoved into his bag and entered barefoot. The pleasantness of his time with

Claremont and the security of the transferred funds gave him a sense of invincibility tonight, like nothing could go wrong with his plan. Still, it was not the time to take unnecessary risks.

The door lock always made a clicking noise, but Jacques tried to open it as gingerly as possible. It seemed very dark, and his heart skipped only a beat when the bathroom light wasn't on for him. Something out of the ordinary, but probably nothing. He was making his way to the bathroom on tiptoe when a light switched on. It wasn't the one by the bed as if Mark had accidentally awakened, but one from behind him. When he saw the bed was empty, his blood started to pound in his head.

"Where were you?" Mark asked. Jacques noticed a few empty beer bottles on the counter. "And don't say at work because someone called here asking why you weren't there tonight."

Jacques started toward the bathroom again, afraid to turn around and reveal his face, but Mark was too quick. There was sudden pain as Mark gripped his upper arm, pivoting him. Jacques gasped as Mark's countenance contorted from anger to confusion and then to rage.

"What the hell is this?"

"Please let me explain," said Jacques. Mark let go with a push, landing Jacques against the wall.

"What the hell is going on?"

"I went to meet a friend of my father's."

"You what? How could you?" Mark looked maddened.

"No, it wasn't..." But Jacques had no time to explain because Mark slapped him, grabbed him by the throat and elevated him. He then soccer-punched him hard with his other fist, and Jacques lost his breath, so he couldn't respond when Mark demanded he tell him why he betrayed him. All he could feel was the intense need for air. Was it just a minute ago that he took his breath for granted?

Reprieve lasted only a moment when he hit the floor because Mark kicked him in the gut and dragged him across the room by his hair.

"Wash it off!" he demanded, ostensibly about the make-up. Jacques was dropped by the bathroom sink but was feeling too bad to lift himself off the floor, even when he clung to both sides of the blue towel hanging from the rack, the same towel he had used earlier to wipe his face after shaving. Things had not gone as he'd hoped since then.

Mark kicked him in the gut again, harder, and yelled. Somehow it seemed to make him angrier that Jacques was vulnerable. Somehow Jacques could never be anything but.

"Get up!" Mark grabbed him by his right arm, lifted him, and threw him so roughly into the shower stall, that Jacques' left arm sent shockwaves of pain to his head from the impact.

Had something broken? At least he could inhale again now. Mark turned the water on and again told him to wash it off. Jacques started to scrub his face with his right hand. He was seated, having slid down the wet tile from the pain in his arm. But the make-up was water-resistant. Semi-delirious by now, he managed to say, "I need make-up remover."

He got kicked in the ribs instead, and this time nearly screamed from the agony. Mark's shoe came full speed into his ribcage again. Jacques was crying in pain. He heard questions, remotely. Mark was ranting, wanting to know how long ago Jacques had returned to prostitution. Had he not feared contracting a virus? Why would he risk death?

Jacques started to fade in and out, and Mark disappeared somehow. At one point, he choked on blood, woke himself up coughing, which also seemed to awaken his lover from the raging trance he'd been in. The water had been turned off. Jacques felt damp and cold from lying in wet clothes, or maybe from bleeding. He recoiled when Mark walked into the bathroom, and Mark cringed in response.

"Are you okay?" he asked him.

Jacques muttered something inaudible. There was blood on his shirt from when he spit up. Mark looked afraid suddenly.

"How much pain are you in?"

Jacques started to grow faint again, although he was trying to cooperate. He recognized that Mark had returned to his senses, but it was too late to comply with his orders.

THIRTY-ONE

"Jacques, try to stay awake," Mark said. Mark noticed severe bruising on his lover's left arm and remembered kicking Jacques directly in the ribs, although he couldn't have meant to do that, could he have? If he called an ambulance, he'd have to explain what happened to the police. He called a cab instead.

"I'm taking you to the hospital," he said as calmly as he could. Jacques seemed to understand; his eyes were open at least. "I need to lift you, okay?" Before he did, though, another wave of panic rushed in. What if Jacques' spine had been hurt? He tried to remember how hard he'd thrown him against the wall and into the shower.

"Try to move your legs for me."

Jacques complied now.

"Okay, good." He was still taking a chance but positioned himself to raise Jacques, one arm under his legs and the other around the back. He forgot to be careful with Jacques' left arm, and Jacques winced with the slightest movement. He carried him directly downstairs.

"Where to?" the driver asked when the cab arrived.

"Get us to the hospital," Mark said, trying to figure out how to maneuver Jacques into the cab without causing further damage.

"Hey!" the cabby said. "Maybe you need an ambulance."

"No time." Mark crawled in holding Jacques against him. "Hurry."

"Yeah, no kidding," the driver said.

Jacques was losing consciousness despite Mark's attempt to keep him awake.

"Shit," Mark shouted. "Watch the jerky turns, will you?"

"You want me to hurry or not?"

Mark saw Jacques' eyes. He looked terrified, or in severe pain, or both.

"It's okay, baby. You'll be okay," he whispered to him. He instinctively held Jacques' head to his chest to soothe him with his heartbeat, although his own was racing.

When they pulled up to the emergency room, Mark told the driver to wait while he rushed Jacques in. They made a spectacle, and he hated it. An intake nurse was already coming around the desk, asking for a gurney. She must have heard the cab screeching to a halt outside.

In the midst of instructions to others, she asked, "What happened?"

"He was beaten."

The nurse gave Mark a disapproving look that Mark had no time to argue. She suspected a domestic dispute swifter than he would have predicted. He left quickly to pay the cab fare after she handed him insurance paperwork to complete.

When he returned, the nurse asked him for identification.

"Mine or his?" Mark asked.

"Both."

"We're students at Tufts. We have their insurance."

Mark caught a glimpse of a police officer walking toward him, and he felt the blood rush from his head. He finished the documents shakily as Jacques was wheeled off for diagnostic images. He saw the cop and the nurse talking, both were shaking their heads. For the first time since he left home, he pined for his parents and for the safety of home.

"Mark, is it?" Officer Marshall held a pad and pen. The cop's accent revealed a South Boston upbringing and his middle-aged gut a tendency to overindulge.

"Yes."

"How'd this happen?"

"I'm not sure." At least that part was true. He had no idea how he could have let this happen. "He gets off work late. I guess someone attacked him."

"Where do you suspect this might have happened?"

"Outside the apartment building. He wouldn't have gotten very far."

"I see you live together," the officer said as he shuffled through some paperwork the nurse had just brought over.

"Ah...yeah."

"May I inquire as to the nature of your relationship?"

"Why?"

"Listen, young man, I need to know what happened." Officer Marshall pinched the bridge of his nose like he had a headache.

Mark looked away, feeling perilously nervous.

"Did you do this?"

"No," said Mark, but he didn't look the cop in the eyes.

"Are you homosexuals?"

Should he answer the question honestly or should he lie? He didn't know which direction to take, and he was starting to feel riled as well as scared. He also didn't know if he should say he wanted to speak with an attorney. Would that imply guilt? Was he being charged with something?

"Well?"

"What difference does it make?"

By the look on his face, the officer hadn't expected the overt defiance. "I'll take that as a refusal to answer the question."

Mark looked at the cop but said nothing.

"Are you sure you're not responsible for this?"

"Yes, I'm sure."

"Well, I'll be asking him soon enough. Have you had any recent threats?"

"What do you mean?" Mark asked him, confused.

"There have been a few incidents of 'gay bashing' these days. With the AIDS problem and all."

"Oh, right." Mark became pensive thinking of stuff he'd seen on the news. "Yeah, I think it may have been that." His forehead furrowed. "Ironically," he said.

"What's that?" the cop asked.

"Um…nothing." He shook his head and wondered if he could he be so fucked up that he would gay bash his own boyfriend.

"One more thing. How come you didn't call an ambulance? Most people would have called an ambulance."

"I don't know. I didn't know if it would cost money, I guess."

"Okay, I'm going to have to insist that you wait here, or I could just arrest you if you prefer."

"Are you asking my preference?" Mark couldn't help sounding disdainful even though he should be respectful. "I won't leave him."

"Fine." The cop eyed him in an unsettling manner before moving on.

Mark thought about what had just transpired. He would need to face his own prejudices, his fears, unadulterated. Would he leave Jacques now? What would happen? A knot the size of a country was taking hold of his stomach. God damn it, he was heartbroken on top of everything else. He didn't want to lose Jacques. He had believed the Frenchman was all his, and that had been a deception. He didn't know what was real and what wasn't.

A resident doctor approached him next and sat with him. Similar questions ensued regarding who he was in relation to the patient. He asked about Jacques' family, and Mark told him they were estranged with no way of contacting them overseas.

The doctor said, "We need some history on him. Any serious medical illnesses or allergies you know of?"

"No, I...he never mentioned anything."

"How long have you known him?"

"About a year, I guess." Mark wasn't capable of the simple calculation at the moment.

"He's badly hurt."

Mark gave the doctor an exasperated look that begged him to go on.

"He probably has internal bleeding, could be from a ruptured spleen or a lacerated liver. The x-rays will show any broken ribs. Looks like a pneumothorax, and a fractured left elbow, as well. Must have been thrown around pretty hard." He looked at Mark in a critical way, and Mark gave him as empty a look as he could rally. "Of course we won't know the extent of anything until we get more pictures. Could we get you to sign some consent forms since he's been in and out? I want to do a CT scan and we're drawing blood now. I'll get a urinalysis as well to rule out any kidney contusions."

"Whatever you think is necessary. What's a pneumothorax?" Mark asked the doctor.

"A punctured lung, which could collapse. Depending on the severity, we may need to do a thoracotomy. Place a tube in. It's called a t-tube."

Mark hadn't really breathed during the report. He gasped for air now as he kept his eyes riveted on the doctor's. "He did cough up some blood, if that helps you figure it out."

"Yeah, he still is. Just a bit. That's why all the tests. The CT will help, but probably it's a hemo-pneumothorax."

"Meaning?"

"Blood may be pooling where the lung is punctured."

Mark looked down, aghast again. "But, is he going to be okay?"

"Well, he's otherwise young and healthy, so he should recover. We need more information."

The resident stood to walk away.

"Wait," Mark asked him. "What about the other organs? If it's the liver or his spleen, what will you do?"

"Take the spleen out. The liver, well, probably nothing but watch it till it heals. But, let's take it one step at a time."

Marshall caught the resident on the way to the restricted area, and they seemed to argue momentarily. The cop followed the doctor into the back area, and Mark's heart began to pound.

———

"Jacques?" The officer said, although he pronounced the name more like Jack. "Can you hear me?"

Jacques sort of nodded. He was hooked up to an IV and wore an oxygen mask. He was waiting to be told what was going to happen to him.

"You've got less than two minutes," the doctor reminded the cop.

"Yeah," he waved the resident off. "Can you tell me who did this to you?"

Jacques held back tears.

"I suspect it was the young man who brought you in."

Jacques mouthed No. It was as adamant as he could be.

"Are you sure? Are you afraid to tell me the truth?"

Jacques started to cough.

"That's it," the resident warned.

"One more thing," the cop pushed. "Your friend said you were attacked at your work site; is that right?"

Jacques nodded.

"Could you recognize who attacked you in a line up?"

Jacques thought about his answer, removed the mask with his good arm and whispered, "Too dark."

The cop shook his head, and he and the doctor exchanged a look. "I'll talk with you again. It's important you tell me everything you remember."

———

When the cop stepped out from behind the barrier, his eyes met Mark's. Perhaps the officer kept his own statistics on domestic violence, maybe prompted by his own family history. Perhaps he took personal offense when he investigated domestic crimes. Mark would never know for sure by the look he gave him, but he certainly seemed invested in his work.

"I hope it was worth it," Officer Marshall was ambiguous, perhaps on purpose.

Mark felt his eyes water over and suppressed his feelings.

"You'll probably get away with this. Seems he's as stuck on protecting you as you are. But, I'm filing a report with certain discrepancies. If it happens again, I'll come after you."

Was that an empty threat? Or, would he somehow be tracked after this? He told himself to stop being paranoid. They could prove nothing so long as Jacques had lied for him. And, he had. Not surprisingly, either.

Mark sat alone in the waiting room for hours; he was afraid of himself again. He had almost killed Jacques. He had completely lost control. He still wanted to call his parents, but what would he tell them? The sting of disappointment was intense—in himself mostly, but also in Jacques for the infidelity that he was sure had occurred. What he wished for most was redemption, and his parents could never give him that now. He was too embarrassed to tell them what happened even if they could.

THIRTY-TWO

Jacques stared out the window of the recovery room; he had a view of the Boston weather and nothing else. The food tray was empty but for a cup of ice, and it was early morning now. The hospital staff didn't allow him to see Mark, although they had told him Mark was still in the hospital, waiting. That must be a good sign; Mark must be willing to listen to him explain.

His ribcage was wrapped to decrease motion and help the ribs to heal. He had earlier been in enough respiratory distress for the doctors to place a tube in him, very temporarily, just long enough for his lung to stay inflated on its own. His liver and spleen had both been uninjured. He saw Mark outside the room, speaking with his nurse. She nodded, and he walked toward Jacques now.

Mark set half a dozen yellow roses on the bedside table as soon as he was inside. He looked exhausted and his eyes were downcast.

"Flowers," Jacques said, pleased.

"Yeah, yellow roses are supposed to mean 'I'm sorry.' Or so the gift shop lady says."

"I'm sorry, too. I should have told you—"

"We don't need to talk about that right now," Mark interrupted him.

"Please let me finish," Jacques said, and he moved the annoying oxygen cannula over his head like a headband.

Mark pulled up a seat, looked unsure of himself and tense.

"I only had dinner with the man, and it was only this one time."

Mark seemed to roll his eyes and said nothing.

"I swear it, Mark. I hope you wouldn't believe that of me."

"I just assumed–"

"I know what you thought, but..." he felt short of breath and must have appeared in distress.

Mark reached over to replace the cannula, "Leave this in," he said.

Jacques explained the phone call, told Mark about half the money, the amount he held in accounts in the US. He wasn't sure what prompted him to keep the other half a secret after the damage the last lie had done.

"Were you planning on leaving me? Is that why you wanted the money?" Mark asked.

Jacques was so astounded at this suspicion, he didn't answer immediately. "Of course not," he said finally. He felt his breath labored again. His heart was pounding. "Why would you think that?"

"I don't know." Mark was holding the fingers of Jacques' left hand, what stuck out from the cast. He started to cry and hid his face in the crook of his arm.

Jacques wasn't sure how to handle this uncustomary behavior. He grabbed a tissue with his right hand and gave it to Mark.

"What do you want to do now?" Mark asked, swallowing some of the tears.

"What do you mean?"

"Do you want to break up?" Mark asked.

Where there were perhaps numerous solutions, Jacques mused at how Mark could think of only one. "Non," he said, a little puzzled. "Of course not. I love you, Mark." He had to hold back tears himself. He removed the cannula again and closed his eyes for a half minute. When he reopened them, Mark was looking into them with intensity.

"But, this was really bad. I don't think you understand the gravity of our situation. I could have killed you. This can't happen again," Mark said with such vehemence that Jacques wondered if he were expected to contain Mark's violence for him. If he knew how, he would have done so already.

"Please don't talk about breaking up. I don't have the strength to go on without you," Jacques pleaded. How could he ever explain that nothing had ever meant so much, not even air? This assertion was confirmed by recent events.

"Okay," Mark quieted him and leaned over to kiss Jacques on his forehead and cheek. He replaced the cannula into Jacques' nostrils again and laid his face on

Jacques' cheek. He jumped when someone knocked and walked in, wiped his face dry before turning around. Mark's awkwardness over crying was so palpable that Jacques could feel it.

"Hi, are you Jacques?" A petite woman stood in front of the bed holding a clipboard. He nodded. "I'm Nancy, the unit social worker. The ER doctor asked for a consultation." She had medium length brown hair and a comforting smile.

Mark introduced himself, reached over and shook her hand.

"I'm okay financially. I have student insurance," Jacques said.

"Oh, good. But, that's not why I'm here."

Jacques felt nervous suddenly. Mark fidgeted and pulled the chair around for her to sit.

"How do you pronounce your name?"

Jacques told her the way English speakers said it, but she said she wanted to know how he would say it in Paris.

"Oh, well, *Zacke*," he said. Mark gave him a quizzical look like he didn't know.

"How are you feeling, *Zacke?*" Nancy asked him.

"Better, thank you."

"Do you want to talk about what happened? Maybe privately?" She glanced at Mark.

"Oh, I'll excuse myself," he said right away.

"No, please stay. He can stay," Jacques said. "I don't want to talk about it again. I gave the police a full report just a little time ago. Do I have to?" He wondered if this was part of a mandatory investigation even though he already told the cops that he didn't remember much. He needed to keep replacing and displacing the cannula because it bothered him.

"No, you don't. We're concerned that you were a victim of so-called gay bashing or of domestic violence. Either way, it may help to talk about it. What we talk about is confidential; I don't report to the police. But, I may be able to help."

"How?" Mark asked, surprising Jacques again.

"Well, if, in fact, you have a problem controlling your anger, I can refer you to groups that deal with anger management. Some batterers are remorseful and even ashamed of their behavior—"

"Wait. Mark isn't like that. I'm sorry, the hospital staff misunderstood." Jacques did not want people to see them like that.

The social worker didn't respond but looked at Mark instead. "Still, if either of you is interested in change, here's my card." She held it out to Mark who hesitated but took it.

———

After Jacques was moved to a regular room the next day, his attending physician was less gentle than the social worker had been.

He called Mark into his office and introduced himself as Dr. Fishburne. "Sit down, please."

Mark did. The brown, wooden chair felt like a remnant of the last century.

"Did you beat your friend?"

Mark didn't reply. He looked away, instead, and noticed the picture of the doctor's family on the desk. He wondered why it was nearly facing him, instead of the other way around.

"Look, I don't know how you can live with yourself after something like that," the doctor said.

Mark glared at him aggressively as he had almost done the police officer, but inside he recognized a great disgust; it wasn't a glib, intellectual distaste for what he did, but the physical presence of something akin to vomit. The doctor told him about anger management classes, he droned on about services available, but Mark could hardly hear him. He was focused on the bile in his stomach.

Afterward, he went to the men's room and wept again. He didn't know how, but the situation had to change. He made his way back to Jacques and turned the television off. He cradled Jacques' head in both his hands very gently. He vowed to never lay a violent hand on him again. He swore on everything sacred. This would never happen again, no matter what.

THIRTY-THREE

Jacques spent most of the next two months at doctors' offices and in rehabilitation. He qualified for "incompletes" at school and finally got the "quality time" with Mark he'd coveted. Mark had been more solicitous than ever, and he had kept his word about not becoming violent. But, behind the courteous exchanges and the apologetic underpinnings, Jacques deliberated over his situation. He watched Mark for any sign of tension or irritation and then modified his own behavior to avoid upsetting him. He wanted to enjoy this version of Mark, but he wasn't sure if he could trust it.

Presently, Mark was relaying a funny day's events at the lab, and Jacques laughed aloud, holding his sides to diminish the pain in his ribs.

"He's so the absent-minded professor," Mark commented about one of his mentors, but not with any malice. He moved books and papers off the couch and slouched down next to Jacques. They were more crowded since Mark was bringing as much work and class assignments home as he could in order to keep Jacques company. He rubbed Jacques' thigh and muttered, "We need more room."

Jacques had wanted to broach an idea he had and took advantage of Mark's remark. "Well, I was thinking about that. We haven't talked about the money my father gave us. We could afford something bigger."

"No way." Mark let out a moan. "I don't want anything to do with the money your father bribed you with."

Jacques hadn't viewed it the same way, but he didn't want to start an argument. "Perhaps we could get something positive out of all this, though. I've been reading about investments, and housing is a good way..."

"No. I said no. Please don't push me." Mark stood up abruptly and picked up the mail that had been sitting on the desk.

"I'm not. It was just a suggestion."

"We'll figure something out," Mark said softer.

Jacques nodded but was disappointed. He also recognized how quickly Mark lost his temper. Mark walked back over to lie on the couch with his head on Jacques' lap, and Jacques rubbed his stomach, ran his fingers along the taut washboard muscles Mark had developed over the last year. He suspected Mark was growing impatient with not having intercourse, but he was still in too much pain.

"That feels good," Mark said.

He didn't offer to blow him. He told himself he felt too weak, but it was just an excuse. He was angry with Mark and didn't want to look at his feeling or really own it. He learned a long time ago that being angry with the people you needed just sucked the life out of your soul and left you with nothing but self-pity.

The phone rang, and Mark got up to answer it. Jacques heard him struggle with the caller's name.

"Hold on." He handed Jacques the phone. "I can't make out the name, sounds very French."

It was a friend of Jacques' from Paris, from the theater, who planned to visit the US in a few weeks. He said he was hoping he could stay with Jacques a couple of nights. Jacques caught Mark's curious expression as he explained to the queen on the other side of the line that it was a bad time. He felt guilty denying his friend's request but knew the circumstances would be impossible. Mark could not handle transsexuality. He was comfortable only in his masculinity, and men who weren't made him extremely uneasy. Jacques had known this from the start. What he hadn't known until more recently was that when Mark felt uneasy, things became very dangerous.

He explained to Mark who the caller was.

"Do you want him to stay? It'd be tight," Mark said.

"No, it's fine. He understood."

Mark sat down and caressed Jacques' face. "You're upset?"

Jacques shrugged.

"Talk to me. I won't lose my temper," Mark said.

"It's nothing," Jacques said. He wasn't sure where he would even begin an honest assessment of their relationship. He couldn't live without Mark, so all else was moot.

When he was feeling much better, and days became more ordinary, Jacques sometimes stopped by the lab in which Mark was employed. Mark seemed to grant these visits now, although he hadn't before. They would leave, get something to eat, and spend time together. Jacques enjoyed having the free time since the semester was over, and he hadn't yet resumed work. It was a typical New England June day with brisk, promising air. For a moment the lab seemed deserted because he didn't see anybody, but then he heard soft murmurs.

"It's all so wrong, beyond comprehension, and mostly my fault." Jacques recognized Mark's voice. He felt tied to the spot, although guilty he was eavesdropping. "I warned myself that getting involved with Jacques was miscalculated ever since I met him," Mark continued. Jacques wasn't sure who else was there. With whom was Mark talking about this, about him? He listened on, although he started to feel sick. "I don't know what to do. I don't trust myself to—you know, not hurt him. I don't know what's wrong with me."

The other voice was female, soothing, but Jacques couldn't catch what it said. He slipped out and ran back to the apartment.

A couple of weeks of nauseous worry later, Jacques had still not heard anything from Mark in regard to the mysterious conversation. He obtained a new job at Mark's suggestion at a local restaurant where the tips were even higher and with fewer tables to serve. He could apply as a seasoned waiter now.

He was finished with his last orthopedic follow up. He would undergo more physical therapy, if needed, for his arm, but he could almost use it as well as before and was only tentative about putting too much weight on it. His ribs had healed, and he didn't hurt whenever he bent for something—as he had certainly done for Mark again by now. His spirits were up today as he arrived home because Mark had mentioned the possibility of a summer vacation.

"What are you doing?" Jacques asked wide-eyed. Mark was packing a suitcase and had two boxes taped up by the door.

"I have to leave. I don't want to discuss it or lose my resolve. I meant to be gone by time you got home."

For a moment these words floated in the air like tiny germs seeking lint on which to attach themselves. Jacques instinctively held his breath to avoid contamination.

"I'm sorry. I didn't mean to sound disrespectful," Mark said.

Jacques stared at him in disbelief, his mouth agape. Unapproved tears were rolling down his face.

"I'm sorry. I didn't think I could face you. I know I'm acting like a coward," Mark said as he grabbed him and held him tightly. "It's for the best. I can't be sure I won't hurt you," he whispered. "Please don't cry, Jacques, we really tried to make things work, didn't we?" He let go and resumed packing.

Jacques started to sob and hated himself for it because Mark would. "But, I do everything you say. You won't get mad."

Mark's face crinkled as if pained by the statement. "That's the point. Don't you want someone you can be yourself with?"

"No! I want you," Jacques said between sobs. He was grabbing Mark's hands and trying to unpack the suitcase.

"Jacques, stop!" Mark caught his forearms, and Jacques writhed with the throbbing it caused to his previous injury. "Shit, I'm sorry. I didn't mean to grab you there. Just let me finish packing."

With this request, Jacques fell to the floor and watched the love of his life pack the last few things in a frenetic manner. A knock on the door startled him, but Mark seemed to be expecting it. He reached over for the larger of the two boxes and gave it to unknown and unrecognizable hands. He grabbed the other box and his suitcase, careful to avoid Jacques' eyes.

"I've taken only my books and clothes. I left everything else for you including a few hundred dollars in the checking account. The rent is paid for July."

Jacques gasped for air; he had the feeling of falling. It was the most barren of places, and the onslaught of loneliness was so rich it gagged him. If he could only breathe, maybe he could think of something to say to change the course of things, but Mark was already gone.

THIRTY-FOUR

Mark's flight into Billings was postponed after "the equipment' was grounded at a scheduled layover. Five hours late now, he'd had too much time to regret what happened. The lab assistant, Mike, who drove him to the airport and agreed to store his boxes, had asked him how bad it was when they got to the car; Mike had heard "the wailing." Mark was stunned the first two hours, but the shock wore off after that and started making room for remorse.

"Are you Mark?" A middle-aged, overweight Native American man pulled his sunglasses off. His hair was tied in a ponytail and a cigarette hung loosely from his lips.

"Yes," Mark reached out to shake the stranger's hand, but the man cackled and swatted Mark on the back in response, walking away.

Mark hurried to reach him. "I guess my grandmother sent you."

"Yeah. I'm William," the stranger said without turning back.

"She didn't mention in her letter how I'd get to her place from the airport. I appreciate the ride."

William smiled but kept walking. "You can throw your bag in the back," he said as they reached the faded blue pickup truck.

"I don't remember how long the trip is. The last time I visited my grandmother, I was really little. She's moved again since then, anyway." He surveyed the mountains in the distance and admired the landscape.

William didn't respond but started the engine, put his cigarette out in the ashtray and pulled out a handmade map. Mark tensed as he watched William trace a route with his finger. It took so long Mark wondered why he'd bothered to start the car.

"We're in a bit of a rush today," William said finally as he put the truck in drive.

"We are?" Mark almost laughed. "Uh…don't you know the way?"

"Nope. Never been there." William turned the radio on.

"Maybe I'm not the right Mark," he spoke loudly now.

"Yeah, I knew your mother."

"Humming?"

"Yeah. You look like her."

The disclosure failed to put Mark at ease, and he started doubting his decision to run from his problems. They headed west on I-90, Mark deciding to keep a mental record of the directions in case they got lost. The mountains in the distance provided landmarks by which to navigate. Gallatin was southwest.

Over an hour passed. William had taken a sudden left off the Interstate and Mark was getting sick from careening unpaved roads. He could no longer keep track. Finally, William pulled over and dug the map out from the paper-covered floor under his feet.

"I think we may have made a wrong turn," the Native said nonchalantly, and Mark wondered if his grandmother was senile sending this guy.

"Where are we going exactly?" Mark made an effort not to sound miffed but failed.

William looked at him from over his glasses. "What's the matter?"

"What's the matter?" Mark's voice was raised. "I'm tired, I just spent about ten hours traveling, and I'm hungry."

"I don't think so."

Mark glared at him, confused.

"I think something else is bothering you," William said.

"Well, think what you want. Do you mind if I at least get out of the truck to take a piss while you're trying to figure out where we are?"

"Don't mind, but grass might," William rejoined.

Mark noticed the South Dakota license plate as he walked past the truck. He couldn't help but recall the last time he went on a journey with a virtual stranger and how it had changed his life.

William started driving in the same direction as soon as Mark closed the door. The dry air seemed to be browning everything as far as the horizon stretched, and they were climbing. An hour or so later, Mark noticed three teepees among the greener hills with the sun setting just behind them.

"I didn't know people still lived in teepees."

William lit up again and informed him that most of the People didn't.

"Do you mind? The smoke bothers me," Mark said, hoping William would care.

"Oh, yeah," William nodded, "me, too. Probably die of cancer."

Mark clenched his fist and stuck his head slightly out the window in response.

"Hi, Unchee. I didn't think we'd ever get here," Mark said when he reached his grandmother.

"Let me look at you," she smiled and grabbed his face, kissed him by pulling his head to her height. "You're so handsome," she said.

Mark laughed. "You look great, too." Although sixty-six now, his grandmother was a replica of how he remembered her. If it weren't for the grey hair, it would have been as though she had been held in time. It fell in a long single braid on her back. Her eyes held a mysterious look about them, like a child with an old soul. There were more lines around the corners, but he barely noticed them. He remembered the warmth he felt whenever her gaze fell on him and felt sad that they hadn't seen each other for so long.

She held onto his hands while she introduced Mark to her friends. One man who looked over a hundred years old addressed him in a language he didn't recognize. Mark shrugged his shoulders and shook his head to signify he couldn't understand.

"Did she teach you none of the People's language?" his grandmother asked, her eyes downcast. Her question appeared rhetorical. "How long are you going to stay?" She looked uplifted by the prospect of his visit.

"Till school starts, I guess," Mark said in a non-committal way, but his grandmother kept her eyes on him until he clarified, "about six weeks."

"Good, that gives us some time to work with, but right now there are preparations to be made," she said, and with this caveat, she sent him off with several of the men, still wondering fifteen minutes later what she'd meant by *work*.

The men walked in the dark brush till they reached a small, round hut made of canvas. Mark noticed a round ditch near the makeshift lodge where a fire was burning. At least eight rocks lay at the bottom, some nearly red as coals, as if they'd been in the fire for hours. He wondered if they were going hunting and thought of food.

"Have you been in a sweat before?" A young man sidled up beside him, Mark guessed a few years older than he. He had brown hair tied back in a ponytail and was white. He wore a Gaelic medallion and a small buckskin pouch around his neck. Mark flashed back to his own "medicine bag," the one he wore with him on his travels when he was a boy. His grandmother had given it to him, and inside it, he kept a small pebble from her yard, a white feather he found in Germany, and a garnet ring his mother had given him for safekeeping. He hadn't seen it in years and tried to remember now where it was, distraught that he could be so negligent about something once so important to him.

"What's a sweat?"

"It's like an old-fashioned steam room but used for prayer and detoxification," the man answered.

"And we're going in there now? I haven't eaten for hours."

"That should be interesting then," the guy said, laughing good-naturedly. "Don't worry, we'll eat right afterward. The shaman, or medicine man, is Lakota, but he lives in northern New Mexico most of the year, in the Sangre de Cristo Mountains."

"Lakota?" Mark asked.

"Sioux Indian."

"Oh, right. I'm Mary's grandson, Mark, by the way." They shook hands.

"I'm Scott Reading. Aren't *you* Lakota? If your Mary's grandson?"

"Well, yeah, but I didn't grow up around here," Mark answered.

"I guess you didn't," Scott said, laughing before he continued. "I'm from Connecticut, but I've spent a few months here, mostly working with the Crow by Bighorn. I came to see Buffalo, though. The medicine man. We're lucky he's around; some might not let us near anything like this." He pointed to another white man at the edge of the encampment.

"Who's Buffalo?"

"Buffalo with Big Horns, actually is his whole name. He's coming there," Scott pointed to a tall and solid man approaching the sweat lodge. "Oh, it's time," Scott said as the other men started to remove their clothing. He instructed Mark to follow their lead and gave him a towel to wrap around his waist.

"When you enter, bow your head and say *Mitakye Asin*, an invocation of sorts that roughly translates as 'To all my relations.'"

Mark followed directions with some reservation. He crouched down to his knees to enter the lodge through a large flap that was pushed aside as a door. The canvas itself encircled twigs and branches that comprised the skeleton of the circular lodge. William and another man started shoveling the rocks into a pit in the center of the lodge. Mark was seated next to the flap and could see the shovel's head enter with the red coal-like rocks. It quickly grew hot within the confines of the canvas.

A heavy, Native man moved out of the way across from him to allow the rock bearers into the lodge and then Buffalo entered, settling back in by the flap and closing it behind him. The heat became oppressive shortly afterward, and Mark questioned the pride that had led him to follow the others into the lodge, the same pride that now made it impossible to leave. No verbal preparation could have helped him deal with the scorching of his membranes with every breath he took.

The shaman threw water, then sage and tobacco onto the rocks in the pit. Soon the lodge was as smoky as it was hot. In the blackness, a hand from the left grabbed his head and pushed him to the ground.

"If it's too hot for you, lower your head to the Mother," the medicine man said.

Mark noticed the air was somewhat cooler as it rose from the dirt, but he didn't appreciate the shaman holding his head down. He fought the urge to buck the hand off. Buffalo with Big Horns started to chant and several of the men joined in. They were praying for peace among nations from what Mark could make out. The shaman spoke English intermittently, perhaps in translation. Mark felt nauseated and kept his head as close to the ground as possible, praying silently for the sweat to be over. Buffalo started to speak of power and control, female and male energies. He recommended allowing an opening for the unknown, for the feminine, to enter and balance their lives and the fate of Mother Earth. He said the sweat lodge was a place of rebirth and that the lives and spirit of the men present were now entwined. Mark didn't like the sound of that at all. Next, the medicine man spoke of the power of the pipe to plant the seeds of their new dreams. Mark wished he were in his lab or anywhere else familiar.

Instead, he found himself on the African plain with Papap's niece, a step-cousin he hadn't seen in years. Last Mark had heard, she had moved to England with her new husband. Presently, though, they were hunting, and she wore a Western Safari outfit like one from old black and white films featuring colonists in Africa, although she remained indeed very black-skinned. Mark tells her she's beautiful, and the turned-up corners of her lips are the only sign she liked the compliment. I'd like to eat those lips, he thinks, disregarding how he sees her as family. Out of nowhere, the roar of a lioness signals an imminent attack on her. His rifle is out of range, but he must act immediately if he is to save the woman's life. He musters the courage to run toward the beast and subdue her by hand, but her claws rip across his chest and expose his heart with a spray of blood. He hears a shot, as his cousin grabs the rifle and kills the beast.

Mark blacked out. When he awakened, he saw stars through the slanted poles of a teepee. He tried to sit up but a flash of pain in his head knocked him straight back down.

"Hey, you're awake," someone said, maybe Scott.

"What happened?"

"You passed out during the sweat. I'll get Buffalo."

When he returned with the medicine man, the latter appeared larger and more intimidating than Mark remembered him from the sweat lodge. He wore his hair pulled back, as William had, and seemed to be in his fifties, maybe late forties. He poured a thick, greenish substance into a cup and handed it to Mark.

"Drink this."

"What is it?" Mark didn't recognize the aroma.

"You don't like when someone else is in charge, do you?"

"No, I guess not," Mark said as he sniffed the contents again. He wasn't sure what to make of the stuff, or the comment.

"That doesn't seem to be working too well for you," Buffalo said. He placed a cool rag on Mark's head.

"What do you mean?"

Buffalo reached over for the cup. "You drinking or not?"

"I don't know what it is." Mark eyed the shaman defiantly, and the latter retrieved the cup, returned its contents to a container. "Where's my grandmother?"

"Oh, she left."

"Where to?" Mark asked. He wondered what the hell was going on. He started to feel nervous and displaced.

"Home."

"Without me?"

Scott walked out of the teepee in response to a call from outside leaving Mark alone with Buffalo.

"You were in no shape to leave."

"Can someone take me there now?" Mark asked, as he tried to sit up again. The movement was still too much for his head.

"You're pretty badly dehydrated."

"I was sweating to death!"

The medicine man laughed heartily.

"Could I at least have some water?" asked Mark. He was still naked under the sheet someone had thrown over him.

"Sure. It'd be better to drink some of this stuff first, though." Buffalo pointed to the container.

"Fine. Whatever."

Buffalo patiently poured another cup and handed it to Mark. "Tell me about your vision, if you want."

"What?" The green fluid tasted putrid. "Are you sure this is safe?"

The medicine man smiled and nodded. "Tell me about the big cat."

Mark's eyes met his immediately. He held the cup to his mouth, motionless. "How do you know about my dreams?"

"It wasn't a dream. It was an indication you're ready to begin. A good thing, because we don't have a lot of time from what your Unchee says." He spoke deliberately, as if each word was significant.

"Time for what?" asked Mark.

"I'm willing to help you know your destiny."

Mark considered the words dubiously.

"You know how I got my name Buffalo with Big Horns?"

"No."

"I was like you when I was a young man, always struggling against instead of flowing with. Destructive even."

"How do you know what I'm like?"

"You'll see how, if you accept the challenge," Buffalo said.

"What challenge?" Suspicious but curious, Mark started to notice more of his surroundings as Buffalo spoke of challenge.

"To stay with me as my apprentice."

"I can't do that. I'm visiting my grandmother," Mark said, perplexed.

"Answer in the morning. Ask your dreams for some guidance on this."

"Well, can I call my grandmother in the morning? It's too late now, I guess." His watch was nowhere in sight.

"Sure."

"Do you have a phone?"

"No."

"No. Of course not." Mark closed his eyes, too tired and spent to worry about his strange circumstances.

THIRTY-FIVE

Mark fell into a restless sleep, his waking and dreaming thoughts both consumed by fantasies of Jacques with sporadic awareness of the stranger's presence in the tee-pee, also sleeping. How disconcerting that he couldn't stop thinking of Jacques, even after he had just supposedly left him for good. Toward morning he dreamt more sequentially.

Jacques was in a bathroom, shaving. It was a delight for Mark to see Jacques shave, and he remarked so. He was vividly aware of Jacques' sex appeal, and he wrapped his arms around him, from behind kissing his neck and earlobe, suddenly shocked by the sight of Jacques' smile, holes where there should be teeth. He pulled away horrified and asked, "What happened?" Jacques turned to him gently and responded, "You knocked them out. Don't you remember?"

Mark woke with a start. It was sunny, and he could hear Buffalo's voice outside the teepee, talking to someone whose voice he didn't recognize. He found his jeans on a table and slid them on. The teepee was spacious enough with the two cot-like beds, a couch, and a small card table with two chairs. A fire pit occupied the center of the round space. Dried herbs hung vertically from the "walls," at sixty-degree angles from the canvas. His own suitcase was by the foot of his bed, and several gas lanterns were placed around the teepee floor, a large one on the table. The dirt floor was well swept and scattered blankets carpeted and warmed it.

Outside the teepee, the blue of the sky extended farther than he'd seen in a long time and reminded him of the natural beauty of Kenya. Mark saw that he'd been moved last night to an area more remote and elevated than where the sweat had been held. For a moment he felt trapped, but he was also awed by the majestic views.

Buffalo left his visitor's side and approached Mark. "Did you decide?" It didn't seem to matter to him one way or the other.

"Can you help me with my temper?" Mark asked him.

A nod.

"Then, yes, I'll stay," his voice seemed to answer for him, the image of Jacques without teeth propelling him.

The shaman waved the stranger off and told Mark to help himself to some breakfast. There was a spread of tea, toast, hard-boiled eggs, jelly, and fruit on a nearby dilapidated picnic table.

"Thanks," Mark said, unprepared for the selection.

"Thank your grandmother when she comes back. She's supplying the grub."

She's paying you to babysit me, Mark thought to himself. At least she was coming. In fact, she came at least twice per week after that, and always trailing behind her was William, or Scott, or someone Mark had never met. She sometimes brought a delectable variety of treats to please Mark, once a sweater, another time a letter from Africa with news from both his sister and his mother. Mark spent the first week stacking woodpiles, tending fires, and learning about native plants. He wondered how it all would help him manage his anger. He spent the second week drumming and learning chants, stacking woodpiles, tending fires, and learning about native animals. He was upset but enjoyed being outdoors.

He spent the third week collecting rocks for the next sweat, as the new moon was approaching. He was having difficulty with the assignment, as most of the rocks he chose didn't seem to meet Buffalo's approval. Not that one, he'd say. He'd laugh aloud and wave another one off, shaking his head, or have other incomprehensible reactions. His counsel was for Mark to choose more wisely, which was frustrating. The only concrete advice he'd gotten was from Scott, not Buffalo, who suggested Mark steer clear of any rocks near the water, as these would sometimes explode when heated too quickly. This week, he'd also learned to concoct some herbal remedies, which, at least, was not a complete waste of time.

A few days before the full moon, Mark asked for the fifth time how all of this was going to help him not destroy things. He was tired of euphemisms and used the dream memory of Jacques' missing teeth to focus whenever he thought of leaving.

"Are you ready to talk about it honestly?" This was the first time Buffalo bothered to respond at all.

Mark wiped the dirt off his hand onto his shorts and looked at Buffalo with contempt.

Buffalo laughed. "Tell me about your vision," he prompted seriously now.

Mark recalled it to the medicine man as detailed as he could. He even seemed to remember the fear he felt as the lioness charged.

"Do you know what it all means?" Buffalo asked him.

"Don't you?" Mark asked. He wanted answers fast. He was due to start the fall semester at Tufts in three weeks.

"Nope."

"Nope?! What am I supposed to be getting from all this? I've done everything you told me to do the last few weeks, even when I didn't want to. For what?" He lowered his voice, "You said you'd help me."

"You're right. First, you learn how to move into a meditative state on your own, to use Western terminology."

"How do I do that?" Mark asked.

"Start to follow your breath, in and out." Buffalo demonstrated in silence. "Then allow your feelings to arise, taking note of them, and placing them in a space outside yourself to dissect at a later time. Then watch your thoughts, like sands in an hourglass, watch them drop, without judgment." He sat in quietude, eyes revealing he had removed himself from time.

Mark cleared his throat to speak. "Is that supposed to relax me when I get angry?"

"Don't know."

A rush of infuriation mounted again. "I could read about meditation in a book!"

"But, you haven't," the medicine man reminded him.

Mark started to pace, kicking rocks, as Buffalo watched him.

"Hmm," the medicine man sounded.

"What!?"

"You seem a bit spoiled," he observed.

"Spoiled?" Mark told him about life in Africa, working on the fields, volunteering to bring supplies to the impoverished in remote areas, seeing people sick and starving. He was indignant. Jacques was spoiled. John was spoiled. *He* wasn't spoiled!

"What does all of that have to do with you?" Buffalo's left eyebrow rose. "Were you the one starving? In what ways did the experience of these things shape and change you exactly?"

Mark didn't answer.

"Any experience can mean different things to different people. One person may become bitter and angry from an event, another humble, and yet another wise, or compassionate." Mark was embarrassed by the likely answer. He kept on pacing in the same way, trying to walk off his irritation.

"Tell me about the young man in your life, the one you dream about, even when you're not sleeping."

"It's none of your business," said Mark. He wondered if his grandmother had told everyone about his personal life. He shouldn't have told her.

"What are you, queer? A fairy? A faggot?" Buffalo stood less than a foot away from him in a confrontational stance.

Mark struck out with a left hook to the jaw. It wouldn't be the first time he fought someone to defend his sexuality or at least to shut someone's mouth about it. Presently he missed the target entirely and stumbled with the weight of his thrust to his knees. He turned swiftly and stood to face the medicine man.

"How the hell did you do that?" Mark asked.

"Do what?"

"You were standing right here, I know you were." Mark put a hand through his hair, confusion supplanting the anger.

"Maybe you don't know much at all. You're a disgrace. You speak none of your people's tongue, save for the chants I taught you, and know nothing of our ways. You're ungrateful when someone offers you their help, or their heart, and you lack control over yourself, which doesn't stop you from strutting around here like you're a commanding officer. I can't help you till you accept that your way hasn't worked."

Mark listened with his eyes averted, tearing over slightly. Buffalo's words stung.

"You don't know how to channel your emotions, and your love is limited, and limiting, when it should be expansive and expanding. But, the choice is yours." Buffalo hesitated, as if to give Mark a moment to let the ideas germinate and his heart soften.

sound negative? How about maternal, nurturing, gentle, soft? Loving, giving? Creative? He thought of stereotypical female traits: indecisive, weak, or weaker at least, insecure, nagging, although his experience of women was limited and he hadn't *known* any of these things to be true. In fact, the one woman he did know very well, his mother, was one of the strongest people he knew. And, couldn't these characteristics be reinterpreted? What he thought of as weak could be seen as tender or soft; indecisive also meant someone was flexible or accommodating; insecure could mean needing protection or living out on a limb. He sighed, and hit the side of his head with his palm. This was harder than he had suspected, difficult to define. The most mundane difference: men penetrated while women were penetrated. The feminine was more open and receptive, while the masculine was more aggressively resistant.

What did this mean? Why had Jacques been so willing to open to him, and why had he never insisted that Mark reciprocate? Well, he wouldn't have, Jacques must have known. But, why? What was the basis of this adamant denial? His mind lurched ahead, not wanting to consider the possibility in any detail.

Why did he punch him that day? What about the crying bothered him? Was he just afraid that Jacques would not need him if he acquired too many friends? Then again, was Jacques exactly what Mark wanted? Someone weak and submissive? So many questions, too many unanswered.

Who am I? The question popped into his mind suddenly, radically, ripping into his preconceptions. It made his mind stop for an instant, stumped. He didn't know.

THIRTY-SIX

It was early afternoon when Mark arrived back at the teepee the day of the sweat. He helped Scott pile rocks into William's truck, changed his clothing, and threw together a bag of dirty laundry for his grandmother to contend with. He ate granola bars in an effort to keep his blood sugar level from bottoming out like it apparently had the last time.

Mark hugged his grandmother when they reached the ceremonial site. She wore a long purple dress, wrapped with a beaded belt. She and several other women were there for a couple of hours and had prepared a banquet to share later that night. Some older men had also arrived, a fire had been started, and William was presently adding the chosen rocks onto the pyre.

"Don't worry so much," his grandmother said as she disengaged his embrace and smiled. "You're doing just fine. Making good steps."

"I'm not so sure," he said, not bothering to ask what she meant and how she knew how or what he was doing.

She pulled him to a trailer parked nearby and suggested they talk together alone. He was more than glad to do so. In fact, he was disappointed that they had spent so little time together. As soon as they were seated on the worn, inset "couch," she invited him to tell her of his journey into the wilderness alone.

Mark thought about it before answering. "Not the best. I always knew I was bull-headed, but I never realized how strong the current of my mind is."

She gave him an eerie look and said, "I've missed your mother very much over the years. Sometimes I wish I hadn't been so bull-headed, too. Perhaps she never would have left me if I had just given her the space to be who she was. It's much harder to accept the things which are different from us than we realize." She resumed her smile. "But, then, had she not left, I wouldn't be sitting here with my beautiful grandson, seeing him blossom with the light and wisdom of the Great Spirit."

Mark blushed, feeling unworthy. He wanted her to speak more about his mother and their relationship. He'd missed the connection all these years, too.

"I know how hard it is for you to make sense of the things of the world. You are like most young Lakota today, even though you think otherwise. When I was a girl, the elders taught us about Great Spirit, and the medicine men and women provided the guidance we needed to understand how mystery reveals itself in everyday life." Her eyes drifted away.

"Unchee, how do you resolve your anger against the white man?"

She looked at him questioningly.

"It's just that the white race has decimated everything in its path to more: more money, more status, more power and control." He searched her face as he spoke. "I've had such difficulty dealing with the revolting exploitation and enslavement of one human by another."

"Crimes against humanity," his grandmother echoed.

"And nature, too, and God, perhaps. I know that I'm far from unique in these concerns, but the anger is so personal for me. I swell like a tide sometimes and can't control myself. I've taken it out on Jacques and I'm afraid of..." Mark stopped for a second to swallow the knot in his throat, and then said, "of myself and what I'm capable of."

"Have patience. That's the best advice I can give you. If you were not capable of repairing this damage, you wouldn't have conceived it."

Mark nodded his head but felt disappointed, wanting someone to provide the answers, wishing everything were easier.

She laid her hand on his knee and continued, "It's been only a hundred years since our people were defeated, forced onto reservations, stripped of our pride, and murdered. The powerlessness, what some believe to be betrayal of the Great Spirit's protection, created a lot of pain."

Mark thought of the irreparable spoils of genocides around the world. Perhaps it's why his mother left this place and detached from the past. Perhaps it was the only way to survive now.

His grandmother looked at him lovingly when he turned back to her gaze. "I have come upon some knowledge I thought you might find interesting, grandson. Have you heard of the word berdache? I believe it is from the French."

Mark shook his head no.

"French colonists are said to have referred to some tribes' medicine men they came across as berdaches because they seemed to show the feminine face."

"What do you mean?"

"It seems the word was originally used for men who sold themselves for sex, and the white settlers did not understand the power of the medicine, the supernatural ability, of people who would present themselves as both sexes, male and female."

"What, did they dress like women?" Mark asked.

"Actually, sometimes they did." They laughed, she especially heartily, Mark with underlying nervousness. "The point is, as I am sure you've heard by now..."

"I have to incorporate the feminine; yeah, right, so I've heard." His sarcasm concealed his need to mull over this information.

Although the sweat was less eventful without the type of dramatic vision he had the last time, it was also less strange to Mark, who had by then learned traditional chants and what to expect. When it was his turn to speak, he prayed for forgiveness and for clarity, for the strength he would need to become the man he was destined to be.

The women finished in their lodge just ahead of the men. Afterward, the sound of the native drum emanating from the encampment brought Mark a deep sense of appreciation for his heritage. He felt like one of his own kind, like Lakota for the first time, and the beat, like the heart of the Mother, was helping him find his way back home.

The morning air held the whisper of winter, reminding Mark that school was soon to start. He'd miss the freedom of the natural rhythm of his time here but would make the most of his last ten days. He reminded himself to get a message to his grandmother to confirm his flight. He stepped out of the teepee, squinted from the sun's rays and found Buffalo sitting at the picnic table.

"I'll be returning to New Mexico in a couple of days."

"What? Already?" Mark tried to screen his reaction.

Buffalo shook his head without raising it. He was working on a piece of suede-like material.

"But, what about me?" Mark asked, surrendering to his concern.

He then repeated the last several months in a whirlwind of memory, ruminating over the mistakes he'd made, the times he hadn't apologized enough, the incident for which he'd been beaten, his inability to make love for so long. If only he'd done things differently, Mark might have stayed. Why didn't he know how to hold onto him?

He jumped out of his thoughts when John knocked on the door. "You all right, mate? Do you need anything?"

"Oh, I'm fine," he responded by rote. He motioned for John to come in and walked to the sitting area by the window. He was charmed by the accommodations and told John how appreciative he was to have such a beautiful room.

"I thought you'd like this one best, but you're welcome to move into any of the others," John said gratuitously. The room he'd chosen was closest to a separate entrance and the ceiling-to-floor windows lit the copious space. John had even relocated a desk from another guestroom, so Jacques would feel as self-contained in the room as he needed.

Jacques sat on the Queen Anne-style chair beside the window and fidgeted somewhat. "Could I ask you something?" he asked as John spread out on the settee. "Do you believe there's something...wrong...with me?"

"Like what?" John asked.

"I don't know, but something...something that makes people, men, want to hurt me?" Tears rolled down his cheek, and before John dismissed his question, he described the extent of the violence that had occurred, not just with Mark but also with his father, and by the men who had assaulted him. He searched John's expression for any clue that would explain his apparent flaws.

Instead, John seemed to have difficulty with such intimate information; he shook his leg in rhythm and appeared frightened. Perhaps he shouldn't have spoken about disquieting things to John. He was considering how to change the subject when John spoke.

"I think you should see my psychiatrist. I've been a little better since I started to see him regularly, well, I go three times a week, actually, but I've been stable and taking my medication. And he's not so bad, really, I mean, if you'd like," he trailed off and looked away.

Jacques made a mental note to be more careful with John's mental health. He decided he would pursue treatment with John's doctor, but he would refuse medication—there was something of John's presence simply gone, and it could be because of the pills.

Over the next few weeks, healing came slowly for Jacques, but he grew in strength and confidence just by making it through each day. Mornings were thorny for him, when waking once again met him with the shock of his loss. Frequent rides to the countryside to picnic were helpful, as were the sessions Jacques arranged with John's doctor. The coziness of the cottage warmed his mood over time.

Being with John was helpful. However mysterious he was about it, John seemed to know about pain. His English friend was also generous with his solicitation—and with his money, although Jacques had repeatedly declined such offers. John informed him that he would give all his money to charity in the end, anyway. He said he had already drawn up his will. He wanted assurance that he'd be useful in death in a way he'd never managed to be in life. Jacques had failed to convince John how valuable he'd been in his own slow recovery over the summer, although that certainly issued no great deed, as Jacques understood himself to be little more than meaningless in the "grand scheme of things."

John held out a cup of tea. Jacques took it but set it down, knowing it was too hot to do more than sip; he lacked the English enthusiasm for the beverage, but John continued to serve it daily for almost two months now.

John cuddled up beside him on the sofa. He'd just turned the television on, but the sound was low. Neither wanted to get up to increase the volume, which led to self-deprecating humor about their lethargy.

"In America, we'd have a remote control," Jacques said. "Of course, Mark would complain it has led to the…what was it?" His eyes looked up and to the right, his mind searching for the memory. "Ah, oui, the stupefaction, is that a word? of the American people."

"I'll have to remember that!" John laughed.

John's body was so close to his that he had to concentrate on not responding merely by instinct. He shoved himself up to the edge of the couch to create some distance.

"I don't want you to leave," John said, with sudden impact.

"What?"

"You heard me." John pulled him back and fit his head into the crook of Jacques' neck, placing Jacques' arm around him as snugly as a blanket. "I suppose you'll want to return to Boston now that summer's nearly over."

"Yes, to see Mark, to try…"

"To try what? You did everything you could. You were the one who made all the concessions. What more can you do?"

"Perhaps, but I'm not ready to give up." Jacques wiped a tear from the corner of his eye before it had time to fall on John. John was astute, and he was right.

John wrapped his arm around Jacques' waist as if holding on to a bed pillow and kissed Jacques on the neck, making him fidget. He wondered if John was so anxious about being left alone that he was offering sex in exchange for something Jacques couldn't promise. He stiffened, and John let go of his grasp a little.

"Why not simply call first, to see if he's even interested in talking?" John asked.

"What if he isn't? Just accept it?" Jacques sniffled in between words, in awe that he could be brought to tears after the time that had passed, and wondering how much of his so-called recovery had depended on a fantasy that Mark would take him back. What if it were just that, a fantasy, and it had been the only foundation of his growing confidence all along? Would he fall apart? He felt gripped by fear, and his companion sensed it.

"Are you all right, then?" John lifted his head and looked at him long enough for Jacques to meet his eyes. "Come on," John said in a soft voice. "He really means that much?"

Jacques shrugged, afraid to admit to his friend the apparently unacceptable.

"Would you like me to wank you?" asked John.

Jacques laughed at the English word, and the suggestion. It must have been John's intent to lighten things up, although he wasn't sure the Englishman wouldn't oblige him if he said yes.

"Call now. I'll get the phone."

"Now?" Jacques asked.

"Why not?"

"It's still too early. Although, maybe he got back earlier to start work. It's possible."

"Good, so we can try." John brought the phone from the end table across the room, but it only went halfway to the couch before the cord was taut.

Jacques stood and envisioned pieces of himself lying around them on the floor. He dialed the lab number, prepared to plead for a second chance if a miracle brought Mark to the phone. It would be 11:00am in Boston.

A stranger's voice answered after the fifth ring, and Jacques asked for Mark with fluttering heartbeats. The young woman didn't know a Mark but agreed to put some-one else on the line when the Frenchman insisted Mark worked there.

"This is George."

"Yes, I need to find Mark. Has he returned to the lab yet from summer vacation?" Jacques tried to control the shaking in his voice.

"Nope. Who's this?"

"Jacques. His roommate, ex-roommate."

"Oh." The voice sounded confused. "He wrote a letter explaining he wasn't coming back this semester."

Jacques hesitated, almost shocked by the news.

"Are you still there?" George asked.

"Yes, thank you. Did he quit school, or transfer? Were there any details?"

"I think he's coming back after the fall semester, but don't quote me on it. I doubt he'll have a job at this lab, though, by then. Sorry I don't know more."

"Okay, thank you very much." Jacques' shaking had stopped, but he panicked at a deeper level.

"What is it?" John grabbed the phone back from him because Jacques was about to drop it. "Go on."

"He's not there. He's not going back."

"He quit?" asked John.

"I'm not sure. They didn't seem to know."

"So, let's call Kenya," John suggested, "We may still have some resolution before night's end. I have the number somewhere."

"It's too late there."

"Only about ten, I think."

Jacques hated to put it off now, too. "Okay," he took the phone back and waited for John to retrieve the number.

"Here you are. Want me to dial it?"

"No, it's okay." Jacques dialed the number and listened to the foreign ring.

"Go ahead," it was Humming. Jacques had hoped it'd be Papap but remembered he never did like to answer the phone.

"Good evening, it's Jacques. How are you?"

"I'm fine. What can I do for you?" she sounded put out.

"Well, is Mark there, by any chance?"

"No, he's not here. He's not in Kenya. But, I can tell him you called."

"Thank you," Jacques said, still as intimidated by Mark's mother as ever, but struggling to get some answers, he added, "Do you know how I can get a hold of him?"

"If he wanted you to know where he is, I'm sure he would have told you," she said with some edge. Jacques wished he could figure out exactly why she disliked him so much. She must know how much he loved Mark. He calmed when she softened suddenly, "But, I can tell you he's fine. And I will let him know you called, when—or if—I hear from him."

"Did he get my letter, do you know?" he asked.

"Well, we haven't forwarded it yet, but I guess I may as well now. I'll send it to him this week." Jacques heard a hint of irritation in her voice aimed at Mark this time.

"I'd appreciate it," he said, irritated she had held onto it for so long. "If I write again, will you forward it for me, too?"

There was a slight hesitation before she answered. "Yes, I will. Good luck to you," she said.

"Thank you."

Thus ended Jacques' chimera of a reunion following a summer hiatus. The next few weeks were unrelenting. Every time he believed he could go on without Mark, something would contradict him, a memory, a sense of loss over something small, like the breathy touch of Mark's lips on his face. No one had ever touched him in the same way. He didn't want to believe that he had lost Mark forever.

"You've become one big, swollen ouch," John said one night before turning in. Jacques had smiled, the first time that day, and licked his fingers clean of jam he'd gotten into, something he had never been permitted to do, even when he was five.

———

Humming washed the remainder of the dinner dishes and decided to let everything air dry tonight. She'd had a rough day. In addition to the usual farm-related duties, she'd had to deal with the calls from creditors since she never paid the bill for the tractor they purchased over a year ago. The equipment was supposed to make the farm labor easier but so far it only served as a reminder that the farm was failing again this year. And she missed her son. How was she ever supposed to get used to his being gone, and so far away? She doubted he would return when he finished school. How often would she actually see him? The irony wasn't lost on her. Her mother was repaying her by stealing her son for the summer. Not that they would have had enough money to bring him home. Not this year. She wrapped some raw dough in a towel and left it on the counter to rise overnight.

Papap was sitting in his favorite chair reading the day's paper. "Who was that on the phone?" he asked, peeking over the turned down corner.

"The French boy," she sighed, using Papap's term of endearment for the first time.

"Oh? What's wrong?" he sounded alarmed, to her irritation.

"Nothing's wrong. Apparently, he doesn't know where Mark is." She tried to hide her satisfaction at that. She had thus far successfully avoided debate about their son's choice in a romantic partner.

"And you say nothing is wrong?" He clucked his tongue in disapproval, and she pretended to be busy with her own reading.

"What?" she asked, since he was still looking at her.

"I am trying to figure out what you hold against that young man."

"I don't hold anything against him," she rejoined, but he kept looking at her. "Kisau, I just want to read my book."

"Like mother, like son."

"What do you mean?"

"It's just easier for you not to explore your feelings about things. Or talk at all. It would have been nice for him to tell us what happened between them."

"Sometimes I wish you were more like other men, Kisau, and not so damned enlightened," she said with a little smirk.

He laughed in his resounding way and when he finished, he asked her, "Why not read that book I bought a few years back?"

"Oh, God, the one about homosexuality?" she rolled her eyes with disdain.

"Yes, that one. It helped me to understand a little better."

"To be honest, I guess I was hoping he'd grow out of it. Instead it got worse," she said, realizing she was in too deep now to stop and placing her book back on the coffee table. Papap stayed quiet but seemed expectant. "When it was Kyle, it was just another boy. They could be friends, no one would notice." She sighed. "I know I'm a monster saying that."

"No, you're not a monster, my Dear," he said softly.

"Do you think it was because of my relationship with Andreas that Mark's, you know," she said, not wanting to admit it aloud.

"Oh, I don't know. There are genetic tendencies," he said. She gave him an incredulous look.

"Really! Did you know that there are homosexuals in other species? It's true," he smiled when she laughed. "It's all in the book," he added. She was still laughing, a release of sorts, and he joined her. She could always count on him to make her laugh and to brighten her mood, even if inadvertently this time.

"I miss him so much," she also confessed when the laugh died down. He nodded. "You know, Kisau, I have come to believe you missed your calling."

"Which calling?" he raised his eyebrows in the lovely way she admired.

"You should have become an animal behaviorist."

"Oh, that. Yes, or more likely an anthropologist," he said.

"Why not go back to school now?" she asked.

"Now, I am resting in my retirement as a farmer." He laughed again but good-naturedly. She understood it would completely turn their lives upside down.

"Why didn't you do it sooner?" she wondered aloud.

"Well," he placed the paper down next to her book on the table before them. "I suppose because I had a job with the government and then," he smiled seductively, "Why, then, my Dear, I met you and your bright-eyed little one. I had to be responsible."

She sighed and felt sad, never having known this about the man with whom she was so intimate. "So, you gave up on your dream because of us?"

He shook his head thoughtfully. "No, I wouldn't say that at all."

"What would you say, my husband?"

"I would say that my dream changed when I met you," he said and smiled.

She got up and joined him in his chair, laying her legs on his lap to make room. "Thank you." She felt better already, feeling very lucky indeed to be with her best friend.

THIRTY-EIGHT

8/28/83 I am alone. The finality, the absoluteness, of this fact has revealed itself to me. We are never anything but alone. My time is marked only by the rhythms of nature and my own breath. My grandmother still comes once a week. She brought me this pen and journal "to record," although to record what exactly was left to my not so keen imagination. Imagination, I left it to people who had nothing better to do. I could use a little about now. The monotony of me knows no bounds. I miss my books.

9/4 I decided to clean the area where the truck is usually parked. It looks like a dump, and I wonder why my nature-loving Lakota guide would allow it to exist like that. I've spent days going through stuff and piling it in such a way that I could easily transfer it to William's truck next visit.

What am I still doing here? I've spent some time criticizing myself, again, for the decision to forgo classes this semester. My ambivalence toward having a career outside of home and the farm had already put me back over a year, and now this absurd foray into what-exactly-I-don't-know makes it a full 2 years. Despite my initial reluctance to go to college, I have to admit that it really suits me. I think of everyone there and what they must be doing. I feel like I'm missing out on things.

9/8 I'm discovering how difficult it is to write without an awareness of some invented reader. Often I think of Jacques reading this journal, but the notion requires I censor what I say.

Time has taken on an entirely odd sense now. No schedule. No deadlines. No electricity. It's getting cooler—I'm wondering how much longer I'll be able to bathe in the lake. I look forward to my grandmother's visits the way children look forward to holidays. I doubt I have impressed

dance trio with two other men featuring homoerotic themes. In the men's dressing room afterward, he had the uncomfortable sensation of being watched. All this time after the assault, he was still jittery around too much sexual attention or when something felt similar in his gut to that night.

"Hi."

Jacques jumped back and struggled to appear collected.

"Oh, sorry, I didn't mean to startle you." The young man held his hand out to shake. "I'm Luke."

"Jacques." He shook hands and noticed the sweat on Luke's palm with distaste.

"I hope I didn't make you uncomfortable, I mean, I couldn't stop looking at you." Luke was still looking at him in a most impudent fashion.

Jacques tried to smile but managed only an inept grin.

"You want to grab some coffee? You're done, right?"

"Ah, yes, I am finished, but my boyfriend is waiting for me at the hotel."

"Oh, your boyfriend?"

"Yes." He wasn't sure what made him lie. Probably Luke was safe, but he wasn't ready to be sexually active with anyone. Luke walked away looking a bit deflated, and Jacques had a glimpse of remorse. What if he never even saw Mark again? Maybe he needed to face some of his fear of men, and New York might eventually help. He ended up being hit on three times while there, and although on a self-imposed sexual moratorium, feeling desirable started to boost his confidence. He knew he'd be offered a "gig," and that it would be a short stay in England once they returned. For this he barely rejoiced, though. Despite feeling driven to move on, he also finally felt part of a household, maybe even a family.

He had considered a trip home to France but still felt too weak to face his father who had said, "It's advantageous the Indian boy is gone." What Indian boy? Jacques had almost asked, absent-mindedly, taking a few moments to see that his father was referring to Mark. "No, it's dreadful he's gone," he'd said, but didn't expect his father to understand. He would instead view the debacle as proof of his son's incompetence. Furthermore, he might not be strong enough to resist his father's influence. These miscellaneous doubts about himself and his life besieged him at inopportune times.

Jacques therefore decided to spend the time at the English cottage with John's sister, Lilith, who had returned to England from Moscow, where she studied

Russian language and history. When they met, he was only fifteen but performing in Paris already. She had accompanied friends to the show and ended up backstage. Jacques and Lilith hit it off and were instant friends; they developed a heightened bond due to feeling commonly misunderstood. Despite the brief amount of time spent together then, they maintained contact and shared everything in their letters for years.

That was until Mark entered the picture. Jacques never could reveal in writing what transpired over the length of his relationship with Mark. In the English country-side now, John acting as host to both, and after only three days together, they grew familiar enough to finish each other's sentences.

"So, when are you going to give me all the details? What happened with you-know-who?" Lilith asked, now sitting beside him at the cottage home in which he'd had the marvelous experience of friendship and mutual support.

"Hasn't John told you?" he asked.

"You know how secretive he is," she smiled in some mockery, albeit good-natured for the most part.

Jacques had forgotten how pretty she was. She shared her brother's features, but her skin was softer, her lips fuller, and her legs longer—or so it seemed.

Hours passed by time they finished discussing in detail the nuances of his rela-tionship with Mark.

"I love your new look," she referred now to his short haircut, nearly buzzed on the sides. "You look like a boy," she added with determined glee.

Jacques shrugged, a little self-conscious and not quite over missing his tresses at times. He had cut his hair before auditioning in New York and after losing faith of regaining the past. It thereby represented his hope, and his heartache. After a few more words, Jacques decided to retire to the room that had housed him during his metamorphosis—a room, ironically, feminine in its decor: very florid and warm, comforting in the way surroundings can be when care has been taken to them. He undressed and climbed into bed to say his nightly prayers, a ritual from childhood he resumed when he started missing the chapel at Tufts, and lastly, thought of Mark.

He quickly entered the place between wakefulness and sleep, the portal to the next world, and he saw Mark covered in snow. An overwhelming sense of fear hit him as he realized that Mark was dying, slipping away from him. The snow was so thick it was like looking at Mark through layers of gossamer veil. The image was haunting yet still disappeared in a flash when he was suddenly awakened.

It was Lilith, standing at the side of his bed. He blinked, his arm lying outside the sheet, dividing them and outlining the shape of his body. The moonlight was so generous tonight that he could see her, her silk robe slipping off her shoulders, revealing her breasts. When his eyes caught hers, they were entreating. He looked to her waist. Taking in her request, he reached for the soft belt, tugged it loose, and saw the look of happiness on her countenance. When the robe hit the floor, she slid into bed beside him. They kissed, both meeting halfway with little pressure. He thought to ask her what it would mean for them, what she would expect from him, but it would come out tactless no matter how delicately he phrased it.

She asked him if he'd ever been with a woman. He told her once and that he would not sulk at constructive criticism. She laughed and took him up on it, guiding his hand. He wanted to please her, but he also just plain wanted her, passionate about her body, scent, and sex the way he never felt at liberty to be. After Lily rolled the condom on him, she also helped him enter her. He followed the movement of her hips, followed her lead at every turn. He planned to wait for her to orgasm before letting go, but failed and had to rely on his mouth to finish her off, the taste of latex the only deterrent. Her back arched, and her breath accelerated, and Jacques almost mirrored her pleasure the way he had so often with Mark.

Afterward, they talked again, although Jacques' eyes burned and kept closing on their own. Despite his somnolence, he had one last question, "Lilith?"

"Yes?" She rolled closer to him.

"Should we not tell John about this?"

Lilith lifted herself over him, swept his face with her palm, and kissed him on the cheek. She tiptoed out of the room.

——

John had been awake and had heard them having sex, however muffled. He braced against the bedpost. The pressure to hurt himself had already been building the last few weeks as he dealt with Jacques' imminent departure. If he lit a cigarette, he could burn his arm and let the pain preoccupy his mind. He fought the urge, trying to remember how he and his doctor planned to manage such a state. He welcomed numbing. The music in his mind was loud and comforting in its encompassing quality. It persisted throughout the night, so that he made it without resorting to physical self-harm. He wished he could write some of the notes in the sequence he heard them, but he didn't trust himself to get out of the bed.

THIRTY-NINE

The next morning, Jacques greeted John as usual, perhaps a bit brighter. "Did you sleep?" he asked the Englishman, worried ever since their trip to New York that John was gradually falling apart.

But, John did not respond. He poured coffee with a trembling hand, which Jacques gripped with his own.

"Are you well, John? Let me."

"You shouldn't."

"Why not?" Jacques asked, amused, as he poured two cups.

"It's a disgrace, is why." John was staring at Jacques as he placed the coffee pot down.

Jacques turned away for a moment and contemplated how to deal with the statement. Whenever John's mind seemed to fray, Jacques had been able to soothe him by telling him he was safe, or that his illness was confusing him, but something in John's voice sounded wilder than before.

"Have you been taking your medication?" Jacques asked as politely as such a question could ever really be delivered.

"Have I been taking my pills?" John laughed. "Oh, the pills, so I can't hear anything!" He threw his hands over his ears, and shot Jacques a look of contempt. "The pills that make me deaf then? Is that what you're on about? How convenient!" He brought the volume of his voice down, but Jacques suspected it was a poor attempt to disguise feeling out of control.

"What do you hear? The doctor said we should let him know if you hear any voices."

"Voices…" John choked up some of his coffee, threw the rest into the drain, hesitated, and then threw the cup across the room. It splattered into shards just as John told him to sod off. Jacques shook and took a breath.

Lilith stood in the doorframe, apparently hesitant to step into the kitchen. John knocked open the door to the yard and left.

"He must have heard us last night." Jacques was still addled by the scene, by John's words and reaction, but that much seemed clear now.

Lilith shot him a glance before chasing John. Jacques could see them through the window, but they were soon swallowed by the expanse of lawn that made the backyard so verdant. John took off in his car recklessly as his sister continued to move farther away from the house.

Jacques decided to catch up with her, heard her crying as he kept a few paces behind out of respect. Finally he asked her what was going on.

To her reticence, he asked, "Is it me? Did I miss that John has feelings for me? Is he jealous?"

"No, it's much more heinous than that," she replied, more to herself than to him.

"What is it?" Jacques felt frustrated but unwilling to show it just yet. Lilith appeared bothered by something profound. She sniffled, wiped her face on her sleeve, and walked back to the house.

———

October 6th I have two choices: Either be at peace, or not. Not at peace is where I end up when the anger invades me. In my meditation now, it has formed into a separate entity, an ugly one, a degrading force within me that renders me powerless, destructive at best. Every time it moves away from me, the vacuum left behind sucks it right back in. The peaceful state is nevertheless becoming more familiar. A sign of progress perhaps. Another gift: the extraneous thoughts no longer pile one on top of the other when I sit.

One thing I am sure of now is that change cannot take place through violence. Since I have so clearly seen my own anger as an energetic mass, I know that action taken in its path only adds to the collective pain. Our heroes, our elected officials, even our visionaries, can only reflect ourselves. To think we can change the world when we are too angry to feel the world in all its complexity is human frailty at its apex. You can't extract righteousness riding the back of your own rage.

10/7 I wonder if the conscious experience of pain can be conveyed genetically. If the hurt, disappointment, and anger could be the result of my ancestors' lives, as much as my own. I had never really thought about being an Indian and what it meant for me because I believed I was a product of my environment more than of my genes. How incomplete of me.

I have to admit that I spent an entire day recently thinking about, wondering, questioning myself, about why, WHY, I was wearing those shoes the night I beat him so badly. I guess I'd been considering walking out, so I had my shoes on, but the truth is that I may have intended to hurt him as badly as I did. To make him pay for having hurt me.

October 8ᵗʰ My experience and appreciation of nature have deepened. It's not that I see it as sentient in the same way as I see myself, but there is a consciousness present, instinctual perhaps, and most definitely, actively alive. Never again will I be able to read a "Vacant Land" sign in the same way. There is no such thing. Another fallacy of man's. So many shortcomings to rise above. I thought I felt connected to land before. It's even more now. This place, these trees, they're alive. Furthermore, they're my companions.

Now I'm sure I would sound insane. Anyway, it's too cold. I'll need to leave soon.

October 9ᵗʰ Why had I systematically worked at not loving him? I was afraid—afraid to stay in the authenticity of my feeling and desire for him, because I was afraid of what that meant about me. So simple, now that the thoughts have surfaced. All along I'd felt untrue to myself by feeling what I did for him, when in fact, I was untrue to myself by not allowing myself to love him.

I'm aware now that Jacques was, or my experience of Jacques was, an extension of my own inner projection, mostly the denied parts of myself, the flip side of the coin by which I defined "me." And, why does anyone deny parts of themselves, anyway? What inherent sense of unworthiness takes precedent, and from where? I've been thinking about this, and as trite as I know this conclusion sounds, it appears to be equally valid. I don't blame my "father" for the rejection he has always met me with, but I do finally understand the power it has held over me.

God, am I making any sense? I thought this was about Jacques and me, about 2 guys in relationship to one another. But, Buffalo was right. It's always been about my own integration.

Is it too late to be new?

October 10ᵗʰ I understand something that hadn't made sense to me before. I was just sitting here when I realized that thought is movement, and as such, it creates time according to the laws of physics. Time is defined as movement through space. This inevitably implies that the Eternal Now that Buffalo has spoken to me about can be reached by stopping the movement. I never understood because I knew I could sit still for a while and time would unavoidably pass. What I didn't grasp until today is that my thoughts haven't been stilled, my mind hasn't stopped work-ing—ever—and I, therefore, have not managed to find myself in forever-space. I will work harder at stilling my mind and being in the moment beyond thought.

Mark hit the lake with a whack. The ice broke unevenly, stretching out like wrinkles in a wizened face. It was not enough to reach liquid water. He wanted to fish, hoped to find living fish under layers of frozen fresh water. It had been cold with blizzard condi-tions for days, and no one had come to bring supplies. Mark assumed the roads were blocked and the way treacherous. He could melt snow in a tin over the fire he came to banking in the teepee, but his staples (granola bars, crackers, cheese) had run low and then out. In the summer, the cheese and other perishables were kept unopened in the cool lake to keep them from putrefying, but such measures were unnecessary once the fury of winter arrived. He'd eaten everything edible around. He was tired of being hungry, and he was tired of feeling cold. He'd begun to pack himself first with pages from his journal, then with leaves as he grew desperate, between layers of clothes.

He whacked at the ice again, aiming for the same point, and careful to step back from the lake. He didn't want to lose his footing. If he weren't so hungry, he'd have convinced himself the plan was foolhardy. He'd had almost no experience with winter. The strike cracked the ice where it was most vulnerable—he'd made sure to pick the site by its seeming lack of profundity. He quickly threw the string into the water and planted the branch pole into the snow. But, the pressure he placed on his stabilizing foot brought it to slip with directness into the triangular break, causing the rent to spread while soaking his shoe and sock.

"Shit," he hissed to no one. He waited for the lake to freeze over the small open-ing, which took longer than he'd calculated, and he was colder because of the slip. He realized he might pay for this break from the monotony of the teepee's confines, and the possibility of dying from hypothermia suddenly evolved into a fully blossomed fear inside the heart of him.

October something ... I can feel the objects around me. They are pulsating. Everything has life. The floor's presence is more imposing than my own. I'm having trouble breathing, and I can only figure that my body is absorbed with this specific problem. As I write this, it's as if thoughts are arising in waves or shapes. I am painfully, yet peripherally, aware of the fire dwindling, and I am too cold, too tight, to move. How is it possible I don't "see" myself dying here, like this? Still, regrets arise. The most important is that I didn't love better. It seems now that it was always about me, and I've grown sufficiently tired of myself. Why has humanity gone searching for intelligent life somewhere out there? The search is right here, within the human heart. Perhaps this time spent tending the teepee, this sojourn away from my life as I had known it, was about finding that intelligence. I hope it has not been in vain.

His hands lacked cooperation at this point. He had to put his pen down and concentrate just on breathing. Shivering became violent. Before long, he started to fade between dreaming and waking reality. When he could no longer discern the difference between them, he surrendered to the idea of departing with no trepidation. He felt Jacques was with him somehow.

"Mark!" William was standing over Mark's body near a dead fire in the middle of the teepee and moving his limbs back and forth. "Get some more," he directed an adolescent boy to bring some water and had also wrapped Mark in several layers of heavy blankets. He was dribbling a homemade remedy onto Mark's lips, rubbing it in. "Should have worked by now. We need to carry him out, get him to the clinic." Just then the boy returned from the van with more water. William sprinkled some on Mark's chapped lips. Was he hallucinating? Did he die? Following the movements of the men in the tepee was demanding, but then the scene slowly started becoming more concrete to him.

They packed Mark's things with dispatch, but William took more care with the shield that Mark had had the instinct to hold close to him before he lost consciousness.

"Where am I?" Mark suddenly spoke but was barely able to move and his words sounded slurred. "My feet," he mumbled. He thought he must still be alive if these men were here helping him.

"Frostbite," William said with his usual neutrality. "Try to move around a bit to get your blood flowing."

"They feel almost like they are burning," Mark slowly articulated. "Should they be burning?" He hoped the men would take them out of the fire and felt consumed with panic.

"That's how frostbite feels sometimes." William waved another man over, one Mark didn't recognize, and the three carried him to the van. Once they situated him in the back seat, horizontal, they discussed which route to take back—Mark listened in total passivity, laughing to himself, or thinking laughter, at least. He thought how William would have been the last man he would have trusted with his life. Now he felt resigned to his circumstances because he had no other option.

The unrecognized man climbed into the backseat and lifted Mark's lower legs onto his lap while William and the boy got in front. He removed Mark's shoes and socks with care and studied Mark's feet with caution, paying particular attention to the bluish toes.

"They're not too bad. I've seen worse. You should be able to keep them."

This statement, too, struck Mark as humorous. They were moving. Mark could hear chains on the tires.

"Who are you?" he managed to ask.

"I'm Michael; I know your grandmother. She said you were in trouble."

At this, Mark felt satisfied, glad even, that his feet were in good hands.

A droning voice on the radio was describing the weather conditions. *More snow expected with dropping temperatures... The coldest October in years... Dangerous travel on the roads... Advise to stay indoors until further notice.*

Mark could see out the far window past Michael's profile. Almost everything was white, a portrait of colorless blur. He was glad his companions were taciturn by nature. He only wanted to feel himself moving against the din of the motorized vehicle.

FORTY

"Shush...Don't tell Mother and Father," she said, the golden blond of her hair cascading over her eyes. "I hate them, anyway."

"We'll get in trouble, we will." Her seven-year-old brother pulled the covers closer to his chin, but she just laughed at him.

Crawling in beside him, she wrapped her arm around him while laying her head on his small chest. He seemed to strain under the pressure, and there was the familiar and coveted sense of excitement and quickening. She started laughing again, her hand now covering her mouth to stifle the noise.

"Be quiet," he whispered.

"They won't hear us," she said between giggles. She had the same problem in church last Sunday, only he had joined her then, hardly able to look at her without exploding.

"What's that, then?" They both heard a door creak. "Was that the attic?" His young eyes, already dilated in the dark, now wild with fear. The footsteps on the creaky boards of the foyer floor magnified one after the other, matching the rapidity and volume of her heart.

The door swung open, and there stood their father, a tall, somewhat gaunt man with wavy blond hair, sharp features, and minimal facial lines. "What the hell is going on in here?" His voice was tense, and it scared her.

Lily jumped out of bed and started to cry against the harsh accusations aimed at her small brother. She wanted to explain that it wasn't he who had done anything wrong, but, as usual, her father wouldn't see the truth. He called his son "disgracefully deranged," and forbade him ever again to have his sister in his bedroom. He told him he'd never come to anything, that he'd be just like his uncle and perhaps he should go to the attic and stay with him now.

"No, Daddy, please!" Lily screamed. She could not let that happen to him.

At that, she woke, breathless. The pressure in her chest felt burdensome and painful. It was her fault that her brother was so sick, that he'd never had a chance to gain his father's approval and feel safe. How could she ever remind him he'd been ruined by her need to seek solace in his innocence and warmth?

After a quick breakfast, she folded the last of her items and packed them fastidiously, ensuring that each lay on the next in perfect lines. She pulled the last turtleneck off the pile and refolded it with caution. Having things in order seemed to relax her sharpened edges, especially in times of heightened stress. She jumped back when Jacques knocked at the door and pushed it open.

"Sorry." Jacques looked chagrined.

Lilith suspected he was frustrated since their night together but knew he was too polite to pry. John had become more withdrawn after settling down from his outburst. She didn't trust that he wasn't finding ways to hurt himself without their knowing.

"You packed already. How efficient." Jacques smiled. He was obviously trying to get her attention off him, where her eyes had remained fixed since he walked in.

"Yes." She closed the valise, somehow feeling exposed, and then walked across the room to get her coat. "It's turned a bit colder, hasn't it? Feels like the dead of winter already." A frisson overtook her by the sound of her own words, and she wondered if they would ever regain a more comfortable intimacy.

He smiled meekly. "You're ready?"

"Of course. Nothing to be nervous about," said Lilith, although, in truth, she'd been anxious ever since John's psychiatrist requested her presence. His secretary had told her that the doctor found something lacking in John's history and wanted her to fill in the gaps, especially after their last session. "Are you sure you don't mind? Staying, I mean, to make sure he's all right, just for a couple of weeks."

"It's okay," Jacques assured her. "Rehearsal doesn't begin for another month."

"Rehearsal? You were offered the part?"

"Yes, an off-Broadway theater production called me last night. Dance mostly."

"That's great news! Congratulations." She smiled but avoided his eyes. He was putting off his plans just to stay with John, and she felt guilty about that and about so many other things. "I don't know how to thank you," she said.

———

They rode together, the three, without a single word, Jacques in the backseat observing the strain among them from a unique perspective.

Lilith pulled in and parked the car by the front office. They all opened their respective doors and walked toward the entrance. Jacques wanted to say something, anything, and felt the vacuum of silence more than the siblings, who hardly seemed to notice.

"May I help you?" Dr. Silver's receptionist asked Lilith.

"Dr. Silver's expecting us," John said.

"Oh, John, I didn't see you. How do you do?"

"Thank you, fine."

"Dr. Silver will see you in a minute, Miss Chatfield. Please take a seat." She smiled at Jacques as she turned away to paperwork.

Jacques had seen Dr. Silver a few times himself over the summer and respected his opinion. There must be something specific the psychiatrist was after, but he feared he'd be the last to know, if at all. The secrecy of his English companions was distressing the past few days.

"Miss Chatfield?" Dr. Silver stood in the doorframe. "Oh, I didn't know everyone was coming along," he added as he saw Jacques and John.

"You know I don't really have a life," John said, not bothering to look up.

The doctor nodded at both the young men but didn't move toward them or comment on John's statement.

———

Lilith alone got up and walked into the next room with Dr. Silver, her heart thrashing.

"Take a seat, please," he smiled fully at her, sitting in the large chair behind his desk. "I'm glad you were able to make it."

"What can I do to help?" she asked him.

"As my secretary advised you by telephone, I'd like you to fill in some gaps for me." He adjusted his glasses on the bridge of his almost perfect nose and began to shuffle through paperwork in John's file.

Lilith noticed she'd been holding her breath, squirmed a little and felt unsettled. No doctor had ever asked to speak with her before.

"For instance," the man continued, either oblivious to or ignoring her discomfort, "John doesn't appear to know if there's any history of mental illness in the family." He looked at her for a reply.

"Oh, I see, well, yes, I suppose you could say that."

"As I suspected. Who was it?"

"My uncle," Lilith said, aware of sounding obtuse.

"Which uncle?"

"My Dad's brother. Henry was his name."

"Was?"

"Yes, he died a while back, I would say about eight years ago. Well, actually he killed himself," she answered.

"I see. That's certainly important. Do you know what was wrong with him?"

"I'm not certain, but..."

"Yes?" Dr. Silver's brow furrowed, and he gave her a quizzical look.

"He used to hear things, also, like John. We didn't know him for long, so perhaps I can't really be of any assistance, after all."

"Actually, that's quite helpful. What about your grandparents? John indicated he was close to your maternal grandmother. Can you comment on that?"

Lilith shifted in her seat. "That's a lie. We never met her."

"Do you know why he would have told me that?"

"No." But she recalled something. "Actually, maybe I do. We used to pretend that we were going to visit with her in summers, that we'd have a hiatus of sorts from our parents' scrutiny." She stopped abruptly with caution and looked away.

"Why were you under scrutiny?" the doctor asked her.

"It's just a phrase."

"Perhaps," he said but wrote something she couldn't see. "Why did the two of you want to get away from your parents so much that you would fabricate a grandmother? She's quite real to your brother. He's told me numerous stories of times with her," he said with his glasses off now, the tip of one of its arms between his front teeth.

"Well, we don't like our parents, didn't even more so then."

"By your brother's description, they were cold," the doctor said.

"Yes."

"And distant."

"That too, yes." Her mind wandered then as she remembered her brother in his younger years, saw him standing in the sunlight with Italian children giggling as they insisted he say more English words. They were on holiday in the mountains in Italy. John enjoyed himself that day, they both did, walking to a pay phone from a farm owned by some local relatives of their nanny. Where were their parents? In Rome or Naples, or as far away as they could go while still ostensibly overseeing the family trip. Their nanny, who was probably around seventy at the time, was well in the distance behind them, walking with the ladies, who transported food in baskets on their heads. John was laughing, and she heard him now in her mind's ear, the locals pointing to everything around for him to provide the English translation. At thirteen, she was a world apart from his eleven-year-old sense of play, and she was more interested in the aesthetic beauty and simplicity of the place. She didn't know why John told them they were from Australia instead of from England.

"Was your brother ever sexually molested?" the doctor asked now.

Lilith was caught off guard and became agitated. She had dawdled in her memory for too long.

"Miss Chatfield?" He sighed. "I apologize if I startled you—"

"No." She let out a stifled laugh. "Why would you suggest that?" She held his eyes this time, almost in confrontation.

"I believe some event triggered John's illness to manifest, perhaps something sexual in nature, although I don't subscribe in full to Freudian fixation on sexuality. Nevertheless, I have questions, and he doesn't seem to have the answers."

She continued to look at him and repeated her response.

"I see. Were you?"

"I'm afraid I don't see how my life pertains to this," she defended.

"Don't you?"

She felt obtuse again. "It's just that my brother is so sick, and he needs me to hold things together, so if you don't mind, I'd like to refrain from answering this line of questioning."

"Miss Chatfield, I'm merely asking you these questions because I'm trying to help your brother. I don't mean to be intrusive."

Lilith wiped a tear from the corner of her eye before it had time to run down her face. "It's not something I talk about, is all."

Dr. Silver sat back in his chair, giving her the literal space she needed.

"My uncle..."

"The one who was also mentally ill?"

"Yes," she said. She suppressed her emotions well.

"Do you have any reason to believe he approached your brother as well?"

"No, I don't think so. Actually, I'm sure he didn't."

"How can you be sure?"

"Well, as I said, our uncle wasn't around for an extended time, and John and I had spoken about it, the way children talk about such things."

"And he told you that your uncle hadn't done anything to him."

"Right, that's right."

"Excuse the nature of this next question, but it's critical. Did anything ever happen between the two of you, between you and John?"

"No, not at all," she answered very quickly, and again the doctor wrote something down.

"Have you had analysis over this issue with your uncle?"

Something of the sterile nature with which the doctor asked the question repelled her. "No, I haven't," she rejoined. "Is that all?"

"Well, I'd like for you to call if you think of anything else that might be important."

"Certainly," she said as she stood to leave.

"It's a bunch of bull shit, if you ask me," she whispered to Jacques as the three returned to the car. Jacques had asked her what she thought of the session.

"They used to say that the doctors knew too much to be held innocent, but too little to actually heal anyone," John said. He had heard her despite the whisper.

"They who?" Lilith climbed in behind the wheel.

"They, the other patients at the loony bin," John snapped.

FORTY-ONE

The following day, Lilith returned to London to stay in her old room at her parents' estate, surrounded by the very things that made her feel most at home and most afraid. Why it should be both at once was not a mystery to her. She looked at her journals, the pages of text she'd written during her studies thus far. The cramped box of stuff gave off wafts of mustiness and incense. On page after page were notes to herself, poems, stories, excerpts from her letters and diary entries. Plenty of ideas for creative writing. She had thought to write about their childhood, to see it in print and redress it with the charms of youth. John would forgive her, wouldn't he? If he could see how she managed to hate herself at the most inopportune times.

In Moscow she had befriended an elderly lady named Olga, who lived next door to the student housing. Every morning Olga would be outside tending to a few plants she tried to keep alive through the brutal winters. Over time, Lilith stopped longer and longer just to chat. Olga had traveled to England as a young woman, been keenly interested in metaphysics and even espoused the teachings of Ouspensky. You would never have guessed it now, all shriveled up and watering dying plants on a dilapidated patio in the cold USSR. Her English was still impeccable, though, after all those years, and Lilith enjoyed their discussions.

One day, Lilith asked if Olga thought the plants might be beyond reviving. *Perhaps,* Olga answered. *Still, I won't give up on one more thing. No, dear, I will just keep trying until I take my last breath. Oh, there goes the bladder again,* she cried. *Will you wait?* Of course, Lilith agreed. She had wanted to return the woman's books—they were too difficult to get a hold of in the current regime to inconsiderately fail to do so. When Olga returned, which took several minutes more than one would imagine, she looked

Lilith deep in the eyes and said, "*Don't give up on yourself, dear, not ever, no matter what you face. Create your life as you will, despite the hardships and the disappointments. Create art in some form or another, and even if the people don't understand it, love them anyway.*" She sighed. "*It's been such a terribly long life in many ways.When I was young, I had great plans, but I delayed them, always finding an excuse; well, sometimes the threat of imprisonment was my greatest excuse,*" she smirked here unusually. "*Now I find I can't even hold in my urine. How's that for fine aging?*" The grief of lost dreams echoed in her voice and in the shake of her head.

Six months later and back in London, Lilith was on the Underground on her way to the theater district to meet a friend when she suddenly had an intense urge to relieve herself. She had to use all her might to contain herself. The image of gushing out, an overwhelming sense of letting go of her bladder, her uterus, her entrails, besieged her. She felt stripped by the emptying of herself. She realized that evening she'd been given a majestic gift—to feel what she might feel as an old woman who didn't realize her own dreams, who never managed to birth her own life in the ways she had conceived.

The terror of that first time, when John was so sick that his parents had no choice but to bring him in for evaluation, still teetered just under the surface for her. He was only fourteen years old when the insanity started, when he began to believe in magic in a way they never even achieved as children. *It's just a phase, dear,* their father repeated whenever she heard her parents arguing about his latest mishap in school or an embarrassing moment in public. They certainly would have sent them to boarding schools had it not been for his incessantly unstable moods, his temper, and his auditory hallucinations. When he became so depressed he couldn't even pull himself out of bed, she was the one who had begged her parents to seek guidance. Their argument was that he was petulant and indolent; hers that he was unwell, impaired in a way he never should have to be. Finding him with his wrists cut up, the blood in the bathtub, was so horrifying that she cried for weeks afterward. She could still see the jagged flesh under the dull knife he had selected, and, although he didn't cut deep enough to lose much blood that first time, it was the most brutal he'd ever been to himself or to anyone. He was such a gentle soul till that point.

And then two years later, after a short time of apparent normalcy, perhaps a year, during which he wrote and played music and excelled at class and spoke to a few peers, it all got out of hand again. He became so unmanageable in his ideas, in his energy, unmatched by anything she'd ever witnessed. He didn't sleep for days, often keeping her awake as well. He consumed alcohol in large doses, initially often vomiting in the early hours of morning. There were sharp edges to everything he said, and she was afraid to disagree with him and his farfetched schemes for fear of being at the brunt of his outbursts. Again, she had asked her parents to find him a doctor, and again they had delayed until it was too late. Perhaps accidentally, she never knew, he drove the car into or rather *at* the garage at full speed, demolishing the entire structure as well as the gardener's shop. At this point, her parents were irked enough to ask the family doctor to place him on sedatives.

The medication helped to some extent, but it wasn't enough, and it wasn't precise. John survived his adolescence despite his parents and the support they reluctantly provided. He was rarely evaluated and was never encouraged to talk about his symptoms. These recent days since his last and most lengthy hospitalization were a change. John had never before demonstrated such perseverance in the face of psychiatric assistance, and she had just basically undermined his efforts instead of helping them. If only she didn't get so nervous about talking with Dr. Silver. If only she didn't have her own demons, she would have been a much better sister. Now, as then.

FORTY-TWO

Having returned to school for the spring semester, Mark resumed work at the same biology lab as before. He had work to do, not simply to make up credits, but also on his "integration." He studied the teachings of mystics and practiced meditation with unbridled devotion, glad for the lack of distraction his solitary life provided. Living alone was especially advantageous when he woke in the middle of the night to record his dreams. He paid particular attention to dreams with visionary content.

In some ways, these visions served as a testimony to the state of consciousness he'd experienced out West and seemed more real to him than his daily life. If it weren't for them, he feared he would lose himself in the academic rat race and the incessant mind chatter, or that he would simply adopt his previous existence. It was with a true diligence that he approached his expanding insights, never wishing to fall back into destructive patterns. He felt blessed when Buffalo with Big Horns appeared in his dreams. On the night of March 4th, he woke and recorded the following:

I found myself walking on a trail someplace West and North; it was cold, and there was a thin layer of snow at my feet, each step imprinting the ground with my presence. I could feel Buffalo, and then paused to look around. A shriek from a hawk landing on a nearby branch pierced through me. The hawk instructed me to proceed; I entertained arguing that I needed to find my teacher first. It was strange that a bird could speak with me in words, so I was suddenly aware that I was in a dream state. I closed my eyes and willed Buffalo to me, and when I opened them, I saw him up ahead and followed him to a teepee. I must have forgotten again that I was dreaming at this point. Next to the teepee, there was a tree trunk whose inviting opening revealed a home.

"What's that?" I asked (aloud?) to an already vanished Buffalo, so I approached the entrance and saw a young woman brushing her hair. As she looked at me, I sensed the compelling desire to devour and to be devoured.

I seemed to close in on her, and again became aware that I was dreaming, and yet the intensity of the feeling was even more real than any I recall previously. If I close my eyes, I can be there again. I can feel myself erect, but it's all over my body and in my mind that I sense it.

When she parted her lips and welcomed me, her dark hair glided gently down her arm. Her mouth opened wider, and without thinking I covered it with my own, surprised at the strength with which she met me. In reciprocity, she retracted, placed her thumb in my mouth and gladly gave of herself, her energy, while I sucked on it. I can almost still sense her energy all the way through me, like warm jelly. I woke up in orgasm, followed by a deep sadness to be stuck back in my room.

The next day, Mark fell asleep at the lab for about twenty minutes, not unlike other days since he began his nocturnal journeys. He was just waking when he spotted Sanjay walking in. Although Mark kept a low profile since his return and fixated on his school schedule instead of his social contacts, he had to admit that he noticed the Indian boy was still around on more than one occasion. Seeing Sanjay now reminded him of his crush while he was still living with Jacques. Grief over Jacques passed fleetingly, and Mark decided to approach the wiry figure.

"Hey, Sanjay, how are you?"

"Mark! Good to see you." Sanjay placed some papers he was reading onto the lab bench next to him as he twirled the stool he straddled around to face Mark. He added quickly, "I'm good, thanks, and you?"

"I'm good; I'm back," Mark said, glimpsing momentarily at the other's crotch, spread out and inviting as it was, and then catching Sanjay's eyes.

"Sorry," Mark said too quickly to conceal. "I mean... shit," he grinned and blushed.

Sanjay laughed, "It's okay. Don't mind you noticing me really."

Mark appreciated the honest reply and smiled. He asked Sanjay if he'd like to spend some time outside the lab.

"Sure," Sanjay smiled and his golden brown skin seemed to shimmer against his white teeth.

Mark was almost shocked at how aroused he felt suddenly. Although he had planned a trip to the library, he changed his mind. "Can you come back to my place now?" He asked with an intensity that would make anyone a little nervous. Mark had never been so honestly forward in his life. It seemed his libido was back with a vengeance.

Sanjay hesitated, his eyes almost bulging. "Well, that was quick."

"No, sorry, I didn't mean to rush things. I'm not sure what's gotten into me," Mark said.

"I guess it's true then what I've heard?"

"What's that?" Mark always hated the idea of people talking about him.

"That you separated from your live-in boyfriend. I mean I'm just curious about the details of your disappearance and all. We all were; sorry, I hope I don't sound nosy or meddling."

Mark realized that he was staring at Sanjay and probably making him uncomfortable. "I don't like conjecture about my life. We can make it another time if you're busy." He felt a little angry now and upset with himself for saying what he just did. It was the first time he felt angry for a while. He acknowledged it and let it move away. Sanjay looked embarrassed.

"Never mind. Forget I asked. It's okay," Sanjay smiled sheepishly, "Today, I mean. I'm just surprised."

"Can you get away?"

"Yeah, I think so." Sanjay repacked the things he'd taken out from his sack, turning his back to Mark, whose ravenous appetite returned. The lab manager was across the room looking at them. Sanjay called out he'd be back in a bit. Nobody cared when he put his hours in at this lab, so long as he did. Mark was glad the manager was so very laid back about it. It allowed him to stay till ungodly hours at night whenever he felt like it.

Mark brought Sanjay to the apartment he rented in Somerville. He had looked Jacques up when he first got back, eager to ascertain his whereabouts. He concluded Jacques had left Tufts, and probably Boston. His mother might have forwarded Jacques' letter but he never received it. He didn't like to imagine she would lie, despite her unexplained animosity toward Jacques, but he also saw it improbable that the letter was lost on its way to Montana. Mark had no idea where Jacques was or what he was up to. He hadn't taken the money from their joint account, even though Mark had told him to; in fact, Jacques had deposited a couple thousand more in it before he left.

"I'm a bit nervous, I guess," Sanjay said as he stepped in behind him.

"Why?" Mark stroked Sanjay's face with the back of his hand. "I won't do anything you don't want." He smiled and Sanjay did, too, but he looked even more timid.

"Tea?" Mark asked him.

"Sure."

"Iced or hot?"

"Hot. It's cold in here." Sanjay laughed, as he pulled his jacket off.

"Winter has been particularly brutal this year, especially for those of us used to warm climates." Mark took Sanjay's jacket, noticing his delicate, sexy fingers. "Take a seat," he said with the superfluous gesture of pointing to the couch. There was no other place to sit but the floor. The couch was a cast off from a doctoral student who left to start a fellowship just as Mark was getting back. There was a small round rug by the front of the couch. The spacious living room opened into an empty semi-formal dining room; both had long, Queen Anne-style windows indicative of the year and the area in which the house was constructed. Mark thought he had taken some time to make the place his own, but now that he looked at it through someone else's eyes, it seemed bare and almost unlived in. He went into the kitchen to get the tea.

"How many apartments are in this house?" He heard Sanjay call out. The small kitchen was not visible from the couch.

"Four," Mark peeked out at him. "Like it?"

"Yes. Do you live in this one alone?"

"Imagine that." Mark smiled, feeling lucky to have been able to bypass dormitory life ever since he started college.

"You really have no roommates?"

"Not at the moment, although I may need one soon for financial reasons. I prefer to live alone as long as I can."

"Is there just the one bedroom?"

"Yes." Mark handed Sanjay the teacup, as he sat down. He noticed the Indian boy's hands again; he had a thing for hands. "I haven't managed to get a table yet," he said. "And, the bedroom is quite plain. I use a futon with a sleeping bag."

Sanjay smiled and looked down.

"I don't mean to make you uncomfortable," Mark said as he raised Sanjay's chin and looked, almost against his will, lasciviously at the Indian's full lips. "You have beautiful lips."

"Thanks," Sanjay's face contorted slightly under the strain of trying to appear cool.

Mark sighed, "Sorry, I keep making it worse. How about a back rub?"

"Okay," Sanjay turned away from him quickly. Mark started to caress Sanjay's back as the Indian read aloud titles of books he glanced on the floor. Mark never did right his habit of keeping books and paperwork all over the place. Sanjay seemed to notice the only other piece of furniture in the room, a wooden cabinet that served as a makeshift bookcase, above which two African masks peered out at them. Mark followed his gaze.

"The masks are from home. Do you hate them?" Mark asked.

"No, they're just different."

"Jacques never warmed up to them. They scared him." He realized he'd spoken of him.

"I've never done this before," Sanjay blurted out.

"I can tell. Don't worry about it."

"I don't want to get sick—anything we do, we need to be safe. You're okay with that?"

"Of course." Mark felt apprehensive about the risks he had taken with his ex. He didn't know for sure that Jacques was healthy right now, and no one seemed to know how long an incubation period might last. He had since learned that AIDS had been identified in France as early as 1982, the year they met. His fingers found their way to Sanjay's thick hair and massaged, and he willed his mind to refocus on the present moment and on being healthy.

Sanjay took a few deep breaths with his massive, brown eyes closed.

"How old are you?"

"Nineteen," Sanjay said.

"Can you look at me?" Mark asked a compliant Sanjay. "We're not going to do anything except this." He kissed Sanjay on the cheek and rough housed him just enough to get the younger man to relax and laugh.

"Was last year your first year in the States?" Mark asked him after they stopped laughing.

"Yeah," Sanjay said.

"You're from Bombay?"

"Yeah." He nodded again, looking pleased.

"Didn't think I knew anything about you?" Mark smiled.

"Well," Sanjay didn't finish his thought. He lifted his teacup from the floor where he'd placed it and sipped.

"Are you Hindu?"

Sanjay nodded.

"Do you know about this?" Mark pointed to a book on the teachings of an Indian Swami. "It's about yoga."

"I'm not an expert on yoga." Sanjay laughed, his eyes betraying astonishment.

"Well, what do you think?"

"You want to have an intellectual discussion on spiritual philosophy, now?"

"Why not?" Mark asked, serious but smiling in a mischievous way. "Are you Brahmin caste?" Mark assumed Sanjay was from the highest social caste, since he was studying in the States.

"I hate being asked this question. I am opposed to the caste system, and I'm sure you don't approve of it, either." He explained to Mark that many from the business class surpassed the Brahmins, especially economically, and could more easily afford private universities. He then reluctantly nodded again, "Yes, if you must know, I am. But I would vote against continuing the caste division given the chance."

"I wasn't holding you responsible for it." Mark smirked, realizing there was a time when he might have.

"No, but I could have chosen not to be born into it, or so my religion dictates."

"You don't believe that?" Mark asked him.

"I'm not sure. Do you believe in reincarnation?"

"I don't know." Mark had been struggling with the idea of Karma since he returned to Boston. How did cause and effect work if reality were actually non-linear? He asked Sanjay if he believed in Karma.

"Oh, yes, I suppose the idea has been duly indoctrinated in me. It's rational, isn't it? There are always consequences for actions, sometimes merely delayed. I'm not sure what I believe otherwise."

"Do you believe that all the major religions can be compared to the different yoga's?"

Sanjay gave him a quizzical look.

Mark picked up the Bhagavad-Gita. "For instance, Bhakti Yoga, the practice of love for a personal face of God or an incarnate version of Him, an avatar, I suppose it's called. There are a lot of people who worship an incarnate version of God like Krishna, or in general, a prophet, a saint, a bodhisattva, or a Son."

"I guess I never thought of it like that, although I have heard it said that everyone in the world is Hindu, just on a different path in one incarnation or another," said Sanjay with a hint of sarcasm.

Mark noticed that Sanjay had relaxed in the comfort of his intellect. His own mind returned to a previous point in the conversation. "Last year was my first year here, too."

"Do you miss Africa?"

"Sometimes."

"I didn't know you were born there. I assumed you lived here before."

"No, but actually I was born in Germany."

"Weren't you in Montana or something? I thought you came from there."

"My Mom did," Mark said.

"What were you doing there for so long?"

Mark's eyes, which had been on Sanjay's, glanced away, and the latter seemed to mistake it to mean he had crossed an unspoken line. He stirred. "I didn't mean to pry, again," Sanjay retracted, shaking his head.

"It's okay, but just difficult to explain. Ask me anything you want," Mark said.

"Did you notice me last year?" Sanjay asked him next.

"You know I did."

"Yeah." Sanjay smiled and blushed, looked down at his tea and placed the cup back on the floor.

"But I wasn't available then."

"What happened?"

Mark recounted an abridged but intact version of his break up with Jacques. He wanted to be honest but felt stymied and embarrassed at spots, never before having spoken of the events aloud.

"Are you going to call him?" Sanjay asked.

"I don't think so."

"Why not?"

Mark closed his eyes for a moment, then lay on his side on the couch, pulling Sanjay down next to him. The Indian was light, although almost as tall as Mark.

"I don't believe it's the right thing to do. Maybe someday."

"Did you love him?"

Without averting his eyes, Mark said, "Not so well."

The impact of his words was visible on the Indian's face.

"May I kiss you?" Mark asked him. He'd kept his hands off him since he'd pulled him beside him.

"Yes, but I'm a little worried. You just finished telling me you beat the crap out of your last boyfriend."

If the subject didn't hurt him so much, Mark would have laughed at Sanjay's predicament. "I can tell you I won't ever strike you, but I totally understand if you'd rather not take the chance." Mark thought of the Karmic ramifications of his previous behavior while he waited for Sanjay's decision. His companion suddenly leaned forward and kissed him on the lips.

"I believe you, as crazy as that may sound," Sanjay said, his movements easy now.

It had been such a long time since Mark had experienced the novelty of a first kiss that he let the next one seep into him like a spoonful of hot soup. When he re-opened his eyes, he grasped Sanjay's head to get a fuller taste of the Indian's lips and mouth. He could feel the other's erection and wanted to act on it, but he wanted even more to let the less experienced of them set the pace.

"Should we go to your bed, or futon?" Sanjay smiled.

"I thought you wanted to move a bit slower?"

"I changed my mind," Sanjay said and quivered in response to Mark's breath in his ear.

"I'd love to... but," he looked at Sanjay, "I think maybe you should consider this some more."

"Consider what?" Sanjay almost whined. He let his fingers flow to Mark's zipper like a pianist's hand and bit Mark gently on the chin.

Mark groaned with pleasure as he grabbed the mellifluous hand and brought it to his lips with tenderness. "You need to know I'm not fully over Jacques, even though it's been...almost a year now, since I left him."

"But, you said you weren't going to call him."

"And that's true, but I can't guarantee he won't try to contact me. Even then, we'd probably not get back together...but for some reason, I don't see him entirely out of my life, either, and I don't want to mislead you." Mark had noticed himself become more psychically aware of things like premonitions or intuitions. He was still analyzing the signs and symptoms of this greater knowing and when to trust it. Sanjay's eyes filled with water, about to overflow, and he comprehended how much more the encounter had meant to the Indian than he had let on. He felt resolute about not letting this go any further today because the last thing he wanted to do was hurt someone else. He forced himself to stand up.

"Then, why did you invite me here?" Sanjay asked him pointedly.

"I wanted to be with you."

"Which is it, then?"

"It's both. That's why I want you to think about it."

"But…" Sanjay held his head in his hands, his disappointment palpable. "Can't we just, you know, kiss or something."

Mark laughed. "In fact, I don't think we can. Come on," he pulled the Indian up. "The cold'll do you good."

"That's not at all funny," Sanjay said, but Mark was already holding Sanjay's coat out to him. He knew Sanjay would be back even as he closed the door and picked up his mail, absent-mindedly shuffling through it. The lusciousness of the Indian's kiss lingered on his mouth, and he planned to jerk off.

At first he noticed it only because every other envelope owned his address in type. The handwriting was unrecognizable, but the post date revealed it had been sent from Montana. Mark opened the letter only to find a smaller envelope folded in half inside–the letter from Jacques his Mom had forwarded to his grandmother's. He'd asked his grandmother to send him anything he missed, and she had, or she had one of her sidekicks do it. Jacques' letter was postmarked almost immediately after Mark left town, so it was bound to be an emotional one. He hesitated to open it now, after so long. It seemed almost voyeuristic to read about Jacques' pain so late after he'd intended him to. He placed both envelopes in his bookcase and walked away. Then he walked back, picked up Jacques' letter, and opened it.

8 June

Dearest Mark,

I don't know where you went. The last few days have been the most awful of my life, and I don't want to ruin any chance to be together again. But, I can't stay here. I know you think I'm shallow, but I will die here alone. With this in mind, I have agreed to visit John in England. I enclose the address and phone number, so you know where to reach me. I hope you will call me. I know I was never really what you wanted. I am so sorry for this.

Maybe I can be better, but we won't know unless you give me another chance. Please call me as soon as you can. I don't want to beg, but I fear I will, anyway. You have been the center of my life. You have been everything. How can you just be gone now? Please don't stay away from me for long.

I love you with every part of me.

Jacques

PS I send this to your home in Kenya in hope you will receive it swiftly.

He didn't try to control the tears as he read over the words a second time. He didn't want to think himself capable of such harm. His mind somersaulted trying to figure out how it had arrived so many months later. Had his grandmother held on to it? Had she known he would not have been able to ignore it? As much as he knew it was too late, he almost felt compelled to run to Jacques. He had to remind himself that the letter had been written nearly nine months earlier and to call now might jeopardize any healing that took place since. And there was no chance for them, he was nearly certain of that. Why re-open the issue now, especially if led to do so by pity?

FORTY-THREE

Mark and Sanjay were much more compatible than Mark and Jacques had ever been. Still, he feared moving too quickly. A month into their relationship, Sanjay was already discussing "co-habiting," and Mark was attempting to arrest, or at least slow down, Sanjay's passion. He worried a little that he had still not gotten Jacques' letter off his mind, or Jacques. Besides, he recalled feeling pressured into a long-term commitment when Jacques was nearly panicked by leaving his parents' estate. He wanted to stop repeating things he regretted the first time around. Presently, he was sitting in a trendy teashop situated in a basement cafe in Cambridge. The modern decor offset the cave-like feel to the place.

"I've never felt this way before. I know what I want," Sanjay said as he cut the carrot cake he'd ordered in half. "I don't want anyone else, and we need to be safe," he added before he looked up from the plate.

Mark almost laughed, "I'm not saying we should see other people, just that I'm not ready to have you move in. I'm really content with how things are for the moment." Mark hesitated to defend his position, and he didn't want to rehash all the reasons it "made sense" to move in together. He was Sanjay's first lover. They had eased into sexual relations that turned out to be pleasant, even ardent. Sanjay lacked the skill and expertise Jacques had, but he had the same open quality to his heart. "Listen, let's re-open the subject in another month," Mark said.

Sanjay looked ready to argue again but then seemed to respect himself enough to resist pleading. He sulked instead, which Mark found exasperating.

"What about your doctor's appointment?" Mark asked.

"It's tomorrow."

"You want me to go with you?"

"No need."

Mark was sure Sanjay wanted him to go. Sanjay was highly neurotic, if not hypochondriacal. His most recent concern was gastrointestinal, but it was almost always something. Mark was growing accustomed to reassuring Sanjay, but this time he was the one who encouraged his lover to get examined. He believed Sanjay had an ulcer.

"I know you don't need me there, but I asked if you wanted me there." He touched Sanjay's knee under the table, which seemed to reduce the latter's perturbation. Sanjay shrugged just as the waitress walked over and asked if either wanted anything else.

"Just the bill," Sanjay smiled shyly at her before looking Mark's way. "How about we go to my place tonight, for a change?" Sanjay's intonation was too sarcastic; he suddenly looked contrite.

"That's fine. Your place it is," Mark agreed to a still sulking boyfriend.

Sanjay lived with three other international students in an older Medford home, three stories high. It was not so noisy and intrusive as a college dormitory, plus Sanjay had his own room, albeit a bit small with a slanted ceiling. The house contained aromas of Indian cuisine and incense. Mark had only been there a couple of times. He didn't mind the curry scent, but the roommates were strangely distant. Sanjay greeted two of them, who were sprawled out in the living room with the television on, books open on their laps. One looked up long enough to say, "Hey," as Mark and Sanjay climbed the narrow stairs.

"It's more comfortable at your place, I guess," Sanjay said as they entered his tight quarters. "I thought they'd be in class."

Mark sat down on the small bed, "It's fine."

"Want something to drink?"

"No, thanks, I'm full."

Sanjay sat next to him and said, "I guess it makes more sense to be at your place." He sounded apologetic.

"Whichever," Mark said, a little irritated. "Do you want to go there now?"

"No, I'm just disappointed."

Mark lifted Sanjay's face to his and kissed his cheek, then his neck. "Can you forgive me?" he whispered into his lover's ear. He figured they were back on the topic of cohabitation, and, as usual, preferred to be physical.

"I'm in love with you," Sanjay said.

"I know that," Mark said gently.

"You don't feel the same?"

"Yes, I do," Mark enjoined.

"You do?"

"Can't you tell?"

"It's just that you seem so independent."

Mark looked at him confused.

"And, you still have Jacques' picture on your dresser," Sanjay said.

Mark hadn't considered this a problem. He had several photos around, all unframed, of family and friends. Still, he wasn't sure he was ready to make the concession he was being asked. "You're rushing me," Mark said as he leant his head back on the bed.

"Okay, I'm sorry," Sanjay said all of a sudden.

"No reason to be sorry, Sanjay. I'm the one who's sorry. I think I should go think things through." Mark felt completely liberated to walk out of the room. He felt mad, but not really at Sanjay, who just wanted reassurance, but at himself for once again not having clarity about his own intentions. He stood up to go.

"No, come on. It's not serious." Sanjay went to embrace him. "It's me, I'm just neurotic."

Mark chuckled before he grew serious again. "Yes, you are, but you're also right about some things. When I met Jacques, and even after we got together, I wasn't over my previous boyfriend, and that held me back...for far longer than it should have."

"So, you are still not over him?" Sanjay crossed his arms and stared at him.

"I should go see him."

"No!" Sanjay almost shouted, but Mark wasn't surprised by the reaction. "So, I'm like a passing fling?"

"No, of course not," Mark said, this time feeling surprised. "But, Jacques and I were a couple for a long time and went through a lot together. I mistreated him badly, as you know. I need to do something right, even if it's just to have proper closure and apologize for my actions," and as he spoke the words, it did seem clear to him. Mark's eyes beseeched Sanjay's for understanding but found them tearful instead, an unbearable sight, especially because Sanjay looked as if he were trying so hard not to cry. Why did he always make his boyfriends cry? He wrapped his arms around Sanjay's waist and held him.

"If you go to him, it will mean the end of us."

"It doesn't have to be that way," Mark said, not sure what Sanjay meant.

"I know it will. With all your intuition," Sanjay said quietly, not letting go of Mark.

"What?"

"I can't believe you don't know it."

FORTY-FOUR

Jacques threw the news magazine onto the coffee table in his psychotherapist's waiting room. Once again he read the inspirational posters that occupied the wall spaces, and yet again he oscillated between disdain and awe. It was a mere curiosity that he could re-read the same words week after week and still have thoughts about them. Was the mind so repetitive about everything? In general, Manhattan had treated him as it treats everyone: anonymously, busily. His eyes fell on the calendar now, images from the Metropolitan Museum of Art, and he felt slight disbelief that several months had gone by since he moved there. At first, he had kept track of the days like razor cuts on his arm, but New York was easy to adapt to, felt like home because it had the same international feel of his home "town." He thrived on the level of energy available around him.

"Jacques?"

"Hi, Barbara," Jacques tried to sound upbeat on purpose. Her hair was done differently today, but he would not comment on it. He felt chastised when he tried to talk about her. He guessed she was in her forties or fifties, and she had mentioned she had a son about his age once. Otherwise, personal data seemed off limits.

"Sorry I'm a few minutes late today, take a seat," she said.

Jacques sat in his usual spot, the right hand corner of a white fabric couch, abutted by an end table and lamp. The office mimicked a den space, warm with dim lighting. A large round-ended bookcase lined the wall opposite them. Barbara sat perpendicular to him in a leather armchair, small pad and pen in her hands. She asked her usual question:

"What's different and what's the same?"

"Things are the same. Well, I spoke with Lily, John's sister, this morning." More commonly he'd respond with an abysmal nothing, but on occasion he'd applaud himself for small triumphs such as spending money on an elaborate meal without fearing the cost, or enjoying his time at the theater.

"The one who's been distant? You never finished telling me about what happened and why your relationship was strained."

"I didn't? No, I suppose…" He looked out the window. "I told you we made love, and then…"

"You made love? No, you didn't tell me that. That was this past summer, at the cottage?"

"Yes, at John's. He wasn't happy, flipped out about it, and I never found out why. It was all very weird. I don't think it was because he was interested in me. Maybe, I thought, because some men have problems thinking of female relatives having sex at all; maybe he felt betrayed by me in that sense. Anyway, I did not ask her about it. Things finally sounded better in her voice. Why mess it up again?"

"What was that like for you?" Barbara asked him.

"Great. I really missed her, especially with everything going on, all the changes."

"Yes, but I meant the sex. You've never mentioned being with a woman."

"Oh, that, it was terrific. I really liked it."

"You did?" She looked a little stunned.

"Yes, very much."

"So, tell me which you prefer, sex with men or sex with women?"

Jacques realized he was in a cultural warp of sorts, Americans being much more prone to defining sexuality or categorizing it. The truth was the easiest way to answer, "Sex with Mark." He smirked.

"I see. And, if there were no Mark?"

"I really don't know. Men, I suppose, but not definitely. So, I am bisexual, if that's what we are getting at, but you know, these days, I am asexual."

"Elaborate."

"I don't want to be anyone's…I don't want to have sex, get involved. I don't want to worry about AIDS." He shrugged out of impatience, already harassed by his acquaintances at work about this on a regular basis. Barbara said nothing and kept looking at him, which irritated him. "Really, it's not something I am uncomfortable about. I've had enough sex to last me a lifetime."

"Even if Mark were back in the picture?"

He hated when she did that. He spent the rest of the session crying on and off about his sense of isolation. He vowed not to return to therapy. It's not that he felt worse when he left but just that he'd rather not have to analyze everything all the time. He decided to walk the eleven blocks home, walk off the loss of his ex-lover, if only he could. Still believing sometimes that he'd never feel the same way about anyone again, he had to remind himself that he was young and probably wrong in reaching such an unfounded conclusion. He had a lot to be grateful for. He had the theater, and nothing could replace the feeling he had when he was on stage, even the smell of it was unique. He was dancing again and in a reputable production. He had even made new acquaintances, perhaps a couple of friends. He felt more confident than he had before, and his investments had increased in value—thanks to the advice and guidance of his broker and accountant. While others in his production were sharing one-bedroom apartments, sometimes three or four dancers in one, he had his own place, modest but classy. He was grateful to have Lilith back in his life, although he could not say the same about John, who had failed to return his phone calls.

Despite his progress, Jacques spent most of his time alone. He avoided the overtures of men and women alike, but his cautiousness was based less on fear of AIDS than he wanted to admit. It was true that a steady stream of information about the spread of the disease bombarded him daily. With Barbara's encouragement, he had been brave enough to get tested, receiving the news that he was negative. Jacques would never have forgiven himself if he had infected the love of his life, which brought him to the underlying reason he was still single and rarely even masturbated—because it was almost always Mark about whom his mind insisted on concocting its fantasies. Barbara had been right to bring this to consciousness again, as he had buried it the past couple of months, had convinced himself Mark was not in his thoughts as often as he actually was. He reconsidered. Sometimes he did feel better when he saw Barbara; she was, after all, one of the few people he could really talk to.

It was with this in mind that Jacques entered her office a week later. "I think I'm over him," Jacques stated, ready to answer this time when she asked what was different and what was the same. Today's eye-opening news would take some proof.

"Tell me about it," she said.

"The other night I went out with some friends, and it's true it was not the first time, but I didn't think of him disapproving this time. You know that constant, critical voice I hear in my head. Then, the next day I got a phone call, and at first, I thought it was Mark, the voice was almost the same. I reacted only a little."

"What do you mean, you reacted a little?"

"My heartbeat went faster, but not too bad, and when I realized it wasn't him, I did not feel the deep longing and disappointment usually there. I even felt a small relief."

"So, your heart rate didn't accelerate as you expected, and you didn't experience profound feelings," Barbara reflected.

"Right. That's it." Jacques felt awkward for a moment. "It's great." He despised himself when he felt so self-conscious and wondered if he should mention it.

"What about the part of you that isn't so sure you're over him?"

Jacques hesitated, not sure of her train of thought.

"You said, 'I think I'm over him,' which implies you don't know you are."

"Yes, well, it would be hard to believe after so much time."

"How does it feel to make your own plans with your own friends?"

Jacques laughed, "It took me awhile, didn't it?"

Barbara continued to hold his eyes without commenting.

"It feels good. I was thinking that I am twenty now, and I don't want the next twenty years to go by too fast. I don't want to be forty and still stuck feeling not-at-home with myself." Jacques looked down, considered the arduous work he'd put into healing. When would he be done finally? When would he summon the magic to let go of the struggle that had defined his life for so long?

"I don't want to wish my life were someone else's," he added. Although Jacques was clear now that he did not exist to fulfill other people's needs, feeling better about himself was tough. And the lack of completion to his relationship with Mark was unsettling.

"I'd just like for him to see me now," he continued without having to worry she didn't follow where his mind led him.

"To what end? What do you really wish for?"

"It's not that I want him back in my life, but I guess I still care what he thinks."

"You want his approval?"

"I don't know. I suppose so," Jacques leaned over, his head hanging closer to the floor, avoiding her eyes.

"Who else would you like to see approve of you?"

"I don't know. My father?"

"Are you asking me?" she smiled. "Do you want him, Mark, to see what he's missing out on?"

"Maybe. I can't accept that low position any more. I don't want to be....subordinate," he remembered the word from a previous discussion. "I'm worth more than what he ever offered me."

"Jacques, you sound like you're reading a script."

He shuffled his feet. *Merde.* She seemed to be waiting for something. He was pissed at her again. He could feel his blood pulsing, as if the pressure was rising. What did she want from him? He didn't want to cry again–they'd been doing so well, and now at some kind of impasse, he was frustrated and kept his head low.

"What is it, Jacques?"

"Nothing."

"Don't you feel safe here, with me?" She leaned over, closer to his face.

"What do you mean?" He looked up at her, feeling like a child.

"What are you feeling? It's safe to say."

"I don't know. I'm upset."

"Upset is a big word that means a lot of things. I know you've been sad for a long time, but you didn't look sad for a minute. You looked something else."

"What?" His question was genuine.

"Can't you tell me?" She reached over and squeezed his hand.

"I guess." He looked away. "I was a little angry."

"What? Please speak up." She squeezed his hand again.

"Angry, I guess." He shrugged, and she smiled. "Why? Is that good?"

"It's perfect. Anger is a perfectly healthy response to unbearable circumstances." She leaned back in her chair. "You're angry a lot of the time, but you ignore it. Do you agree?"

He nodded, tears welling up against his will.

"Tell me about feeling angry with me."

"It's just that..." He wiped his eyes.

"I know it's uncomfortable for you, but do it anyway," she encouraged.

"What do you want from me? I try so hard, I do my homework, you know, I thought you would be happy that I'm over him, and instead..." Jacques was purposely not looking her in the eye as he spoke. He was afraid of what he might find there, afraid that he might disappoint someone yet again.

"Keep going," she said.

"You criticized me again."

"Did you want to please me, Jacques?"

242

He stared at her, shocked at the insight.

"Is that why you work so hard, and pay me all this money? To please me?"

He was appalled. "So, I've not improved at all?"

"What do you think? Really think about it." She added, when he was about to answer too swiftly.

"Yes, I think I am, but…"

"You are. Period. No but. You are much better. You've had a number of grief and loss issues to work on, and abuse is never easy to process. You've done a truly awe-inspiring job with all this and should feel proud of yourself. There's just so much anger under the surface we need to help you release. But first you need to acknowledge it."

"I have reasons to feel angry." He looked at her for approval.

"You know feelings are not facts, and feelings don't have to be rational, we've been over that."

"Yes," he nodded.

"But, I'll admit, you have some damn good reasons to feel angry." She smiled gently.

His phone was ringing as he entered his apartment. He tripped over the new loveseat he purchased. He needed to move it.

"Hello?"

"Jacques, it's John."

"Mon Dieu, I have been thinking about you. How are you?"

"I'm managing. You?"

"Good, good, I'm glad to hear from you. I've missed you." He considered mentioning Lilith's call but thought better of it. There was silence. "John, are you there?"

"Yes, I'm here."

"Talk to me. It's been too long."

"How about a visit? Can you take a vacation to come over?"

Jacques wondered what had happened. "Not much, I'm afraid, but I could take a few days perhaps. I'd like that very much. Are you all right?"

"Yes."

"You're not still angry? I felt very sorry about things when I left."

"No, I'd prefer to drop the whole thing. I do need to ask you something."

"What?" Jacques was curious.

"Do you want to see Mark again?"

"What? Why?"

"He called me. Wanted to know how to get in touch with you."

Jacques noticed his runaway heartbeat after all. "I don't believe it." He gasped, partly wondering if John were lying. "Did he say why?"

"Not really. He sounded different from what I remember."

"How so?"

"Can't really explain it. What should I tell him? Actually, he's willing to come here if you agree to meet with him. He didn't know you were in New York, and I didn't tell him. I remember now he said something about wanting to chat you up."

"To chat me up? He didn't use those words, did he?"

"Mate, I'm not sure which bloody words he used."

"Was he okay? Did he sound sick, or say anything about that?"

"Not at all. He sounded...good. Actually, he asked the same about you and me. I guess we'll all quite lucky right now."

Jacques wasn't certain how to respond. He was too superstitious to say something about feeling lucky. "I'll make the trip to see you, but I'm not sure I'm ready to see Mark. Let me think about it." He also intended to speak to Barbara about it.

He and John talked for a while after that. John told him that he was "stable," and proud of the work he'd done with Dr. Silver. They spoke about Lilith and her adventures in Russia, both sidestepping any exchange about her romantic life. All during their conversation, though, Jacques had to remind himself to breathe. He was sweating and looked pale when he happened to catch a glimpse of himself in the mirror. What did Mark want, and could he live with never finding out? John and he settled on a date. He couldn't pass up seeing Mark again. What was the point in waiting?

"Tell him we already had plans for the week-end, so you don't think I'd care one way or the other if he happened to be there. What do you think about that?"

"Brilliant. I'll see you then," John said.

FORTY-FIVE

Mark buckled his seatbelt, feeling fortunate. He managed to pull enough cash together for an economy fare flight to London on short notice, even if he had to go "stand-by" and wait at the airport for six hours. Now thinking back to almost three years ago when he first flew to Europe, he could hardly remember when Jacques was not in his life. Although he felt aged compared to that time, he felt a youthful anticipation. His motives were partially clear: he wanted to apologize, to provide resolution. Perhaps he also wanted to prove to himself that he no longer had feelings for Jacques, but then why did he feel almost excited? He couldn't concentrate on his reading.

John had arranged a car for him at Heathrow, but Mark's flight had arrived a little early. He suspected Jacques was already at the cottage, although John had been vague, even evasive, about their plans. In the men's restroom, he tied his hair into a ponytail and splashed cold water on his face. He had a backpack over his right shoulder. He spent an hour or so reading biology before the car picked him up, but then was too anxious during the ride to concentrate. He was eager to get past any awkwardness that might arise between Jacques and him, and of course between John and him, as well. The car pulled up a long drive, and John was already on the lawn, walking toward him with his hand outstretched "How was the flight, mate?"

"Not bad." Mark smiled. "You seem well."

"I'm all right, indeed." John's step was more assured as he veered back toward the door. "Come on in. You don't have any other bags?"

"No," said Mark. He surveyed the large abode John had called his family's cottage home. "Nice place."

"Right, I remember your disapproval of anything overstated."

"Not at all," Mark assured him, chuckling.

John showed him to the modest bedroom off the living room, and Mark thanked him in return for his hospitality. "And, thanks, for arranging this...meeting with Jacques."

"It wasn't a problem. Jacques said he didn't mind when I mentioned it the other day."

Mark was dumbfounded at that. It seemed rather casual. "Is he here?"

"No, he's out at the moment. Probably be back by evening."

Mark wondered where Jacques could've gone.

"Do you care to spend time with me?" John asked in an offhanded manner.

"Of course; I assumed we would." Mark studied the Englishman. "Mind if I shower?"

"Not at all, the bathroom's across the hall." He pointed to it, looking brighter. "In the mood for some supper?"

"Definitely. Listen," Mark caught John on his way out. "I'd like to apologize if I ever offended you." John gave him a quizzical look. "I mean, you're very charitable, and despite certain mental handicaps, you've been very kind. I'm sorry I haven't been as good a friend to you as I should have been."

John looked even more befuddled at that. "Cheers, mate," he said and smiled, and Mark was glad he said something.

Mark took a quick shower, and with his hair still wet, walked into the kitchen where John was sitting at a small dinette set. Mark could see a more formal dining room through a door that was left ajar. Before he could say anything, John was up and reaching for his keys. He led Mark to a separate garage to the left of the house. An antique car was partially covered. "What are you doing with this?" Mark asked, curious to know if John had mechanical skills.

"Oh, that. Good God, nothing. It belongs to my father."

"I thought maybe you were working on it. The tarp looks like it was moved off."

"Right, well. No idea. He just stores it here." John shrugged. "This is mine here," and he pointed to a black Jaguar.

"I thought we'd go for fish and chips at a nearby pub." John spoke through the window as he maneuvered his Jaguar out of the tight spot, so Mark could climb in unencumbered.

"I'm really hungry now," Mark said as he got in. They were both quiet on the way to the pub, but it didn't feel awkward as Mark had feared. Instead, it was comforting, and they felt like old friends. He remembered the feeling he got at the train station after their night at Andreas'. The small town came up suddenly, and John pulled into an even smaller lot.

"Right, then. So, mate," John said as they exited the car. He came around and put an arm over Mark's shoulder. "What 'ave you been up to?"

Mark smiled, remembering John had a tendency to switch accents. "Working at the lab, school, studying biology and medical sciences. I'm hooked on research."

"Sounds a bit drab."

"I like it." Mark chuckled again. They sat themselves in a booth.

"What else? Anything new since you and Jacques split up?"

Mark filled John in on parts of the last year, time in Montana, Sanjay. He deleted most of the details.

"Did you like being by yourself for so long?" John asked him.

"I wouldn't say I liked it, but I learned a lot, grew up, let go of some of the anger and hate I was constructing."

"Some?"

Mark smiled at the laconic wit. "What about you? You seem much...better, more balanced. Christ, the last time I saw you, you were in a psychiatric ward, immobile and moot."

"And now look at me," John sounded sarcastic.

"Yes, now look at you. You look great. We're conversing without you talking nonsense."

"Um, thanks, I guess. You have a frightfully interesting way of complimenting me," John said.

"I'm sorry. I did mean it as a compliment."

"Good enough. I'm taking my medication as prescribed, not as I want to, and not doing any drugs. I'm not supposed to drink more than a beer a day. No worry for me, since I was never a dipsomaniac when I wasn't high," he said, "another kind of maniac, perhaps." John revealed the slightest fear around the corners of his eyes as he spoke. "I've grown accustomed to myself, this life, I suppose. Drab. You know, anything can grow comforting in its familiarity. My dysphoria, which basically means my bad mood, should you be uninformed or otherwise too normal to know, has become as worn as an old pair of slippers, just too easy to slip into."

Mark nodded but didn't comment.

"I always felt like I was jumping rather uncontrollably on a tightrope, never had much cause to be careful. Anyway, now," John said, after the waiter brought their non-alcoholic beverages, "I feel a bit bored, truth be told. I've been looking forward to this visit from you and Jacques more than you know. All my old chaps were druggies, so I don't associate with them any more. I live a very solitary, structured life now."

Mark took in the stench of overcooked oil. He finished his last chip, having listened keenly to John's account of his existence. "You're welcome to visit me in Boston if you want to."

"Cheers," John said, looking amused," I know you wouldn't extend an invitation flippantly."

An English punk band played in the background. They all sounded the same to him.

"You fancy this band?" John asked him.

"I guess so. The song's quite cynical, isn't it?"

"Suits me," John said.

Mark looked away. "Will you drop the cynical attitude long enough to help change the things you're cynical about...isn't that the real issue?" He turned back to look at John.

"I'm not sure anything's worth that much to me."

"Well, I wasn't meaning you in particular, just anyone who's cynical. Think about it. When you're not participating or contributing, it's easy to be cynical." Mark emptied his mug.

"Is that supposed to make me feel better or worse, mate?"

"Neither," Mark gave him an apologetic look. "It's an observation that may not even apply to you. I think we need to move forward toward positive change in the world."

"Are you still a communist, then?" The question seemed to come from nowhere.

"You and Jacques *have* been talking," said Mark.

"I ask because I was wondering if you'd ever been to Eastern Europe or the Soviet Union."

"No, but I know the practice falls short of the ideal, if that's what you're getting at."

"Exactly what I'm getting at," John said smoothly, and Mark smiled at the subtle criticism. Indeed, John had been talking with Jacques quite a lot.

"I can only speak for myself," Mark said, "because I know I wanted to change things in the world, the disparity of resources, the motivating force of greed, the imbalance of power...I wanted to do that without confronting those very things within. It's harder to look at myself, but change can't really be done any other way. How can anyone raise the consciousness of others, if they're blind to their own limitations?" He saw that John seemed captivated by him, by his words, and added, "But, I'm still growing in this direction and don't have the answers."

"But you make sense. My life is at odds with yours, it would seem. I can't function without taking my medication, but, in turn, the pills rob me of who I really am. The battle inside me blows up without them, but taking them doesn't create the real balance of forces I'm looking for, just a sort of truce."

"I wouldn't advocate for not taking your medicine," Mark said.

"I know, I know. It's just that I want things resolved. When I'm on them..." he grimaced at Mark's worried expression, "Don't bother so, mate, I'm not going to stop taking the pills," he promised. "I just wish there was another way."

"What do you want to resolve?"

"Phantom memories. Half-understood feelings or convictions I have about myself."

"Such as?"

"I don't want to go into detail about it, but it's just that I know there's something terribly wrong with me. I don't mean sick, but evil, and I have no idea why. It's a ghost of a memory. Anyway, I don't want you to have to rescind your compliment by speaking nonsense again," he smiled crookedly, revealing a propensity in his face to frown more often.

Mark assured him that his opinion didn't change. "Besides, it sounds like you're being haunted by something in your past you don't remember. Maybe you pushed it into a type of oblivion because it was something painful."

"That's what I believe, too," John said.

"Things have a way of expanding in importance when you don't look at them head on." Mark had thought this exact thing of himself, of his feelings for Jacques, of his anger.

"I've considered hypnosis, but I fear whatever it is that may be behind this conviction of mine," John said.

Mark gave him an understanding look, and John tittered, looking a little uncomfortable. "Enough of this serious talk. I'm afraid I'm not used to socializing much. Why don't you drink?"

"I do, sometimes, but I prefer not to touch the white man's poison," Mark said with a straight face.

"Ah, duly noted, as if you didn't pay us back with tobacco," John retorted, quick as ever, and they both laughed.

In the car lot, Mark was startled when John reached for his hand. He looked around to see if anyone was watching.

"Doesn't matter," John said. "No one will hurt me if I'm with you."

"Sure, but how will I fare?" John's assumption that Mark would protect him was perceptive. "Are you coming on to me, or just wanting affection?"

John looked at him in his customary askance manner, "Which would you prefer?"

"The truth."

"I don't feel very sexual, not without being high. But, I haven't been touched in a long time and wouldn't mind some affection. How's that for truth?"

"It's perfect." On many layers, Mark thought. He realized he'd enjoyed the conversation so much he'd forgotten to wonder where Jacques was.

When they reached the house, it was still empty. Mark wanted to provide comfort to John and was almost glad for some time alone. He pulled him to his lap and let him sit there as a child might, encouraging him to take all the affection he needed. It felt good to be with him.

But as Jacques walked in, John jumped with a start and pulled away from Mark. John's behavior made him wonder a little, and he gave the Englishman an inquiring glance before he really looked at Jacques.

"Hey," Mark said. He wasn't sure how to greet Jacques. He thought he'd extend a hand, or hug, or kiss both cheeks if that's what Jacques initiated, but his ex-lover was just staring at him instead.

"Sorry. Wow, you look different," Mark said. He noticed Jacques' very short hair and the suit, but beyond that, he saw the memorable, emerald green eyes now looking back at him with—was it contempt?

Mark finally extended a hand, which Jacques met while maintaining eye contact.

"Nothing happened," said John suddenly.

"It doesn't matter," Jacques said.

"I know, of course, but just so you know." John was facing the floor as he spoke.

The three stood uncomfortably about for a moment, and then John offered drinks.

"You've been drinking already," Mark said to Jacques.

"What does it matter to you?"

Mark took a deep breath and sat down. Parsimonious as ever, he didn't want to say something he judged too obvious.

Jacques sat on the other end of the couch, flipped his shoes off, and rested his feet on the coffee table. Just then John returned with two glasses of wine, which he placed near Jacques' feet.

"I'll be off to bed," he announced. When the sound of his bedroom door closed behind him, Jacques spoke.

"John told me you asked to see me."

"Yes, that's true." Mark nodded.

Jacques turned to face Mark, his back now against the arm of the couch, his feet and legs crossed in front of his torso in a very protective posture. Again he was staring at Mark who started to feel uneasy. He had expected Jacques to be warmer. Jacques had always been comforting and open toward him.

"Is everything going well?" Mark asked him finally.

"That's why you wanted to see me? To ask me how things are going?" Jacques asked.

Mark felt bewildered, not having prepared for this level of hostility.

"Let's see...hmm...yes, everything is going well." Jacques spoke at length and rapidly about his life. He told Mark about his decision to audition for productions in New York, that he was proud to be dancing on stage, and that he enjoyed having money after a year of living in poverty.

"You're happy," Mark said in a neutral tone.

"And you? Now that you're free of me?"

Mark sighed, "I'm okay."

"You must be better than okay now."

"I didn't realize you'd be so incensed."

"Is that what I am?" Jacques took his glass and drank from it. "I felt such elation when my therapist validated my right to feel angry. And in the last few weeks, I have felt almost consumed by it, for once not praying for it to pass and not afraid of it." He placed the glass back on the table and turned back toward his ex-lover a little softer. "Yes, I see a therapist now."

"Want a foot massage?" Mark offered, wanting very much to change the subject. Was Jacques saying he sought help to deal with their break up? After everything else he'd been through?

"Sure, why not?" Jacques extended one leg in Mark's direction.

Mark enveloped Jacques' right foot with both hands, glad to have something physical to do. He slipped the sock off and started to rub and probe. He opened up about some of his experiences since they parted, told him about the hypothermia he suffered. He wasn't sure why he was telling Jacques about how he almost died. Maybe he wanted sympathy from his ex-lover and wanted to know Jacques still cared.

"Ask me," said Mark when he saw a distant, confused look on Jacques' face.

"What?"

"Whatever it is that's almost to your lips." At the thought of Jacques' lips, Mark's mouth watered. The memory of the taste of their combined saliva when they were intimate sent a frisson down his spine.

"I don't know—some strange sense that I knew this somehow," said Jacques.

"I don't see how you could have."

"Right." Jacques closed his eyes and leaned his head back. "Why did you hate me so much, Mark?"

"I didn't hate you. Why would you think that?"

Jacques snapped his head forward and gave Mark a frigid look.

Mark stifled a nervous laugh and said, "I guess one might have reason to believe that, but I see it more as fear, certainly not hate. I was angry I'd fallen in love with you."

"What? Did you? Love me?" Jacques looked incredulous.

"Of course," Mark stated. Jacques had to know that even if he never told him.

"And so…this made you angry?"

"I saw you as spoiled, your former life as ostentatious."

"And now?" Jacques asked.

"Pretty much the same."

"You are the most arrogant son-of-a-bitch I've ever known," said Jacques with a particularly thick accent, obviously inebriated. He pulled his foot from Mark and stood up. "That's all you'll ever see when you look at me," he said.

"No, I see an attractive, confident, and stronger man than I've known before, too."

"So, now I'm attractive?"

"You were always that to me," Mark muttered. The two were silent for a moment. "Not just that, though. In fact, I think quite highly of you and did then, too."

Jacques didn't respond but looked like he might laugh.

"Could we spend some time together? Tomorrow?" Mark asked. He clasped his hands together.

"Why?" Jacques paced on the other side of the coffee table.

"We clearly have unresolved feelings. Can't we help each other get past them?"

"I'll think it over," Jacques said. "Right now I am going to go to sleep. I've had a long day." He picked up his shoes and walked out, leaving Mark more than a little curious about how changed his ex-lover was.

FORTY-SIX

Mark had jetlag but was awake and hanging around Jacques' bedroom by 10:00am the next morning. John assured him Jacques would be asleep for sometime, maybe past noon, and invited him to join him in the kitchen.

"Aren't you tired, mate?" John asked as they walked to the kitchen. "Want some biscuits? I'm afraid I don't have much in the way of breakfast food." He busied himself with plates.

"I wouldn't mind some juice if you have it."

"Doubt it. So, how'd it go?"

"What?" Mark was rubbing his eyes at the table. He felt clumsy around all the fine china.

"Your talk with Jacques."

"Oh, that. Different from what I expected." Mark slopped a little jam onto a biscuit.

"How so?"

"He's so angry with me. Also, he's changed."

"I should say. Looks like a guy for one thing."

"Yeah," Mark chuckled, "more so, anyway. It suits him. See, he was never a drag queen at heart."

"He looks good, doesn't he?"

"Really good."

"Hmm…" John poured honey onto toast. "What about Sanjay?"

"What about him?" Mark asked. "Oh, I should call him. May I use your phone?" Mark wouldn't have asked except that the cost wouldn't mean anything to John.

"Feel free," said John, "I was just wondering if you realize the dreamy look about you when you mention Jacques."

"That's ridiculous," Mark said as he dialed.

"Hey, it's me. It's really early there, but you're probably already at the library studying by now. Um, the trip was fine. I'll call you as soon as I get back. Good luck on your microbiology exam. I'm sure you'll do fine. I'll talk to you soon." Mark hung up. "Answering machine."

"I see. Well, anyway, Jacques and I are attending a chamber music concert this evening. You are welcome to join us." John had a mysterious smile on his face as he spoke.

"Thanks, I will," Mark said.

The two spent the next few hours reading in the study, Mark with the text book he brought, John with the newspaper, then a magazine, then a few chapters of a fictional paperback he picked up. John was amazed at Mark's presumed attention to his one book, and Mark just laughed because he alone knew he had no idea what he was reading. His mind was too taken by Jacques–his different look, his attitude toward him, his anger.

Finally, Jacques walked in, wearing pajama pants and carrying a mug of coffee. His chest and abdomen were a little more developed. He commented to John in French that the coffee was horrible.

"Yeah, a few hours old, it is," John said.

"Not as old as some." Both Jacques and John laughed at that.

"Was a friend–well, not actually a friend–of ours, last summer, who used to keep his coffee for days. Kept reheating it," John explained.

"It was disgusting," Jacques said, laughing again. "He was disgusting."

"Why?" asked Mark.

"Let's say, Willy could satisfy himself as unabashedly as a domestic pet," John said.

Jacques sprayed some of his coffee through his guffaw at John's description. "Excusez-moi," he said as he still laughed. "John, you have a couple of strange acquaintances, n'est-ce pas?"

"Well, had," John said. "Besides that, Willy was a self-proclaimed misanthrope, and Jacques kept taking offense to him."

"I guess I've heard enough," Mark said. John and Jacques appeared to share a level of intimacy he hadn't expected.

John was wiping tears from his eyes from the hysteria. He assumed an aloof appearance and spoke to the air with his head turned to his right, "Sorry. Are you in a testosterone hell?" he said in a falsetto voice, in a mock performance, turning to face the other direction and imaginary speaker now, he responded to himself, "Yes, and if I don't start thrusting soon, I'll lose all capacity for logic."

He and Jacques started laughing anew, but Jacques seemed to curtail his enthusiasm when he saw Mark watching him. "How do you say, you'd have to be there. Willy was very entertaining as well as offensive," Jacques spoke to Mark.

"It's good to see you laugh," Mark told him.

Jacques looked flabbergasted and then quite visibly raised his guard against Mark. "So, you want to make sure your feelings about me are all finished?"

"Maybe he's not sure he's over you," John added in the spirit of Jacques' tone.

"Maybe not," Mark said, good-naturedly watching their faces. He was ready for the hostility this time but saw only shock in their expressions.

Jacques cleared his throat and fidgeted. "So, let's picnic. I'll take a shower while you fix the basket."

"I'll help you," John stood up and walked at a brisk pace through the French doors into the kitchen. "Come on, then!" he yelled over his shoulder.

Mark caught up to him as he was opening cupboards and placing containers on the counter. "I have loads of picnic food." He tore into the refrigerator.

"What the hell does that mean?" Mark asked.

"Olives," he handed the jar to Mark. "Pate, Caviar, vegetable terrine, cucumber salad, hummus, stuffed grape leaves, curried chicken salad, and the selection of fruit on the counter."

Mark's dropped jaw was his only response.

"I also have French bread, cheeses, wine, and, if I'm not mistaken, ah…yes," as he repositioned items, "pastries."

"Jesus."

"Jacques and I usually picnic, so I was prepared. You want all of it?" John asked.

"Um, I don't know. What does he like?"

"Weren't you two living together, for Christ's sake?"

Mark felt shame for an instant, remembered they ate mostly pasta, pizza, Chinese food, and anything cheap. He never ascertained his lover's actual tastes.

John helped Mark decide on choices.

"It's an actual basket," Mark remarked as John pulled out the neatly lined container. They stuffed the items in.

"So, that's it, then, you're set," John smiled as he said.

"Yes, I'm set," Mark stated, wondering how the day would go.

FORTY-SEVEN

Jacques stepped out of the bathtub and vigorously dried himself off. He nearly scoured the skin right off a couple of times, so befuddled he felt. All night he tried to rid himself of Mark—again. How can one person have so much control over him? He needed to stay sharp, to guard himself from falling for him all over again. He was barely recovered from the last heartbreak. He should never have agreed to this preposterous outing. He should have said he was busy with some old friends in London, or made up any number of things.

Jacques dressed in quick but meticulous motion. He wore casual slacks and a white v-neck t-shirt. He balled the shirt up in his fists a bit to rumple it up. He shouldn't look like he cared too much how he looked. Then he felt foolish all over again. He was afraid to release his anger. If he let go of that, God only knew what might happen this weekend.

He walked into the kitchen and grabbed the keys to the Jaguar.

"Let's go, I'll drive," he announced in French, and Mark grabbed the basket. Jacques tried not to check Mark out but saw he was wearing his usual—jeans and t-shirt. He had noticed Mark's skin had gradually lightened since he'd left Kenya, but it had been even more apparent when he saw him yesterday.

As they were pulling out, John ran up to the car with a large tablecloth for the ground to double as a blanket.

"He's quite solicitous, isn't he?" Mark said.

"He's been a good friend to me." Jacques drove with ease on the left side of the road, hoping Mark would be impressed. He had learned to drive for the first time the summer he spent with John.

"Jacques, I want to apologize to you."

Jacques felt eager to hear what Mark might say, but all he did was smirk.

"I'm sorry for so many things, I'm not sure where to start. Of course, I'm still sorry for assaulting you, but...I regret other things, too." Mark's face was turned toward sheep safely grazing on the side of the road, and Jacques thought it must be hard for him to apologize like this.

"The way I always treated your opinions and preferences as if you weren't entitled to them. For bullying you. How could I ever make amends for these things?"

"You want to relieve your guilty feelings?" Jacques felt unable to manage his confrontational tone. He veered off the main drive onto an unpaved road.

"It's beautiful here," Mark's eyes rolled over the landscape.

"Yes, John and I used to come here often. We used to picnic here, when I was living at the cottage with him."

"What else did you two do?" Mark asked as they stepped out of the car. Jacques led him to a knoll overlooking a valley.

"Just stuff," he said and smiled at Mark's pleased expression at the location.

"Like what?"

"We made dinner, we watched the telly, we ate at a local pub and met some mates there from London, as John calls them, sort of supervised visits, I guess. John's been very dedicated to staying off drugs. He had his regular appointments with his doctor. Just stuff."

He laid the spread out on the tablecloth. "Lilith visited us. We got closer, but then...alors, shortly after that, I moved to New York City."

"What do you mean, you got closer?"

"We slept together," Jacques stated in a matter of fact tone.

Mark spit out the bottled water he'd just gulped.

"Oui. John reacted even more poorly than that," Jacques said, and he couldn't help but laugh. "I never did get any explanation. Maybe he was jealous, but I doubt it. He never gave me any sign he wanted to be more than friends. I think he hasn't come to terms with his own heterosexuality," he joked.

"Was he getting high then?"

Jacques turned back toward Mark. "No, as I said. Why?"

"Just curious." Mark shrugged.

"Anyway, we didn't talk for a while after that."

"How was it?" Mark asked.

"How was what?" Jacques slipped just then as he was slicing a pear and cut into his right middle finger, "Merde!"

"Are you okay?" Mark grabbed a napkin and pressed it against the slight wound. "Hold it up a little."

"You are not afraid to touch my blood?"

"No. Should I be?" asked Mark.

"I tested negative, miraculously."

Mark nodded. "I figured that, but it's good to know."

"Did you get tested?"

"No."

"No? Why not?"

Mark looked at him and smiled. "I don't know. I figured you would, and if you were positive, you would let me know."

"It's bleeding a lot. Maybe I need a..." but he didn't recall the English word, a rare occurrence at this point.

"A stitch? No, I don't think so. Fingers tend to bleed a lot. It may scar, though."

Jacques' eyes fell on Mark's countenance only several inches away, but he tore them away quickly when Mark met his look. "You think of being a doctor?"

"I'm more interested in research," Mark said.

"Medical doctors do research, don't they?" Jacques asked.

"I never thought of myself as good with people."

"You never *were*."

"And now? You're enjoying my bedside manner?" Mark asked, grinning.

Jacques blushed and hated himself for it. "I can do it," he said as he took his hand and the napkin away from Mark.

"So?"

"Oui?"

"Sex with Lilith? How was it, if you don't mind my asking? You know, I've never been with a woman."

"I liked it a lot." Jacques smiled at him. "But it hasn't changed me entirely if that's what you mean."

They were silent for some time after that, just part of the landscape. Then Jacques shoved an assortment of food aside and lay down.

Mark remained propped up by both arms, legs outstretched, and stated suddenly, "It's not just that I want to relieve my conscience. I'm genuinely remorseful.

I don't feel I can move on, I guess, without making it up to you. Unless you don't want me to, of course, in which case, I'll respect your wishes. For once."

Jacques had closed his eyes and fought back tears fiercely. "In what way?"

Mark rolled onto his side to face Jacques. "You tell me."

Keeping his eyes closed, Jacques asked, "What can you do? Go backward in time, undo the damage?"

"What bothers me most of all is to hear bitterness from you. It was never your nature, despite everything that happened…things that would have thrown people over the edge long ago. I hate to think my…behavior…may have been what did it."

"Don't credit yourself that much."

Mark closed his eyes and lay back. "You were always so open and loving regardless of the things in your past. You gave me so much. I hope you understand that there was nothing inadequate about you. It was me, my incapacity to love well. You have so much to offer, and I hope you'll be happy." Mark sounded rehearsed but sincere at the same time.

"I used to think it was my fault, that I provoked your anger." Jacques opened his eyes and watched the birds overhead. "I tried to change, but I could never please you."

"It was my fault, Jacques. It became easy to go off. It was a bad habit. It even seemed justified until…that night I brought you to the hospital. Something shifted then, but I was still unable to love you the way you did me. I'm sorry I failed you."

Jacques tried not to react emotionally about what he perceived to be yet another reminder of Mark's rejection. "I envied you your power," he said instead.

Mark chuckled. "I kept giving my power away, kept losing control. That's not powerful."

"I always thought of you as powerful." Jacques looked at him, but Mark avoided his probing eyes.

"On the surface, maybe. Acting out of control is never truly powerful, is it?"

"I don't know." Jacques tried to abate his own confusion, conscious his brow might furrow.

Mark smiled, "What I'm trying to say is that I admire how strong you were, still are. Would you ever be able to forgive me?" Mark's speech was soft and far from hollow.

"Why does it matter?" Jacques felt angry again. The last thing he could abide was Mark being nice to him. Not now. Not this late. And not just because he was remorseful. Damn it, he still wanted Mark to want him.

"It just does," Mark answered.

"I forgive you for...for so much. I'm just angry about how you left me. You were a coward."

"Yes!" Mark turned away with an abruptness that made Jacques sad. "Exactly, I was."

A few minutes went in quiet. Finally, Mark said, "I wanted to patch things up. I missed you. I know you don't believe me, but I did. At the same time, I knew you were better off without me. No one would argue that, right?"

"Right," Jacques whispered. He stood up and stretched.

"Are you–I mean, do you have a guy now? In your life?"

"No, not interested, really."

"You mean you went straight? Or, just, what, celibate?"

"Not exactly. I have wondered this myself, why I haven't gotten involved with anyone. Aside from the obvious," he glanced at Mark and decided to explain, "You know, my ex was a monster, and I'm nervous to try again." He grinned but stopped when he noted Mark's look of dismay, and then continued, "It comes to this. When I meet men, available men in New York or wherever, I have no desire for them. Why step in a puddle when I used to swim in the ocean?"

Mark appeared thoroughly perplexed, and Jacques smiled at him. He had nothing to lose now by being entirely honest. He had already lost.

"You will always be the ocean to me, Mark. Or, more correct, my love for you was the ocean. I can't just settle for a puddle now, and most people don't seem deep enough to hold me." He started to yank the blanket out from under his former lover. "You're ready to go?"

Mark looked suspended in thought.

"We have that concert tonight. I'd like to..."

"What?" asked Mark, standing now.

"Nothing. Nothing important. I just can't believe I'm standing here having this conversation with you. You have no idea how devastated I was. It felt worse than being attacked by those men. Worse than anything."

Mark took the cloth and finished folding it for him. "I'm sorry. I'm really sorry," he said, not exactly to Jacques.

"Well, we all have our demons, n'est-ce pas?"

"Yeah. Our angels, too," Mark said with a gentleness Jacques wasn't used to hearing.

FORTY-EIGHT

Mark felt underdressed as he walked out of his guest room. He hadn't packed anything suitable for a chamber music concert in London. He was sure John would deride him, but instead his host walked over looking ill.

"What's wrong?"

"I feel sick in my stomach."

"Eat something rancid?" Mark asked, concerned.

"Dunno." John held his hands over his abdomen and was bent over a little.

Mark laid his palm on his forehead, "You feel warm."

"I think I'll pass tonight," John said as Jacques was within earshot. "Do you two mind going without me?"

Mark would've believed John was faking illness if he hadn't just felt his forehead himself. The three stood uneasily in the corridor.

"Do you want us to stay with you?" Jacques asked him in French, but John declined, indicating he'd like to just go to bed.

"I hope I'm dressed well enough," said Mark as the two walked toward the car.

Jacques commented neither way, and Mark felt embarrassed about his jeans.

"Do you mind if I drive to an underground station and park there? I don't want to drive all the way into town," Jacques said a minute later.

"No, not at all." Mark closed the passenger door with a thump. "Do you know which composers are being played?"

"No...do you prefer not to go?"

262

"No, that's not what I meant," Mark said and felt shocked once again at Jacques' level of opposition. "I was just curious."

For a while, they sat in silence. Mark took a moment to enjoy the tour of English suburbia. He stole a surreptitious look at Jacques whenever he could, and his heart beat a little faster when he did.

"We'll take the Underground from here," Jacques announced as he pulled the emergency break on a slope.

Descending the stairs, Mark turned Jacques toward him, his hand daring to hold his former boyfriend's waist. "Why can't we look at each other?" He stopped climbing down.

Jacques' eyes drifted to Mark's lips and then down the stairwell. "It hurts too much. Please move away from me," he said in the smallest of voices.

Mark followed him down, a step behind. His eyes roamed the length of the tracks, and he could hear the roar of an approaching train.

"Good timing," Jacques said, and Mark was fascinated by the frivolous mood. His eyes watched Jacques from behind as they climbed in.

The swiftness of the start made him lose his footing for a moment. Jacques had already found two seats ahead. He had forgotten how strangers admired Jacques everywhere, not any less so now that his hair was short.

They reached the concert hall just as curtain time approached, not having judged properly the many stops the underground would make along the way. They ushered themselves to seats side by side, the darkness starting to envelop them.

Mark felt grateful for the diversion the music provided, though his mind continued to regurgitate their previous conversations, the sight of the countryside, Jacques' finger bleeding. He heard the violin chase the viola, moving faster and faster. He didn't recognize the piece and had forgotten to grab a program in the rush. His thoughts moved along just as quickly, the violin, then the viola. No matter how he chewed on them or swished them around his palate, he couldn't find anything but the sour taste of Jacques' words from the past couple of days. He and his fucked up version of love had moved the Frenchman, who had always been committed to him, whose feeling for Mark was, in his own words, as deep as the ocean, from sweet to sour.

Applause ruptured his musings. The violin had been caught in the end, and the ensemble began a new piece. This time, the sound of the bassoon drifted in the air like a prank, the ever-rising notes resonating whimsy, mocking his own, more somber mood. He saw Jacques' profile; he too appeared bemused by the music.

Jacques had been quick enough to grab a program, but he held it in his hand opposite Mark. He must have mistaken Mark's touch at first, the back of a hand on the back of a hand. It sent goose bumps like dominoes down Mark's legs, and Jacques moved away.

"Can you pass me the program?" Mark whispered near Jacques' ear, hoping it explained the touch that sent shivers everywhere. He loitered in the vicinity of Jacques' ear a little too long. He took in the Frenchman's scent, made it a part of him as it had once been.

He moved away only when Jacques pushed the paper into his hand. It was too dark to read, of course, and Mark gave up after a slight strain. The bassoon taunted again, and Mark reached into his jacket for a pen but had forgotten to bring one. For what would he have needed it? Again, his skin touched Jacques', this time he let the back of his fingers find the spaces between Jacques': a crook here, a knuckle there. In a flash of silence from the ensemble, he thought he could hear the beating of a heart.

"Do you have a pen?" he whispered when the music restarted. Jacques used the hand Mark had fondled to grab one from his jacket's inside pocket and nearly flicked it at him.

Armed with paper and pen, Mark started to write. He wrote, *I'm sorry* in the margins several times. Then he wrote, *I can't find the words that carry enough weight. Instead, they disappear into the paper, like invisible ink. Could the paper itself give birth to our words, as if they're already there, waiting for our hand to write them? If so, I wish I could find them and change the course of things gone by. I wish we could make a non-linear equation of this world.*

He thought to push it into Jacques' hand, force him to find it sometime by serendipity, force him to see something other than loss. But, he was done with force. He slipped the program into his own pocket and leaned as far back as he could in order to watch Jacques as inconspicuously as possible.

Mark excused himself to use the restroom when the concert ended. He left Jacques in the lobby, and splashed cold water on his face, watched it run off his hands over the sink. Let it stand in for his tears. He couldn't figure out what it was that he wanted from Jacques. He no longer trusted himself.

He relieved himself and walked out, seeing Jacques over by a woman and two men. When he saw they were conversing, he felt disinclined to intrude. Jacques turned abruptly, "Ah, there you are. I am being accused of having an imaginary friend." The four laughed.

He introduced them in French then: the woman he knew from the stage in New York, her husband, and a friend of theirs. Mark smiled and shook the woman's husband's hand. The other man seemed effeminate and appeared to turn his nose up a bit as he asked Mark how he met Jacques. His command of French tentative, Mark responded in English.

"We met about two and a half years ago, in Paris."

Jacques asked the others to excuse Mark's aversion to the French language, and Mark seemed to lose popularity points. Jacques went on to tell them that Mark had been his boyfriend but that they were barely friends now, or something like that from what Mark discerned. The three seemed to appraise him unabashedly, and then they all kissed Jacques good-bye with a flair of showiness.

"Why are you so rude?" Jacques accused Mark as soon as they walked out of the theater.

"How was I rude?" he asked.

"Never mind." Jacques walked ahead, but Mark grabbed him by the crook of his arm, accidentally snapping him back a little.

"Let go of me!"

"Sorry." Mark was exasperated. They stared at one another until Jacques looked away at a couple passing them. They had been a "couple" once, but that was a long time ago. He needed to remember that. "I didn't mean to be rude. Please help me to understand."

"By insisting on speaking in English, even though you knew we were conversing in French."

"You said you met them in New York, so I figured they'd understand me. I haven't spoken French in years," he said, feeling defensive.

"Exactement!"

"What?"

"You were living with me and never practiced your French. If you remember, I was practically not permitted to speak my own language!" Jacques was yelling, and passersby were staring. It started to rain.

Mark recalled that Jacques had spoken in English to his friends when Mark had first approached them, but the point was moot now because Jacques had moved to deeper ground.

"You're right. J'avais tort. Je suis désolé," he offered.

"From now on we speak in French," Jacques stated.

"Bon," Mark complied, his heart pounding in his chest. Christ, he wanted him again. What was he going to do with this now? They walked in the rain apart from one another, Mark's conflicting thoughts accompanying their silence.

FORTY-NINE

Mark felt both anticipation and dread when he woke the next morning. Jacques was quiet the rest of the way home the night before, even when Mark had tried to make light conversation about people and places in Boston. He had never had to work this hard around Jacques, had never felt so inadequate in his presence. He strategized to regain Jacques' admiration, then questioned his own motives. He dreamt about Jacques and himself all night, them as a couple, them as enemies, them as co-conspirators in the drama of their lives. Now that there was this enormous space between Jacques and him, he found himself wanting to cross it more than ever.

John was already up and sitting at the kitchen table when Mark walked in. "How do you feel?" Mark asked him as he poured himself a cup of coffee. The usual makeshift breakfast spread had a few new additions.

"Much better, thanks. How was the concert?" John asked, fanning the newspaper in front of him.

"Confusing."

"How so?"

"I can't figure out what's going on between us. Sometimes, he seems so different, I'm enthralled, and other times, it feels just like the past. Our interaction fits its own, mutually destructive pattern," Mark stated as he dug into a cereal box John had picked up yesterday. "He's going to speak to me in French from now on, or so he announced last night. I don't understand why the language thing is such a big deal."

John gave him the side-glance Mark remembered too well. "Oh, don't you now? You're the one who's made it a big deal." John walked over to get more coffee. "Course, the French have always been hung up about that."

Jacques walked in, and Mark wondered if he'd heard the conversation. The Frenchman was dressed in an exquisite, very expensive looking suit with shirt and tie. Mark was wearing boxer shorts and a ribbed t-shirt Jacques had bought him in Boston. The sense of being ill fitted to the moment seized him again while his mind concocted a legitimate way to impede Jacques' departure.

"I suppose I should wish you a good journey back to the States," Jacques said in a sudden burst.

"I'm not leaving till tomorrow morning," Mark rejoined.

"Oh." Jacques shot a look toward John that Mark couldn't decipher. Instead he decided to ask Jacques in French where he was going, and a grin flashed across Jacques' face for an instant. He looked as good or better than Mark ever remembered him. The business clothes generated an air of confidence around him.

"I have a business meeting," Jacques said in French.

"You're meeting with your broker?" John asked.

"Oui. Quest-ce que vous faites?" Jacques asked them.

"No idea, um, a film?" Mark's French was stilted and at times poorly pronounced, but Jacques looked as satisfied as if Mark were groveling. How simple it would have been to please him.

"Let's do," John said, as he pulled the entertainment section from the paper. "The three of us—you'll be done by then, Jacques?"

Mark studied Jacques to see if the suggestion pleased him.

"That's fine with me," Jacques said as he glanced at his watch. A taxi pulled up front.

"Meet us at half past at the theater," John yelled as Jacques walked out.

"But, how does he know when and where?" Mark asked him, actually worried.

"It's our favorite theater, it's old and lovely, pre-World War II. There's a cafe next door, so we usually pick up something whenever we have to wait."

Mark was getting tired—or was it jealous—of the "we this" and "we that."

"The films either start at 1:50 or 2:05, and there are usually two selections. See, all very routine." John said as he slid his finger across the paper and showed Mark the selection. "Looks like an American movie and a French one."

Mark shrugged. He couldn't care any less what they saw.

"Don't try so hard," said John.

"What?"

"With Jacques, just be yourself, or the new, improved version, anyway."

"I need some quiet time, I need to settle myself. Could you tell me where the theater is, and I'll meet you?"

"Sure. Want a map?" John asked.

"That's perfect. Thanks," Mark exhaled.

He hurried to shower and dress while spectral feelings continued to haunt him. Although he missed Sanjay when he thought of him, he rarely thought of him. Wasn't that how it always was with Jacques? His balance started to sway under the burden of his insights.

At the end of the dirt path bordering John's cottage was a small wooded area in which he could immerse himself in meditation with little concern of being watched. He found a large oak tree to lean on and tried to move into an elevated state of consciousness. Although his practice was mind-altering at times, more often than not, it simply evoked the still, small voice within, the one so often drowned out by the noise of modern life, the one obscured most of the time by the mind's inexorable ranting. Finding that voice was miracle enough, but the most profound experiences came in the form of bliss and were rare. Buffalo had referred to these as "the pearl of sitting."

He hadn't felt this out of sorts in a long time. His first priority was to create harmony with Jacques. It took a lengthy thirty minutes, but he received the guidance he sought. He saw what it meant to open his heart when it threatened to close, how it would look to expand and trust when his tendency was to close down or feel angry. If he could face being vulnerable, his words and actions would flow from an internal state of love instead of fear. His rational mind told him that risk was inevitable.

He next called for clarity of purpose in regard to Jacques because fleeing was no longer an option. Entering the void that followed brought a deluge of divine love to every cell. A transcendent opening tore through him, and he arrived at the other side deeply in love with his life, his very breath. Although he'd met this experience before, it had never been quite so encompassing. The joy overcame him and caused him to tear up.

And he understood the full scope of his love for Jacques now. The feeling was internal—not a result of the Frenchman—because such a state could never truly result from anything outside the self. Yet, it provided a doorway to Jacques nonetheless, one he'd been searching for since the day they met. Mark sat stunned by the enormous desire to love Jacques and by having now the freedom to do so.

He walked about a mile toward the theater, the sense of loss at each decreased notch in vibration mitigated by the excitement at seeing Jacques with his new eyes. The rail stop was easy to find, and Mark enjoyed caressing everyone and everything near him with the tentacles of ecstasy that emanated from his soul.

FIFTY

John waited on the bench by the marquee. He hadn't been out to the movies since Jacques lived with him. A faint contentment grew as he watched the cars go by and waited for his two companions. It was unusual for him to be in the company of others. The feeling of happiness was transient, replaced by the knowledge that they would both be gone very soon. He would return to his aloneness, not his aloneness as a concept, as in an existential sense of never being able to share the same space with someone, but the actual being-alone-all-the-time in which he lived. If he ruminated too much on it, he became moody and difficult to please. If his temperament became obvious to others, his doctor would raise his dose of medication, which would then lead to not thinking about it for a time, and so forth. The secret was to be able to contemplate his seeming lack of meaning without allowing it to move him in any way, which he hadn't yet mastered.

Just then he eyed Mark a bit off in the distance, keeping a swift pace. He found no reason not to outright stare at Mark's approach, for he had no reason to give pretense he was above waiting. There was an almost-radiant aura around Mark. He had always been sensitive to energetic changes in ways mysterious and sometimes scary.

"Hey—what's got into you? You're beaming," he said as Mark came close enough to engage.

"Yes, I am. Pearl day." Mark smiled.

"What's that? You all right?"

"Better than that. Are you?" Mark asked him.

"I suppose." Sadness had crept in while he thought about being alone, but there was no reason to point it out.

"Jacques here yet?" Mark asked.

"No. It's only quarter past, though." John lit a cigarette and motioned toward the cafe with a question on his face.

"No, thanks, I'm set. Unless you want to go in," Mark said.

"Nah." He hesitated. Mark appeared completely different in the short span of time. "Well, what's going on?"

"I want him back."

"You're joking, you are." John felt his eyes dilate a little, if that was possible.

"Not at all," Mark said as he smiled mischievously.

"And, I'm the bloody crazy one 'round 'ere?"

"You think that's crazy?" Mark said as he laughed.

"You think he should even entertain the idea? After how you treated him?" John shut an eye to close out the glare of the sun as he looked at Mark.

"I thought you'd be pleased. The way you've been pushing us together."

"I did no such thing."

"Then you're more duplicitous than I imagined," Mark said as he laughed again.

"Cheers, mate. Anyway, why tell me? I could tell him, and you'd be exposed. My loyalties lie more with him than with you." John noticed Mark seemed pleased with his candidness, which John wasn't used to. People usually hated him for being so incisive.

"I am strong enough, finally, to be so exposed. Even if Jacques rejects me, I've managed to move beyond mind." He smiled. "I'll be fine either way, but I want him back."

John felt momentarily speechless. He took a couple of drags from his cigarette and asked, "Shall I tell him then?"

"If you wish. It seems irrelevant since I'm going to tell him myself," Mark said.

"You are? Just like that?"

"Of course. Why not?"

John had the feeling that they were having two separate conversations.

Just then, a taxi pulled up, and John and Mark watched as Jacques paid the fare. His jacket was over his shoulder, his tie loosened, so that the top buttons could be undone. He sauntered over, smiling at John.

"How'd it go, then?" John asked him.

"In the end, good."

John was anxious for details but felt it was not his business to ask. Jacques would tell him about his finances if he wanted.

"You look gorgeous," Mark told Jacques, whose eyes darted away.

"Merci." The Frenchman blushed.

"No, I thank you," Mark said in French before reverting to his more comfortable tongue. "I thank you for once again being so kind as to indulge me by letting me spend time with you, so I could make sure I'm over you, no less." He looked away for a second. "You're as generous as ever. The truth is I'm not over you." He laughed aloud as John and Jacques exchanged an incredulous glance. "Not by a long shot! I don't even want to be over you."

Jacques' jaw had dropped.

"You don't need to comment. You owe me nothing. I'm just thrilled to be here right now," Mark said. "Let's go watch the film. I didn't mean for you to feel uncomfortable," he added.

"What about me?" John asked. "Does my discomfort mean anything?" He was a little offended when his friends laughed at that because, once again, he hadn't meant to be funny.

John had already purchased the three tickets beforehand. He wanted to be remembered as a good host, hoping they would return. He saw Mark stop Jacques on the way in and overheard him ask the Frenchman to dinner.

Jacques smirked. "You can't afford my choice in restaurant," he said.

John turned to pass in his ticket. He wished he could give Mark the money without offending him. In a way, he felt like a child watching his separated parents try to patch things up, which might have accounted for his sudden sense of peace and security. Everything was going to be okay.

Mark stopped Jacques again. "I have a credit card. I can charge it."

John was too close behind them to pretend he hadn't heard, so he weighed his options and decided to get involved. "Bloody hell, did he just say charge it? Sounds like an offer you can't refuse, Jacques."

———

That evening Mark enhanced his wardrobe by borrowing a blazer from John. He was trying on shirts, too, looking for one that wouldn't look so tight, as his physique was broader and more muscular than John's.

Mark grimaced at the pink pinstripe on beige background, "Keep looking."

John announced he would go in search of clothing his father may have stored at the cottage. Mark felt utterly mystified by his situation. Lifting a tiny teakettle made of porcelain from the dresser, he wondered why anyone would acquire such a thing.

"Jackpot!" said John. Mark almost dropped the trinket. "Try this suit on."

"What?"

"This suit. My father's. I'll bet it almost fits, although you may need a belt."

Mark grabbed it from John summarily and put it on. The slacks were a little loose, as John predicted.

"You could keep the jacket buttoned. It'd be hardly noticeable. Of course you'll have to give this shirt a try despite hating it. I'll fetch the tie that goes with it."

"There's a tie that matches this?"

"Indeed," John answered through the doorway. He was back in no time, handing Mark a rose-colored tie just the right color of the stripes.

As Mark was starting to feel disheartened, Jacques walked in and whistled with a teasing grin. "You look nice."

"Well, the shirt's ugly, and the pants are too big." It was incredible how sophisticated Jacques looked in comparison in his black slacks and suede jacket.

"Nonsense," John muttered, cut off by Jacques' laughing.

"Not at all. I don't think I've ever seen you dressed. The pink suits you," Jacques said with a smile.

"I guess we'll take a cab," Mark said as they walked toward the door. "I don't even know if this is the wrong side of the road for you or not."

"The wrong side?" Jacques laughed, and Mark joined him.

"You know what I mean."

"Oui, je sais. I will drive. Did you choose the restaurant?"

Mark glanced at John as he opened the back door. He'd forgotten to ask about restaurants. "Yes, he's taking you to *Chez Nous*," John declared. "You won't have to drive into town and it's French, and you have a reservation."

Jacques seemed pleased, and Mark thanked John in a whisper as he kissed him on the cheek, the uncustomary attention turning John a light crimson.

"Do you want me to drive?" Mark opened the driver's side door.

"No, I can do it," Jacques said with a tone of exasperation.

"Sorry. I just thought I've never taken you out on a proper date." He climbed in the other side and noted Jacques made no comment. After pulling out, Jacques asked about Sanjay instead.

"What about him?"

"I'm curious what you would say to him if I agreed to take you back," Jacques said.

"I would tell him the truth."

"Don't you care not to hurt him?"

"Yes," Mark said, feeling sad about the unpreventable because he would tell Sanjay how he felt regardless of the outcome here.

They were silent until Jacques pulled into the lot of a small house, aglow with little white lights as piercing as the stars. "Too romantic for you?"

"No, not at all," Mark said. Jacques' words were prickly so far, and Mark wondered if he'd be confrontational the whole evening.

"Do you want me to pay the bill?" Jacques asked him.

"No, I'm taking you out, remember?"

"Yes, you said."

Mark grabbed Jacques' hand as they walked toward the entrance. He tried to slow the Frenchman's brisk pace to take a look around. He lifted Jacques' hand to his lips and kissed it and then pulled him under the cover of a tree, Jacques' face alarmed with uncertainty.

"May I kiss you?" he asked him.

Jacques jerked away in response and shook his head.

"Won't a kiss help you decide?'

"No," Jacques said.

"No?"

"Non. Je ne sais pas."

Mark wanted to slip his arm around Jacques' waist and hold him but feared Jacques would find it too aggressive.

"Okay, let's go eat," Mark tried to sound light. "Have you been here?"

"Oui—food is prepared well," Jacques said, quickly turning back toward the entrance.

"When you came to Kenya, did I ever tell you about honey guides?"

"What? No. And, you never took me to Mombasa or to the Mt Kenya Safari Club. I still have the brochure. I kept it all this time."

Too many unresolved resentments to calculate, Mark thought. "Well, I apologize for that. Maybe next time." Jacques seemed to roll his eyes. "Anyway," Mark continued, "in Kenya, there are birds that align with badgers in the wild, or sometimes even with people, to help them find honey. It's all very symbiotic in the end, of course."

The *maitre-de* showed them to a small round table in a corner.

"Mark, what the hell are you talking about?"

"I don't know," he said, laughing. "I guess I was thinking you're like a honey guide to me, showing me the sweetness of life."

Jacques gave him a somewhat grave look, but then asked, "You miss home?"

"Yes, very much," Mark said.

"Why don't you go visit your family? How is everyone?"

"The flights are too expensive. They're well. Thanks for asking. Papap asked if I'd heard from you. I never told them what happened, what I did." It took a moment before Jacques seemed to catch on that he meant the abuse. "I was too ashamed to tell them. Anyway, we're forgetting to speak in French," Mark said.

"I know. It's not easy to break habits, n'est-ce pas? I will pay for you to go, if you want." When Mark started to decline, Jacques cut him off, "I would really like to do that for you."

Mark nodded. "Thanks." He refrained from arguing because it was clear that Jacques needed to know that he could accept his money, and thereby, his position in life. He looked over at the Frenchman and noticed for the first time a shiny little bauble on his ear.

"What's this?" Mark asked. He outlined Jacques' left earlobe with his finger. A diamond studded earring glistened. Touching Jacques' ear sent an electric impulse directly to Mark's groin, and Jacques smiled, looking a little less in control than a moment before.

The waiter came by and filled their glasses while Jacques ordered in French for the both of them. Mark trusted Jacques' choices, as Jacques had always paid attention to the types of details Mark tended to ignore.

"What?" Jacques asked as his attention returned to Mark.

"It's just...it's just that you're so beautiful. I'm sorry if I didn't tell you that enough. I did think it often."

Jacques' expression changed. It was Mark's turn to ask, "What?"

Jacques shrugged. "Is it just that you want me? For sex?"

Disappointment surged through Mark for a moment. "Why would you say that?"

"With my history?"

Mark lowered his eyes. "Then lets make a toast. To new life and new memories." He raised his glass, and they drank. "I wasted so much time being despicable toward you when we could've been so happy. I wish I could take it all back." It was useless to foster so much regret, but he felt unable to stop himself.

———

The waiter brought a few selections to the table. "Try the *escargot*," Jacques suggested. "You like it?" he smiled as Mark popped and chewed.

"Kind of. It's not as salty as I expected. Why haven't you made me try it before?"

"I could never make you do anything." He glimpsed Mark's saddened expression. "I'm sorry, I know I sound very angry," he said. They ate in silence for a while, Mark then commenting on the other appetizers. Jacques was still astounded by the unfamiliarity of the experience and his own regrets. As difficult as things had been with Mark, he was, after all, a changed man because of him. Had he stayed in Paris, he might be dead already from AIDS, or at least addicted to drugs. What else would he have done to soothe himself? It had already become an issue the year they met, although he'd never told Mark about the tranquilizers, or the cocaine back stage that grew more and more appealing. He was looking at Mark pointedly without realizing it.

"Maybe we'll never overcome our past." Mark smirked. "But, I'd like to."

"Let's talk about something else," Jacques said.

"Like what?"

"Tell me about Sanjay." His curiosity was too high to resist.

"Why?"

"I want to know."

"He's someone I know from the lab. I've known him since last year. He's Indian, has golden brown skin, dark hair and eyes. He's smart. A bit nervous."

"You have that effect on people."

The waiter dropped off their salads and took further direction from Jacques. Mark asked, "Are you nervous around me right now?"

Jacques was perplexed by the question before he recalled what he'd said. "Not now," he said at last. "I feel fairly secure that you're not going to hurt me. I don't care to impress you, and the wine has kicked in, to be honest." They both smiled. "But, to be serious, I could never be sure you're not going to hurt me if we did get back together."

"So, you're considering it?"

Jacques laughed at Mark's take on the comment and felt too astonished to respond.

"Will you consider it?"

"Non."

"You're not used to me doting on you. Don't you want to get used to it?" Mark reached over to touch his hand, and Jacques did feel nervous now despite the wine. He wasn't sure how long he could hold him off, or if he wanted to. There were so many times he'd prayed exactly for this moment.

"Let me love you, Jacques."

"I'd be a fool."

"You've never been the fool. I was the one who was the fool."

"We live in different cities now, and I won't fit into your life any more. I won't be poor," Jacques said, knowing this would break the deal.

"Of course not. I understand that. And I'd come to New York as often as I could until I'm finished," Mark said.

"It would never work," Jacques stated, although he felt much less declarative than that.

"Why?"

"What would happen the first time you got tired of me not doing your bidding?"

"That's not fair, Jacques. Now you're the one refusing to see a change in me."

"Don't you think violent men often say they've changed?" Jacques asked him. Mark looked startled by this frank acknowledgment. They looked away from each other for a second.

"Yes, I guess that's true. But, I left you for fear of hurting you again. I wouldn't be here, persisting as I am, if I thought there was any possibility of my losing control. Not that you're any less a challenge now." Mark placed his napkin on the table, as if he were done eating, and looked defeated. "Atonement isn't a cheap ticket. I learned that in the wilderness. But, I'll do whatever's needed to make amends. I can tell you still love me."

"Love doesn't matter."

Mark winced. "Of course it does. Give me another chance to prove it."

"Don't ask me again. I won't give up my life."

"I'm not asking that." Mark lowered his voice after another couple looked their way. Jacques wanted him to let the subject drop for the remainder of the meal, and

Mark seemed to catch on. Instead, he asked for details about Jacques' life, his friends, his dance, what it was like in New York. Jacques was delighted he could share stories he felt proud of, that he felt independent and strong now.

———

Once they returned to the cottage, Mark gently pinned Jacques to the wall of the corridor between their bedrooms, wanting to kiss him more than he'd ever wanted to before, more than that evening in Jacques' home in Paris, when they kissed for the first time and Mark felt that seductive gush of desire.

He pleaded instead that Jacques let him pursue the relationship, but Jacques was unyielding.

"Let me kiss you," he insisted next.

Jacques relented to the unavoidable. Jacques had never denied him anything. It was a slow kiss at first, Mark barely brushing his lips against Jacques', but when he let go of the Frenchman's arms and wrapped his own around Jacques' waist, Jacques moved with grace toward Mark and embraced him by the neck. It was insufferably the most heartfelt kiss they'd ever shared; how could Jacques not admit it? Mark groaned and said, "It's intoxicating."

"Maybe it's the wine," Jacques said as he wiped a tear from his right eye.

"No, it's not the wine. I'm in love with you, and it feels so incredible. Give me a chance, Jacques, please let me show you."

"Non," Jacques was pushing away again, "I am too familiar with the power of this attraction, and for you it is brand new."

"No, it's not brand new, you know that, but it's transformed. It's your choice, of course," Mark said as he stepped back a little. He was again very conscious of the need not to force Jacques into anything.

"If you really want to prove you've changed, that you truly love me, you'll drop this. You won't contact me or try to change my mind," Jacques said as he looked down rather than at Mark.

Mark felt blind-sided by this challenge and dropped his voice. "Is that really what you want?"

"Oui."

"Then I'll do it, under one condition."

"What condition?" Jacques asked as he seemed to regain his composure. He met Mark's eyes again and grabbed his face unexpectedly, kissing him hard. Mark didn't want to let him pull away when he was done.

Leaning his forehead on Mark's cheek, Jacques asked again what the condition was.

"That you call me, if you change your mind. You'll come back to me if you decide it's what you want. Promise me that." Mark suspected it was exactly what Jacques wanted, and he struggled with how to make the option viable for him.

"Okay, but I won't," Jacques' voice sounded higher as if he was holding back tears.

"Maybe you will," he consoled Jacques in a strange twist of positions. "I'll be there, waiting."

"You can't wait…I won't come." Jacques was shaking his head and moving back again.

"It's my choice to wait. Just promise you won't hold out on me if you change your mind."

"I promise, but don't expect it."

Mark closed his eyes to ward off the tears, but one escaped and slid down his cheek. Jacques wiped it with his thumb. "Ninapenda wewe sana."

"Excuse me?" Jacques asked.

"I love you, in Swahili. You asked me once…how to say it."

"Yes, I remember…" Jacques' expression strained, and Mark tried to suppress the enormous anguish he felt.

FIFTY-ONE

Six Months Later

Mark rummaged through old text books, eager to find the answer to Steve's riddle. "I know I'm right," he laughed.

Steve feigned he was out of earshot and walked into the bedroom carrying two glasses of wine. "Excuse me?"

"I'm right, you're wrong," said Mark, smiling, still looking down from page to page.

"Keep dreaming. I'm the mathematician here," Steve said.

"Which just proves your propensity toward megalomania."

Steve walked over to Mark and kissed the latter on the cheek, then bit him softly, teasing. "Just can't stand to be wrong, can you?"

"I'd tolerate it better if I were more accustomed to it," Mark said as he took one of the glasses.

"Okay, prove it another time. Come watch the movie I rented."

Mark looked up from his book. "Now?"

"Yes, now."

Mark complied, enjoying the banter and Steve's self-assuredness. After returning from London, Mark had tried to reach Sanjay for a week before he pushed his way past the Indian's housemates to confront him. "Why are you avoiding me?" he'd asked, well aware that the precarious relationship couldn't, in any event, survive Mark's confession of his feelings for Jacques. Still he'd wanted the elusive closure, and Sanjay gave it to him, however unlikely a definitive refusal from his part would have seemed.

A few months later, Steve and Mark united after meeting at a campus rally to support Tibetan independence. Steve was from a middle class Greek-American family in Providence, Rhode Island, and obtained his Bachelor's degree at Brown before starting his Ph.D. in math at Tufts. They were the same age and had similar temperaments. A much better match for Mark, Steve did not only boast high aptitude, he was downright cocky, something Mark found irresistible. Steve had been involved in a serious relationship with another student at Brown, his only other sexual encounter, and was attractive on many levels. Mark felt attached to him. But, he presented his heart with an unheard-of caveat: that it belonged, in fact, to an ex, a Frenchman involved in theater in New York. Steve accepted this fantasy because he considered it just that. He saw a photograph of Jacques and stated it was unlikely he'd be pining over Mark. *Hate to tell you*, he'd said, but Mark knew better.

Presently, Steve hooked a finger around one of Mark's and tugged, "Come on."

Mark yielded, threw the book on the floor, ready to swear he'd find the evidence of his math if given the time to search when instead he received an intuitive omen. A flash of his future revealed itself to him without disguise and without solicitation. They were walking hand in hand, he and Jacques, as if it were the most natural thing. The meaning was clear. Somehow, he would reunite with Jacques. The revelation left him feeling compassionate for the friend and lover who stood before him now.

"What is it?" Steve asked.

Mark had never concealed his sudden shifts, premonitions and otherworldly experiences. He shrugged. "Did I ever tell you why I've left myself open to reconciling with Jacques?"

"Fuck, not this again." Steve breathed out hard. "What? Go on."

"Jacques and I are somewhat incompatible."

"To say the least."

"Yes, and when I'm with him, I need to stretch a whole lot. I have to see myself in alternative ways, deal with constant growth."

Steve visibly tightened his muscles. Mark ran the back of his hand along the stubble on Steve's cheek, feeling sad and happy at once. "Are you going to tell me what the hell you're saying?" Steve asked him.

———

The doorman held open the door for Jacques and handed him his post. "These came for you today, sir." He was a balding, polite gentleman, whose consistency was comforting.

"Thank you, Reynolds." Jacques tipped him offhandedly, not because he was expected to, but simply because he could. He was feeling generous and strong today, was returning from a session with Barbara. He had moved uptown a bit, his place a little more posh. Mark would be even more uncomfortable here, and that had been part of the attraction when he rented it.

"Thank you kindly, sir." Reynolds tipped his hat and hit the elevator call button. "You have a pleasant evening. If there's anything I can do, please ring."

"I will." Jacques looked up from his mail for a moment and smiled. Returning to it, he noticed a British postmark. He hadn't heard from John in over a month, had started to worry, especially when his phone calls went unanswered. He had written a note to Lilith asking for an update on her brother's condition, but it appeared he was about to get the news first hand. It was John's erratic and interesting handwriting on the envelope. He tore it open, smiled at a neighbor riding up from the 5th floor when the doors opened prematurely, and then read,

Dear Jacques,

I'm sorry to have worried you. Heard from Lilith just today, and she admonished me for not getting back to you sooner. I had an unfortunate side effect from the medicine and had to be hospitalized for a short time. Apparently, too much "medication" can be toxic. I had the worst stomach problems, but I'm told I was lucky not to have developed kidney failure. Can you bloody believe it? I guess it'd been my fault, in a way, because I hadn't kept my appointments for blood tests. Anyway, all's right now, except that I'm on a new medication. It's a bit daunting after all this time to think I might start to hallucinate again, or start to falter in my ideas. I've made lots of progress with my music—even leased a piece to the London Philharmonic, if you can believe that (this after a smaller outfit had performed it). I struggle with missing the highs sometimes and suppose I'll never be able to trust myself entirely. I cannot relay what it felt like, to be on top of the world in that way. I have to remind myself of where it inevitably led, and even so must rely on my doctor to persuade me it's for the best this way.

I miss you, my friend. It's so lonely here. There's just so much enthusiasm I can feel when I meet with my shrink once a week (yes, I've cut down, and you?). Have you decided what you want to do about Mark? The last time we spoke, you were still deliberating, painfully, if I recall. You didn't seem quite so resolved as what I remembered a few months before. Funny, really. I thought

I sounded like the sane one when we last spoke. I do miss the contradictions in my life, though. I used to (so desperately) need security, so I'd throw myself into unsure situations. I'd leave when I was content to stay, and remain where I'd wish to depart. More things I do make sense now. There's complacency if nothing else. You told me once that Mark was like the ocean to you, and I wonder how long you can really stay away from the ocean. Do you?

Why don't you visit again? We haven't seen in each other in ages, mate.

Yours, John

There was no date, but the envelope was postmarked a week ago. He had read the last bit outside his apartment door, not wanting to put the letter aside before he was finished. The words stung. Complacency. How long *could* he stay away from the ocean? He dipped into his pocket and scanned the bundled keys for his apartment door. It swung open heavily, as if it were on an incline, or a precipice. He dropped the rest of the mail, junk and a couple of bills, and his keys, onto the small entrance table, and then he tugged his shoes off and sat down on the couch, almost ceremoniously. What if Mark wasn't available now? What if it was too late, anyway?

The last six months had been relatively easy. He had ended things; he made a decision he never thought he could. Barbara helped him through the rough days, when he felt sad or lonely, or felt he lacked purpose. But, the days were generally good now. His work was great, although he started to look forward to a change, perhaps an opportunity in a musical, earn his way onto Broadway. His money was earning more money, and it was far surpassing his expenses. He met someone, Patrick. They had met at a friend's anniversary party ("Ten Years in the Biz") and hit it off. Patrick had been born in Ireland but raised in New York City. He was a writer, well-educated, older, handsome, sensitive, and smooth. Nothing was taken for granted.

At first, Jacques enjoyed the spontaneity. He didn't know when Patrick would call or return his calls, didn't know when he'd be out of town; it always felt new and different. The sex was interesting, if not great. But, then, a couple of months ago, Jacques had dared to ask where things were going. He wanted to be safe in a post-AIDS world, to stay alive, he explained. He wanted a relationship, a commitment. That was enough to shove Patrick away, far away. He next heard from him from California, "Doing some research for a new book." Didn't matter, maybe it's what he wanted: an excuse to consider Mark again, to compare him to Mark. Does life happen to you, around you, or because of you?

What had Barbara said? Something about him "not leaving himself," even when he'd been sad or afraid the last several months. She reminded him of how he used to dissociate from himself, how that had been a defense mechanism, or a survival skill when he was growing up, and how he'd grown out of it. He told her he wondered sometimes if the profound sadness was his own, or if he was spinning on the dreidel of Earth's woes, some collective pain. He'd been reading Jung. And meditating. He'd also been studying the Christian mystics, wanting to clear his mind to make way for the divine presence, to become a vessel, in a sense, and to hold the vibration of love. Mark had spoken about such mystical experiences, too.

He snuggled into his bed early, reflecting on his circumstances while he savored the feel of the sheets. Life had been good in New York. He had friends here now. He was well respected in his company, was considered unusual, which was valuable in New York. He could *afford* to live in New York City, another gift. Once, when he'd first moved to "the city," as New Yorkers called it, he'd considered killing himself, seriously enough to have envisioned a plan. He had pills from John's psychiatrist and had never used them. He'd wanted to stay off any medicine which might dull him or otherwise take his life slowly, or which might turn him into an addict. But then for a few days, he had considered ending it all himself, quietly, over a weekend. He would tell everyone he was going away, so no one would come looking for him. He thought for a moment why he hadn't gone through with it. Perhaps it was because of John and some odd sense of responsibility to model endurance. He'd never told anyone, but he'd sought therapy after that and had found Barbara.

Since his rendezvous with Mark in England, he worked on self-validation, the art of confidence in the ability to comfort oneself, acknowledge and treasure that same self, to parent it as needed, and to love the self. He mastered the definition, anyway.

He couldn't sleep now that his mind was pulling him in so many directions. If only he could come to relieve some of the tension, but he was afraid his mind would wander to Mark as it always did when he masturbated. He resented this and then did it anyway, eventually falling asleep, wanting to fly to London to see John as soon as he could.

"I had to get away from New York suddenly," Jacques explained. "I don't want you to feel indebted to me for visiting." He took the obligatory cup of tea, glad to see that not too many things had changed at the cottage. John purchased a gorgeous piano, which now took center stage in the salon. Jacques offered praise at what John likely saw as an act of capitulation—he'd refused for so long to enjoy playing music that would have remotely pleased his parents. John offered to play something now, and Jacques asked for Chopin or Debussy, something soothing and warm, just like the cottage.

When he finished, John sat on the divan next to Jacques and studied him a bit. "What's on your mind, mate?"

"What? Oh." Jacques shook his head never mind, but then changed it. "Are you interested in Mark?"

"Romantically? No, I'm not. Why would you ask that?"

"I don't know. I needed to make sure." Jacques looked at him directly until John averted his eyes. "How are you, really? I still never forgot how upset you were about Lilith and me. I never meant to hurt you in any way."

"No, please," John said before he could go on. "I'm all right, mate. Just sort of reminded me of things, perhaps." He seemed far away. "Do you think it's terribly abnormal for..."

"For what?" Jacques prompted, although feeling apprehensive about John really divulging anything despite his seeming composure.

"It's nothing."

"You recall my life? How strange it's been? Sometimes I think about my past, and even I think it's incredible." Jacques shook his head and said *encroyable* in his native language. "Abnormal is my *shtick*." They laughed at the New York in him.

"Well, then, do you think children experiment sometimes, with siblings and such?"

"Excuse me? Oh, I think maybe, it's possible, but I never had any. What does your doctor say?"

"Has Lilith ever spoken to you about our uncle? My father's brother? He spent a couple of summers with us when we were young. Used to spend quite a bit of time in the attic. He was crazy, I suppose."

Jacques said she hadn't.

"I think he molested her, but she's never willing to speak of anything. Not that I've asked her to in many years, but..."

"I'm a little surprised she never said," Jacques said.

"Perhaps I'm the one who molested her. I don't know." John held his head in his hands.

"But, you were just a child, how could you? And younger than she was. That makes very little sense, John."

John looked as though he had discovered something. "You're right, mate, that makes little if any sense." He was gone from there in his thoughts, and Jacques didn't interrupt.

Finally, John spoke again, "Maybe someday I will ask her once more. Maybe my entire life of guilt stemmed from a mere illusion." He recalled to Jacques a conversation he'd had with Robin a few weeks after his discharge from the hospital. *It's not real*, she'd said. *None of this is real. We're just dreaming, mate. We can rejoice because it's all been a projection of some kind. Or, perhaps a story in someone's imagination.* He had looked out of the window that morning and wished himself happy dreams for the day. "It had been comforting rather than threatening to see it all as purely fictional," he explained to Jacques.

Jacques wasn't sure how to respond and felt an unnerving twinge of discomfort by the conversation. He redirected John to something he'd said earlier. "What do you mean about guilt?"

John shook his head, as if throwing a burden from himself. "I don't know. I've done so much work in therapy. Stuff has grown clearer than I ever thought possible, but still I can't remember everything." He dropped his head and ran a hand along his neck, suddenly looking tired. Jacques said so.

"A little. I'm not ready to say good night. You're the one who should be ready for a lie down after your trip," John said.

"Have you heard from him?" asked Jacques.

"You're referring to Mark, I assume. Yes, I have."

"How is he?"

John seemed to hesitate, as if he were deliberating something. He went to his bedroom and returned with a letter. "Here, if you'd like."

It was written on loose-leaf paper in black ink. It spoke of studies, a new apartment, a young man named Steve, despite his continued commitment to Jacques should Jacques change his mind. It was two pages, thoughtful, and genuine. He sounded happy. It was dated a couple of months before.

"Nothing since?" Jacques asked.

"No, I was incognito, if you recall. Haven't had a chance to write back."

"Yes, right, of course."

"So, what do you think?" John asked.

"Mon Dieu, I don't know. My head is spinning; my heart is all over the place."

"And your stomach?"

"My stomach? Hmm...butterflies."

"Butterflies," John repeated, looking pensive. "I guess we know what that means, then, don't we?"

CPSIA information can be obtained
at www.ICGtesting.com
Printed in the USA
LVOW10s2353210617

538958LV00010B/228/P